"You are good with a rapier," said Logar.

"I am better with a saber," Chareos answered.

"In that case we will take no chances," hissed Logar. "Kill him!"

Two swordsmen leapt forward. Chareos blocked a wild slash, spun to avoid a second thrust, and backhanded his blade across the first man's throat. Blood spurted and the attacker fell, thrusting his fingers at the wound in a vain attempt to stem the flow of his life. The second attacker sent a cut at Chareos' head, but he ducked. The swordsman fell back, eyes widening.

"Well?" Chareos glared at Logar.

Logar attacked. Chareos leapt back from a slice that would have disemboweled him. Then he swept a riposte that plunged into Logar's groin, severing the huge artery at the top of the inner thigh. Logar stared at the blood drenching his leggings; then his legs gave way and he fell to his knees before Chareos. He blinked up at his killer before toppling to the ground . . .

By David Gemmell
Published by Ballantine Books:

LION OF MACEDON
DARK PRINCE

KNIGHTS OF DARK RENOWN

MORNINGSTAR

The Drenai Saga
LEGEND
THE KING BEYOND THE GATE
QUEST FOR LOST HEROES
WAYLANDER*

The Stones of Power Cycle
GHOST KING*
LAST SWORD OF POWER*
WOLF IN SHADOW*

THE LAST GUARDIAN*

**Forthcoming*

QUEST FOR LOST HEROES

David Gemmell

A Del Rey® Book
BALLANTINE BOOKS • NEW YORK

A Del Rey® Book
Published by Ballantine Books

 Published in the United States of America by Ballantine Books, a division of Random House, Inc., New York. Originally published in Great Britain as a Legend Book, published by Arrow Books Limited, an imprint of Random House UK Ltd., in 1990.

ISBN 0-345-37904-7

Manufactured in the United States of America

First Ballantine Books Edition: July 1995

10 9 8 7 6 5 4 3 2 1

Dedication

Some men climb mountains or found empires; others make fortunes or create classics. But *Quest for Lost Heroes* is dedicated with love to Bill Woodford, who took on the role of stepfather to a shy, introverted, and illegitimate six-year-old boy and never once let him down. Through his patient encouragement, his quiet strength, and his endless affection he gave his son the pride and the confidence to fight his own battles—both in life and on the printed page. Thanks, Dad!

Acknowledgments

Grateful thanks also to Liza Reeves for the direction, Jean Maund for copy editing, and Tom Taylor, Stella Graham, Edith Graham, and Val Gemmell for the test reading.

Prologue

THREE MEN WERE down; the other four formed a half circle around the huge, ugly man in the bearskin jerkin.

"You want to know what it's like on the mountain?" he asked them, his voice slurred. He spit blood from his mouth, which stained his red and silver beard. His attackers hurled themselves forward, and he met the first with a crashing blow to the chin that sent the victim sprawling to the sawdust-covered floor. Blows rained in on him. He ducked his bald head and charged at the remaining three, but his foot slipped and he fell, dragging a man with him. A booted foot lashed into his face, but he swung his arm to knock the man from his feet. The ugly man staggered upright and leaned back against the wooden counter, his eyes narrowing as two of his attackers drew daggers from their belts. Dropping his right arm, he pulled a long skinning knife from his boot. It was double-edged and wickedly sharp.

The innkeeper moved silently behind him, and the blow to the back of the ugly man's neck was sudden. His eyes glazed. The knife dropped from his fingers, and he fell facedown to crash alongside his victims.

"I'll cut his puking heart out," said one of his attackers, moving forward.

"That would not be wise," the innkeeper told him. "The man is a friend of mine. And I would be obliged to kill you." The words were spoken softly but with a confidence that cut through the atmosphere of anger and sudden violence.

The man slammed his dagger home in its sheath. "Someone will kill him one day," he said.

"Sadly, that is true," the innkeeper agreed, opening the flap on the counter and kneeling beside the unconscious man in the bearskin. "Are your friends alive?"

Two of the men were groaning, and a third struggled to sit. "Yes, they're alive. What was that nonsense about a mountain?"

"It's not important," replied the innkeeper. "There's a pitcher of ale by the barrel. You're welcome to it—and there'll be no charge for your drinks this evening."

"That's good of you," said the man. "Here, let me give you a hand with him." Between them they hauled the ugly man upright and carried him through to a room at the rear of the inn, where a lantern burned brightly and a bed was ready, the sheets drawn back. They laid the unconscious warrior on the bed, and the innkeeper sat beside him. He looked up at his helper; all the man's anger had disappeared.

"Go and enjoy your ale," said the innkeeper. "My wife will bring it to you."

After the man had gone, the innkeeper checked his friend's pulse. It was beating strongly.

"You can stop pretending now," he remarked. "We are alone."

The ugly man's eyes opened, and he eased himself up on the thick pillows. "I didn't want to have to kill anyone," he said, smiling sheepishly and showing a broken tooth. "Thanks for stopping it, Naza."

"It was nothing," Naza told him. "But why do you not let it rest? The past is gone."

"I was there, though. I was on the mountain. No one can take that from me."

"No one would want to, my friend," Naza said sadly.

The ugly man closed his eyes. "It wasn't what I dreamed of," he said.

"Nothing ever is," replied Naza, standing and blowing out the lantern.

Later, after Naza and his wife, Mael, had cleared away the tankards, pitchers, and plates and locked the doors, they sat together by the dying fire. Mael reached over and touched her husband's arm; he smiled and patted her hand.

"Why do you put up with him?" asked Mael. "That's the third fight this month. It's bad for business."

"He's my friend."

"If he was truly your friend, he would not cause you so much grief," she pointed out.

He nodded. "There's truth in that, Mael, my love. But I feel his sadness; it hurts me."

Moving from her seat, she leaned over to kiss his brow. "You are too softhearted. But that is one of the reasons I love you, so I won't complain too much. I just hope he doesn't let you down."

He pulled her into his lap. "He will; he can't help it. He climbed the mountain, and now he has nowhere to go."

"What mountain?"

"The worst kind, Mael. The kind that first you climb and then you carry."

"It is too late for riddles."

"Yes," he agreed, surging to his feet and holding her in his arms. "Let me take you to bed."

"Which bed? You put your drunken friend in ours!"

"The upper guest room is free."

"And you think you're still young enough to carry me there?"

He chuckled and lowered her to the floor. "I could, but I think I'll conserve what little strength I have for when we get there. You go up and light the lantern. I'll be with you in a little while."

He wandered back to his own room and pulled the boots from the sleeping man. A second knife clattered to the floor. Covering his friend with a blanket, he crossed the room.

"Sleep well," he whispered, pulling the door shut behind him.

◊ 1 ◊

SEVENTEEN PEOPLE WATCHED the duel, and not a sound could be heard above the whispering of the blades and the discordant music of steel on steel. The earl rolled his wrist and sent a lancing stroke toward the face mask of his opponent, but the man dropped his shoulder and swayed aside, flashing a riposte that the earl barely parried. For some minutes the two duelists were locked in a strategic battle, then the earl launched a blistering attack. His opponent—a tall, lean man wearing the gray habit of a monk beneath his mask and mail shirt—defended desperately. With a last hissing clash the swords came together, the earl's blade sliding free to touch the monk's chest.

The duelists bowed to each other, and a light ripple of applause came from the spectators. The earl's wife and three sons moved out onto the floor of the hall.

"You were wonderful, Father," said the youngest, a blond-headed boy of seven. The Earl of Talgithir ruffled the boy's hair.

"Did you enjoy the exhibition?" he asked.

"Yes, Father," the boys chorused.

"And what was the move by which your father defeated me?" the monk asked, pulling off his mask.

"The Classic Chare," replied the eldest.

The monk smiled. "Indeed it was, Lord Patris. You are studying well."

The earl allowed his wife to lead his sons from the hall and waved away his retainers. With the hall empty, he took the monk's arm, and the two men strode to the south gallery, where a pitcher of fruit juice and two goblets had been set aside.

The earl filled the goblets. "Are you really content here?" he asked.

The monk shrugged. "As content as I would be anywhere, my lord. Why do you ask?"

The earl gazed into the eyes of the man before him. The face he saw was strong, the nose long and aquiline, the mouth full below a trimmed mustache. "There are many legends concerning you, Chareos," he said. "Some have you as a prince. Did you know that?"

"I have heard it," Chareos admitted. "It is unimportant."

"What is important? You are the finest swordsman I ever saw. You were one of the heroes of Bel-azar. You could have been rich beyond the dreams of common men."

"I am rich beyond the dreams of common men, my lord. And *that* is what is important. This life suits me. I am by nature a student. The libraries here in Gothir are among the best anywhere. Far south, they say, the libraries of Drenan contain more books, but here are the complete works of Tertullus. It will take me many years to study them all."

"It doesn't seem right," said the earl. "I remember my father putting me on his shoulder so that I could see the heroes of Bel-azar as they marched through the streets of New Gulgothir. I remember everything about that day. You were riding a white stallion of some seventeen hands and wearing a silver mail shirt and a helm with a white horsehair plume. Beltzer was behind you, carrying his ax. Then Maggrig and Finn. People in the crowd reached out to touch you as if you were a lodestar. It was a wonderful day."

"The sun shone," agreed Chareos, "but it was only a parade, my lord—and there are many parades."

"What happened to the others?" asked the earl. "Did you remain friends? I have heard nothing of them for years."

"Nor I," Chareos answered. The dark-eyed monk looked away, seeing Beltzer as he had been on the last day: drunk, red-eyed, and weeping, his ax auctioned to settle his debts. The farmer had become a hero, and it had destroyed him in a way the Nadir could not. Maggrig and Finn had been there; they had left Beltzer alone in the back room of the inn and walked with Chareos out into the sunshine.

"We are going back to the mountains," Finn had said.

"There's nothing there," Chareos had told him.

Finn had smiled. "There's nothing anywhere, Blademaster." Without another word the black-bearded archer had taken up his pack and moved off.

The youth Maggrig had smiled, offering Chareos his hand. "We will meet again," he had said. "He probably only needs a little time to himself, away from crowds."

"How do you suffer his moods and depressions?" Chareos had asked.

"I do not see them," Maggrig had answered. "I see only the man."

Now Chareos sipped his fruit juice and gazed out of the tall window. He was sitting too far back to see the courtyard and the gardens beyond. But from here he could look over the high wall of the monastery and off into the southern distance, where the forest lay like a green mist on the mountains. His gaze swept across to the east and the ridges of hills that led to the Nadir Steppes. For a moment only he felt the touch of icy fear.

"You think the Nadir will attack come summer?" asked the earl, as if reading his thoughts. Chareos considered the question. The Nadir lived for war—a dour, nomadic tribal people, joyous only in battle. For centuries Gothir kings had held them in thrall, sure in the knowledge that the tribes hated one another more than they detested the conquerors. Then had come Ulric, the first great warlord. He had united them, turning them into an invincible force, an army numbering hundreds of thousands of fierce-eyed warriors. The Gothir were crushed and the king slain, and refugees fled to the northwest to build new homes. Only the great Drenai citadel of Dros Delnoch, far to the southeast, had turned them back. But a century later another warlord arose, and he would not be thwarted. Tenaka Khan had crushed the Drenai and invaded the lands of Vagria, his armies sweeping to the sea at Mashrapur and along the coastline to Lentria. Chareos shivered. Would they attack this coming summer? Only the Source knew. But one point was as certain as death—one day the Nadir would come. They would sweep across the hills, their battle cries deafening, the grass churned to muddy desolation under the hooves of their war ponies. Chareos swallowed, his eyes fixed to the hills, seeing the blood-hungry hordes flowing across the green Gothir lands like a dark tide.

"Well?" queried the earl. "Do you think they will attack?"

"I could not say, my lord. I do not listen to the reports as once I did. It is said that the Drenai are in rebellion again, led by yet another who claims to be the Earl of Bronze reborn. I think that makes it the fifth in the thirty years since Tenaka Khan stormed Dros Delnoch. But perhaps such an uprising will put off the Nadir plans."

"He went the way of all the others," said the earl. "He was caught and crucified; the rebellion was crushed. It is said the new khan has ordered his troops north."

"People have been saying that for years," said Chareos. "There is little here for them. The spoils they took from the conquests of Drenan, Vagria, and Lentria made them rich. We have nothing to offer them; we are not even a gateway to richer kingdoms. Beyond New Gulgothir is the sea. Perhaps they will leave us alone." Even as he spoke, Chareos felt the lie sitting cold in his throat. The Nadir lived not for plunder but for blood and death and conquest. It would matter nothing to them that the riches were few. No, they would be fired with thoughts of ancestral revenge on the Gothir people.

"You do not believe that, Blademaster. I see it in your eyes," said the earl, standing. "No, the Nadir hate us for the past, and they are tormented by the memory of Bel-azar, the only defeat to stain the reputation of Tenaka Khan."

Chareos rose and assisted the earl into his caped coat. He looked into the younger man's face. "Bel-azar was a miracle. I do not know how we did it or why Tenaka Khan *allowed* us to hold. But it was twenty years ago; I very rarely think of it now."

"The old fortress is in ruins," the earl said. "It's as good as Nadir territory now. Thank you for the lesson. I think I am getting closer to you."

"Better than that, my lord. You beat me today."

"Are you sure you did not let me win just because my sons were watching?"

"You won fairly, my lord. But next week I will be better."

"Next week you come to the castle. Afterward we will ride out into the Hunting Woods and see if we can flush out a boar or two."

Chareos bowed as the earl strode from the hall. There was still some juice in the pitcher, and he refilled his goblet and wandered to the window, watching as the earl's retinue rode from the monastery.

It had been a long time since those names had been voiced: Beltzer, Maggrig, and Finn. He could still see the red-bearded giant hammering his battle-ax into the Nadir as they swarmed over the gate tower wall. And each evening the bowmen, Maggrig and Finn, would compare scores and write them in charcoal on the granite wall: "Maggrig killed eleven today, making his tally thirty-one. Death to the Nadir!" Old Kalin would dispute their figures as he cooked the evening meal over the brazier. Such a way with food, that man, Chareos remembered—he could make sirloin steak taste like sheep's bowels. He had died on the last day.

The gate tower section took the most casualties throughout. Of the original complement of forty-five, only Beltzer, Maggrig, Finn, and Chareos had survived. The Nadir had taken the fortress, but Beltzer had leapt from the gate tower and single-handedly retaken the Gothir standard, hacking and cutting his way back to the tower door. Once inside, the soldiers had barricaded themselves in and defied the encircling Nadir warriors. For most of the day the enemy had scaled the wall, only to be repulsed by the swords and axes of the defenders.

That night Tenaka Khan himself had walked, with his shaman, below the gate tower.

"Surrender to me and you may leave here alive," he had called.

"That would be contrary to our orders," Chareos had answered him.

"What is the most important to you, duty or freedom?" the khan had asked.

"An interesting question, sir," Chareos had replied. "Why not come up here and debate the point."

"Throw down a rope," the khan had answered.

Chareos smiled at the memory now as he heard footsteps in the hall behind him and turned to see the senior brother approaching.

"Am I disturbing you?" asked the old man.

"Not at all, Parnio. Please join me."

The white-robed senior sat by the table and gazed up at the sky. "The heavens are incredible," he whispered. "Ever-changing yet constant in their beauty."

"Indeed they are," agreed Chareos, sitting opposite the old man.

"Have you touched the power of the Source yet, my son?"

"No, Father. I am still a doubter. Is this a concern to you?"

The senior waved a slender hand. "Not at all. Those who seek him find him . . . but in his own time. But you have been here two years now, and I wonder what holds you. You do not need to wear the robes in order to use the library."

Chareos smiled. "There is comfort in belonging, Father. There is a certain anonymity."

"If it was anonymity you were seeking, you would not have kept your own name, and certainly you would not have acceded to the earl's request to teach him the finer techniques of swordsmanship."

"True. Perhaps the answer is simply that I do not know. Yet I have no desire to leave."

"By my lights, my son, you are a young man. You should have a wife and children; there should be love in your life. Am I at fault in my thinking?"

Chareos stood and moved once more to the window. "Not at fault, Senior Brother. I loved once . . . and in truth

I could love again. But the pain of loss was too much for me. I would rather live alone than suffer it."

"Then you are here to hide, Chareos, and that is not a good reason. The gift of life is too great to waste in such a fashion. Think on it. Why should the famed hero of Bel-azar fear such a wondrous joy as love?"

Chareos swung on the old man, his dark eyes hooded and angry. "Bel-azar! I have heard that name twice today. It means nothing. I had a sword . . . I used it well. Men died. I see nothing heroic in that, Senior Brother. A long time ago I watched an old man, crippled in the joints, try to aid a woman who was being attacked. One blow from a fist killed that old man. But his action was heroic, for he had no chance. Do you understand what I am saying? The soldier always has a chance. There are men and women in the world who perform heroic acts daily, and no one sees them. But I—because of a good eye and a fast arm—I am one of the heroes of Bel-azar. My name is sung in the long halls and the taverns."

"You are wrong, Chareos. *Men* sing of you. But the action of that old man was sung before God. There is a difference."

"There would be—if I believed. But I do not."

"Give it time—and beware of the earl, my son. There is strength in him, but there is cruelty also. And when you go to teach him at his castle, do not wear the gray. We are not warriors here; this is no Temple of the Thirty."

"As you wish, Father."

The old man rose. "When I came upon you," he said softly, "you were lost in thought. Will you share your memories?"

"I was thinking of Bel-azar and Tenaka Khan. I was wondering about that last night when he climbed the wall alone and sat with us until the dawn. He talked of his life and his dreams, and we spoke of ours. Beltzer wanted to hold him for a hostage, but I overruled him. At dawn he climbed down from the gate tower and led his force away. We still had the Gothir standard, so—in theory, at least—the victory was ours."

"You admired the man?"

"Yes. There was a nobility of spirit. But I do not know why he let us live."

"Did he not tell you?"

"No. But he was not a man to act without a reason, and it has haunted me for years. When he died, I journeyed into Nadir lands and stood before the great tomb of Ulric, where Tenaka Khan was buried. I was drawn there. I rode into the camp of the Wolves and knelt before the shaman. I asked him why we were spared on that day. He shrugged. He told me we were the *Shio-kas-atra*, the ghosts-yet-to-be."

"Did you understand him?"

"No. Do you?"

"I will pray on it, my son."

Beltzer awoke to a roaring sea of pain within his skull. He groaned and hauled himself to a sitting position, his stomach heaving. He pulled on his boots and staggered upright, wandered around the bed to the window, and opened it. Fresh air drifted in on a light breeze. He hawked and spit; his lip was split, and a little blood could be seen in the phlegm. There was a mirror on the dresser, and he sank down into the seat before it and stared at his reflection. One eye was swollen and dark; his forehead was grazed, and there was a shallow cut on his right cheek; his red and silver beard was matted with dried blood. He felt sick. The door opened behind him, causing the curtains to billow. He turned to see Mael entering, bearing a tray on which was a platter of toasted bread and cheese and a jug; he prayed it contained ale.

"Thank you," he said as she set down the tray. She looked at him and shook her head.

"You are a disgrace," she told him, planting her hands on her ample hips.

"No lectures, Mael. Have pity! My head . . ."

"Your pain is your own affair. And I have no pity for drunken louts. Look at the blood on these sheets! And the stink is enough to turn a decent man's stomach. How long since you bathed?"

"It was this year, I know that."

"When you've finished your breakfast, you will go to the

woodshed. There you will work until you have settled your bill. Ax and saw will clear your head."

"Where's Naza?" he asked, straining to focus on the flaxen-haired woman.

"He's gone into the city. It's market day. When he returns, you will be gone—you understand that?"

"He . . . owes me."

"He owes you nothing. You hear me? Nothing! You've been here two months. You've not paid a single Raq for food, lodging, or ale, and in that time you've insulted our customers, picked fights, and generally done your best to ruin the trade my husband lives on. You will chop wood and then you will go."

His fist slammed down on the dresser, and he surged to his feet. "You dare to talk to me like that?" he stormed. "You know who I am, woman?"

"I know," she said, moving closer. "You are Beltzer. Beltzer the drunkard. Beltzer the sloth. Beltzer the braggart. And you stink. You stink of sweat, sour ale, and vomit. Of course I know who you are!"

He raised his hand as if to strike her, but she laughed at him. "Go ahead, mighty hero of Bel-azar. Come on!"

Beltzer pushed past her and out into the empty room beyond, but she followed him, her anger lashing him with whips of fire. He stumbled out into the yard beyond the tavern, blinking in the harsh sunlight. The woodshed was to his right; open fields lay to his left.

He took the left path and headed off into the high country, but he had traveled only a half mile when he sat down on a rock and gazed over the rugged countryside. Three miles ahead was his cabin. But there would be no one there: no food, no drink, merely the howling of the wolves and the emptiness only the lonely could know.

His heart full of shame, he turned back toward the woodshed.

Stopping at a stream, he stripped himself of his bearskin jerkin and grey woolen tunic. Then, placing his boots beside his clothes, he stepped into the water. With no soap to cleanse himself, he scrubbed at his body with mint leaves and washed the blood from his beard. When he returned to the bank and lifted his tunic, the smell from it almost made him nauseous. "You've fallen a long way," he told himself aloud. He washed the tunic, beating it against a rock to drive out the dirt, then wrung it clear of excess water and struggled into it. His bearskin jerkin he carried over his arm.

Mael watched him walk back into the yard and cursed softly under her breath. She waited until she heard the sound of the ax thudding into the tree rounds and then returned to the kitchen, preparing the pies and pastries the farm workers and laborers would require at noon.

In the woodshed Beltzer worked hard, enjoying the heft of the single-bladed ax and the feel of the curved wood. His arm had lost none of its skill, and each stroke was clean, splitting the rounds into chunks that would burn on the iron-rimmed braziers at each end of the tavern's main room.

Just before noon he stopped and began to cart the wood across the yard. Then he carried it into the tavern to stack beside the braziers. Mael did not speak to him, and he had no desire to feel the sharpness of her tongue. She handed him a plate of broth and some bread when the noontime custom died down, and he ate it in silence, longing to ask for a tankard of ale but fearing the inevitable refusal.

Naza returned at dusk and carried a pitcher of ale out to the woodshed.

"How are you feeling, my friend?" he asked, filling a tankard and passing it to the grateful Beltzer.

"Worse than death," he replied, draining the tankard.

"You didn't have to do all this," said Naza. "You should have rested today. You took quite a beating last night."

Beltzer shook his head. "Your wife understands me better than you. This is what I need," he said, lifting the tankard. "You know, there's an insanity to it all, Naza. I was the most famous person in Gothir. I was the standard-bearer. I was wined and dined; money and presents poured into my hands. I was on top of the mountain. But there was nothing there. Nothing. Just clouds. And I found that you can't live on that mountain. But when it throws you off—oh, how you long for it! I would kill to climb it again. I would sell my soul. It is so stupid. With fame I thought I would *be* someone. But I wasn't. Oh, yes, the nobles invited me to their castles for a while, but I couldn't talk to them in their own language about poetry and politics. I was a farmer. I can't read or write. I stood with them and sat with them, and I felt like the fool I am. There is only one skill I know—I can swing an ax. I killed a few Nadir. I took the standard. And now I can't even become a farmer again. The mountain won't let me."

"Why don't you visit Maggrig and Finn? They still have that house in High Valley. They'd be glad to see you, and you could talk of old times."

"They were always loners, and we were never close. No, I should have died at Bel-azar. Nothing has gone right since then."

"Death comes soon enough to all men," said Naza. "Don't wish for it. Come inside and have a drink."

"No, tonight I will sit out here and think. No drinking. No fighting. I will sit here."

"I'll send a jug out to you—and a hot meal. I'll have some blankets brought out, too."

"You needn't do this for me, Naza."

"I owe you, my friend."

"No," said Beltzer sadly, "you owe me nothing. And from now on I work for my food."

Forty wooden pegs two inches in diameter had been driven into the lawn; each was set some three feet apart in rows of eight. The eight young students stood before the pegs, awaiting instructions from Chareos. The morning sun was bright, and a light breeze caressed the elm trees that bordered the lawn.

"Now, gentlemen," said Chareos, "I want you to walk along the pegs, turn, and come back as swiftly as you can."

"Might I ask why?" Patris, the earl's eldest son, inquired. "Are we not supposed to learn the use of the sword?"

"Indeed you are, my lord. But you hold a sword in the hand, and that is only one aspect of the bladesman's skill. Balance is everything. Now kindly take your positions."

The youngsters stepped on to the pegs and made a wary

start. Patris moved smoothly out, turned, and ran back to where Chareos waited. The other youths followed more carefully. Three slipped and had to make the attempt a second time; these three Chareos took aside.

"You will continue on the pegs until I return," he told them. One was the fat child, Akarin, son of the city's elder magistrate. He would never be a swordsman, but he was a game boy and Chareos liked him.

He took the other five youths to the run. It had been finished the day before, and Chareos was well pleased with it. A long plank was angled up to join a platform of logs some six feet above the ground. The logs were balanced on greased spheres of wood, allowing them to roll gently. At the end of the log run was tied a knotted rope. With this it was possible to swing the twenty feet to the second set of logs and down a greased plank to the ground. The youths looked at the structure, then gazed one to the other.

"Who wishes to be first?" asked Chareos. No one spoke. "Then it will be you, young Lorin," the monk said, pointing to the redheaded son of Salida, the earl's captain of lance.

Gamely the boy ran up the plank and onto the logs. They rolled and twisted under his feet, and he half fell but righted himself and slowly made it to the rope. With a leap he sailed over to the second run, released the rope, and missed his footing, tumbling to the soft earth. The other youths did not laugh; they knew their turn would come. One by one each of them failed the run until at last only Patris was left. He nimbly ran up the plank and onto the logs. Moving carefully, he reached the rope and then swung. Just before landing he angled his body sideways and, bending his knees, dropped into a crouch. Although the log rolled, his balance was perfect. But the greased plank at the end of the run foxed him, and he slipped and fell sideways to the mud.

Chareos called them to him. Their fine tunics of embroidered silk were covered in mud and grime.

"Gentlemen, you are in sorry condition. But war will render you yet more sorry. The soldier will fight in rain and mud, snow and ice, drought and flood. It is rare that a warrior ever gets to fight in comfort. Now make the attempt twice more—in the same order, if you please. Patris, walk with me a moment." He led the earl's son some way from the others. "You did well," he said, "but it was not innovative thought. You watched, and you learned from the errors of your friends. The greased plank fooled you because you did not consider the problem."

"I know now how to descend it, Master Chareos," said the boy.

"I don't doubt it. But in real war an officer may have only one chance to succeed. Consider each problem."

"I will."

Chareos wandered back to the three youths on the pegs. Each was coping more ably with the course, except Akarin. "Let me look at you," said the monk, and the boy stood red-faced before the swordmaster as Chareos gripped the flesh above the youth's hips. "You know, of course, that you are carrying too much weight. Your legs are strong, but your body is out of balance. If you truly wish to become a swordsman, then limit your diet to one meal a day. Make it a broth, with meat and vegetables. No honey cakes. No sweetmeats. You are a fine boy, but your mother spoils you."

The other two boys were allowed to attempt the run, but they fared badly. Akarin pleaded with Chareos to be allowed to try.

"They will make fun of me," he pleaded. "Please let me attempt it."

Chareos nodded, and the fat youngster ran at the plank, made it to the logs, and wobbled toward the rope. Under his great weight the logs did not roll as badly as they had with the other youths. He swung on the rope but lost his grip and dropped into a mud pool. A huge splash went up, followed by a roar of laughter from the other boys.

Akarin hauled himself clear of the pool and stood blinking back his tears.

There was always one, Chareos knew, who had to endure the taunting. It was the nature of the pack.

He led them to a nearby pasture and opened the chest containing swords, masks, and mail shirts. Then he paired off the youngsters, partnering Patris with Akarin. The earl's son stalked across to the monk. "Why must I have the piglet?" he demanded.

"Because you are the best," answered Chareos.

"I do not understand."

"Teach him."

"And who teaches me?"

"As an officer, my lord, you will have many men under your command, and not all will be gifted. You must learn to use each man to his best advantage. Akarin will gain more from partnering with you than he would with any other boy . . . and I will teach you."

"So from now on he is my problem?"

"I believe that will be in his best interests—and yours."

"We will see," said Patris.

When the afternoon session ended, Akarin had learned a great deal from Patris, but his arms and legs were bruised from the countless blows the older boy had landed with their wooden practice blades.

"I will see you tomorrow, gentlemen," said Chareos, watching as they trudged wearily back to their homes. "Wear something more in keeping tomorrow," he called after them.

The following afternoon the youths assembled by the pegs, and Chareos came out to them. Akarin was not present; instead, a slim boy stood beside Patris.

"And who is this?" Chareos inquired.

"My cousin, Aleyn," answered Patris.

"Where is Akarin?"

"He has decided not to continue his lessons."

"And you arranged this, my lord?" Chareos asked softly.

"I did. You were wrong, Master Chareos. When I am an officer, I will have no one in my force who is not excellent in every department. I shall certainly have no pigs."

"Neither will I, my lord. I suggest that you and your cousin remove yourselves immediately. The rest of you gentlemen can begin on the pegs."

"No one move!" ordered Patris, and the youths froze. "You dare to insult me?" the boy demanded of Chareos.

"You have brought discredit on yourself, my lord," Chareos answered him icily, "and I will no longer be at your service. Since these youngsters are your friends and in some way dependent on your good graces, I shall not ask them to remain and incur your displeasure. There will be no more lessons. Good day to you."

Chareos bowed to the group and walked away.

"You'll pay for this!" Patris shouted.

The monk ignored him and returned to his rooms, his fury hard to control. He was angry not with Patris but with himself; he should have seen it coming. The earl's son was a fine athlete, but his personality was flawed. There was in him an arrogance that could not be curbed and a cruelty that would never be held in check.

After a while he calmed his emotions and walked to the library. There in the cold, stone quiet of the reading hall, he sat and studied the writings of the philosopher Neucean.

Lost in his studies, he did not feel the hours flow by. A hand touched his shoulder.

"The earl is waiting for you in the Long Hall," said the Senior Brother.

Chareos left the library and walked through the arched gardens toward the steps to the Long Hall. He had expected some reaction to his dismissal of Patris—but a visit from the earl? And so swiftly? It made him feel uneasy. In Gothir the old feudal laws had been much revised, but the earl was still the ultimate power in the Southlands, and on a whim, he could have a man flogged or imprisoned or both.

Chareos gathered his thoughts and climbed the stairs to the hall. The earl was standing alone by the south window, his fingers tapping rhythmically at the sill.

"Welcome, my lord," said Chareos, and the slim young man turned to him, forcing a smile. His face was fine-featured, his hair long and blond, heat curled in the manner of the lord regent's court.

"What are we to do about this business, Chareos?" asked the earl, beckoning the monk to a seat by the window. Chareos sat, but the earl remained standing.

"You are speaking of the lessons?"

"Why else would I be here? You have caused quite a stir.

My wife wants you flogged; the captain of the guard wishes to challenge you; my son wants you hanged—though I pointed out that withdrawing from lessons is hardly a crime. So, what can we do?"

"Is the subject so important, my lord? There are many swordmasters."

"That is not the point, and you know it, Chareos. You have insulted the heir to the earldom, and in doing so, it could be argued that you have insulted me."

"The question of right and wrong must be considered," said the monk.

"The fat boy? Yes. But I want this business resolved. I suggest you invite the child—what's his name? Akarin?—to return to the classes. You can then pair him with someone else, and the lessons can continue."

Chareos considered the question and shook his head. "I am indeed sorry that you feel the need to be involved in this . . . petty matter. What with thoughts of the Nadir, the slave raids, and the many duties you face, this is an unnecessary irritant. However, I do not see that the resumption of lessons is what is called for here. Your son is highly gifted but arrogant. Resumption of lessons will, for him, be a victory. It will be better for the boy if he is placed with another master."

"You speak of arrogance?" snapped the earl. "He has every right to be arrogant. He is my son, and we of the House of Arngir are used to victory. The lessons will resume."

Chareos rose and met the earl's icy stare. "I should point out, my lord, that I receive no pay. I chose—as a free man—to administer the lessons. I choose as a free man to cease them. I am contracted to no one and therefore am not under the law."

"Then you are telling me that the insult to my family stands? Be careful, Chareos. Think of what that means."

The monk took a deep, slow breath. "My lord," he said at last, "I hold you in the highest regard. If you feel that my actions have brought discredit to you, then accept my sincerest apologies. But at the beginning it was made clear to the students that in the matter of my lessons they had no rank. There would be no privilege. Patris not only dismissed one of my pupils but stopped the others from obeying a command. By all the rules that he—and you—agreed to, he had to go. I cannot reverse that decision."

"Cannot? Say it honestly, man. You *will* not."

"I will not." A cold silence grew between the men, but the earl seemed unwilling to end the meeting and paced by the window for several minutes.

"Very well," he said finally. "It will be as you say. Logar will take over the duties of swordmaster. I will see you, as agreed, at the castle hall on Petition Morning."

"You still wish me to practice with you, my lord?"

"I do. Or are you withdrawing from that duty also?"

"Not at all, sir. I will look forward to it."

The earl smiled. "Until then," he said, turning on his heel and striding from the hall. Chareos sat down, his hands trembling and his heart beating wildly.

It did not make sense for the earl to retain him, and he had an uneasy feeling that the next practice would not be a pleasant experience. Was he to be publicly humiliated?

He wandered to the window. Now would be a good time to leave. He could travel north to the capital or southeast into Vagria. Or even south through the lands of the Nadir and on to Drenan and the great library.

He thought of the twelve gold coins he still had hidden in his room. He could buy two horses and supplies for a journey. His gaze flickered around the hall; he had been almost content here.

His mind journeyed back to the last night on the gate tower as they sat with Tenaka Khan, the violet-eyed lord of the Nadir.

"Why did you let us live?" whispered Chareos.

The two-hour service was drawing to a close. Chareos enjoyed the singing of hymns, the chanting of the ritual prayers, and the feeling of belonging that accompanied the morning worship. It did not matter to him that his faith was less than that of his brothers. He felt at one with the Gray Order, and that in itself was enough for the former soldier.

He rose from his knees and filed out with the others,

head bowed, face shadowed by the deep hood. The morning sunshine was welcome after the cold of the nave as Chareos stepped out into the Long Garden and down the terraces toward the southern gate. Once beyond it, the peace of the monastery was lost within the noise of the crowds heading for the market meetings. Chareos allowed himself to be swept along until he reached the main square, where he pushed clear of the crowd and moved down a narrow alleyway to the livestock market. Daily auctions were watched there by discerning farmers and noblemen, with the pedigrees of bulls and horses discussed at length in the stalls surrounding the circular arena. Chareos eased himself onto the front bench by the rail and sat in silence while the bulls were led into the circle. The bidding was brisk, especially for the Drenai bulls—powerful beasts, short-horned but weighed down with flesh. After an hour the horses were led in. Chareos bid for a bay gelding but lost out to a young nobleman sitting three rows back. He bid again for a dun mare but this time was beaten by a bid from the back of the arena. Most of the other horses were swaybacks or past their prime, and he began to lose interest. Then the gray was brought in. Chareos had no wish to bid for a gray; out in the Wildlands they stood out too much, unlike the bay or the chestnut. But this animal had the look of eagles about him. His neck was long and arched, his ears flat to his skull, his eyes fierce and proud. The man leading him had a nervous look, as if fearing that at any moment the beast would rear and smash his skull. Bidding was slow, and Chareos was surprised to find himself raising an arm and even more surprised when he won the auction with a price less than half the sum he had bid for the gelding.

The man beside him leaned in close. "Beware, Brother, that is the mount that killed Trondian—threw him, then trampled him to death."

"Thank you for your concern," said Chareos, rising and moving to the rear of the arena. The stallion had been stabled there, and the monk moved in alongside him, stroking his gleaming flank. "I understand you are a killer, white one. But I daresay there is another side to your story."

Carefully he checked the stallion's legs. "You are a fine beast." Edging back, he made his way to the auction table.

"I will ride him this afternoon," he said, "but I wish him stabled with you until Petition Day."

"As you wish," replied the auction clerk. "That will be twelve silvers for the horse and six coppers for the week. Will you require a saddle? We have several that would suit you."

Chareos chose a Vagrian saddle with a high pommel and a good harness, settled his account, and left the market. After a short walk he entered Wool Street. There he purchased riding clothes: soft leather boots, dark woolen trews, two thick white shirts, and a leather topcoat that was double-shouldered and vented at the ribs to allow for ease of movement. He also bought a cloak of shining black leather lined with fur.

"A fine choice, sir," the merchant told him. "The leather is Ventrian and will stay soft through the fiercest winter. It is deeply oiled and will repel rain."

"Thank you. Tell me, who is the finest swordsmith here?"

"Well, that is a matter of debate, of course. But my brother . . ."

"Does your brother supply the earl?"

"No, but . . ."

"Who does supply the earl?"

The man sighed. "It is not far from here. You are seeking Mathlin; he has a forge by the eastern gate. Follow Wool Street until you reach the Gray Owl tavern, turn right, and continue to the temple. Then it is the second on the left."

Mathlin—a dark-bearded, powerfully built Drenai—took the monk through his workshop to a building behind the forge. On the walls hung swords of every kind: broad-bladed glaives, short stabbing swords, sabers, and the rapiers carried by the Gothir noblemen. There were even tulwars and double-headed axes on display.

"What blade were you seeking, sir monk?"

"A cavalry saber."

"Might I suggest that you try Benin's establishment. His

weapons are cheaper than mine and would probably suit you just as well."

Chareos smiled. "What suits me, swordsmith, is the best. Show me a saber."

Wandering to the far wall, Mathlin lifted clear a shining weapon. The blade was only slightly curved, the hilt topped with a cross-guard of iron. He tossed it to Chareos, who caught it expertly, then hefted the blade, slashed the air twice, rolled his wrist, and executed a lunge. "The weight is wrong," he said. "The lack of balance makes it unwieldy. Perhaps you should direct me to Benin."

Mathlin smiled. "That was made by my apprentice, and he has much to learn. Very well, sir monk. Perhaps you would follow me." He led the way through to a second room. The swords there were beautifully fashioned but without adornment—no gold leaf, no filigree silver. Mathlin took down a saber and passed it to Chareos. The blade was no wider than two fingers and sharp as a razor. The hilt guard extended around the fist, protecting the sword hand.

"Forged of the finest Ventrian steel and tempered with the blood of the smith," said Mathlin. "If there is a finer saber, then I have not seen it. But can you afford it?"

"What are you asking?"

"Three gold pieces."

"I could buy five horses for that sum."

"That is the price. There is no haggling to be done here, sir monk."

"Throw in a hunting knife and a good scabbard and we will strike the bargain," said Chareos.

Mathlin shrugged. "So be it. But the knife will be one made by my apprentice. Nothing I make comes cheap."

◊2◊

THAT AFTERNOON, IN his new clothes, Chareos prepared to ride the gray for the first time. He checked the saddle's underblanket for rucks or folds that would rub at the beast's back, then examined the bridle and bit. The latter was heavy and ridged.

"Take it out," Chareos told the hostler.

"This is a troubled beast, sir. You may need that bit."

"I want a sound horse. That . . . monstrosity . . . will tear his mouth to pieces."

"Maybe so. But it will keep him in check."

Chareos shook his head. "Look at his mouth—there are scars there already . . . old scars. And on his flanks. His masters have been hard men."

He took an apple from the barrel by the door and cut it into quarters with his new hunting knife. Then he offered a quarter to the gray, which turned its head away. Standing to one side of the horse, Chareos ate the first quarter himself; then he offered another. This time the gray accepted the gift, but his eyes were still wary.

"I reckon he'll be fast," said the hostler. "He's built for it. And with that color he'll need to be. You using him for afternoon rides, sir?"

"Perhaps. I may take him on a journey or two."

The hostler chuckled. "Don't try the Wildlands. They'll see a horse of this color from a mile away, and you'll have robbers around you thicker than flies on dog droppings."

"I'll bear that in mind," Chareos said irritably. Stepping

into the saddle, he steered the stallion out into the back street behind the auction yard.

Twenty minutes later he was in the foothills to the south of the city, with the wind in his hair and the stallion galloping at full stretch. He let the beast have his head for a full quarter mile and then drew him back, pulling left to climb a gentle rise. At the top he allowed the horse to walk for a while, watching the beast's breathing. He need not have been concerned; within a few minutes the stallion was no longer snorting, and there was little evidence of sweat on his flanks.

"You are strong," said Chareos, stroking the long sleek neck, "and fast. But when will you let me know why you are such a troubled beast?"

The stallion plodded on, but when Chareos urged him into a canter over the hills, the horse responded instantly. At the end of an hour's riding the city was far behind, though Chareos could still see its turrets in the misty distance. He made up his mind to turn back, for dusk was fast approaching and the great stallion was finally tired. Angling the beast down a short slope, he spotted billowing clouds of smoke from the south, beyond the hills. He rode on, entering a circle of trees. In a clearing he came on a group of soldiers sitting around several small fires. He recognized the officer, who was sitting apart from his men, as Logar, the earl's champion.

"There is a large fire south of you beyond the hill," Chareos told him. "Have you not noticed the smoke?"

"What business is it of yours?" asked Logar, rising smoothly. A tall, lean young man with cold eyes and a dark trident beard, he moved forward to stand close to the stallion. The horse did not like the proximity of the soldier and backed away; Chareos calmed him.

"It is not my business," he said. "Good day to you." He rode from the clearing, topped the rise, and gazed down on a scene of devastation. There were twelve homes burning, and several bodies lay sprawled on the ground. Elsewhere people were trying to bring the blaze under control at a large communal barn. Chareos cursed and returned to the soldiers' camp.

Logar was dicing with a junior officer, and both men looked up as Chareos rode in. "There is a village close by," said Chareos, "which has been under attack. You will take your men and help with the fire fighting. And know this: I shall report you to the earl for dereliction of duty."

All color fled from Logar's face as he rose and grasped the hilt of his saber. "Step down, you whoreson! I'll not be insulted by the likes of you."

"You have been," said Chareos. "Now do as I told you." Swinging the stallion, he rode to the village, tethering the horse upwind of the smoke before running to help the villagers. The fire at the barn was out of control. As a man ran by him bearing a bucket of water, Chareos dragged him to a halt. "You must get out what you can. The barn is beyond saving," he told him. The man nodded and ran on to the others as the soldiers arrived and hurled themselves into the work. Three of the homes were saved, but the barn fire raged on. Several axmen hammered an entrance at the rear of the building, allowing others to enter and drag clear what grain sacks could be saved. The battle went on long into the evening, but finally the fires died down.

Chareos walked to a nearby stream and washed his face and hands of grime. He looked down at his new clothes. The jerkin was singed, as were the trews; the shirt was blackened by smoke, the boots scuffed.

He sat down. His lungs felt hot, and his mouth tasted of wood smoke. A young man approached him.

"They took eleven of our women, sir. When will you ride after them?"

Chareos stood. "I am not a soldier; I was merely passing by. You need to see the officer with the troop; his name is Logar."

"A thousand curses on him!" spit the young man. Chareos said nothing but looked more closely at the villager. He was tall and slender, with long dark hair and keen blue eyes under thick brows. The face was handsome despite the blackening of smoke and charcoal.

"Be careful what you say, youngster," warned Chareos. "Logar is the earl's champion."

"I don't care. Old Paccus warned us of the raid, and we

sent to the earl for aid three days ago. Where were the soldiers when we needed them?"

"How did he know of the raid?"

"He's a seer: he told us the day and the hour. We tried to fight them, but we've no weapons."

"Who were they?"

"Nadren. Outlaws who trade with the Nadir. For slaves! We must get them back. We must!"

"Then see the officer. And if that does not satisfy you, go to the earl. It will soon be Petition Day."

"Do you think he will care about what happens to a few poor farmers?"

"I do not know," said Chareos. "Where is Paccus?"

The young man pointed across the ruined village to where an old man was sitting on the ground, wrapped in a blanket. Chareos made his way over to him.

"Good day, sir."

The old man looked up, his eyes bright in the moonlight. "So, it begins," he said softly. "Welcome, Chareos. How can I help you?"

"You recognize me? Have we met?"

"No. How can I help you?"

"There is a young man who claims you knew of the raid. He is angry—understandably so. How did you know?"

"I saw it in a dream. I see many things in dreams. I saw you in the clearing beyond the hill asking the vile Logar about the smoke. He and his men have been camped there all day, but he did not want to be involved in a battle. Who can blame him?"

"I can. There is no place for cowardice in an army."

"You think it cowardice, Chareos? We are talking of a man who has killed sixteen men in duels. No, he was paid by the slavers. Since slavery was outlawed in Gothir lands, the price per head has quadrupled. Our eleven women will fetch perhaps fifteen gold pieces each; Ravenna will fetch more."

"That is a great deal of money," Chareos agreed.

"The Nadir can afford it. Their treasuries are bulging with gold and jewels from Drenan, Lentria, Vagria, and Mashrapur."

"How do you know that Logar accepted a bribe?"

"How do I know that you are planning to leave the city on Petition Day? How do I know that you will not travel alone? How do I know that an old friend awaits you in the mountains? How? Because I am a seer. And today I wish I had never been born with the talent."

The old man turned his head away, gazing down at the cinder-strewn ground. Chareos rose, and as he walked back toward his stallion, a tall figure stepped into his path.

"What do you want, Logar?" he asked.

"You insulted me. Now you will pay the price!"

"You wish to duel with me?"

"I do not know you; therefore, the laws of the duel do not apply. We will merely fight."

"But you do know me, Logar. Look closely and picture this face above the robes of a gray monk."

"Chareos? Damn you! Will you hide behind the rules of the order? Or will you meet me like a man?"

"Firstly I will see the earl and discuss your . . . curious behavior today. Then I will consider your challenge. Good night to you." He moved on, then turned. "Oh, by the by . . . when you spend the gold you made today, think of the bodies that lie here. I noticed two children among the corpses. Perhaps you should help bury them."

The stallion stood quietly as Chareos stepped into the saddle. The rider looked back once at the smoldering remains of the village and then rode warily for the distant city.

"I am deeply sorry that you have decided to leave us," said the senior brother, rising from his chair and leaning across the desk with one hand extended. Chareos accepted the handshake.

"I also am full of regrets, Father. But it is time."

"Time, my son? What is time but the breath between birth and death? I had thought you were coming to understand the purpose of being, to establish the will of the Source in all things. It saddens me greatly to see you armed in this way," he said, pointing to the saber and the hunting knife.

"Where I am traveling I may have need of them, Father."

"I learned long ago that the sword is no protection, Chareos."

"I have no wish to argue, Father. Yet it must be said that the monks exist here in peace and security only because of the swords of the defenders. I do not belittle your views; I wish all men shared them. But they do not. I came to you as a broken man, and you made me whole. But if all men lived as you and I, there would be no children and no humanity. Where, then, would be the will of the Source?"

The Brother smiled. "Oh, Chareos, how narrow is your thinking! Do you believe that *this* is all there is? You were an acolyte, my son. In five or ten years you would have been ready to study the true mysteries, and you would have seen the magic of the universe. Give me your hand once more."

Chareos reached out and the monk took his fingers and turned his palm upward. The senior brother closed his eyes and sat statue-still, seeming not even to breathe. Slowly the minutes passed, and Chareos found his shoulder stiffening as he sat with arm outstretched. Easing his hand from the brother's grip, he waited in silence. At last the monk opened his eyes, shook his head, and reached for a goblet of water.

"Your journey will be long, my friend, and perilous. May the Lord of All Harmony travel with you."

"What did you see, Father?"

"Some sorrows are not for sharing before their time, my son. But there is no evil in you. Go now, for I must rest."

Chareos took a last stroll around the monastery grounds before walking on toward the keep at the center of the city. Several centuries earlier the keep had been built to guard the northern toll road, but when the Nadir hordes of Ulric first gathered, they destroyed the great southern city of Gulgothir, the capital of the Gothir kingdom, and the land was torn in two. Refugees streamed north, over the mountains and far from Nadir tyranny. A new capital was built on the western edge of the ocean, and the keep at Talgithir became the southernmost point of Gothir lands. It had grown in size since those early days, and now the keep was but a small island at the center of a bustling metropolis.

The great gates of oak and iron were shut, but Chareos joined the line at the side gate that slowly filed through to the outer courtyard. There were the petitioners, men and women with grievances only the earl could settle. There were more than two hundred people already present, and each carried a flat disk of clay stamped with a number. When that number was called, the petitioner would walk inside the main hall and present his case to the earl. Of the hundreds waiting, only about a dozen would be dealt with, the rest returning the next Petition Day.

Chareos walked up the wide stone steps toward the two guards at the top; their spears were crossed, but they lifted them to allow him to pass through into the inner chambers. Three times already he had tried to contact the earl, to inform him of the deeds of his soldiers. But on each occasion he had been turned away and told that the earl was too busy to be interrupted.

A servant led Chareos through to the dining hall. The long tables had been removed, and now the earl and his retainers sat facing the doors. The first petitioner was already before them, talking of a broken promise in the matter of the sale of three bulls; he had received half the payment on delivery, but the remainder had been denied him. The accused was a nobleman, a distant relative of the earl. The case was found to be proved, and the earl ordered the money to be paid, plus five silver pieces to be given to the plaintiff to offset the waste of time the case had incurred. He also fined the nobleman twenty gold pieces.

The plaintiff bowed low and backed from the chamber. The next person to be called was a widow who claimed that her inheritance had been stolen by a man who had claimed to love her. The man was dragged into the hall, weighted down with chains. His face was bruised and bloody, and he admitted the charge against him. The earl ordered him hanged.

One by one the petitioners came forward until, at noon, the earl rose. "Enough for one day, by the gods," he said.

A young man pushed through the main doors, the guards

running after him. "My lord, hear me!" he called. The two guards seized the man's arms and began to drag him away.

"Wait!" called the earl. "Let him speak."

Chareos recognized the tall young villager and eased himself forward to hear him.

"My village was attacked by raiders. Eleven of our women were taken to be sold to the Nadir. We must get them back, my lord."

"Ah, yes, the village. A sad affair," the earl said. "But there is little we can do. We followed their tracks to the mountains, but they escaped into Nadir lands, and I have no jurisdiction there."

"Then you will do nothing?" the man shouted.

"Do not raise your voice to me, peasant!" roared the earl.

"We pay taxes to you, and we look to you for protection. But when we asked for it, your men stayed hidden in a wood while our people were slaughtered. Do cowards now rule the Gothir?"

"Take him!" shouted the earl, and the guards leapt on the villager, pinning his arms. "I want him flogged. Get him out of here."

"Is that your answer?" yelled the youth. "Is this justice?"

The earl ignored him, and the youth was hauled away, the doors closing behind him. "Ah, Chareos," said the earl. "Welcome. Are you ready for the exhibition?"

"I am indeed, my lord," replied Chareos, stepping forward. "But may I first say a word about the young man's claims?"

"You may not!" snapped the earl. "Logar!" The champion rose from his seat and walked out to stand with the two men. "I hurt my shoulder during last week's exhibition," said the earl, "and it is troubling me still. But rather than disappoint our guests, would you take my place against the hero of Bel-azar?"

"It would be a pleasure, my lord," replied Logar. "Might I suggest that it would imbue the spectacle with greater tension were we to exhibit our skills without masks and mail shirts?"

"Is that not dangerous?" the earl queried. "I would not like to see a tragic accident."

"There is danger, my lord, but it might add spice to the exhibition."

"Very well," agreed the earl, ignoring Chareos. "Let it be as you say."

A page came forward bearing two rapiers. Chareos chose the left-hand blade and moved away to loosen his muscles. He laid his saber and knife on a ledge, his mind racing. He had no doubt that Logar would try to kill him, yet if he killed Logar, the earl would have him arrested. Mechanically he went through his exercises, stretching the muscles of his arms, shoulders, and groin. He glanced at the two rows of spectators, his eye catching the young Lord Patris. The boy was grinning wolfishly. Chareos turned away and approached Logar.

The two men lifted their blades high, saluting each other, then touched swords.

"Begin!" called the earl.

Logar launched a sudden attack, rolling his wrist in the Classic Chare, but Chareos parried the blow, moving smoothly to his right. Logar's eyes narrowed. Three times the soldier hurled himself forward, and on each occasion he was parried. Chareos was growing angry. Logar was making no attempt to defend himself, sure in the knowledge that Chareos could not—in an exhibition—deliver a killing thrust. Twice his blade flashed by Chareos' throat, and the monk knew it was only a matter of time before the earl's champion found a way through his defenses. Chareos blocked a thrust and leapt back, wrong-footing Logar. As the champion cursed and moved forward, Chareos took a deep breath and prepared to meet the attack, knowing now that Logar intended to kill him. But was it the earl's plan or merely the result of Logar's wounded pride? Logar's sword blade lanced for his eye, but he sidestepped, spun on his heel, and jumped back. Logar swung and grinned broadly. Back and forth across the hall the two swordsmen battled. The spectators could not hold themselves in silence and began wildly cheering every attack made by Logar. Several minutes passed, and still there was no resolution to the encounter. Logar lunged. Chareos only partly blocked him and felt his opponent's sword blade slice into the skin of his cheek.

At the sight of blood a hush fell on the spectators, who looked to the earl to end the exhibition. But he made no move. So it was the earl's plan, thought Chareos, and anger flared within him, but he held it trapped. He could not kill Logar, for then the earl would have him arrested and on trial for murder. Coldly furious, Chareos circled, then moved swiftly to his right. Logar lunged forward. Chareos parried three thrusts, then slashed his own blade high over Logar's sword. The point of Chareos' rapier split the skin above Logar's right eye and sliced on across his brow. Blood billowed into the swordsman's eyes, and he fell back.

Chareos turned to the earl. "Is the exhibition over, my lord?"

"That was foul work," said the earl. "You could have killed him."

"Indeed I could, for he is not very skillful. But for good luck, this blow," said Chareos, pointing to the cut on his own cheek, "would have pierced me to the brain. Happily there is little harm done; his cut is not serious. And now, with your permission . . ." A sound from behind made him spin on his heel. Logar had wiped most of the blood from his face and was running at him with sword extended. Chareos sidestepped and rammed his hilt guard behind Logar's left ear, and the champion fell unconscious to the marble floor. "As I was saying," said Chareos coldly, "with your permission I will leave."

"You are not welcome here," hissed the earl, "or anywhere within my jurisdiction."

Bowing, Chareos backed three steps and took up his saber and knife. He marched from the hall with head held high, feeling the hostility following him.

Out in the courtyard most of the petitioners had remained to watch the flogging. Chareos descended the steps, his eyes locked to the writhing form of the villager as the lash snaked across his skin.

Approaching the captain of the guard, he asked, "How many strokes has he suffered?"

"Eighteen. We'll stop at fifty."

"You'll stop at twenty," Chareos told him. "That is the penalty for insubordinate behavior."

"The earl did not specify the number," the officer snapped.

"Perhaps he thought you would know the law," remarked Chareos as the lash sounded once more.

"That's enough," said the captain. "Cut him down." They dragged the villager out through the postern gate and left him lying beside the path.

Chareos helped him to his feet. "Thank you," the man whispered.

"You'll not get home in that state," Chareos told him. "You'd best come with me. I'll book a room at the Gray Owl tavern, and we'll see to your back."

The Gray Owl tavern was a rambling building built around an ancient inn that sat on the mountain road leading to Gulgothir. At its center was an L-shaped hall where drinkers and diners were waited on by serving maids. Two new buildings had been constructed on the east and west sides, and a stableyard had been added to the rear.

As Chareos eased his way through the milling taverners, his jutting scabbard cracked against a man's leg.

"Watch what you're doing, you whoreson!" hissed the drinker. Chareos ignored him, but as he walked on, he gripped the hilt of his saber, holding the scabbard close to his leg. It was a long, long time since he had worn a sword belt, and it felt clumsy, out of place.

He passed through a doorway and mounted the circular stair to the first-floor corridor. At the far end he entered the double room he had paid for that afternoon. The villager still slept, his breathing deep and slow; the draught of *lirium* administered by the apothecary would keep him unconscious until dawn. Chareos had cleaned the whip wounds and covered them with goose grease, pressing a large square of linen to the villager's back. The lash cuts were not deep, but the skin around them had peeled back, burned by the leather of the whip.

Chareos banked up the fire in the hearth on the south

wall. Autumn was approaching, and a chilly wind hissed through the warped window frames. He removed his sword belt and sat in a wide, deep leather chair by the fire. He was tired now, yet his mind would not relax. The sanctuary of the monastery seemed distant, and depression hit him like a physical blow. Today the earl had tried to have him killed—and for what? All because of the actions of an arrogant child. He glanced at the sleeping villager. The boy had seen his village razed and his loved ones taken, and he had now been whipped to add to his agony. Justice was for the rich . . . it always had been. Chareos leaned forward and threw a chunk of wood on the fire. One of the three lanterns on the wall guttered and died, and he checked the others. They were low, and he pulled the bell rope by the west wall.

After some minutes a serving maid tapped at the door. He asked for oil and ordered a meal and some wine. She was gone for half an hour, during which time a second lantern failed.

The villager groaned in his sleep, whispering a name. Chareos moved over to him, but the youth faded back into slumber.

The maid returned with a jug of oil. "I'm sorry for the delay, sir, but we're full tonight and two of the girls have not come in." She refilled the lanterns and lit them with a long taper. "Your food will be up soon. There is no beef, but the lamb is good."

"It will suffice."

She stopped in the doorway and glanced back. "Is he the villager who was scourged today?" she whispered.

"He is."

"And you would be Chareos the monk?"

He nodded, and she stepped back into the room. She was short and plump, with corn-colored hair and a round, pretty face. "Perhaps I shouldn't speak out of turn, sir, but there are men looking for you—men with swords. One of them has a bandage on his brow."

"Do they know I am here?"

"Yes, sir. There are three men in the stable, and two others are now sitting in the main hall. I think there may be more."

"Thank you kindly," he said, pressing a half silver piece into her hand.

After she had gone, he bolted the door, returned to the fire, and dozed until there was another tap at the door. He slid his saber from the scabbard. "Who is it?" he called.

"It's me, sir. I have your food and wine."

He pulled back the bolts and opened the door. She came in and laid the wooden tray on the narrow table by the chair. "They are still there, sir. And the man with the bandage is talking to Finbale, the owner."

"Thank you."

"You could leave through the servants' quarters," she offered.

"My horses are in the stable. Do not fear for me."

She smiled. "It was good what you did for him," she said, and then she left, pulling the door shut behind her. Chareos pushed home the bolt and settled down to his meal. The meat was tender, the vegetables soft and overcooked, and the wine barely passable; even so, the meal filled his belly, and he settled down to sleep in the chair. His dreams were troubled, but when he awoke, they vanished like smoke in the breeze. Predawn light had shaded the sky to a dark gray. The fire was almost dead, the room chilly; Chareos added tinder to the glowing embers, blowing the flames to life, then piled on larger chunks. He was stiff and cold, and his neck ached. With the fire blazing once more, he moved to the villager. The youth's breathing was more shallow now. Chareos touched his arm, and the villager groaned and opened his eyes.

He tried to sit up, but pain hit him and he sank back.

"Your wounds are clean," said Chareos, "and though they must be painful, I suggest you rise and dress. I have bought a horse for you. And we leave the city this morning."

"Thank you . . . for your help. My name is Kiall." The youth sat up, his face twisted by the pain clawing at his back.

"The wounds will heal well," Chareos told him. "They

are clean and not deep. The pain is from the whip burns, but that will pass in three or four days."

"I do not know your name," said Kiall.

"Chareos. Now get dressed. There are men waiting who will make our departure troublesome."

"Chareos? The hero of Bel-azar?"

"Yes," snapped Chareos, "the wondrous giant of song and tale. Did you hear me, boy? We are in danger. Now, get dressed."

Kiall pushed himself to his feet and struggled into his trews and boots but could not raise his arms to pull on his shirt. Chareos helped him. The lash marks extended all the way to Kiall's hip, and he could not fasten his belt. "Why are we in danger?" he asked.

Chareos shrugged. "I doubt it has to do with you. I had a duel with a man named Logar, and I would imagine he is feeling somewhat humiliated. Now, I want you to go down to the stable. My horses are there. Mine is the gray, and the saddle is by the stall. You know how to saddle a horse?"

"I was once a stable boy."

"Good. Make sure the cinch is tight enough. Two stalls down there is a swaybacked black gelding; it was the best I could find for you. He's old and nearly worn out, but he will get you back to your village."

"I will not return to the village," said Kiall softly. "I will hunt down the raiders who took Ravenna and the others."

"A sound and sensible idea," said Chareos irritably, "but for now be so good as to saddle my horse."

Kiall reddened. "I may owe you my life, but do not mock me," he said. "I have loved Ravenna for years, and I will not rest until she is free or I am dead."

"The latter is what you will be. But it is your life. My horse, if you please."

Kiall opened his mouth but said nothing. Shaking his head, he left the room. Chareos waited for several minutes and then walked down the stairs to the kitchen, where two scullery servants were preparing the dough for the day's bread. He summoned the first and asked her to pack some provisions for him: salt beef, a ham, corn biscuits, and a small sack of oats. With his order filled, he paid her and wandered through the deserted main hall. The innkeeper, Finbale, was hanging freshly washed tankards on hooks above the bar. He nodded and smiled as Chareos moved toward the door, and Chareos stopped and approached the man.

"Good morning," said Finbale, a wide grin showing the gaps in his teeth.

"And to you," responded Chareos. "Will you have my horse brought to the door?"

"The stable is only across the yard, sir. And my boy is not here yet."

"Then do it yourself," said Chareos coldly.

"I'm very busy, sir," Finbale answered, the smile vanishing, and turned back to his chores.

So, thought Chareos, they are still here. Holding his provisions in his left hand, he stepped out into the yard. All was quiet, and the dawn was breaking to the east. The morning was chilly and fresh, and the smell of frying bacon hung in the air. Glancing around the yard, Chareos saw a wagon close by and a short wall leading to the chicken run. To the left the stable door was open, but there was no sign of Kiall. As Chareos moved out into the open, a man ran toward him from the side of the building; he dropped his provisions and drew his saber. Two more men came into view from behind the wagon, and then Logar appeared from the stable. His forehead was bandaged, but blood was seeping through the linen.

"You are very good with a rapier," said Logar. "But how do you fare with the saber?"

"I am better with a saber," Chareos answered.

"In that case we will take no chances," hissed Logar. "Kill him!"

As two swordsmen leapt forward, Chareos blocked a wild slash, spun on his heel to avoid a second thrust, and backhanded his blade across the first man's throat. Blood welled from the cut, and the attacker fell, dropping his sword and thrusting his fingers at the wound in a vain attempt to stem the flow of his life. The second attacker sent a cut at Chareos' head, but the monk ducked under it and thrust his own blade through the man's chest. A third swordsman fell back, his eyes widening.

"Well?" said Chareos, glaring at Logar, and the earl's champion screamed and launched an attack. Chareos blocked the first slash, leapt back from a sweeping slice that would have disemboweled him, then swept a flashing riposte that plunged into Logar's groin, severing the huge artery at the top of the inner thigh. Logar dropped his saber and stared in disbelief at the blood drenching his leggings; then his legs gave way, and he fell to his knees before Chareos. He looked up at his killer and blinked before toppling sideways to the ground. Chareos moved to the body, pulling free the sword belt and sliding the dead man's saber back into the scabbard. When Kiall rode into the yard, leading Chareos' gray, the former monk tossed Logar's saber to the villager, gathered his provisions, and swung into the saddle. The last swordsman stood by, saying nothing. Chareos ignored him and steered his mount toward the southern gate.

The yard had been roped off, and guards stood by the entrances. Behind them a crowd had gathered, straining to see the stiffening corpses. The earl stood over the body of Logar, staring down at the gray, bloodless face.

"The facts speak for themselves," he said, pointing at the body. "See, he has no sword. He was murdered, and I want the killer brought to justice. Who would have thought that a hero of Bel-azar would stoop to such a base deed?" The retainers grouped around him said nothing, and the surviving swordsman turned his eyes from the earl.

"Take twenty men," the earl ordered Salida, his captain of lancers, "and bring Chareos back here."

Salida cleared his throat. "My lord, it was not like Logar to walk unarmed, and these other two men had swords drawn. Chareos is a master bladesman. I cannot believe . . ."

"Enough!" snapped the earl, and swung to the survivor. "You . . . what is your name again?"

"Kypha, my lord," replied the man, keeping his eyes fixed on the ground.

"Was Logar armed when Chareos slew him?"

"No, my lord."

"There you have it, then," said the earl. "And you have the evidence of your eyes. Do you see a sword?"

"No, my lord," said Salida. "I will fetch him. What of the villager?"

"He was an accessory to murder; he will hang alongside Chareos."

The twenty-two captive women sat close together in four open wagons. On either side warriors rode, grim men and fierce-eyed. Ravenna was in the second wagon, separated from her friends. Around her were women and girls taken in two other raids. All were frightened, and there was little conversation.

Two days before a girl had tried to escape; she had leapt from a wagon at dusk and run for the trees, but they had ridden her down in seconds and dragged her back. The captives had been assembled in a circle to watch the girl being whipped, and her whimpering screams still sounded in Ravenna's ears.

After that several of the men had dragged her away from the camp and raped her. Then her arms had been tied and she had been flung down near the other prisoners.

"There is a lesson to be learned here," said a man with a scarred face. "You are slaves, and you will begin to think like slaves. That way you will survive. Any slave who attempts to run will be treated more harshly than this one. Remember these words."

Ravenna would remember . . .

The time to escape would not be while the Nadren held them. No, it was necessary to be more cunning. She would wait until she was bought by some lecherous Nadir. She would be pliant and helpful, loving and grateful . . . and when he had grown confident of her emotions—then she would run.

"Where are you from?" whispered the woman beside her. Ravenna told her.

"I visited your village once. For the summer solstice fair." Ravenna looked at the bony figure, scanning the lean, angular face and the shining black hair. She could not remember her.

"Are you wed?" she asked.

"Yes," said the woman, shrugging. "But that does not matter anymore."

"No," Ravenna agreed.

"And you?"

"I was due to marry. Eighteen—no, seventeen—days from now."

"Are you a virgin?" the woman asked, her voice dropping lower.

"No."

"You are from now on. They will ask. Virgins fetch higher prices. And it will mean these . . . pigs . . . will not touch you. You understand?"

"Yes. But surely the man who buys me . . ."

"What do they know? Men! Find yourself a sharp pin and on the first night cut yourself."

Ravenna nodded. "Thank you. I will remember that."

They lapsed into silence as the wagons moved on. The raiders rode warily, and Ravenna could not stop herself from scanning the horizon.

"Do not expect help," the woman told her.

"One should always hope."

The woman smiled. "Then hope for a handsome savage with kindly ways."

The mountains towered before them like a fighting line of white-bearded giants, and an icy wind drifted over the peaks into the faces of the riders. As Chareos pulled his fur-lined cloak about him and belted it, he glanced at the villager. Kiall's face was gray and he swayed in the saddle, but he offered no complaint. Chareos gazed back toward the city. It was far behind them now, and only the tallest turrets could be seen beyond the hills.

"How are you faring?" he asked Kiall. The villager gave a weak smile. The *lirium* was wearing off, and pain was eating into his back like hot coals. The old swayback gelding was a serene beast, and normally the ride would have been comfortable, but now every movement pulled at

Kiall's tortured flesh. "We will stop in a while," said Chareos, "once we are in the trees. There are lakes there with crystal-clear water. We will rest, and I will see to your injuries." Kiall nodded and gripped the pommel of his saddle. He felt sick, and sweat had formed a sheen on his face. Cursing inwardly, Chareos moved alongside the swayback. Suddenly the white stallion arched its neck and flashed a bite at the older animal. Chareos dragged on the reins, and the gelding reared. Kiall all but toppled from the saddle. The stallion bucked and dipped its head, but Chareos clung grimly, his thighs locked tight to the barrel of the animal's body. For several seconds the horse tried to unseat him; then it settled down as if nothing had happened and stood calmly. Chareos stepped down from the saddle, stroking the stallion's long neck. Moving to stand before the horse's head, he rubbed at its nose, then blew a long slow breath into each of its nostrils. "Know me," whispered Chareos, over and over again. "I will not harm you. I am not your master. I am a friend."

At last he remounted and continued the journey south. Chareos had never traveled those hills, but travelers spoke of a settlement built around a tavern. He hoped that the village was close and that they had a healer. Kiall's fever was climbing, and for all Chareos knew the wounds could be festering. As a soldier he had seen many men die from what appeared to be small wounds. The skin would swell and discolor, fever would deepen, and flesh would melt away. He recalled a young warrior at Bel-azar who had cut his hand on a thorn. The hand had swelled to three times its size, then had turned blue and finally black. The surgeon had cut it from him. But the boy died . . . And he died screaming. Chareos glanced at Kiall and forced a smile, but the youth did not respond.

By late afternoon Kiall could ride no more. He was feverish and moaning, and two of the long wounds in his back had opened. Chareos had lashed the young man's wrists to the pommel and was now leading the gelding as he guided the horses along the shores of a wide lake; it was smooth as a mirror, and the mountains were reflected on its surface. Dismounting, he hobbled the horses and helped

Kiall to the ground. The villager sagged, his knees giving way. Chareos let him lie and built a fire. As a soldier he had seen many men flogged. Often the shock of the beating was what laid a man low, the humiliation more than the agony. With the fire blazing, he turned Kiall onto his stomach and sniffed at the wounds. There was no smell of corruption. Chareos covered him with a blanket. The young man was strong and proud. He had not complained about his pain, and Chareos admired that.

He sat by the fire, staring out over the mountains and the stands of pine which grew green through the snow. There had been a time when such a view had made him think of freedom, the wide beauty, the towering grandeur of the peaks. Now, he realized, they spoke only of the futility of man. Wars, plagues, kings, and conquerors were as nothing to these peaks.

"What do you care for my dreams?" asked Chareos, his mind drifting back to Tura as it so often did when the reflective mood came upon him. Beautiful, black-haired Tura. She had made him feel more of a man than he could have wished for. With her he was complete. But what she had seemed to give so freely, she had cruelly stolen back. Chareos' face reddened with the memory. How many lovers had she taken before Chareos had discovered her infidelity? Ten? Twenty? How many of his friends had accepted the gift of her body? The hero of Bel-azar! If only they knew. Chareos the bladesman had not gone there to fight; he had gone there to die.

There was little heroism in that. But the bards did not care for realism. They sang of silver blades and dashing deeds; the cuckold's shame had no place in the saga of Bel-azar.

He stood and wandered to the lakeside, kneeling to drink, closing his eyes against his reflection. Returning to the fire, he saw that Kiall was sleeping peacefully. The sun drifted low in the west, and the air grew cooler. Chareos loosened the saddle cinches on the horses and stretched out his blanket close to the fire.

Lying back, he stared at the stars. He had wanted to forgive Tura, to take her far from the fort and start a new life, but she had laughed at him. She liked it where she was, where there were men at hand, strong men, lusty men, men who would give her presents. In his mind's eye he could see himself striking her and smashing her beauty beneath his fists. But he never had. He had backed from the room, forced by the strength of her laughter, the love he had allowed into his heart torn away by the talons of treachery. He had never loved again, never taken a woman to his heart or his bed.

A wolf howled in the distance, a lonely mournful sound. Chareos banked the fire and slept.

Birdsong drifted through his dreams, and he awoke. He did not feel refreshed for his sleep and knew that he had dreamed of Tura. As always, he could remember little save her name echoing in his mind. He sat up and shivered. The fire was nearly gone, and he knelt before it, blowing the embers to life and adding twigs to the tiny flames. Then he rose and wandered from the campsite, gathering dead wood.

With the fire blazing once more, he moved to the stallion, stroking its neck. He took some cold meat from his sack of provisions and returned to the warmth of the blaze. Kiall woke and carefully sat up. His color had returned, and he smiled at Chareos.

The former monk sliced the ham with his hunting knife and passed it to the villager.

"Where are we?" asked Kiall.

"About ten miles from the old toll road. You look better."

"I am sorry to be a burden to you. And even more sorry that you had to kill for me."

"It wasn't for you, Kiall. They were hunting me. A haughty child is disciplined, and now three men are dead. Insane."

"You were amazing in the fight. I have never seen anything like it. You were so cool."

"You know why they died?" Chareos asked.

"They were not as good as you?" ventured Kiall.

"No, they weren't, but that's not the whole reason. They

died because they had something to live for. Finish your breakfast."

For three days they moved higher into the range, crossing streams and rivers. Above them the snow geese flew, heading for their distant breeding grounds. In the waters the beaver battled against the floods, building their dams. Kiall's wounds were healing fast in the clean mountain air, and now he wore Logar's saber at his side.

The companions had spoken little during the climb, and at night, at the campfire, Chareos would sit facing north, lost in thought.

"Where are we going?" Kiall asked as they saddled their horses on the fifth morning.

Chareos was silent for a moment. "*We* are heading into a settlement called Tavern Town. There *we* will purchase supplies. But after that *I* will be riding south across the steppes. And I will be riding alone, Kiall."

"You will not help me rescue Ravenna?" It was the first time since the tavern that the villager had spoken of the raid. Chareos tightened the saddle cinch on the stallion before turning to face the young man.

"You do not know which direction the raiders took. You do not know the name of their leader. By now the women will be sold. It is a hopeless cause, Kiall. Give it up."

"I cannot," said the young man. "I love her, Chareos. I have loved her since I was a child. Have you ever been in love?"

"Love is for fools. It is a surging of blood in the loins . . . there is no mystery and no magic. Find someone else, boy. By now she has been raped a dozen times, and she may even have found she likes it."

Kiall's face went white, and Logar's saber flashed into the air. Chareos leapt back. "What in the devil's name are you doing?"

"Apologize! Now!" Kiall ordered, advancing with the saber pointing at Chareos' throat.

"For what? For pointing out the obvious?" The saber lanced forward, but Chareos swayed aside from the point and drew his own sword. "Don't be a fool, boy. You are in no condition to fight me. And even if you were, I could cut you to pieces."

"Apologize," repeated Kiall.

"No," said Chareos softly. The villager attacked wildly, but Chareos parried with ease, and, off balance, Kiall tumbled to the ground, dropping the saber. He reached for it, but Chareos' boot trapped the blade. Kiall twisted and dived, his head ramming into Chareos' belly, and both men fell. Kiall's fist cracked against Chareos' chin. The former monk blocked a second blow, but a third stunned him, and he lost his grip on his saber. Kiall swept up the blade and lurched upright. Chareos tried to rise, but the point of his own saber touched the skin of his throat.

"You are a surprising lad," remarked Chareos.

"And you are a whoreson," hissed Kiall, dropping the saber to the snow and turning away. His wounds had opened, and fresh blood was seeping in jagged lines through the back of his tunic.

Chareos rose and slid the saber back in its scabbard.

"I am sorry," he said, and Kiall stopped, his shoulders sagging. Chareos moved to him. "I mean it. I am not a man who likes women very much, but I do know what it is to be in love. Were you married long?"

"We were not wed," Kiall told him.

"Betrothed?"

"No."

"What, then?" asked Chareos, mystified.

"She was going to marry another man. His father owns the whole of the east pastureland, and it was a good match."

"But she loved you?"

"No," admitted Kiall. "No, she never did." The young man hauled himself into the saddle.

"I don't understand," said Chareos. "You are setting off on a quest to rescue a woman who doesn't love you?"

"Tell me again what a fool I am," Kiall said.

"No, no, forgive me for that. I am older than you, and cynical, Kiall. But I should not mock. I have no right. But what of her betrothed? Is he dead?"

"No. He has made an arrangement with Ravenna's father, and now he will marry her younger sister, Karyn—she was not taken."

"He did not grieve for long, then," Chareos observed.

"He never loved her; he just wanted her because she is beautiful and her father is rich; he breeds pigs, cattle, and horses. He is the ugliest man I ever saw, but his daughters have been touched by heaven."

Chareos picked up the boy's saber and handed it to him hilt first.

Kiall gazed down at the blade. "There's little point in my carrying this sword. I have no skill with such things."

"You are wrong," said Chareos, smiling. "You've a good hand, a fast eye, and a proud heart. All you lack is tuition. I'll supply that as we search for Ravenna."

"You'll come with me? Why?"

"Never count the teeth of a gift horse," answered Chareos, moving to the gray and stepping into the saddle. The horse trembled.

"Oh, no," whispered Chareos. The stallion bucked violently, then reared and twisted in the air, and Chareos flew over his head to land in the snow with a bone-jarring thud. The stallion walked forward to stand over him. He pushed himself upright and remounted.

"A strange beast," observed Kiall. "I don't think he likes you."

"Of course he does, boy. The last man he didn't like he trampled to death."

Chareos touched his heels to the stallion and led the way south.

He stayed some lengths ahead of Kiall as they rode through the morning, aware that he had no answers that the boy would understand. He could have told him of a child thirty years ago who had had no hope, save that a warrior named Attalis had rescued him and become a father to him. He could tell him of a mother also named Ravenna, a proud, courageous woman who had refused to leave the husband she adored even for the son she loved. But to do so would mean sharing a secret that Chareos carried with shame—a duty unfulfilled, a promise broken. He felt the fresh breeze whispering against his skin and could smell the trees and the promise of snow. He glanced at the sky.

There was nothing he could say to Kiall. The boy was happy. The legendary blademaster had agreed to accompany him, and in Kiall's mind success was assured.

Chareos' thoughts turned to the farm girl and the man who loved her, just as he had loved Tura, a hopeless one-sided emotion. Yet even now, after the bitterness and the pain, Chareos would walk through a lake of fire if Tura needed him. But she did not need him . . . she never had.

No, the one in need was a pig breeder's daughter. He twisted in the saddle and looked back at Kiall, who smiled and waved.

Returning his gaze to the mountains ahead, Chareos remembered the day Tura had left him. He was sitting alone in the small courtyard behind the house. The sun was sinking behind the clouds and seemed to burn like red fire. Finn found him there.

The bowman sat alongside him on the stone seat. "She didn't love you, man," said Finn, and Chareos wept like a child. For some time Finn sat in silence, then he placed his hand on Chareos' shoulder and spoke softly. "Men dream of many things, Blademaster. We dream of fame we can never know or riches we can never win. But the most foolish of all is the dream of love, of the great abiding love. Let it go."

"I can't," answered Chareos.

"Then mask it, for the troops are waiting and it is a long ride to Bel-azar."

◊ 3 ◊

THE STAG DIPPED its head to the stream, its long tongue lapping at the clear water. Something struck it a wicked blow in the side; its head came up, and an arrow sliced through one eye, deep into the brain. Its forelegs buckled, and it dropped to the earth, blood seeping from its mouth.

The two hunters rose from the bushes and splashed across the stream to the carcass. Both were wearing buckskins, fringed and beaded, and they carried curved hunting bows of Vagrian horn. The younger of the men—slight, blond-haired, with wide eyes of startling blue—knelt by the stag and opened the great artery of the beast's throat. The other man, taller and heavily bearded, stood watching the undergrowth.

"There's no one about, Finn," said the blond hunter. "You are getting old and starting to imagine things."

The bearded man swore softly. "I can smell the bastards—they're hereabouts. Can't see why. No raiding for them. No women. But they're here, right enough. Puking Nadren!"

The smaller man disemboweled the stag and began to skin the carcass with a double-edged hunting knife. Finn notched an arrow to his bow and stood glaring at the undergrowth opposite.

"You are making me nervous," the younger man told him.

"We been together twenty years, Maggrig, and you still read sign like a blind man reads script."

"Truly? Who was it last year said the Tattooed Men were hunting? Stayed guard for four days and not a sight of the headhunters?"

"They were there. They just didn't want to kill us right then," said Finn. "How long are you going to be quartering that beast?"

Just then four men rose from the bushes on the other side of the stream. They were all armed with bows and swords, but no arrows were notched and the blades were scabbarded.

"You want to share some of that?" called a lean, bearded man.

"We need it for the winter store. Deer are mighty scarce these days," Finn told him. Maggrig, kneeling beside the carcass, sheathed his hunting knife and took up his bow, sliding an arrow from his quiver.

"There's two more on this side," he whispered.

"I know," said the older man, cursing inwardly. With two Nadren hidden in the undergrowth behind them, they were trapped.

"You are not being very friendly," said the Nadren warrior as he and the others began to wade toward the hunters.

"You can stop there," Finn told him, drawing back the bowstring. "We are in no need of company." Maggrig, confident that Finn could contain the men at the stream, notched an arrow to his bow, his blue eyes scanning the undergrowth to the rear. A bowman rose from the bushes with his arrow aimed at Finn's back. Maggrig drew and loosed instantly, his shaft flashing through the man's throat, and the raider's arrow sailed over Finn and splashed down into the water before the four men.

"I didn't order him to do that," said the lean man across the water, waving his arm at the men alongside him. They began to back away, but Finn said nothing, his eyes fixed on them.

"The other one is ready to chance a shaft," whispered Maggrig. "Do you have to stand there inviting it?"

"Hell's gates, I'm tired of standing around in the cold,"

said Finn. "Make the whoreson show himself." Maggrig drew back on the bowstring and sent an arrow slicing into the bushes. There was a yelp of surprise, and a bowman reared up with a shaft through his upper arm. Finn spun on his heel and sent a second arrow into the man's chest, and he fell facedown into the undergrowth. Finn swung back, but the men across the stream had vanished into the bushes.

"Getting old, am I?" Finn snapped. "Your boots have more brains than you." Maggrig grabbed Finn's jerkin, hauling him from his feet as three arrows slashed the air where he had been standing. Maggrig loosed a shaft back across the stream, but he knew he had struck nothing.

"Time to be going home, old man," Maggrig said. An arrow hit the ground before him, striking a stone and ricocheting into the carcass. Hastily the two men dragged the butchered deer back out of range, stacked the choicest cuts of meat inside the skin, and faded into the woods. They moved warily for several miles, but there was no sign of pursuit.

Finally they angled across the slopes of the mountain to the partially hidden cabin set against the north face. Once there, Finn built up the fire and tugged off his wet boots, hurling them against the stone of the hearth. The cabin was two-roomed. A large bed was against the wall opposite the fire, and a single window had been fashioned beside the door. Bearskin rugs covered the floor. Maggrig opened the door to the workshop beyond, where they crafted their bows and arrows and beat the iron for the heads. He heard Finn swear.

"Damn Nadren! When I was your age, Maggrig, we had mounted patrols that scoured the mountains for scum like that. It's a bad day when they feel they can come in, bold as a brass mirror, to steal an innocent man's supper. Damn them!"

"Why so annoyed?" asked Maggrig. "We killed two of them *and* kept our supper. They haven't caused us a problem, save for three lost arrows."

"They will. Murderous savages, the lot of them. They'll be hunting us."

"Ah yes, but we have the great hunter Finn, the smeller

of trouble! Not a bird can break wind in the mountains without Finn picking up the scent."

"You're as funny as a broken leg. I've got a bad feeling, boy; there's death in the air smelling worse than winter." He shivered and stretched out his large, bony hands to the fire.

Maggrig said nothing. He could feel it, too.

Carrying the quartered stag through to the back of the workshop, Maggrig hung it on iron hooks by the far wall. Then he spread the skin and began the long job of scraping the fat from it. He'd need a new shirt for the winter, and he liked the russet color of the hide. Finn wandered in and sat at the workbench, idly picking up an arrow shaft and judging the line. He put it down. Normally he would cut feather flights, but now he merely sat staring at the bench top.

Maggrig glanced up at him. "Your back troubling you again?"

"Always does when winter's close. Damn! I hate going down to the Tavern Town but needs must. Have to pass the word about the raiders."

"We could look in and see Beltzer."

Finn shook his head. "He'll be drunk as usual. And one more insult from that pig and I swear I'll gut him."

Maggrig stood and stretched his back. "You don't mean that. Neither does he. He's just lonely, Finn."

"Feel sorry for him, do you? Not me. He was cantankerous when he was married. He was vile at Bel-azar. There's a streak of mean in the man—I can't stand him."

"Then why did you buy his ax when they auctioned it?" demanded the blond hunter. "Two years of trapping to pay for that! And what have you done with it? Wrapped it in oilskin and left it at the bottom of the chest."

Finn spread his hands. "No accounting for myself sometimes. Didn't like the thought of some northern nobleman hanging it on his wall, I guess. Wish I hadn't now; we could do with some ready coin. Buy some salt. Damn, but I miss salt. I suppose we could trade some bows. You know, we should have stopped long enough to take the weapons from those Nadren. Could have got some salt for them, right enough."

A wolf howl rent the night.

"Puking sons of bitches!" said Finn, standing and striding back into the main room.

Maggrig followed him. "Got it in for wolves now, have you?"

"Wolf call makes no echo, boy. Don't you remember nothing at all?"

"I was raised to be a priest, Finn. My father didn't think I'd have much need for wolf calls and echoes."

Finn chuckled. "If they find the cabin, you can go out and preach to them."

"How many do you think there are?"

"Hard to say," Finn told him. "Usually they keep to bands of around thirty, but there may be less."

"Or more?" suggested Maggrig, softly.

Finn nodded. The wolf call sounded once more.

And this time it was closer . . .

Chareos drew rein on a hilltop and glanced back down toward the valley. "What is it?" asked Kiall. "That's the fourth time you've checked the back trail."

"I thought I saw riders, sunlight gleaming from helms or lances. It could be a patrol."

"They would not be looking for us, would they? I mean, we have broken no laws."

Chareos looked into Kiall's face and read the fear there. "I have no idea. The earl is a vengeful man and feels I have insulted him. But even he could find no way to accuse me in this matter. Let's move. We should be in Tavern Town by midmorning, and I would sell my soul for a hot meal and a warm bed."

The clouds above them were heavy with the promise of snow, and the temperature had dropped sharply during the past two days. Kiall wore only a woolen shirt and leggings, and just looking at him made Chareos more cold. "I should have bought gloves," he said, blowing at his hands.

"It is not too cold yet," said Kiall cheerfully.

"It is when you are my age," Chareos snapped.

Kiall chuckled. "You don't look much past fifty."

Chareos bit back an angry retort and urged the stallion

down the slope. All life is a circle, he reminded himself, remembering the days when he had chided Kalin for being nearly senile. Old Kalin? The man had been forty-two, nearly three years younger than Chareos was now.

The stallion slithered on the slope. Chareos pulled his head up and leaned back in the saddle. The gray recovered his balance and reached the foot of the hill without incident. The trail widened into a mountain road, flattened by the wide leather-rimmed wheels of the wagons that carried timber to Talgithir. The trees gave shelter from the wind, and Chareos felt more comfortable. Kiall rode alongside, but the gray nipped at the gelding, which reared. The villager clung on grimly.

"You should sell that beast," said Kiall. "There is a devil in him."

It was good advice, but Chareos knew he would keep the gray. "He is bad-tempered and a loner. But I like him. He reminds me of me."

They emerged from the woods above a cluster of buildings at the center of which was a tavern. Gray smoke rose from its two stone chimneys, and men could be seen gathering outside the main doorway.

"Bad timing," muttered Chareos. "The timber workers and laborers are waiting for their midday meal."

The two men rode down into the settlement. The stables were at the rear of the tavern, and there Chareos unsaddled the gray and led him into a stall. He forked hay into the feeding box and brushed the animal's back. Then he and Kiall walked through into the tavern. It was nearly full and there was no room close to the fires, so the two men sat at a bench table.

A plump woman approached them. "Good morning, sirs. We have pies and good roast beef and a rich honey cake served hot."

"Do you have rooms available?" asked Chareos.

"Yes, sir. The upper guest room. I will have a fire lit; it will be ready shortly."

"We will take our food there," he told her. "But for now two goblets of mulled wine, if you please."

She curtseyed and moved back into the throng. The

crowd made Chareos uncomfortable; the air was close and reeked of wood smoke, sweat, and broiling meat. After a while the woman returned and led them through to the stairs and on to the upper guest room. It was large and cold despite the newly lit fire, but there were two soft beds, a table, and four deep leather chairs.

"It will warm up soon enough," said the woman. "Then you'll need to open the window. The left shutter is a little stiff, but a good push will move it; the wood has warped. I will bring your food presently."

Chareos removed his cloak and dragged a chair to the fire. Kiall sat down opposite him, leaning forward; his back was healing fast, but still the wounds were sore.

"Where do we go from here?" he asked.

"Southwest into Nadir lands. There we'll hear of the Nadren who raided your village. With luck, Ravenna will have been sold and we should be able to steal her back."

"What of the others?"

"For pity's sake, boy! They'll be spread all over the Nadir lands. Some of them will be sold twice over, and we'd never find them all. Use your brain. Have you ever been to the steppes?"

"No," admitted Kiall.

"It's a big land. Huge. Endless prairies, hidden valleys, deserts. The stars seem close, and a man could walk for a year without seeing a single tent village. The Nadir are a nomadic people. They could buy a slave in . . . Talgithir, say . . . and three months later be in Drenan. They go where they will unless they are summoned to war by the khan. It will be task enough merely to find Ravenna. Believe me!"

"I keep thinking of her," said Kiall, turning to stare at the fire. "How frightened she must be. It makes me feel guilty to be sitting in comfort by a fire."

"Nothing worthwhile was ever done in haste, Kiall. She is a beautiful woman, you say. Therefore, they will not harm her. Is she virgin still?"

"Of course!" hissed Kiall, face reddening.

"Good. Then they will not rape her, either. They will set

a high price, and that might mean they keep her for a month or two. Relax, boy."

"With respect, Chareos, would you mind not calling me 'boy'? I last heard that more than five years ago. I am nineteen."

"And I am forty-four—that makes you a boy to me. But I am sorry if it offends you . . . Kiall."

The villager smiled. "It does not offend me. I think I am too sensitive. It is just that in your company I feel . . . young and useless. I am an apothecary's assistant; I know herbs and medicines but nothing of swordplay. I wouldn't know where to begin to look for Ravenna. Calling me 'boy' just highlights my . . . lack of worth in this quest."

Chareos leaned forward and added a chunk of wood to the blaze. Then he looked up into the earnest gray eyes of the young man. "Do not speak of lack of worth," he said. "You proved your worth when you spoke out before the earl . . . and more. Not one man in a hundred would set out on a quest such as this. You will learn, Kiall. Every day. And this is your first lesson: A warrior has only one true friend. Only one man he can rely on. Himself. So he feeds his body well; he trains it; works on it. Where he lacks skill, he practices. Where he lacks knowledge, he studies. But above all he must believe. He must believe in his strength of will, of purpose, of heart and soul. Do not speak badly of yourself, for the warrior that is inside you hears your words and is lessened by them. You are strong, and you are brave. There is a nobility of spirit within you. Let it grow—you will do well enough. Now, where is that damned food?"

Outside two hunters were loping into the settlement. The taller man glanced back and cursed.

From the woods came forty riders, swords in their hands.

Finn ran up the tavern steps, hurled open the door, and all but recoiled from the mass of humanity wedged inside. "Raiders!" he bellowed, then turned and sprinted across to the barn, where Maggrig was scaling a rope to the hayloft. The rolling thunder of hooves grew louder. Finn did not look back but leapt for the rope and hauled himself up to kneel alongside his slender companion. Maggrig notched an arrow to his bow. "We should have stayed in the woods," he said. "I don't believe it will be safer here."

Finn said nothing. The riders galloped in to the settlement, screaming war cries and slashing the air with their curved blades. Some among them were Nadir warriors in lacquered breastplates; others were renegade Gothir outlaws bearing axes and knives. All carried small round bucklers strapped to their left forearms. As they leapt from the horses and ran for the buildings, Finn sent an arrow that skewered a man's neck. Maggrig loosed a shaft, but it struck a horned helm and glanced away to tear at the flesh of another warrior's arm. Seven of the raiders charged toward the barn, and Finn cursed. A second shaft sang from his bow but thudded against a raised buckler. Maggrig's next arrow hammered into a man's groin, and the man stumbled and fell. The six remaining raiders ran into the barn below.

Finn stood and scanned the hayloft, seeing a ladder by a trapdoor some ten paces back. He moved to it and began to haul it up, but before he could lift it out of reach, a tall raider leapt and dragged it back. Pulled forward, Finn almost toppled into the trap.

"I remember you, you puking bastard," yelled the Nadren warrior at the foot of the ladder, staring up at Finn. "You are dead meat. I'll rip your guts out through your bowels."

Holding his buckler ahead of him, he began to climb. Finn swore and ran back to Maggrig.

"Good place you chose," whispered Finn. Maggrig drew back on his bowstring and sent an arrow slicing into the back of a man running toward the tavern.

"You think we should leave?" he asked.

"No, I think we should stay and plant flowers," muttered Finn. Behind them the Nadren warrior had reached the hayloft. Finn sent a shaft at him, but the man blocked it with his buckler and began to haul himself through the opening. Dropping his bow, Finn launched himself at the warrior feetfirst, his right foot cracking home against the man's chin. Half-stunned, he slumped back, but he still had a grip on his sword, which he swung wildly. Finn rolled away from the cut. Maggrig ran back to aid him, but Finn waved him away. Rolling to his feet, the black-bearded hunter scooped up his bow and quiver and looped them over his shoulder. "Let's go!" he shouted at Maggrig. "Now!" Dropping to his belly, he grabbed the rope and slithered over the hayloft opening. Halfway down he released his hold and dropped to the ground. Maggrig joined him.

Deep in the barn, behind the winter wood store, Beltzer awoke. His head was pounding, and he sat up and groaned. He blinked and saw the Nadren warriors around the ladder. Worse, one of them swung around and saw him. Staggering upright as the man raised his sword and charged, Beltzer curled his right hand around the haft of a hatchet whose head was half-buried in a round of wood. He dragged it clear and leapt to meet the swordsman. The thin saber slashed for his head, but Beltzer ducked and sent the hatchet blade through the man's ribs. The wooden haft snapped under the impact. Four more warriors came at him, and with a bellow of rage, Beltzer dropped his head and dived at them. Three of the Nadren were hurled from their feet, but the fourth moved in with sword raised. An arrow punched through his temple, and he staggered before dropping to his knees. Beltzer's huge fists clubbed at the men around him; in the close confines of the brawl they could not use their swords. He scrambled to his feet, kicked a man in the head, and ran back toward the wood store. The Nadren surged after him.

At the back of the barn the long-handled tree ax rested against the wall. Beltzer swept it into his hands and swung on the attackers. Two men died in the first seconds of the combat, the survivor first backing away and then turning to spring for the safety of the outer yard. An arrow from Finn stopped him in his tracks, and he pitched facefirst to the floor.

"What in the seven hells is going on?" bellowed Beltzer, but Maggrig and Finn were gone, and he sat down on a tree round and stared at the bodies. A movement from the ladder caught his eye, and a Nadren warrior clambered down from the hayloft. The man took one look at the giant with the ax and made off at speed.

Outside, Finn had dropped his bow and now held two bloodstained hunting knives. Beside him lay two Nadren warriors and the body of Maggrig. Eight raiders circled him. "Come on, my boys," he snarled. "Come in and die!"

Beltzer strolled out into the open with his ax on his shoulder and saw Finn surrounded. "Bel-azar!" he screamed. The circle around Finn broke as the giant charged, and the slashing ax scattered the attackers. A warrior carrying a short stabbing spear rushed at Finn, but Finn sidestepped and rammed his hunting knife into the man's belly.

Inside the tavern all was chaos. The raiders had forced their way in and hacked and slashed at the defenseless workers. Several were dead; others were wounded. The survivors cowered on the floor, eyes averted from the warriors who stood guard over them. One Nadren warrior had climbed over the counter and was holding Naza's wife, Mael, by the throat. A knife blade hovered over her right eye. Naza lay in a pool of blood by the man's feet.

"Where is it, you fat cow?" hissed the warrior, but suddenly a movement at the back of the room caused him to twist, his eyes narrowing. A door had opened, and a tall man stepped into view carrying a shining saber. Behind him came a second man, younger but also armed. The Nadren's eyes flicked back to the first man; he was no youngster, but he moved well. "Don't just stand there," the Nadren told the warriors. "Take them!"

The farm workers scrambled back to form a pathway, and several of the Nadren ran at the newcomers. Swords flashed, and the clash of steel was punctuated by the screams of the dying. The Nadren holding Mael watched as his men were butchered by the tall swordsman. Hurling Mael aside, he vaulted the counter and ran to the door, shouting for aid.

But he stopped in the doorway—and cursed, for galloping from the woods to the north were twenty lancers. He leapt down and stepped into the saddle of the nearest horse, dragging the reins clear of the post around which they had been loosely tied.

"To horse! To horse!" he shouted. Then the lancers were upon them. The raiders, most of them on foot, scattered before the charge, but the lancers wheeled their mounts and bore down on the fleeing Nadren. A dozen of the raiders, mounted now, counterattacked, trying to cut a path to the south.

Inside the tavern Chareos stumbled. A sword flashed for his head, and he hurled himself to his right, landing on the massed forms of the laborers. The last Nadren loomed over him with sword raised, but Kiall slashed his saber across the man's throat. Chareos regained his feet and moved to the doorway. On the open ground beyond he saw Salida and his lancers battling desperately against the raiders. The Nadren, realizing now that they outnumbered the soldiers, were attacking with a renewed frenzy. Chareos sheathed his saber and drew his hunting knife. He ran among the milling horsemen and dragged a Nadren from the saddle, plunging his knife between the rider's ribs. Vaulting to the horse's back, he drew his saber and battled his way toward Salida.

Inside the tavern, Kiall glared at the workmen. "Is this what you will brag about to your children?" he shouted. "How you cringed in the face of danger? Get up! Arm yourselves!"

Seven of the men pushed themselves to their feet, but most of them remained where they were. The seven took weapons from the dead Nadren and followed Kiall out into the open. "At them!" yelled the young villager, running forward and plunging his saber deep into the back of a horseman.

By the barn Beltzer knelt by Finn, who sat with Maggrig's head in his lap. The blond hunter was bleeding from a wound to the scalp.

Beltzer reached for Maggrig's wrist. "He's not dead," he said, but Finn ignored him. Beltzer cursed and stood, pushing Finn aside and grabbing Maggrig by his shirt. He dragged the unconscious hunter back into the barn, away from the slashing, stamping hooves of the milling horses.

Finn blinked and followed him. "Not dead?" he whispered.

"Stay with him," said Beltzer, hefting his ax.

"Where are you going?" asked Finn.

"I'm going to kill a few Nadren. Then I am going to have a drink—many drinks."

The giant vanished back into the fray. Finn sat back and looked down at Maggrig. He felt for the younger man's pulse; it was strong and even.

"You are nothing but trouble for me," said Finn.

Slowly the battle turned. The lancers, fighting with sabers now, were more disciplined than the raiders, and Chareos had linked with Salida at the center. The two swordsmen seemed invincible.

Several of the Nadren turned from the fight and kicked their horses into a gallop. Others followed them. In all, seventeen Nadren escaped.

The others were killed where they stood.

Eleven lancers were dead, four more were seriously wounded, and the open ground before the tavern was blood-drenched. Six horses had been killed, and two others had been crippled and put down. Everywhere lay the corpses of dead warriors. In the sudden calm Salida lifted one leg and slid from the saddle. He wiped his saber clean on the shirt of a dead man and returned it to his scabbard. Chareos dismounted alongside him.

"A timely arrival, Captain," said the former monk.

"Indeed, Chareos. My thanks. You fought well."

" 'Needs must when demons rise,' " quoted Chareos.

"We need to talk," said Salida, leading his horse away from the slaughter field. Chareos followed him to a well at the rear of the tavern, where both men drank, then Salida sat down on the well wall. "The earl has ordered your arrest. He means to see you hanged."

"For what?" said Chareos. "Even an earl must have a reason."

"The murder of Logar."

"How can a man be accused of murder when he is attacked by three swordsmen?"

"Logar was unarmed."

"Un . . . Wait a moment." Chareos moved back to the battleground and called Kiall to him. "Give me your sword for a second." He took the saber to Salida. "You recognize this?"

The captain examined the blade and looked up. "Yes, it is Logar's saber. But that means nothing, Chareos. There is a witness against you, and the earl wishes you dead."

"Do you believe me?"

The captain smiled wearily. "I believed in you even before I saw the sword. Logar was a snake. But that is not the point at issue, and you leave me with a problem. My orders are to take you back. If I do, you will hang for certain; if I don't, I will be stripped of my command. Why in Bar's name did you cancel those cursed lessons?" Without waiting for an answer, Salida stood and returned to the tavern. He summoned an underofficer and gave instructions for the clearing away of the bodies.

Chareos sat by the well with Kiall beside him. "What will you do?" the villager asked. Chareos shrugged. "You can't go back," Kiall said.

"No," Chareos agreed, "I can't go back." A shadow fell across them, and Chareos was suddenly lifted from his feet and held in a crushing bear hug. Beltzer spun him around several times, then kissed him on both cheeks.

"I couldn't believe my eyes," said the giant. "Blademaster? What are you doing here? Did you come to see me? Have you a task for me? Dear gods of heaven, what a day!"

"Put me down, you ape!" thundered Chareos. Beltzer dropped him and stepped back, hands on hips.

"Gods, but you look older. Maggrig and Finn are here. We're all here! It's wonderful. I've been waiting for something to happen. Anything! But to have you here . . . well, say something, Blademaster."

"You look dreadful," said Chareos, "and your breath would make rotting fish smell like perfume. Moreover, I think you've broken one of my ribs."

"Who is the boy?" asked Beltzer, jerking a thumb at Kiall.

"His name is Kiall. We are traveling together."

"Good to meet you," said Beltzer, thumping Kiall on the back. The villager groaned and staggered. "What's the matter with him?"

"He suffered a whipping," snapped Chareos, rubbing at his ribs, "which I think you just reminded him of. Do you live here now?"

"After a fashion. I've been helping Naza, the tavern owner. Come, you must be dying of thirst. Let's have a drink or two . . . or three. Gods, what a lucky day! I'll fetch us some ale." Beltzer ambled away toward the tavern.

"What *was* that?" Kiall asked.

"*That* was Beltzer. Once seen, never to be forgotten."

"Beltzer?" whispered Kiall. "The golden-haired hero of Bel-azar?"

"You will find, Kiall, that song and fable are not reliable. There could once have been a blind sow who would have considered Beltzer handsome, but I doubt it. I've seen whores turn him away while his pockets were bulging with gold coin."

"It's incredible," whispered Kiall. "He's ugly and fat, and he smells."

"Those are his good points," said Chareos. "Wait until you get to know him." He stood and walked toward the barn, where Finn was helping Maggrig stand.

"Still drawn to trouble like moths to candles," remarked Chareos, smiling.

"It would seem so, Blademaster," answered Finn. "The boy here got a crack to the skull."

"Bring him to my room."

"I don't want to stay here too long," said Finn. "I hate crowded places—you know that."

"I remember. But spare me an hour if you will. Kiall will show you the way."

Chareos walked over to where Salida sat on the raised walkway around the tavern.

"I have met some old friends, Captain. I will be in my room if you wish to talk to me."

Salida nodded. "Get your friend another saber. I will take Logar's back to the earl."

"And what of me, my friend? And what of you?"

"You go where you will, Chareos. And may the Source guide you. As for me . . . who knows? I wasn't always a captain of lance; there may be other roles I will enjoy. But I think the earl will send others after you. He is no longer rational where you are concerned."

"Be careful, Salida."

"Yes, this is a world for careful men," he replied, waving a hand at the battlefield.

Inside the tavern the bodies had been dragged away, leaving trails of blood on the wooden boards. The eastern end of the dining room was now a hospital area where soldiers were stitching wounds and applying bandages. Chareos saw the innkeeper's wife sitting beside her husband. With a deep wound in his shoulder and a lump on his temple, Naza was white-faced and deep in shock.

Chareos joined them, and the woman looked up and smiled wearily. "Thank you for your aid, sir," she said. "I thought they would kill me."

"What did they want?" asked Chareos.

"The timber workers are paid tomorrow. We keep the silver coin hidden here. There are four hundred men, and they are paid each quarter year; it is a sizable sum."

"I see. Would you mind if I took some food from the kitchen? My companion and I still have not eaten."

"I will prepare you something presently," she offered, her face flushing.

"Not at all," said Chareos swiftly. "Stay with your husband. It is no trouble to me, I assure you."

"You are kind, sir," said Mael.

Chareos walked through to the kitchen. Several tables had been overturned and there were broken pots and crockery on the floor, but a large pot of stew still simmered on the huge iron stove. A serving maid entered from the rear of the building. Short and slender with dark, curled hair, she curtseyed. "May I help you, sir?" she inquired.

"Bring some food, stew, meat, bread . . . whatever, to the upper guest room. We will also need some wine—five goblets. Oh, yes, and some linen for bandages. Will you do it now?" he asked, handing her a half silver piece. She pocketed the coin and curtseyed once more.

Chareos returned to his room, where Finn was sitting on one wide bed, dabbing with a cloth at the wound on Maggrig's head; it was a shallow cut, and his temple was bruised and swollen. Beltzer was sitting by the fire with a pitcher of ale in his hands; Kiall was standing by the window, looking down at the former battleground. He had surprised himself that day, leading the farm workers into the fight; the excitement had been great, and his fears had vanished in the chaos of the skirmish. Now he felt like a warrior. He glanced up at the sky. How blue it was, how fresh and clean the air. He turned and smiled at Chareos, then switched his gaze to Beltzer. Ugly the man was, but he had swung his ax like a giant of legend. He had not seen Maggrig and Finn in action, but merely to be in the same room as the heroes of Bel-azar filled him with pride.

A serving maid brought food, but Kiall was no longer hungry. Beltzer took his share, while Chareos sat quietly opposite the giant, gazing into the fire. Finn had applied a linen bandage to Maggrig's head, and the younger man lay back on the bed and fell asleep. There was no conversation, and Kiall pulled up a chair and sat in silence. His hands began to shake, and his stomach heaved. Chareos saw this and passed across a chunk of black bread.

"Eat it," he said. Kiall nodded and chewed at the crust, and the nausea passed.

"What now?" said Beltzer, laying the empty pitcher beside the chair. "Back to chopping wood and punching timbermen?"

"What do you want?" asked Chareos softly.

"I want it to be the way it was," the giant answered.

"Nothing is the way it was. And I'll tell you something, Beltzer, old friend—it never was the way it was."

"I'm supposed to understand that, am I? You always were so clever with words. But they don't mean pig wind. I'm not old; I can hold my own with any man. I can drink a mountain of ale and still lift a barrel of sand over my head. And there's no man alive can stand against me in battle."

"That's probably true," Chareos agreed, "but you are not young, either. What are you, Beltzer? Fifty?"

"Forty-eight. And that's *not* old."

"It's older than Kalin was at Bel-azar. And didn't you advise him to go home and leave the fighting to the younger men?"

"It was a jest," snapped Beltzer. "And I didn't know then what I know now. Gods, Blademaster, there must be something for me!"

Chareos eased himself back in his chair and stretched his legs to the fire. "I am on a quest," he said softly.

Beltzer leaned forward, his eyes shining. "Tell me," he invited.

"I am helping young Kiall rescue a woman stolen by the Nadren."

"A noblewoman? A princess?"

"No, a village girl—the daughter of a pig breeder."

"What? Why? Where is the glory in that? The Nadren have been stealing women for centuries. Who'll sing a song about the rescue of a pig breeder's daughter?"

"No one," admitted Chareos, "but if you'd rather stay here and chop wood . . ."

"I didn't say that—don't put words in my mouth. Which group took her?"

"No one knows."

"Which Nadir camp did they head for?"

Chareos shrugged. "We don't know."

"If you are mocking me, I'll break your head," Beltzer said. "What *do* we know?"

"We know she was taken. Now all we have to do is find her and steal her back."

"You'd need the Tattooed Man for that, and he's gone. Probably dead by now."

"My thoughts exactly," agreed Chareos, "but I shall ride into the valley and seek him. Unless you have a better plan."

"Anything's better than that," said Beltzer. "They'll take your head and shrink it down to wear on a belt. You don't even speak the language."

"You do."

"I need some more ale," said Beltzer, lurching to his feet and striding from the room.

"Who is the Tattooed Man?" asked Kiall. "And where is the valley?"

"The Gateway is not of this world," answered Finn, moving to join them. "And only a moonstruck fool would venture there. What game are you playing, Chareos? No one goes into the valley."

"It is no game, Finn," Chareos told him. "The quest, as it stands, is impossible . . . unless we can find a man who can follow spirit trails. Do you know of any as skilled as Okas?"

"None," admitted Finn. "But the valley? I wouldn't go there if my soul depended on it. Neither will Beltzer. They don't like visitors."

"I'll go there with you," said Kiall. "I'll go anywhere if it means a chance to find Ravenna."

"I can remember when *we* sounded like that," Finn mused. "It's a wonder we've survived so long, Blademaster. If you want to die, why not leap from a cliff or open your veins with a sharp blade? The Tattooed People will kill you slowly. But then, you know that."

Chareos turned to Finn and smiled. "I know the perils, Finn, and I won't go without Beltzer. For some reason Okas seemed to like him."

"Perhaps it was the smell," offered Finn. "He was the only man I ever met who stank worse than the big man. Even so, it is not a journey I would undertake."

"What is so terrible there?" Kiall asked.

Finn scratched at his beard. "According to Okas, the land is hot and there are beasts there who feed on human flesh. Also, the Tattooed People collect heads and shrink them down by magic. About twenty years ago a nobleman named Carsis led a small force into the valley; their shrunken heads were left on spears at the entrance. For ten years, whenever a traveler passed by, the heads would shriek warnings. I saw them once—aye, and heard them. They spoke of the terrors of hell."

"They are not there now, then?" said Kiall.

"No. The lord regent sent a section of lancers into the hills. They built a great fire and burned the heads."

"Do the Tattooed People venture into our lands?"

"Sometimes, boy. And that's when a man locks his doors and sits up at night with sword and bow close at hand. You still want to go there?"

Kiall swallowed hard. "I will go wherever I have to."

"Spoken like a hero," said Finn sourly.

The door opened, and Beltzer entered, carrying two pitchers of ale. "I'll come with you," he told Chareos.

"Spoken like an idiot," whispered Finn.

The soldiers dug a shallow trench a half mile from the settlement. The bodies of the Nadren, stripped of their armor and weapons, were unceremoniously flung into it. The corpses of the soldiers, eleven in all, were wrapped in their blankets and reverently placed on the back of a wagon, ready for burial with honors in Talgithir.

Salida ordered the Nadren grave to be filled with rocks to prevent wolves and foxes from digging for food. It was almost dusk, and he was bone-weary. Seven of the dead had been new recruits, unused to war, but four had been seasoned veterans. One of them had been his valet, a bright, amusing man named Caphes; he had a wife and five sons in Talgithir, and Salida did not relish the visit he would have to make to the family home. The sound of a horse's hooves made him turn, and he saw Chareos riding toward him on a huge white stallion.

The former monk dismounted and approached.

"I wanted to make sure," said Chareos, "that you had no second thoughts on the matter of my arrest."

Salida gazed into the man's dark eyes, unable to read the thoughts of the tall swordsman before him. "No, I have not," he said, and Chareos nodded.

"You are a good man, Salida. Here, I have brought Logar's saber." He handed the scabbarded weapon to the officer. Dipping his hand into the sack hung behind his saddle, he produced a wineskin and two leather-covered brass cups. "Join me?" he inquired.

"Why not? But let's move away from the stench of death. I've had my fill of it."

"You look tired," Chareos told him. "And not just because of the battle, I think."

They strolled to a group of boulders and sat down; Salida unbuckled his iron breastplate and laid it beside him. "No, it is not. I am a family man now, Chareos. There was a time when I believed that soldiers could make a difference." He accepted a goblet of red wine and sipped it. "But now? I have three sons and a beautiful wife. The Nadir are gathering again, and one day soon they will cross the mountains and destroy the Gothir. What then of my sons and their dreams?"

"Maybe they will not come," said Chareos. "The Gothir have little; this is not a rich land."

"They don't care about riches; they live for war. And what do we have to oppose them? The army has been cut to two thousand men. We couldn't even hold Bel-azar now." He drained his wine and held out the cup for more. Chareos filled it and sat silently.

"I was born out of my time," continued Salida, forcing a smile. "I should have been an officer in the great days when the Gothir swept across Nadir lands all the way to the Delnoch mountains."

"It is all a circle," Chareos told him. "The Gothir had their day, as did the Drenai and the Vagrians. Now we live in Nadir days. Their time will come, and then an officer just like you will sit at the last outpost of the Nadir empire bewailing his fate and wondering about the dreams of his sons."

Salida nodded. "May that day come soon," he said, grinning. "Is it true that you were once a Drenai prince?"

Chareos smiled and refilled his own cup. "So the singers would have us believe."

"Have you never thought to return to your homeland?"

"This is my homeland. But yes, I have considered crossing the Delnoch mountains . . . one day, perhaps."

"I once visited Castle Tenaka," said Salida. "It is an incredible place: six great walls and a keep with walls three feet thick."

"I knew it as Dros Delnoch," Chareos told him. "It was said that it could never be taken. I was raised on stories of Druss the Legend and Rek, the Earl of Bronze. Strange that it should have been conquered by one of Rek's descendants. Castle Tenaka? I don't like the sound of the name."

"You met him once, did you not? The great khan?"

"Yes. A very long time ago. Another lifetime." Chareos rose. "If you do not object, I would like to find my companion another saber. I doubt the Nadren had anything of similar workmanship, but then, he is no swordsman."

"There's no point in going through the Nadren weapons—poor iron, badly fashioned. I gave a sword to my valet. It is a good blade, and he will have no further use for it. Take it with my blessing." Salida walked across to the wagon and lifted clear a cavalry saber in a wooden, leather-covered scabbard. "The balance is good, the edge keen."

"Thank you, my friend," said Chareos, offering his hand. Salida gripped it.

"At least I can tell my sons I fought alongside a hero of Bel-azar."

"May the Source go with you, Salida."

The captain watched as Chareos swung into the saddle. The stallion reared and came down at a run. Salida stood for several minutes as the rider grew ever smaller, then returned to the task at hand: ordering the wagon hitched and the riderless horses tied to the rear.

It would be a sad ride back to Talgithir.

◊4◊

AN EERIE SILENCE covered the high forest like an invisible cloak as the dawn light bathed the tavern. Kiall gazed around the seemingly deserted settlement. There were few signs now of the battle, save for the dried bloodstains on the snow. Beltzer hoisted his pack to his shoulders and stamped his feet. "I hate the cold," he declared.

"We haven't started yet," said Finn, "and already you're complaining."

Kiall struggled to get his arms through the pack ropes, and Maggrig assisted him, lifting the loops over the thick goatskin jerkin Kiall now wore.

"It's too big for me," said Kiall.

"There's gratitude," snapped Beltzer, "after all the trouble I took to get it for you."

"You stripped it from a dead Nadren," Chareos pointed out.

"Had to kill him first," retorted Beltzer, aggrieved.

Chareos ignored him and shrugged into his pack. Finn had lent him a fur-lined cloak with a deep hood, which he lifted into place and tied under his chin. Moving away from the others, he drew his saber. After several practice lunges and parries, he scabbarded the sword and adjusted the loops of the pack. He dropped his arms, and the pack fell away . . . the saber flashed into the air. Twice more Chareos repeated the maneuver. At last, satisfied, he rejoined the others. The pack was less comfortable now, the ropes biting into his shoulders, the weight too low on his back. But it could be swiftly jettisoned if the need arose, and that was worth a little discomfort.

The group set off on the ice-covered trail. Chareos had never enjoyed walking but on Finn's advice had left the horses in the settlement, paying Naza a retainer to feed and groom the mounts while they were gone.

Both the bowmen had declined the opportunity to join the three questers, but Finn had at least agreed to guide them to the Shrieking Gate. As he walked behind Finn, Chareos considered all aspects of the way ahead. The Nadren were still in the forest, but this was not a great fear. Five well-armed men should prove deterrent enough, especially after the mauling the raiders had received. No, the biggest problem was what awaited them beyond the gate.

The Tattooed People were a mystery. Some said they had once been of this world, forced back by the migration of nations ten centuries before when the warlike Drenai, the Gothir, and the ferocious Nadir tribes had come sweeping from north, south, and east. One legend claimed the Tattooed People used sorcery to open a doorway between worlds, allowing the tribe to escape to a hidden land of riches and plenty. Another maintained that the Gateway had been there from the days before the ice fall, a last remnant of a once-proud civilization, and that beyond it lay mountains of gold.

But whatever the truth the Gateway did exist, and on rare occasions one or more of the Tattooed People passed through it. Such had been the case when Okas had wandered into the army camp six months before the battle at Bel-azar. He had squatted down at Chareos' campfire and waited in silence until Beltzer offered him a plate of meat and bread. He was a small man, no more than five feet tall, potbellied and wearing only a loincloth decorated with pale stones. His entire body was covered in blue tattoos, some in the shape of leaves, others in runic symbols around what appeared to be campfire scenes. His face also was tattooed with curving lines, and his beardless chin was completely blue, shaped like a beard with a waxed mustache above it. Amazingly he spoke a little of the Common Language, and more amazing still, in the four months Okas was with them the uncouth Beltzer mastered the tribesman's tongue. Okas proved invaluable during that time. In the skills of tracking he had no peers, at least not among the Gothir. And he was a great "finder." Chareos' senior officer, Jochell, lost a valuable golden ring and had the quarters of all enlisted men searched. Through Beltzer, Okas told the officer that he would find the missing item.

Jochell was dubious, yet he had seen Okas' skills in action during the hunt for Nadir raiders. Much to the amusement of the men, Okas took the officer's hand and held it in silence for a while, eyes closed. Then he released his grip and trotted from the camp. Jochell saddled his horse and rode after him; Chareos and Finn followed, anxious to see the outcome. Two hours later they were at the scene of the previous day's battle with Nadir outriders. There was a small stream to the west of the battlefield. Okas moved to it and knelt by the waterline. Then he grunted and pointed. Jochell joined him. There, just below the surface, nestling among the pebbles, was the gold ring, its pale central opal glistening blue.

Jochell was delighted and gave Okas two gold pieces. The tribesman stared at them for a while, then tossed them to Chareos. That night Okas left them, but not before he had sat with Beltzer for more than an hour. He said farewell to no one else, merely gathering up his blanket and walking from the camp.

In the morning Chareos had asked Beltzer, "What did he say to you?"

"He told me to stay close to you, Maggrig, and Finn during the coming days. He also told me that Jochell's ring would grace a Nadir hand before the winter moon."

"I wish I hadn't asked," Chareos said.

"He's only been gone a few hours, and already I miss him," said Beltzer. "You think we'll see him again?"

Now, as he walked through the early morning frost, Chareos remembered that conversation and the many that had followed it. Beltzer told him of the land beyond the Gateway. It was hot and humid, with towering trees and vast open veldts and lakes. There were huge animals there, higher than houses, and hunting cats with fangs like long knives. It was a world of sudden storms and sudden death.

"Are you thinking of going there?" Chareos had asked. Beltzer had looked away, his face reddening.

"I would have liked to, but Okas said the Tattooed People kill any interlopers. Their history is full of massacres and the murder of their people by our races. They are terrified it will happen again."

The sky darkened, and thunder jolted Chareos' mind back to the present. Finn called a halt and turned to face Chareos. "It will be dusk soon, and there's going to be a heavy snowfall," he said. "I suggest we look for somewhere to camp and sit it out. We will build two shelters and gather wood for fires." The group walked on into a thick stand of pine. Finn and Maggrig scouted the area, locating two good sites. Kiall watched as the hunters tied twine to the tops of four sapling trees. These were then pulled together and fastened. Finn sent Beltzer and Chareos out to cut branches from the surrounding pines, and they were threaded through the tied saplings to form a spherical shelter some ten feet across. The bowmen left Kiall, Chareos, and Beltzer to complete the walls, then walked some thirty feet away to build their own shelter.

Snow began to fall, gently at first, then thick and fast. The wind strengthened, gusting the snow into the faces of the workers, ice forming on brows and beards. Chareos continued to pack the walls of the shelter while Beltzer and Kiall gathered dead wood for a fire. The temperature plummeted as the sun dipped below the peaks.

Chareos had left a rough doorway on the south side of the structure, and Kiall and Beltzer crawled inside. A tiny fire surrounded by stones was burning at the center of the circle, but there was not heat enough to warm a man's hands, let alone keep death from his body, thought Kiall miserably. The snow fell harder, covering the shelters, blocking the gaps in the walls, and cutting out the icy drafts.

The temperature began to rise. "Take off your cloaks and jerkins," ordered Chareos.

"I'm cold enough already," Kiall argued.

"As you please," said Chareos, removing his fur-lined cloak and heavy woolen overshirt. Adding fuel to the fire, he lay down, his head resting on his pack. Beltzer did likewise, having discarded his bearskin jerkin. Kiall sat shivering for some minutes. Neither of the others spoke for a while, then Kiall unclipped the brooch that held his Nadren cloak in place. As soon as he struggled out of the goatskin jerkin, the warmth from the fire enveloped him.

"I don't understand," he said.

Chareos raised himself on one elbow and smiled. "Wool and fur are made not just to keep cold out but to keep warmth in. Therefore, it will work in reverse. If your body is cold and there is heat outside, the furs will stop it from getting through to you."

"Why did you not just tell me?"

"I find some men learn best by suffering," said Chareos.

Kiall ignored the rebuke. "Why did Finn and Maggrig choose to have their own shelter?" he asked. "Surely there is enough room in here with us."

"They prefer their own company," answered Beltzer. "They always did. But I am sorry they will not be coming with us beyond the gate. I never knew a better shot than Maggrig or a cooler fighting man than Finn."

"Why won't they come with us?" Kiall asked.

"They have more sense," Chareos told him.

Ravenna's dreams were strange and fragmented. She was a child in the arms of her mother—safe, warm, and comforted. She was a doe running through the forest, pursued by wolves with long yellow fangs, sharp as swords. She was a bird, trapped in a gilded cage and unable to spread her wings.

She awoke. All around her the other women lay sleeping. The air was close, and there were no windows. Ravenna closed her eyes. Tomorrow she would stand naked on the auction block. Her heart began to beat wildly; she calmed her breathing and tried to relax.

The dreams flowed once more. Now she saw a knight in shining armor riding through the gates, the Nadren scattering before him. Leaning from his saddle, he plucked her from the auction platform and rode out across the steppes. Safe in the trees, he helped her down and dismounted beside her. He lifted his visor . . . the face inside was rotted and long dead, the flesh hanging in leather strips from the grinning skull.

She screamed . . .

And woke. The other women were still sleeping; the scream, then, had been part of the nightmare. Ravenna was glad of that. Wrapping the thin blanket round her shoulders, she sat up. Her dress of yellow-dyed wool was filthy, and she could smell stale sweat upon it.

I will survive this, she told herself. I will not give in to despair.

The thought strengthened her for a moment only, but the weight of her captivity bore down on her, crushing her resolve.

She wept silently. The woman from the wagon rose from her blankets and walked over to her, putting a slender arm about her shoulders.

"Tomorrow," she said, "when you stand on the platform, do not try to entice a buyer. The Nadir put no stock in women. They view them like cattle. They fear proud women. You understand me? Keep your head down and obey the commands of the auctioneer. Do not think of nakedness. Be meek and submissive."

"If they fear proud women, perhaps no one would buy me."

"Do not be a fool!" snapped the older woman. "If you look defiant, the auctioneer will have you whipped into submission or you'll be bought by a man who enjoys inflicting pain on women. What you need is a master who will treat you casually. There is no such animal as a gentle Nadir, but better to be bedded swiftly by an indifferent savage than to be beaten like a dog."

"How is it you know so much?" asked Ravenna.

"I have been sold before," said the woman. "I spent three years as a whore in New Gulgothir. Before that I was sold to a Nadir chieftain."

"But you escaped?"

"Yes. And I will escape again."

"How is it you are so strong?"

"I was once wed to a weak man. Sleep now. And if you cannot sleep, rest. You will not want dark rings under those pretty eyes."

"What is your name?"

"What does it matter?" the woman answered.

Salida strode into the main hall, his armor dust-stained and dull, his eyes bloodshot and weary. Yet still he kept his back straight, his chin high. There were more than forty noblemen present. He bowed before the earl, and their eyes met.

"Do you bring me Chareos?" the earl asked softly.

"No, my lord. But I bring you Logar's saber." He held the scabbarded blade high and placed it on the dais before the earl. "Also I bring you the owner of the Gray Owl tavern, who witnessed the fight; he is outside. He says that Logar and two others attacked the monk and that Chareos defended himself nobly. The man Kypha was lying."

"You took this investigation on yourself?" said the earl, rising from his ebony chair, his eyes cold.

"I know, my lord, how highly you value justice. I must also tell you that Chareos and the villager, Kiall, fought alongside myself and the men from Talgithir against a large band of Nadren. Chareos slew at least six of them in a pitched battle. Without him and Beltzer, Maggrig, and Finn, we might well have lost the encounter. I judged—perhaps wrongly—that you would not appreciate the waste of time involved in bringing Chareos back."

The earl stood in silence for several seconds, then he smiled. "I like my officers to show initiative, Salida, and this you have done. You also destroyed a band of raiders and showed, I understand, great personal courage. You are to be commended both for your action in battle and for your discretion. Go now. Rest. You have earned it."

Salida bowed and backed two paces before turning and striding from the hall. Aware that all eyes were on him, the earl turned back to his guests. For an hour he moved among them, his mood light, his humor good. Just before dusk he left the hall and walked swiftly through the stone corridors of the keep until he reached the stairway to his private rooms.

He entered the study and pushed shut the door. A tall man was standing at the window. He was lean and hawk-faced, with pale eyes separated by a curved beak of a nose. A scar ran from his brow to his chin in an angry white line. He wore a black leather cloak that shimmered in the lantern light, and three knives hung from a baldric on his chest.

"Well, Harokas?" said the earl.

"The man Kypha is dead. Somehow he contrived to drown in his bath," answered Harokas. "I hear the other business is finished."

The earl shook his head. "Nothing is finished. The man insulted me through my son, then disgraced me publicly. Find him—and kill him."

"I am skillful with a blade, my lord, but not that skillful."

"I did not say fight him, Harokas. I said *kill* him."

"It is not for me to criticize—"

"No, it is not!" stormed the earl.

Harokas' green eyes narrowed, but he said nothing.

"I want him to know why he is dying," the earl continued.

"What should I tell him, my lord?" asked Harokas. "That a hero of Bel-azar is doomed because he disciplined an arrogant boy?"

"Beware, Harokas," the earl hissed. "My patience is not limitless—even with those who have served me well and faithfully."

"It will be as you order," said Harokas. He bowed and left the study.

Kiall's dreams were troubled. Again and again he saw the Nadren sweep down on the village, heard their wild battle cries, and saw the sunlight gleaming on their swords and helms. He had been high in the woods, supposedly gathering herbs for the apothecary, but in reality he had been wandering, dreaming, imagining himself a knight, or a bard singer, or a nobleman on a quest. In his fantasy he was a man of iron courage and lethal skills. But when the Nadren war cries had sounded, he had stood frozen to the spot, watching the carnage, the looting, raping, and burning. He had seen Ravenna and the others hauled across the saddles of the conquering raiders and taken away to the south. And he had done nothing.

He knew then, as he knew now, why Ravenna had rejected him, and he suffered again the pain of their meeting in the high meadow by the silver stream.

"You are a dreamer, Kiall," she had said, "and I like you. Truly I do. But I need more than dreams. I want a man who will build, who will grow. I need a strong man."

"I can do all these things," he had assured her.

"Only in your head. Now you must leave me. If Jarel sees you talking to me, he will be jealous. And it would not be wise for you to make Jarel angry."

"I am not afraid of Jarel. But I *love* you, Ravenna. I cannot believe that means nothing to you."

"Poor Kiall," she had whispered, stroking his cheek. "Still the dreamer. Love? What is love?" She had laughed at him then and walked away.

Kiall awoke. His body was warm under the blanket, but his face was cold. Raising himself on one elbow, he saw that the fire was dying. He added wood and sat up. Beltzer was snoring, and Chareos remained in a deep sleep. The flames licked the fuel and rose. Kiall warmed his hands and wrapped his blanket around his shoulders.

He sniffed. The air inside the shelter was close and full of smoke, but still he could smell the rank odor emanating from Beltzer. This was no dream. Here he sat with the heroes of Bel-azar, on a quest to rescue a beautiful maiden from the clutches of evil. Yet in no way did the reality match the fantasies; a bad-tempered swordmaster, a vile-smelling warrior, and two hunters who spoke barely a civil word to anyone but each other.

Beltzer snorted and turned over, his mouth open. Kiall saw that he had lost several teeth and that others were discolored and bad. How could this fat old man *ever* have been the golden-haired hero of legend?

I should have stayed in the village, he told himself, and learned the apothecary's skills. At least then I would have been able to afford to take a wife and build a home. But no, the dreamer had to have his way.

He heard the crunching of boots on the snow outside, and fear rose in him as he pictured the Nadren creeping up on them as they slept. He scrambled to his feet and dressed swiftly. Then he heard Maggrig's voice. Pulling on his boots, he dropped to his knees and eased himself out into the snow-covered clearing. The sky was a rich velvet blue, and the sun was just rising above the mountains to the east. Maggrig and Finn were skinning four white rabbits, the nearby snow spattered with blood.

"Good morning," said Kiall. The younger man smiled and waved, but Finn ignored the villager. Kiall moved alongside them. "You're out early," he remarked.

"Early for some," grunted Finn. "Make yourself useful." He tossed a rabbit to Kiall, who skinned it clumsily. Finn gathered up the entrails and threw them out into the bushes, then scraped the fat from the furs and pushed them deep into his pack.

Kiall wiped his blood-covered hands on the snow and sat back on a rock. Finn's bow was resting against it, and Kiall reached for it.

"Don't touch it!" snapped Finn.

Kiall's anger rose. "You think I would steal it?"

"I don't much care—but don't touch it."

Maggrig moved alongside Kiall. "Don't take it to heart," he said softly. "No bowyer likes another man to touch his bow. It is . . . a superstition, I suppose. You see, each bow is made for one archer. It is designed for him alone. Finn makes his own bows. Even I am not allowed to use them."

"No need to make excuses for me," said Finn sourly.

Maggrig ignored him. "When we get to the cabin," he told Kiall, "you will see many bows. Finn will probably give you one—a weapon to suit your length of arm and your pulling strength."

"It would be no use," said Kiall. "I have no eye for archery."

"Neither had I when I first met Finn. But it is amazing what a man can learn when he is paired with a master. Finn won every prize worth the taking. He even took the lord regent's talisman against the best archers of six lands: Drenai, Vagrians, Nadir, Ventrians, and even bowmen from Mashrapur. None could compete with Finn."

"Not then or now," muttered Finn, but his expression softened and he smiled. "Don't mind me, boy," he told Kiall. "I don't like people much. But I don't wish you harm, and I hope you find your lady."

"I am sorry you will not be traveling with us," said Kiall.

"I'm not. I have no wish to have my head shrunk on a pole or my skin flayed outside a Nadir tent. My battle days are long gone. Quests and the like are for young men like you."

"But Beltzer is coming," Kiall reminded him.

Finn grunted. "He never grew up, that one. But he's a good man in a scrap, right enough."

"Chareos, too," said Maggrig softly.

"Yes," agreed Finn. "A strange man, Chareos. But you watch him, boy, and learn. His kind don't come around so often, if you catch my meaning."

"I'm not sure that I do."

"He's a man with iron principles. He knows the world is shades of gray, but he lives like it's black and white. There's a nobility in him, a gallantry, if you like. You'll see what I mean, come the finish. Now, that's enough talking. Wake your companions. If they want to break their fast, they'd better be up. I'll not wait for them."

The snow held off for several days, but even so the travelers made slow progress across the peaks. On the fifth day Maggrig, leading the group, came too close to the lair of a snow leopard and her cubs. The leopard seemed to explode from the undergrowth, spitting and snarling. Maggrig was hurled from his feet, a jagged tear across one arm of his tunic. Beltzer and the others ran forward, shouting at the tops of their voices, but the animal crouched before them, ears flat to her skull and fangs bared. Finn dragged Maggrig clear, and the travelers gave the beast a wide berth. Maggrig's arm had been slashed, but not deeply, and the wound was stitched and bound by Finn.

On the following morning they reached the valley where

the hunters' cabin was hidden. A blizzard blew up around them, and they forced their way, heads bowed against the wind, to the frozen doorway. Snow had banked against it, blocking the door and filling the window frame alongside. Beltzer cleared it, shoveling it aside with his huge hands. The inside was icy, but Finn got a fire going; it was more than an hour before the heat warmed the cabin.

"That was good luck," said Beltzer, finally stripping his bearskin jerkin and squatting on the rug beside the fire. "That blizzard could have hit us days ago, and we'd have been trapped out in the mountains for weeks."

"It may be lucky for you, dung brain," said Finn, "but I do not relish my home being filled with sweating bodies for days on end."

Beltzer grinned at the black-bearded hunter. "You're the least welcoming man I've ever known. Where do you keep the drink?"

"In the well outside. Where else?"

"I mean the ale, or the wine, or even the malt spirit."

"We have none here."

"None?" asked Beltzer, eyes widening. "None at all?"

"Not a drop," answered Maggrig, smiling. "Now how lucky do you feel?" His face was white, and sweat dripped into his eyes. He tried to stand but sank back in his chair.

"What's the matter with you?" said Finn, rising and moving to the younger man.

Maggrig shrugged. "I don't . . . feel . . ." He sagged sideways from the chair. Finn caught him and carried him to the bed, where Chareos joined him.

"He has a fever," said Chareos, laying his hand on the hunter's brow. Maggrig's eyes opened.

"Room's going around . . . thirsty . . ." Finn brought him a goblet of water and lifted his head while he drank.

Kiall cleared his throat. "If you boil some water, I'll make a potion for him."

Finn swung on him. "What are you . . . a magician?"

"I was an apothecary's assistant, and I bought some herbs and powders back in Tavern Town."

"Well, come and look at him, boy. Don't just stand there!" stormed Finn. Kiall moved to the bedside. First he examined the wound on Maggrig's temple; it had closed and healed well, but his master had always told him that blows to the head often shocked the system. Perhaps the second injury, caused by the leopard's attack, had caught the hunter in a weakened state. Trying to remember what Ulthen had told him of such wounds, he removed the bandage from Maggrig's arm; the cut was jagged and angry, but there was no pus or obvious sign of infection.

Kiall filled a small copper pot with water and hung it over the fire. Within a few minutes the contents were boiling. Then he opened his pack and took out a thick package wrapped in oiled paper. Inside were a dozen smaller packages, each decorated with a hand-drawn leaf or flower. Kiall selected two of the packets and opened them. Bruising the leaves, he dropped them into the water and stirred the brew with a spoon. Then, lifting the pot from the fire, he laid it in the hearth to cool.

"Smells fine," said Beltzer.

"How would you know?" hissed Finn. "What have you made there, boy?"

"It's a potion from willow leaves and comfrey. Both are good for fighting fevers, but the comfrey helps clean the blood and give strength to a sick man."

"What else is it good for?" asked Beltzer.

"It helps heal bones and reduce swellings and stops diarrhea. It has also—so my master told me—been used to prevent gangrene in wounds. Oh, yes . . . it is good for rheumatic pain, too."

"Then while you have the ingredients there, my boy," said Beltzer, "better make another pot. I have the rheumatism in my knee. Hurts like Hades."

When the mixture had cooled, Kiall carried it to Maggrig's bedside, and Finn held the hunter's head while he drank. At first he choked, but he swallowed half the contents and sank back. Kiall covered him with a blanket, and Finn sat at the bed's head, mopping the sweat from Maggrig's brow. Beltzer strolled over and finished the brew, belching loudly.

For an hour or more there was no change in Maggrig's condition, but at last he drifted off into sleep. "His color is a little better," said Finn, looking to Kiall for confirmation. The youngster nodded, though he could see little change. "Will he be all right now?" Finn asked.

"We'll see tomorrow," answered Kiall cagily. He stood and stretched his back. Looking around, he saw that Beltzer had fallen asleep by the fire and Chareos was nowhere in sight. The back room door was open, and Kiall wandered through. It was colder there but not uncomfortable. Chareos was sitting at the workbench, examining sections of wood shaped for a longbow.

"May I join you?" asked the villager.

Chareos looked up and nodded. "How is Maggrig?"

"I don't really know," whispered Kiall. "I have only been working with Ulthen for a few months. But the potion will reduce the fever. I'm not sure, though, about the arm wound. Perhaps the cat had something trapped beneath its claws—dung, rotting meat . . ."

"Well, he has two choices: live or die," said Chareos. "Keep an eye on him. Do what you can."

"There's nothing much I can do at the moment. That's a thin bow, isn't it?" he went on, looking at the slender length of wood in Chareos' hand.

"It is just a section: one of three. Finn will bond them together for more flexibility. You know what wood this is?"

"No."

"It is yew. A curious wood. When you slice it, there are two shades: light and dark. The light is flexible, the dark compactable." He lifted the piece and showed it to Kiall. "You see? The light wood is used for the outer curve, where maximum flexibility is needed; the dark, for the inner, where it compacts. It is beautiful wood. It will be a splendid weapon."

"I didn't know you were an archer."

"Nor am I, Kiall, but I was a soldier, and it pays a soldier to understand the workings of all weapons of death. I'm getting cold in here—and hungry." Chareos replaced the wood and strolled out into the main room, where Finn was asleep beside Maggrig while Beltzer lay unmoving on the floor. Chareos stepped over the giant and added wood to the fire, then took dried meat and fruit from his pack and shared it with Kiall.

"Thank you for agreeing to help me," Kiall said softly. "It means much to me. Finn told me you were gallant."

Chareos smiled and leaned back in his chair. "I am not gallant, Kiall. I am selfish, like most men. I do what I want, go where I want. I am answerable to no one. And do not thank me until we have freed her."

"Why *did* you come with me?"

"Why must there always be answers?" countered Chareos. "Perhaps I was bored. Perhaps it was because my mother's name was Ravenna. Perhaps it is because I am secretly a noble prince who lives to quest for the impossible." He closed his eyes and was silent for a moment. "And perhaps I do not know myself," he whispered.

By midmorning Maggrig's fever had broken, and he was awake and hungry. Finn showed no relief, gathered his bow and quiver, and, with Chareos and Beltzer, set off into the snow to scout the trail to the Valley of the Gateway. Kiall remained with the younger hunter; he prepared a breakfast of oats and honey and built up the fire. Then he dragged a chair to Maggrig's bedside, and the two men sat and talked for much of the morning.

Maggrig would not speak of the battle at Bel-azar but told Kiall how he had been a student at a monastery. He had run away on his sixteenth birthday and joined a company of bowmen from Talgithir. He had spent two months with them before being sent to the fortress; there he had met Finn and the others.

"He is not the friendliest man I have known," said Kiall.

Maggrig smiled. "You learn to look beneath the harsh words and judge the deeds. Had I not met him, I would not have survived Bel-azar. He's canny and a born fighter. There's more give in a rock than in Finn. But he's never liked company much. Having you all here must be driving him insane."

Kiall glanced around the cabin. "How do you stand it? Living here, I mean? You are days from civilization, and the mountains are savage and unwelcoming."

"Finn finds cities savage and unwelcoming," said Maggrig. "This is a good life. Deer are plentiful, and mountain sheep. There are pigeons and rabbits and many roots and tubers to spice a broth. And you should see the mountains in spring, ablaze with color under a sky so blue that it would bring tears to your eyes. What more could a man need?"

Kiall looked at the blond hunter, at the clear blue eyes and the handsome, almost perfect features. He said nothing. Maggrig met his gaze and nodded, and an understanding passed between them.

"Tell me of Ravenna," invited Maggrig. "Is she beautiful?"

"Yes. Her hair is dark and long, her eyes brown. She is long-legged, and her hips sway when she walks. Her laughter is like sunlight after a storm. I will find her, Maggrig . . . one day."

"I hope that you do," said the hunter, reaching out and patting Kiall's arm, "and I also hope that you will not be disappointed. She may be less than you remember. Or more."

"I know. She may be wed to a Nadir warrior and have babes at her heels. It does not concern me."

"You will raise them like your own?" Maggrig inquired. His expression was hard to read, and Kiall reddened.

"I had not thought of it. But . . . yes, if that is what she wishes."

"And if she wishes you to leave her be?"

"What does that mean?"

"I am sorry, my friend. It is not my place to criticize. But as I understand it, the lady turned you down once. Perhaps she will do so again. When a woman has children, she changes; they become her life. And if their father loves them—and the Nadir are fond of their children—then she may wish to remain with him. Have you considered that possibility?"

"No," answered Kiall honestly, "but how much must I consider? She could be dead or sold as a whore. She could be diseased. She could be wed. But whatever the situation, short of death, she will know that someone cared enough to come after her. That is important, I think."

Maggrig nodded. "You are correct in that, my friend. You have a wise head on those young shoulders. But answer me this, if you can: Does the lady have any virtues other than beauty?"

"Virtues?"

"Is she kind, loving, understanding, compassionate?"

"I . . . I don't know," admitted Kiall. "I never thought of it."

"A man should not risk his life for beauty alone, Kiall, for that fades. You might as well risk it for a rose. Think on it."

Finn walked around the deserted campsite. The snow had been packed tight by heavy boots, and there were three abandoned shelters.

"How many men?" asked Chareos.

"I'd say around seven, maybe eight."

"How long ago?" questioned Beltzer.

"Last night. They moved off to the east. If they come across our tracks, they will be led straight back to the cabin."

"Can you be sure they are Nadren?" Chareos asked.

"There is no one else up here," said Finn. "We should be heading back. Maggrig is in no condition to fight, and your villager is no match for them."

Kiall stood in the doorway, feeling the warm sun on his face. The long icicles hanging from the roof were dripping steadily. He turned back inside.

"How bizarre," he said to Maggrig, who was slicing venison into a large iron pot. "The sun is as warm as summer, and the ice is melting."

"It is only autumn," Maggrig told him. "The blizzard was a foretaste of winter. We often get them. The temperature plummets for several days, and then it is like spring. The snow will clear within a day or two."

Kiall pulled on his boots and took up the saber Chareos had given him.

"Where are you going?" asked Maggrig.

Kiall grinned. "Before they get back, I'd like to practice a little with this blade. I am not much of a swordsman, you know."

"Nor I. I could never master it." Maggrig turned back to the broth, adding vegetables and a little salt. Having hung the pot over the fire, he sank back into a chair. He felt weak and dizzy, and his head was spinning.

Kiall stepped out into the sunshine and slashed the air with the saber, left to right. It was a fine blade, keen-edged, with a leather-covered hilt and an iron fist guard. Many was the time during his youth when he had walked alone in the woods holding a long stick, pretending to be a warrior knight, his enemies falling back from the demon blade he carried, dismayed by his awesome skills. He hefted the saber, cutting and lunging at imaginary opponents: three, four, five men died beneath the glittering steel. Sweat dripped from his back, and his arm was growing tired. Two more opponents died. He spun on his heel to block a thrust from behind . . . his blade clanged against an arrowhead, shattering the shaft. Kiall blinked and gazed down at the ruined missile on the snow.

Then he looked up and saw the Nadren at the edge of the undergrowth. One man held a bow, his mouth open in surprise. There were seven men in all, four of them with bandaged wounds on the head or arm. All were standing silently, gazing at the swordsman.

Kiall stood frozen in terror, his mind racing.

"That was a pretty trick," said one of the newcomers, a short, stocky man with a black and silver beard. "I have never seen an arrow cut in flight or believed any man could move so swiftly."

Kiall glanced once more at the arrow and took a deep breath. "I was wondering when you would show yourselves," he said, surprised that his voice was smooth and even.

"I did not tell him to shoot," said the Nadren leader.

"It does not concern me," replied Kiall loftily. "What do you want here?"

"Food. That's all." He saw the man's eyes flicker to his

right and glanced back. Maggrig now stood in the door of the cabin with his bow in his hands, an arrow notched to the string. An uneasy silence developed. The Nadren were tense, hands on their weapons.

One warrior eased himself alongside the leader and whispered something Kiall could not hear. The leader nodded; he looked at Kiall.

"You were one of the swordsmen back in the town. You were with the tall one, the ice warrior."

"Yes," admitted Kiall. "It was quite a battle, was it not?"

"He cut us to pieces. I have never seen the like."

"He is quite skilled," said Kiall, "but a hard taskmaster for a student like myself."

"He is your swordmaster?"

"Yes. It would be hard to find a better."

"I can see now why you find it so easy to cut an arrow from the air." The Nadren spread his hands. "However, since we must fight or starve, I think it is time we put your skills to the test." He drew his short sword from the leather scabbard at his hip.

"Is this wise?" asked Kiall. "There are four of you wounded. It does not seem much of a contest, and warriors should fight over something more valuable than a pot of broth."

The man said nothing for a moment, then smiled at Kiall. "You would allow us inside?" he asked softly.

"Of course," Kiall told him. "But naturally, as a token of good manners, you would leave your weapons here."

"Ha! And what then would stop you from butchering us?"

"What stops me now?" countered Kiall.

"You are a cocky young snipe," snapped the leader. "But then, I've seen you in action, and I guess you've reason to be." He slammed his sword back in its scabbard, loosened the buckle on his belt, and dropped the weapon to the ground. The other Nadren followed his lead. "Now, where is the broth?" Kiall sheathed his blade and gestured toward the cabin. Maggrig stepped back inside. Kiall took a deep, slow breath, calming himself, then followed them.

At first the atmosphere within the cabin was tense.

Maggrig sat back on the bed, honing a hunting knife with long, rasping sweeps against a whetstone while Kiall ladled out the broth. It was undercooked, but the Nadren wolfed it down. One of the men seemed weaker than the others. He had a wound to the shoulder; it was heavily bandaged, yet blood seeped from it steadily. Kiall moved to him. "Let me see that," he said. The Nadren did not complain as Kiall gently unraveled the bandage. The flesh was sliced back, the cut angry and swollen. Kiall replaced the bandage and took herbs from his pack. Selecting the leaves he needed, he walked back to the man.

"What is that?" grunted the warrior. "It looks like a weed."

"It has many names," Kiall told him. "Mostly it is called fat hen. It is used to feed chickens."

"Well, I'm no chicken!"

"It also heals festering wounds. But it is your choice."

"You are a surgeon, too?" asked the leader.

"A warrior needs to know of wounds and ways of healing them," replied Kiall.

"Let him do it," said the leader, and the warrior settled back, but his dark, slanted eyes fixed on Kiall's face, and the young man felt the hatred in his stare. He pushed the flap of skin in place and stitched the wound, then laid the leaves on top of it. Maggrig brought a section of linen for a new bandage, and this Kiall applied.

The warrior said nothing. He moved to the wall and curled up to sleep on the floor. The Nadren leader approached Kiall. "My name is Chellin," he said. "You have done well by us. I thank you for it."

"I am Kiall."

"I could use a man like you. If ever you travel south past the Middle Peaks, ask for me."

"I'll remember that," Kiall said.

The tension in the room eased, and the Nadren settled back. Kiall built up the fire and helped himself to a little broth. He offered food to Maggrig, who shook his head and smiled.

As the afternoon sun began its slow descent toward the western mountains, Chellin roused his men and walked with Kiall out into the sunlight. Just as they gathered their weapons, Chareos, Finn, and Beltzer appeared. Chareos had his saber in his hand.

Kiall waved to them casually, then turned to Chellin. "Good luck on your journey," he said.

"And you. I am glad the ice warrior was not here when we arrived."

Kiall chuckled. "So am I."

The warrior whose arm Kiall had treated approached him. "The pain has mostly gone," he said, his face expressionless. He held out his hand and gave Kiall a golden Raq.

"That is not necessary," Kiall told him.

"It is," retorted the man. "I am no longer in your debt. Next time I see you, I will kill you—as you killed my brother during the raid."

When the Nadren had gone, Kiall wandered back to the cabin. Chareos' laughter came to him as he mounted the three steps to the doorway. Inside Maggrig was regaling them with the tale of Kiall the arrow slayer. Kiall flushed. Chareos rose and walked to him, clapping a hand to his shoulder.

"You did well," he said. "You thought fast and took control. But how did you deflect the arrow?"

"It was an accident—I didn't even know they were there. I was practicing with the saber, and I spun around. The arrow hit the sword blade."

Chareos smiled broadly. "Even better. A warrior needs luck, Kiall, and those Nadren will carry the tale of your skill. It could stand you in good stead. But it was an enormous risk. Maggrig told me how you threatened to kill them all single-handed. Let's walk awhile."

Together the swordmaster and the young villager walked out into the fading sunshine. "I am pleased with you," said Chareos, "but I think it is time I gave you a little instruction. Then, perhaps the next time you face armed men, you will not need to bluff."

For an hour Chareos worked with the villager, showing him how to grip the saber, how to roll his wrist, to lunge and parry. Kiall was a swift learner, and his reflexes were good. During a break from the exercise Chareos and his student sat on a fallen log.

"To be skillful requires hard work, Kiall, but to be deadly requires a little more. There is a magic in swordplay that few men master. Forget the blades and the footwork—the battle is won in the mind. I once fought a man who was more skillful than I, faster and stronger. But he lost to a smile. He thrusted, I parried, and as our blades locked, I grinned at him. He lost his temper, perhaps feeling that I had mocked him. He came at me with great frenzy, and I killed him . . . just like that. Never let anger, or outrage, or fear affect you. That is easy advice to give but hard to follow. Men will bait you, they will laugh at you, they will jeer. But it is just noise, Kiall. They will hurt the people you love. They will do anything to make you angry or emotional. But the only way you can make them suffer is to win. And to do that you must remain cool. Now let us eat—if the Nadren left us any broth."

Chareos sat beneath the stars, his cloak wrapped loosely around his shoulders, the night breeze cool on his face. Inside the cabin all was silent, save for Beltzer's rhythmic snoring. A white owl soared and dived. Chareos could not see its prey or whether the owl had made a kill. A fox eased itself from the undergrowth and loped across the snow, ignoring the man.

Memories crowded into Chareos' mind, days of youth and ambition, times of wonder and glory, nights of despair and dark melancholy. What have you achieved? he asked himself. Indeed, what was there to achieve? He remembered the parting from his parents and the long, cold journey that had followed it; that had been hard on a young boy. The memories were jagged, and he pushed them away. His adolescence in New Gulgothir had been lonely despite the friendship and guidance of Attalis, his swordsmaster and guardian. Chareos was never at ease among the boys of his own age, but worse than that, he could not adapt to the curious lifestyle of the Gothir nobility. It was on a journey north that he had begun to understand them. He had passed a village that nestled against a mountain. Above the settlement was a monstrous overhang of rocks and boulders.

"That looks perilous," Chareos observed to Attalis, and the old man nodded.

"It will fall one day," he said. "Few will survive it."

"Then why do people live there?"

"They always have, lad. And after a while they don't notice it anymore. You can live with fear only so long, then you absorb it and it loses its power."

The Gothir were like that, living always with the threat of a Nadir invasion they could not prevent. The nobility organized endless feasts, banquets, dances, and diverse entertainments, keeping only a token army to man the ramparts of Bel-azar. Chareos had come to manhood in those days of apathy and instant gratification. An expert swordsman, thanks to the tutelage of Attalis, he won a commission to the Sabers, the elite force formed by the lord regent. He recalled now with embarrassment his pride when the white cloak and silver saber had first been presented to him. He had stood with two hundred other young men before the gallery, his back straight, his eyes fixed on the lord regent on his ebony throne. He had felt like a man, and destiny was smiling on him.

Two weeks later his world lay in ashes. Attalis, always a proud man, became involved in a minor dispute with Targon, the lord regent's champion. The dispute festered into a blood feud, and Targon challenged the old man publicly. The duel was fought in the royal courtyard. It did not last long. Chareos, on patrol with the Sabers, heard of it two days later. Attalis had been crippled by a piercing thrust to the shoulder and had fallen to his knees, his sword clattering to the stone. Targon had then stepped forward and sliced open the old man's throat.

Chareos asked for compassionate leave to attend the funeral, and this was granted. He used his meager savings and a pledge against the next year's pay to purchase a plot of ground, a marble sarcophagus, and a statue above the grave. This done, he sought out Targon. The man was taller by a head than Chareos and whip-lean; he was fast and confident of his talents. Once more the duel took place in the royal courtyard.

Targon flashed a mocking grin at the young officer. "I hope you'll offer more sport than the old man," he said. Chareos did not reply. His dark eyes were fixed on Targon's swarthy features as he drew his borrowed rapier. "Frightened, boy?" asked Targon. "You should be."

The lord regent lifted his arm, and both men presented their swords. The duel began in a blistering series of thrusts, parries, and ripostes. Chareos knew within seconds that he was outclassed, but he remained calm, sure in the knowledge that no matter what, his blade would find its home in the flesh of the man he faced. Back and forth across the courtyard the two warriors fought, their blades shimmering in the early morning sunlight. Three times Chareos felt his opponent's sword nick his skin, twice on the upper arm, once on the cheek. A thin trickle of blood dripped to his chin. But Targon could find no opening for the killing thrust. Beginning to lose patience, he attacked with greater fury, but his young opponent blocked him at every turn.

The two men stepped back from one another, sweat on their faces. "You take a long time to die, boy," remarked Targon.

Chareos smiled. "You have the sword skill of a Nadir tent wife," he said. Targon flushed red and launched another attack. Chareos blocked the blade, rolled his wrist, and lanced his rapier deep into Targon's right shoulder, slicing the muscles and tearing through ligament and sinew. Targon's rapier fell from his hand, and for the first time fear showed in his pale eyes. For several seconds Chareos stood watching his opponent, then his blade cut the air with a hissing slash to rip across Targon's throat.

The lord regent's champion staggered back, clutching the wound. Blood bubbled through his fingers as he fell to his knees. Chareos walked forward and placed his boot against the dying man's chest. With one contemptuous push, he hurled Targon to his back. There was silence among the spectators, and then the lord regent called Chareos forward while pages ran to Targon, seeking to stem the bleeding.

"You took not only his life but his dignity," said the lord regent.

"If I could, my lord, I would follow him into hell and destroy his soul as well," Chareos told him.

That afternoon Chareos had stood alone by Attalis' tomb. "You are avenged, my friend," he said. "He died as you died. I don't know if that is important to you. But I remembered your teaching, and I did not allow my hatred to control me. You would have been proud of that, I think." He was silent for a moment, and his eyes filled with tears. "You were a father to me, Attalis. I never told you how much you meant to me or ever thanked you for your friendship and your company. But I do so now. Rest easy, my friend."

A quarter of a century later, outside Finn's cabin, Chareos the Blademaster wept again for the old man, for the ruin of his hopes and the failure of his dreams.

It had always been Attalis' wish that one day they would return home and restore all that had been lost. Without the old man Chareos had viewed that dream with cold logic and had ruthlessly pushed it aside.

Now he dried his eyes with the edge of his cloak. "What would you think of this quest, Attalis?" he whispered. "The hunt for the pig breeder's daughter? Yes, I can almost hear your laughter."

He stood and entered the cabin, where the fire was low, the room warm and cozy. Kiall and Beltzer were asleep before the hearth, Maggrig deep in dreams in the bed by the far wall. Lantern light was streaming from the back room, and Chareos walked quietly across the cabin floor and looked in. Finn was sitting with his feet on the workbench, idly cutting flights for new arrows.

"I couldn't sleep," said Chareos, moving in to sit opposite the black-bearded hunter.

Finn swung his legs to the floor and rubbed his eyes. "Nor me. What happened to us, eh?"

Chareos shrugged. In the lantern light Finn looked older, his face seemingly carved from teak. Deep shadows showed at his eyes and neck, and silver hairs glistened within his matted beard. "You seem to have found peace, my friend," said Chareos. "Up here in the mountains you have freedom and more land than some kings."

"Not much of a life for the boy, though he doesn't complain."

"The *boy* must be thirty-six years old. If he doesn't like the life, he is old enough—and man enough—to say so."

"Maybe," said Finn, unconvinced. "And then again, maybe it is time to move on."

"You'll find nowhere more beautiful, Finn."

"I know that," snapped the hunter, "but there's more to it. I'm no youngster, Chareos. I feel old. My bones ache in winter, and my eyes are not what they were. One day I'll die. I don't want to leave the . . . Maggrig . . . up here alone. I don't like people much—nasty minds, foul manners, always looking to steal or lie or slander. But maybe that's just me. Maggrig, he gets on with folks, likes company. It's time he learned how to live with people again."

"Think about it some more, Finn," advised Chareos. "You are happy here."

"I *was*. But nothing lasts forever, Blademaster. Not life, not love, not dreams. I reckon I've had more than my share of all three. I'm pretty much content."

"What will you do?"

Finn looked up and met Chareos' gaze. "I never had many friends. Never needed them, I reckon. But you and that fat pig are the closest I got to family. So we'll come with you—if you want us, that is."

"You don't need to ask, Finn."

"Good," said Finn, rising. "That's a burden off my heart. Maybe we'll even find the girl. Who knows?"

Tsudai watched the auction with little interest. He had no taste for these pale-skinned Gothir women with their cold blue eyes and their huge cowlike breasts. He swung away from the window and looked at the dark-haired woman seated on the satin-covered divan. Now there was a *real* Nadir beauty.

The first time he had seen her had been when Tenaka Khan had brought her to Ulrickham. She had been fourteen years old, her skin golden, her eyes proud. Tsudai had always believed proud women were the devil's curse, and he had longed to take a whip to her, to see her kneeling at his feet. Even now the memory brought a surge of arousal.

He moved to sit beside her. As she smiled thinly and edged back from him, his face reddened, but he forced himself to remain calm.

"Your brother, Jungir, sends greetings. He hopes that you are in good health," said Tsudai. "I will tell him that you are, for I have never seen you look more beautiful, Tanaki."

"Why should I not be in good health?" she asked him. "Did Jungir not send me to this desolate land in order that I might enjoy the freshness of the air?"

"It was for your own safety, Princess. There were rumors of plots and fear for your life."

She laughed then, the musical sound doing little to ease Tsudai's physical discomfort. Her eyes met his, and for the first time it seemed to him that she smiled with genuine warmth.

"Why do we play such foolish games, Tsudai? There is no one else here, and we both know why my brother sent me here. He killed his own brothers and, possibly, his own father. Why should he balk at slaying his sister? I'll tell you why. Because I am the only hope the Nadir have for providing a male heir. For all his skill with horses and weapons, Jungir is sterile."

Tsudai blanched. "You must not say that! If I was to repeat that to the khan . . ."

"Not even you would dare to voice that, even at second hand. Now, why are you really here, Tsudai?"

He swallowed his anger, feeling uncomfortable sitting there dressed in the full armor of his rank. He reached for the buckle of his black and silver breastplate.

"Do not undress," she chided him. "That would not be seemly."

"Seemly? What would you know of seemly? You take a succession of barbarian lovers, discarding them daily. That is no way for a person of your bloodline to behave."

Tanaki stood and stretched her arms over her head. Her figure was slim and lithe, and the short silken tunic rode up to show smooth golden thighs.

"You do this to fire my blood," snapped Tsudai, rising to his feet, aware of arousal coursing through him.

"A volcano could not fire you," she said. "Now, for the last time, tell me why you are here."

He looked hard into her violet eyes and suppressed the desire to strike her, to hammer her to her knees before him.

"Your brother merely wishes to know of your well-being," Tsudai said. "Is that so hard to understand?"

She laughed, the sound rippling across his emotions like beestings. "My well-being? How sweet of him! I saw your aide looking over the new slaves. The great warrior Tsudai, now reduced to finding concubines. Have you seen any that please you, Tsudai?"

"I do not find any of them attractive, though there are one or two that may suit. But you wrong me, Tanaki. I came here in order that I might speak with you. You know how perilous your position is. You know that at any time your death could become expedient. Four years ago you had the opportunity to become my wife. Now I offer that gift to you once more. Agree and you will be safe."

She moved closer, her perfume washing over him. Lifting her hands, she rested them on his shoulders and looked deeply into his dark, slanted eyes.

"Safe? With you? I remember when you sought my hand. I considered it with due seriousness. I sent spies into your palace, Tsudai. Not one of your women lacks scars from the whip. I know what you want," she whispered huskily, "and you will never have it!" Then she laughed again and stepped back. His hand lashed out. She swayed out of his reach, then stepped inside. Tsudai froze as the dagger point touched his neck. "I could kill you now," she told him.

It was his turn to laugh as he pushed her hand away. "You still want to live, though, do you not? And an attack on me would bring you down. I offered you my hand, Tanaki. But now I will wait. And when the day comes for you to suffer, it will be Tsudai who rides to you. It will be Tsudai to whom you will beg. And I tell you now that no pleas will be heard. When next we meet, you will not be so haughty."

The warrior spun on his heel and stalked from the room. Tanaki returned the small dagger to its sheath and poured herself a goblet of wine.

It had been foolish to anger Tsudai. He was Jungir Khan's most trusted adviser, and his was a friendship it would have been wise to court. But there was something about the man, a coldness within the soul, a meanness of spirit, that she could not tolerate. Her father, Tenaka, had distrusted him. "I have nothing against a man who disciplines his household," Tenaka had told his daughter, "but any man who needs a whip to deal with a woman has no place in my service."

Tanaki swallowed hard as she pictured her father, his violet eyes full of warmth, his smile like the dawn light, welcoming, reassuring. Her stomach knotted, and tears welled in her eyes. How could he be dead? How could the greatest man in the world be dead?

Blinking away her tears, she wandered to the window and watched the auction, wondering which of the women Tsudai would purchase. Rarely did she feel sorry for any of the slaves. But today . . .

She saw a dark-haired young woman pulled to the block, her yellow dress stripped from her. She had a good figure, and her breasts were not overlarge. Tanaki's eyes flicked to Tsudai's bidder, and she saw his hand rise.

There were several other bidders, but the woman was sold to the Nadir general.

"Tread warily, girl," whispered Tanaki. "Your life depends on it."

◊ 5 ◊

MAGGRIG'S FEVER-INDUCED WEAKNESS lasted a further five days, during which time Chareos continued to teach Kiall the elementary moves of swordplay. Beltzer, his mood foul, took to walking alone in the mountain woods. Finn spent much of the time in his workshop, completing a new longbow.

The snow all but disappeared from around the cabin, and the sun shone with summer warmth over the mountains.

On the morning of the sixth day, as the questers prepared to set off for the Valley of the Shrieking Gateway, Finn called Beltzer to his workshop. The others gathered around as the hunter pulled clear a brass-bound oak chest from its hiding place beneath a bench seat. Finn opened the chest and lifted out a long object wrapped in oiled skins. He placed it on the benchtop and cut the thong bindings with his hunting knife. He gestured to Beltzer. "It's yours. Take it."

The giant unwrapped the skins, and there lay a gleaming double-headed ax. The haft and handle were as long as a man's arm, oiled oak reinforced with silver wire. The heads were curved and sharp, acid-etched and decorated with silver runes. Beltzer's hand curled around the haft, lifting the weapon.

"Nice to have it back," he said, and without another word stalked from the workshop.

"Ignorant, ungrateful pig," stormed Maggrig. "He didn't even say thank you."

Finn shrugged and gave a rare smile. "It is enough that he has it," he said.

"But it cost you a fortune. We had no salt for two years and precious little else."

"Forget it. It is past."

Chareos moved forward and placed his hand on Finn's shoulder. "That was nobly done. He wasn't the same man without that ax. He sold it while drunk in Talgithir and never knew what became of it."

"I know. Let's be on our way."

The journey to the valley took three days. They saw no sign of any Nadren and only once caught sight of a single rider far to the south. The air was thin here, and the questers talked little. At night they sat beside campfires but slept early and rose with the dawn.

Kiall found it a curious time. It was an adventure, full of promise, yet these men, these comrades of war, hardly spoke at all. When they did, it was to discuss the weather or the preparation of food. Not once did they mention the Gateway, or the Nadir, or the quest. And when Kiall tried to introduce such topics to the conversation, they were brushed aside with shrugs.

The valley proved an anticlimax to Kiall. It was just like several others they had journeyed through, its pine-cloaked flanks dropping away into a deep cleft between the mountains. There were meadows at the base, and a stream ran along its length. Deer moved across the gentle hills, and there were sheep and goats grazing close by.

Finn and Maggrig chose a campsite, removed their packs, took up their bows, and moved off to hunt for supper. Chareos climbed a nearby hill and scanned the surrounding countryside while Beltzer prepared a fire and sat, watching the flames flicker and dance.

Kiall seated himself opposite the bald giant. "It is a beautiful ax," he said.

"The best," Beltzer grunted. "It is said that Druss the Legend had an ax from the Elder Days that never showed rust and never lost its edge. But I don't believe it was better than this one."

"You carried that at Bel-azar?"

Beltzer glanced up, his small, round eyes fixing to Kiall. "What is this fascination you have with that place? You weren't there—you don't know what it was like."

"It was glorious. It is part of our history," said Kiall. "The few against the many. It was a time of heroes."

"It was a time of survivors—like all wars. There were good men there who died on the first day and cowards who lasted almost until the end. There were thieves there and men who had raped or murdered. There was the stench of open bowels and split entrails. There was screaming and begging and whimpering. There was nothing good about Bel-azar. Nothing."

"But you won," persisted Kiall. "You were honored throughout the land."

"Aye, that was good—the honor, I mean. The parades and the banquets and the women. I never had so many women. Young ones, old ones, fat ones, thin ones: they couldn't wait to open their legs for a hero of Bel-azar. That was the real glory of it, boy—what came after. By the gods, I'd sell my soul for a drink!"

"Does Chareos feel as you do—about Bel-azar, I mean?"

Beltzer chuckled. "He thinks I don't know . . . but I know. The blademaster had a wife," he said, twisting his head to check that Chareos was still high on the hill. "Gods, she was a beauty. Dark hair that gleamed like it was oiled and a body shaped by heaven. Tura, that was her name. She was a merchant's daughter. Man, was he glad to be rid of her! Anyway, Chareos took her off his hands and built a house for her. Nice place. Good garden. They'd been married maybe four months when she took her first lover. He was a scout for the Sabers, just the first of many men who romped in the bed Chareos made for her. And him? The blademaster, the deadliest swordsman I ever saw? He knew nothing. He bought her presents, constantly talked about her. And we all knew. Then he found out . . . I don't know how. That was just before Bel-azar. Man, did he try to die! He tried harder than anyone. But that's what makes life such a bitch, isn't it? No one could kill him. Short sword and dagger he carried, and his life was charmed. Mind you, he had me alongside him, and I don't kill easy.

When the Nadir rode away, you've never seen a man so disappointed."

Kiall said nothing but gazed into the fire, lost in thought.

"Shocked you, did I, boy?" said Beltzer. "Well, life's full of shocks. It's all insane. There never was a better husband. Gods, he loved her. You know where she ended up?"

Kiall shook his head.

"She became a whore in New Gulgothir. The blade-master doesn't know that, but I saw her there, plying her trade by the docks. Two copper coins." Beltzer laughed. "Two of her front teeth were gone, and she wasn't so beautiful. I had her then. Two copper coins' worth. In an alley. She begged me to take her with me; she'd go anywhere, she said. Do anything for me. She said she had no friends and nowhere to stay."

"What happened to her?" whispered Kiall.

"She threw herself from the docks and died. They found her floating among the scum and the sewage."

"Why did you hate her?" asked Kiall. "She did nothing to you."

"Hate her? I suppose I did. I'll tell you why. Because in all the time she was cuckolding Chareos, she never once offered it to me. She treated me like dirt."

"Would you have accepted?"

"Sure I would. I told you; she was beautiful."

Kiall looked into Beltzer's face and remembered the song of Bel-azar. Then he looked away and added fuel to the fire.

"Don't want to talk anymore, young Kiall?" asked Beltzer.

"Some things it is better not to hear," said the villager. "I wish you hadn't told me."

"Whores' lives don't make pretty stories."

"No, I suppose they don't. But I wasn't thinking of her; I was thinking of you. Your story is as disgusting as hers."

Kiall rose and walked away. The sun was fading, the shadows lengthening. He found Chareos sitting on a fallen tree, gazing at the sunset. The sky was aglow, red banners flowing over the mountains.

"It is beautiful," said Kiall. "I have always enjoyed the sunset."

"You are a romantic," stated Chareos.

"Is that bad?"

"No, it is the best way to live. I felt that way once, and I was never happier." Chareos stood and stretched his back. "Hold on to your dreams, Kiall. They are more important than you realize."

"I shall. Tell me, do you like Beltzer?"

Chareos laughed aloud, and the sound, rich and full of good humor, echoed in the valley. "No one likes Beltzer," he said. "Least of all, Beltzer."

"Then why do you have him with you? Why did Finn buy his ax?"

"You are the dreamer, Kiall. You tell me."

"I don't know. I can't imagine. He is so gross; his speech is vile, and he doesn't understand friendship or loyalty."

Chareos shook his head. "Don't judge him by his words, my friend. If I was standing alone down there in the valley, surrounded by a hundred Nadir warriors, and I called his name, he would come running. He would do the same for Finn or Maggrig."

"I find that hard to believe," said Kiall.

"Let us hope you never see the proof of it."

At dawn the next morning the questers moved north into the shadowed pine woods, following a deer trail that wound down to a shallow stream. This they waded across, climbing a short, steep slope to a clearing beyond. The wind gusted, and an eerie, high-pitched scream echoed around them. Finn and Maggrig leapt from the trail, vanishing into the undergrowth. Beltzer lifted his ax from the sheath at his side, spit on his hands, and waited. Chareos stood unmoving, hand on sword hilt.

Kiall found his limbs trembling and suppressed the urge to turn and sprint from the clearing. The scream came again, an ululating howl that chilled the blood. Chareos walked on, Beltzer following. Sweat dripping into his eyes, Kiall could not bring himself to move. He sucked in a deep breath and forced himself forward.

At the center of the clearing, some fifty paces away, stood a huge stone edifice, and before it, on lances decorated with feathers and colored stones, were two severed heads.

Kiall could not tear his eyes from the shrunken faces. The eye sockets were empty, but the mouths trembled with each scream. Maggrig and Finn stepped back into view.

"Can we not stop that noise?" hissed Beltzer, and Chareos nodded. He walked swiftly to the first lance and held his hand behind the severed head. The scream stopped instantly. Chareos lifted the head and placed it on the ground, then repeated the action with the second. All was silent now, save for the gusting wind. The other questers approached. Chareos squatted down and lifted the silent head, turning it in his hands. Taking his hunting knife, he plunged it deep through the scalp, peeling back the skin, which stretched impossibly before snapping clear of the wooden skull beneath. Chareos stood and lifted the wood to his lips; immediately the bloodcurdling scream sounded. He tossed the object to Finn. "It is merely a kind of flute," said the former monk. "The winds enter through the three holes in the base, and the reeds set in the mouth supply the sound. But it is beautifully crafted." Stooping, he gathered the skin, lifting it by the hair. "I do not know what this is," he said, "but it is not human flesh. See, the hair has been stitched in place."

Kiall picked up the second head and looked closely at it. It was difficult to know now why it had inspired such fear. He turned it. The wind whistled through it, and a low moan came out. Kiall jumped and dropped the head, cursing himself even as the others laughed.

Chareos moved on to the edifice. There were two stone pillars, twelve feet high and three feet square, covered with an engraved script he did not recognize. An enormous lintel sat above the pillars, creating the impression of a gateway. Chareos squatted before it, running his eyes over the script.

Kiall moved around to the rear. "There are symbols here," he said, "and the stone seems a different color. Whiter, somehow . . ." He stepped forward.

"Stop!" yelled Chareos. "Do not attempt to pass through."

"Why?" Kiall asked.

Chareos picked up a round pebble. "Catch this," he said, tossing it through the opening. Kiall opened his hands, but the stone vanished from sight. "Throw one to me," commanded the blademaster. Kiall obeyed. Again the pebble disappeared.

"Well, do we go through?" asked Beltzer.

"Not yet," Chareos told him. "Tell me again all that Okas told you of the Gateway."

"There was precious little. It leads to another world. That is all."

"Did he not say it leads to many worlds?"

"Yes," admitted Beltzer, "but we do not know how the magic works."

"Exactly," said Chareos. "Did Okas give an indication of when he would pass through the Gateway? Daytime, midnight, sunset?"

"Not as I recall. Is it important?"

"Did he say which side he entered, north or south?"

"No. Let's just go through and see what we find," urged Beltzer.

Chareos stood. "Take my hand and hold to it tightly. Count to five, then draw me back." He moved to the entrance and held out his arm. Beltzer gripped his wrist, and Chareos leaned forward, his head slowly disappearing from view. Beltzer felt the body sag; he did not count but dragged Chareos back. The blademaster's face was white, and ice had formed on his mustache; his lips were blue with cold. Beltzer laid him down on the grass while Finn began rubbing at the frozen skin. After a while Chareos' eyes opened; he stared angrily at Beltzer.

"I said count to five," he said. "Not five thousand."

"You were in there for only a few heartbeats," Finn told him. "What did you see?"

"Heartbeats? It was an hour at least on the other side. I saw nothing save snow and ice blizzards. Not a sign of life. And there were three moons in the sky." He sat up.

"What can we do?" asked Beltzer.

"Build a fire. I'll think on it. But tell me everything you can remember about Okas and his tribe. *Everything.*"

Beltzer squatted down on the grass beside Chareos. "It's not a great deal, Blademaster. I never had much of a memory for detail. They call themselves the People of the World's Dream, but I don't know what that means. Okas tried to explain it to me, but I lost hold of it—the words roared around my head like snowflakes. I think they see the world as a living thing, like an enormous god. But they worship a one-eyed goddess called the Huntress, and they see the moon as her blind eye. The sun is her good eye. That's all."

Finn lit the fire and joined the two men. "I have seen them," he said. "In the mountains. They move at night, hunting, I think."

"Then we will wait for moonlight," said Chareos. "Then we shall try again."

The hours passed slowly. Finn cooked a meal of venison, the last of the choice cuts he had taken from the deer killed the previous evening. Beltzer wrapped himself in his blankets and slept, his hand on his ax. Kiall wandered away from the fire, walking to the crest of a nearby hill. There he sat down alone and thought of Ravenna, picturing the surge of joy she would feel when he rode to her. He shivered, and depression struck him like a blow. Would he ever ride to her? And if he did, would she just laugh, as she had laughed before? Would she point to her new husband and say, "He is my man. He is strong, not a dreamer like you"?

A sound came from behind, and Kiall turned to see Finn walking toward him. "You wish to be alone?" asked Finn.

"No, not at all."

Finn sat down and stared over the rugged countryside. "This is a beautiful land," he said, "and it will remain so until people discover it and build their towns and cities. I could live here until my dying day and never regret it."

"Maggrig told me you hated city life," said Kiall. The hunter nodded.

"I don't mind the endless stone and brick; it's the people. After Bel-azar we were dragged from city to city so that crowds could gawp at us. You would have thought we were gods at the very least. We all hated it—save Beltzer. He was in a kind of heaven. Chareos was the first to say 'No more.' One morning he just rode away."

"He has had a sad life, I understand," said Kiall.

"Sad? In what way?"

"His wife. Beltzer told me about it."

"Beltzer has a big mouth, and a man's private business should remain so. I saw her in New Gulgothir three years ago. She is happy at last."

"She is dead," said Kiall. "She became a street whore and killed herself."

Finn shook his head. "Yes, Beltzer told me that, but it's not true. She was a whore, but she married a merchant—bore him three sons. As far as I know, they are still together. She told me she had seen Beltzer—it was the lowest point of her life. That I can believe. Every time I see Beltzer, I feel the same way. No, Beltzer heard of a whore who drowned, and the rest was wishful thinking. She was happy when I saw her—for the first time in her life. I was pleased for her."

"You did not hate her, then?"

"Why should I hate her?" asked Finn.

"She betrayed Chareos," Kiall answered.

"She was sold to him by her father. She never loved him. She was fey and high-spirited—reminded me of a fawn I saw once. I was hunting, and the creature saw me. It did not recognize a bow or a hunter; it had no fear. When I stood with bow bent, it trotted toward me. I dropped the arrow, and the fawn nuzzled my hand. Then it went its way. Tura was like that. A fawn in search of a hunter."

"You liked her, then?"

Finn said nothing but stood and walked back down the hill. The sun was setting, and a ghostly moon could be seen shimmering behind the clouds.

Chareos waited as the moon rose higher. Silver light bathed the clearing, and the ancient stone Gateway shimmered and gleamed like cold iron. He stood and rolled his head, stretching the muscles of his shoulder and neck, trying to ease the tension born of fear. Something deep within him flickered, a silent voice urging him to beware. He sensed himself on the verge of a journey that would take him where he did not want to go, on pathways dark and perilous. There were no words of warning, merely a feeling of cold dread.

"Are you ready, then?" asked Beltzer. "Or would you like me to try it?"

Chareos did not reply. He walked to the Gateway and held out his arm. Beltzer gripped his wrist as he leaned forward, half his body disappearing. Seconds later he drew back.

"I do not know if that is the place, but it fits the description. There is jungle beyond. The sun is bright." He swung toward Maggrig and Finn. "I need only Beltzer with me. The rest of you should stay here and await our return."

"I get bored just sitting," said Finn. "We'll come with you."

Chareos nodded. "Then let us go before good sense can assert itself."

He turned and was gone from sight. Beltzer followed him, and Maggrig and Finn stepped through together. Kiall found himself alone in the clearing. His heart was beating wildly, and fear surged through him. For several heartbeats he stood rooted, and then, with a wild cry, he leapt through the Gateway, cannoning into Beltzer's back and sprawling to the mud-covered trail. Beltzer swore, leaned down, and hoisted Kiall to his feet. Kiall smiled apologetically and looked around. Huge trees festooned with vines surrounded them. Plants with leaves like spears and heavy purple flowers grew at their bases. The heat was oppressive, and the questers began to sweat heavily in their winter clothes. But what impressed Kiall most was the smell—overpowering and cloying, decaying vegetation mixed with the musky scent of numberless flowers, plants, and fungoid growths. A throaty roar sounded from some distance to their left, answered by a cacophony of chittering cries in the trees above them. Small, dark creatures with long tails leapt from branch to branch or swung on vines.

"Are they demons?" whispered Beltzer.

No one answered him. Chareos looked back at the Gateway. On this side it shone like silver, and the runic script was smaller, punctuated by symbols of the moon and stars. He gazed up at the sun.

"It is near noon here," he said. "At noon tomorrow we will make our way back. Now, I would suggest we follow this trail and see if we can locate a village. What do you think, Finn?"

"It is as good an idea as any. I will mark the trail in case any should become lost." Finn drew his hunting knife and carved an arrowhead pointing at the Gateway. Beside it he sliced the number 10. "That represents paces. I will swing a wide circle around our trail, marking trunks in this manner. If we do become separated, seek out the signs." Aware that Finn was directing his remarks to him, Kiall nodded.

The group set off warily, following a meandering trail for almost an hour. In that time Finn disappeared often, moving to the left and reappearing from the right. The small, dark creatures in the trees traveled with them, occasionally dropping to the lower branches, where they hung from their tails and screeched at the newcomers. Birds with glorious plumage of red and green and blue sat on tree limbs preening their feathers with curved beaks.

At the end of the hour Chareos called a halt. The heat was incredible, and their clothes were soaked with perspiration. "We are traveling roughly southeast," Chareos told Kiall. "Remember that."

A movement came from the undergrowth to their right. The spearlike leaves parted . . . and a monstrous head came into sight. The face was semihuman and black as pitch, the eyes small and round. It had long sharp fangs, and as it reared to its full height of around six feet, its enormous arms and shoulders came into view. Beltzer dragged clear his ax and let out a bellowing battle cry. The creature blinked and stared.

"Move on. Slowly," said Chareos. Warily the group continued on the trail, Chareos leading and Finn, an arrow notched to his curved hunting bow, bringing up the rear.

"What an obscenity," whispered Kiall, glancing back at the silent creature standing on the trail behind them.

"That's no way to talk about Beltzer's mother," said

Maggrig. "Didn't you notice the way they recognized each other?" Finn and Chareos chuckled. Beltzer swore. The trail widened and dropped away toward a low bowl-shaped depression cleared of trees. There were round huts there, and cooking fires still burned. But no one would use them. Bodies lay everywhere, some on the ground, some impaled, others nailed to trees at the edge of the village. Huge, bloated birds covered many of the corpses or sat in squat and ugly rows along the roofs.

"I think we've found the Tattooed People," Finn said.

Kiall sat on the slope above the devastated village and watched his companions moving about the ruins. Finn and Maggrig skirted the round huts, reading sign, while Beltzer and Chareos walked from hut to hut looking for survivors. There were none. Kiall felt a sense of despair creeping over him. This was the third time in his young life he had seen the results of a raid. In the first Ravenna had been taken, but other, older women had been raped or abused. Men had been slain. The second he had witnessed—and taken part in—a wild, frenzied slashing of swords and knives, his blood hot, fired by a need to kill. Now here was the third—and the worst of all. From his vantage point he could see the bodies of women and children, and even his unskilled eye could read the mindless savagery that had taken place here. This was no slave raid. The Tattooed People had been exterminated.

After a while Maggrig shouldered his bow and strode up to sit alongside Kiall.

"It is revolting down there," said the hunter. "It seems that nothing was taken in the raid. Some two hundred warriors surrounded the village earlier today, moved in, and killed almost everyone. There are some tracks leading north, and it looks as if small groups of the Tattooed People fought clear and fled. Maybe a dozen. But they were followed."

"Why would anyone do this, Maggrig? What is gained by it?"

The hunter spread his hands. "There is no answer I can give you. I took part in a raid on a Nadir camp once. We had found several of our men tortured over campfires, their eyes burned out. We followed the raiders to their village and captured them. Our officer, a cultured man, ordered all the children to be brought out to stand before the captives. Then he slew them in front of their parents. After that the Nadir were hanged. He told us the Nadir did not fear death, so to kill them was no real punishment. But to butcher their children before their eyes—that was justice." Maggrig fell silent.

Kiall looked back at the village. "There is no justice in any of it," he said. The others joined them, and the group moved back from the slope to make camp. Finn was unable to light a fire because the wood was too damp, and the questers sat in a circle, saying little.

"Was Okas among the dead?" asked Kiall.

Chareos shrugged. "Difficult to tell. Many of the corpses have been stripped almost clean, but I saw no tattoos I could remember."

"Have we arrived in the middle of a war between them?"

"No," answered Finn. "The Tattooed People are small and pigeon-toed. The tracks of the raiders show them to be tall. I found this," he went on, pulling a broken gold wristband from the pocket of his deerskin jerkin. Beltzer gasped as he saw it.

"Sweet heaven!" he exclaimed. "How heavy is it?" Finn tossed it to him. "It must be worth around a hundred Raq," said the giant.

"The owner threw it away when it broke," said Finn. "Gold cannot be worth that much here."

"It isn't," agreed Chareos, producing a small, barbed arrowhead; it, too, was gold.

"I am beginning to like it here," remarked Beltzer. "We could go back to Gothir as rich men."

"Let us be content to be going back as *live* men," snapped Chareos.

"I am with you on that," whispered Finn, holding out his hand to Beltzer, who reluctantly returned the wristband.

Chareos rose. "It is coming on toward dusk," he said. "I think we should make our way back to the gate and camp there." He shouldered his pack and led the others toward the northwest. They moved warily, stopping often while Finn scouted the trail ahead, and Kiall grew increasingly nervous. There would be little chance of hearing the approach of a legion of enemy warriors, not above the chittering of the dark creatures in the trees, the distant roar of hunting cats, and the rushing of unseen rivers and streams. He kept close to Chareos, Beltzer bringing up the rear with his huge ax in his hands.

Up ahead Finn dropped to his haunches, raising his arm and pumping his fist three times in the air. Then he rolled to the left and out of sight. Maggrig ducked into the undergrowth, followed swiftly by Chareos and Beltzer. Kiall stood for a moment alone on the trail. Three tall warriors came into sight, dragging a young woman; they saw Kiall and stopped, perplexed. They were tall men, bronze of skin, with dark, straight hair. Gold glittered on their arms and ankles. Two of them carried weapons of dark wood, while the third had a long knife of burnished gold. They wore necklets of colored stone, and their faces were streaked with many colors. The woman was small, her skin copper-colored. On her brow was a blue tattoo. She wore only a loincloth of animal skin.

Slowly Kiall drew his saber. One of the warriors screamed a war cry and ran at him, his wooden club raised high. Kiall dropped into the sideways crouch Chareos had taught him, then sprang forward, the saber lancing the man's chest. The bronze warrior staggered back as the sword slid clear. He looked down at the wound, saw the blood burst from it, and slumped facefirst to the ground. The young woman tore herself free of her captors and ran down the trail toward Kiall, who stepped aside to let her pass. The remaining warriors stood, uncertain. But from behind them came a score more of their comrades.

Kiall plunged left into the undergrowth as the hunters rushed forward. The ground dropped away, and he lost his footing, slipping and sliding down a mud-covered slope to land in a sprawling heap at the bottom.

Half-winded, he struggled to rise. Gathering his saber, he glanced up: the bronze warriors were coming down toward him. Spinning on his heel, he raced down a narrow trail.

Broad overhanging leaves lashed at his face, thorn-covered branches ripped at his clothes. Twice he slipped and fell, but the bloodcurdling cries of the pursuing hunters fed his panic, giving strength to his flight.

Where were his friends? Why were they not helping him?

He forced his way through a last section of dense undergrowth and emerged on the muddy bank of a great river that was wider than the lakes of his homeland. His breathing was ragged, his ears filled with the drumming of his heart.

Where can I go?

He had lost all sense of direction, and thick lowering clouds obscured the sun. He heard shouts from his left, and swinging to the right, he ran along the riverbank.

A huge dragon reared from the water, its elongated mouth rimmed with teeth. Kiall screamed and leapt back from the river's edge. A spear sliced the air by his head, and he turned in time to see a bronze warrior diving at him. The warrior crashed into Kiall, hurling them both back toward the riverbank. His saber knocked from his hand, Kiall surged up and crashed his fist into the man's face, knocking him sideways. The warrior sprang upright, but Kiall leapt feetfirst, his boots thudding against the man's chest and propelling him back into the dark water. As the warrior struggled to the surface and began to wade ashore, the dragon's head reared behind him, the monstrous jaws clamping home on his leg. He let out an agonizing scream and began to stab at the monster's scaled hide with a golden knife. Blood billowed to the river's surface, and Kiall watched in horror as the warrior was dragged from sight.

Kiall tore his eyes from the scene and took up his saber. He scanned the trees for sign of the enemy. A sudden movement behind made him spin around with sword raised. It was the young woman, and she waved him toward where she was hidden in the undergrowth. He ran to her, dropped to his knees, and crawled inside the spike-leaved bushes. Carefully she eased leaves back across the opening.

Within seconds more of the enemy arrived on the scene. They stood at the riverside, watching the struggle between the dying warrior and the dragon. When it was over, the hunters squatted in a circle and spoke in low voices; one pointed up the trail, and it seemed to Kiall that they were arguing about which direction to take. A large spider, hairless and bloated, crawled onto Kiall's hand. He stifled a scream. The girl swiftly leaned over him, plucking the insect from his skin and carefully placing it on a leaf.

The hunters rose and moved off into the jungle.

Kiall lay back and smiled at the young woman. She did not respond in kind but touched her hand to her breast, then to her brow, then pressed her fingers to Kiall's mouth. Not knowing how to respond, Kiall lifted her hand and kissed it. She settled down beside him, closed her eyes, and slept.

For some time he lay awake, too frightened to leave the sanctuary of the undergrowth. Then he, too, drifted off into a light doze—and awoke with the moon shining high above the trees. The woman sat up and crawled into the open. Kiall followed. She whispered something to him, but it was a language he had never heard.

"Okas?" he asked. Her head tilted. "I am looking for Okas."

She shrugged and trotted off along the riverbank. He followed her through the moonlit jungle, up over hills and rises, down through vine-choked archways and on to a wide cave where she stopped outside and held out her hand. He took it and was led inside. Torches flickered, and he saw more than thirty of the Tattooed People sitting around fires built within circles of stone. Two young men approached them. After the woman had spoken to them for a few moments, he was led farther into the cave.

An old man, nearly toothless, sat cross-legged on a high rock. His body was completely covered in tattoos, and his lower face was stained blue, as if emulating a beard and an upturned mustache.

The woman spoke to the old man, whose face remained expressionless throughout. Finally she turned to Kiall and dropped to her knees. Taking his hand, she kissed it twice, then rose and was gone.

"I am Okas," said the old man.

"I am—" Kiall began.

"I know who you are. What do you want of me?"

"Your help."

"Why should I seek to aid the soul of Tenaka Khan?"

"I do not know what you are talking about," said Kiall. "I am seeking to rescue a woman I love—that is all."

"Where is fat Beltzer?"

"I lost them when we were attacked."

"By the Azhtacs; this also I know! Give me your hand." Kiall reached out, and Okas took his hand and turned it palm upward. "You lost your woman—and yet not your woman. And now you are on a quest you do not understand that will determine the fate of a people you do not know. Truly, Kiall, you are a part of the World's Dream."

"But will you help me? Chareos says you can follow spirit trails; he says that without you we will never find Ravenna."

The old man released his hand. "My people are finished now; the day of the Azhtacs has dawned. But soon another day will dawn, and the Azhtacs will see the destruction of their homes, the torment of their people. Yet that gives me no pleasure. And I do not wish to be here when they come for my children. I had thought to die tonight, quietly, here on this stone. But now I will come with you and die on another stone. Then I will join the World's Dream."

"I don't know how to thank you," said Kiall.

"Come," said the old man, dropping to the floor beside him. "Let us find the ghosts-yet-to-be."

Chareos dragged his sword clear of the dying Azhtac and swung to see if any of his companions needed help. Beltzer was standing over a dead warrior with ax raised. Maggrig and Finn had sheathed their knives and notched arrows to their bows. Nine dead Azhtacs lay sprawled around them. Chareos glanced up at the sun; it was almost noon, and the silver-gray Gateway beckoned.

"Where in Bar's name is Kiall?" hissed Chareos.

Finn joined him. "I marked as many trees as I could, Chareos. I think he must be dead."

Beltzer dropped to his knees beside a corpse and began to tug at the gold circlet the man wore on his brow. At that moment Maggrig shouted a warning, and a large group of Azhtacs raced from the trees. "Back!" shouted Chareos. Beltzer cursed and rose. Maggrig and Finn ran through the Gateway. Beltzer raised his ax and bellowed a battle cry, and the Azhtacs slowed. Beltzer turned and sprinted through the gate, followed by Chareos.

The moonlight was bright on the other side, and the cold was numbing after the heat of the jungle. A spear flashed through the Gateway, striking the ground and half burying itself in the snow. Beltzer moved to one side of the Gateway; when an arm and a head showed through, his ax smashed into the head, catapulting the man back through the opening. Then there was silence.

"All that gold," said Beltzer, "and I didn't get a single piece of it."

"You have your life," Finn told him.

Beltzer swung on him. "And what is that worth?"

"Enough!" roared Chareos. "We have a comrade on the other side. Now cease your arguing and let me think."

In a circle of boulders within sight of the Gateway Maggrig lit a fire, and they all gathered around it. "You want to go back, Blademaster?" asked Maggrig.

"I don't know, my friend. We were lucky to escape the first time. I should think they would place guards on the gate, and that makes it doubly perilous."

"I think we should go back," said Beltzer. "I'm willing to risk it."

"For the boy or the gold?" asked Maggrig.

"For both, if you must know," Beltzer snapped.

Chareos shook his head. "No," he said, "that would be foolhardy. Kiall is alone there, but he is a resourceful lad. Finn marked the trees, and if he still lives, Kiall will follow the trail back to the gate. We will wait for him here."

"And what if you are right about guards, eh?" inquired Beltzer. "How will he get past them?"

"My guess is that they will be watching the gate to see who passes from this side. He may have an opportunity to run at it."

"Aren't you forgetting something, Chareos?" asked Maggrig. "If he chooses the wrong time, there is no knowing where the gate will take him."

"As I said, he is resourceful. We wait."

For some time they sat in silence. The wind picked up, gusting the snow around them; the fire spluttered, and little heat seemed to emanate from it. "We could freeze to death waiting here," grumbled Beltzer. "At least it is warmer on the other side."

"It is colder than it ought to be," remarked Finn suddenly. "When we left, the thaw had set in. The weather should not have turned so swiftly."

"It has not necessarily been swift," said Chareos, drawing his cloak more tightly about his frame. "When I first looked beyond the gate, I seemed to be there, frozen, unable to move, for an hour at least. You said it was but a few heartbeats. Well, we were beyond the gate for a day—that could be a week here, or a month."

"It better not have been a month, Blademaster," Maggrig said softly. "If it is, we are trapped in this valley for the winter. And there is not enough game."

"Rubbish!" snorted Beltzer. "We would just pass through the gate and wait for a few of their days, returning in spring. Isn't that right, Chareos?"

The blademaster nodded.

"Well, what are we waiting for?" asked Beltzer. "Let's go back and find the lad."

Finn bit back an angry response as Beltzer pushed himself to his feet. Just then a spark lifted from the fire and hung in the air, swelling slowly into a glowing ball. Beltzer's mouth dropped open, and he took up his ax. Chareos and the others stared at the floating sphere, watching, astonished, as it grew to the size of a man's head. The color faded until the globe was almost transparent and they could see the gate reflected there and the snow gusting around it. Finn gasped as two tiny figures showed inside the sphere, stepping through the miniature Gateway.

"It is Okas," said Beltzer, peering at the ball. "And the lad with him." He spun around, but the real Gateway was empty. The scene inside the floating sphere shimmered and changed; now they could see Finn's cabin and a warm fire glowing in the hearth. Okas was seated cross-legged before the blaze, his eyes closed. Kiall sat at the table.

The sphere vanished.

"He found the old boy," said Beltzer. "He found Okas."

"Yes, and arrived back before us," continued Finn.

The four men stood. Chareos doused the fire, and they set off through the snow.

In the cabin Okas opened his eyes. "They come," he said.

"I had begun to give up hope," replied Kiall. "Twelve days is a long time to be trapped in that jungle."

Okas chuckled. "They left before we did. But I know how to use the gate." He stood and stretched. A small man, no more than five feet tall, he was round-shouldered and potbellied. He could have been any age from sixty to a hundred and looked as if a stiff breeze could snap his bones. Yet he had walked through the snow clad only in a loincloth and had appeared to suffer no discomfort from cold or exhaustion. And he left barely a print on the snow, as if his weight were no more than that of a bird. He looked up at Kiall. "So tell me all you know about the great khan."

"Why are you interested? I don't understand," said Kiall.

"I was here when he led his armies into Drenai lands," Okas told him. "And again when they marched against Belazar. Strong man, the khan. Great man, perhaps. But he is dead, yes?"

"I don't know much about him. He conquered the Drenai and the Vagrians. He died some years ago; he is buried in the tomb of Ulric."

"No, he is not," said Okas. "He is buried in an unmarked grave. But I know where it is. How did he die?"

"I do not know. His heart gave out, I would suppose. That is how most people die—even kings. Are you sure Chareos is coming?"

Okas nodded. He poured himself a goblet of water. "I sent them a message. They come. Fat Beltzer is disappointed. He wanted to go back through to the jungle to find you—and to be rich. Fat Beltzer always wanted to be rich."

"He is your friend?"

"All men are my friends," said Okas. "We are all of the Dream. But yes, I like very much fat Beltzer."

"Why? What is there to like?" Kiall asked.

"Ask me again in half a year. I will sleep now. I am older than I look."

Kiall thought that barely credible, but he said nothing. Okas sat down before the fire, crossed his arms, and slept upright. Kiall blew out the lantern and lay back on the bed by the wall.

The others were coming. The search for Ravenna was under way.

He slept without dreams.

It was a further two days before the exhausted travelers reached the sanctuary of the cabin. Beltzer was the first inside. He hoisted Okas into a bear hug and spun him around until the little man laughed delightedly. "How come you still live, fat man?" he asked. "How come no one kill you yet?"

"They do keep trying," replied Beltzer. He put the old man down and stared closely at his wrinkled skin and rheumy eyes. "By the Source, you look all but dead yourself."

"Soon," said Okas, smiling. "The Dream calls. But I will stay a little while with my old friends." He turned to Chareos, who had shed his ice-covered cloak and was stripping his wet clothes from himself and standing before the fire shivering. "You and I, we speak," Okas said. "Back room good place."

"This minute?"

"Yes," answered Okas, moving through to the workshop. Chareos pulled a fresh tunic from his pack and dressed, then walked to where Okas waited. The old man reached out and took his hand, holding it firmly for several seconds. "Sit down," he ordered, "and tell me of quest."

Chareos explained about the raid on the village and Kiall's love for Ravenna. "The others are coming along for different reasons. Beltzer is a lost soul down from the mountain. Finn fears his death will leave Maggrig alone."

"And you?"

"Me? I have nothing better to do with my life."

"Is that true, Chareos? Do you not carry a dream?"

"Another man's dream. It was never my own."

Okas clambered up on the edge of the workbench and sat down, his short legs dangling less than halfway to the floor. He looked closely at Chareos. "Not your dream, you say. So, you also do not understand nature of this quest, nor where it take you. Tell me of Tenaka Khan and gatetower night."

Chareos smiled. "Do you know everything, Okas?"

"No; that is why I ask."

"He climbed up to sit with us, and we talked of many things: love, life, power, conquest, duty. He was a knowledgeable man. He had a dream, but he said the stars stood in his way."

"What did he mean by it?"

"I don't know. He was no youngster then. Perhaps he meant death."

"How did he die?"

"As I understand it, he collapsed at a feast. He was drinking wine, and his heart gave out."

"What happened then? After feast?"

Chareos spread his hands. "How would I know? They buried him in Ulric's tomb. It was a great ceremony, and thousands witnessed it. Our own ambassadors—and others from Ventria and the east—attended. Then his eldest son, Jungir, became khan. He killed all his brothers and now rules the Nadir. What has this to do with our quest? Or are you merely curious?"

Okas lifted his hand, the index finger pointed up, and spun it in the air. Golden light streamed from the finger, forming a circle. Other circles sprang up, crisscrossing the first until a sphere hung there. He dropped his hand and traced a straight golden line. "This line is how you see your quest: flat, straight, start, finish. But this," he said, raising his eyes to the globe, "is how it really is. Your line is touched by many others. I know your secret, Chareos. I know who you are. You are son of last Earl of Dros Delnoch. You are heir to Armor of Bronze. And that makes you blood relative of Tenaka Khan and descendant of both Ulric and Earl Regnak, the second Earl of Bronze."

"That is a secret I hope you will share with no one else," whispered Chareos. "I have no desire to return to the Drenai, and I want no one seeking me out."

"As you wish . . . but blood is strong, and it calls across the centuries. You will find it so. Why did Tenaka Khan let you live?"

"I don't know. Truly I don't."

"And the ghosts-yet-to-be?"

"Just another riddle," answered Chareos. "Are not all men the ghosts of the future?"

"Yes. But in the Nadir tongue the phrase could be translated as 'companions of the ghost' or even 'followers of the ghost.' Is that not so?"

"I am not skilled in the nuances of the Nadir tongue. What difference does it make?"

Okas jumped down to the floor, landing lightly. "I will take you to Nadren village where Ravenna and the others were held. Then we see."

"Is she still there?"

"I cannot say. I will pick up the spirit trail at her home."

Okas returned to the main room, where Kiall had lifted a heavy bundle to the tabletop. When he opened it, golden objects fell across the wooden surface, glinting in the lantern light. There were armbands, necklets, brooches, rings, and even a belt with solid gold clasp.

"Oh, joy!" cried Beltzer, dipping his huge fingers into the treasure and lifting a dozen items clear. "Chareos said you were resourceful, but he didn't do you justice."

"With this we should be able to buy back Ravenna," said Kiall.

"With this you could buy a hundred women," countered Beltzer. "When do we share it out?"

"We don't," Kiall stated. "As I said, this is for Ravenna."

Beltzer reddened. "I worked for this, too," he said, "and you must have stripped it from the bodies of the men I slew at the Gateway. Part of it is mine. Mine!" He scooped up a handful of golden objects and began to cram them into his pockets. Kiall stepped back and drew his sword, but Beltzer saw the move and swept up his ax.

"Stop this foolishness!" roared Chareos, moving between them. "Sheath the blade, Kiall. And you, Beltzer, put back the gold."

"But Chareos—" began Beltzer.

"Do it now!"

Beltzer slammed the gold back to the table and stalked off to sit by the fire. Chareos turned his angry eyes on Kiall. "There is truth in what he said. Think on it!"

Kiall stood silently for a few moments, then he relaxed. "You split it fairly, Chareos," said the young man. "I will use my share to buy Ravenna."

Finn stepped to the table, lifted a single ring, and slipped it on his finger. "This will do for me," he said. Maggrig chose a wristband. Chareos took nothing.

Beltzer stood and glared at the others. "You will not shame me," he hissed. "I will take what is mine!" He shoveled a number of items into his deep pockets and returned to the fire.

"We leave at first light for Tavern Town," said Chareos. "We will buy extra horses there. Since you are now rich, Beltzer, you can buy your own—and all the food and supplies you will need."

6

"You tell me I face great danger, and yet you do not know whence it comes?" asked Jungir Khan, his manner easy, his voice cold. He lounged back on the ivory inlaid throne and stared down at the shaman kneeling before him.

Shotza kept his eyes on the rugs below him, considering his words with great care. He was the third shaman to serve Jungir Khan; the first had been impaled, and the second strangled. He was determined there would be no fourth. "Great Khan," he said, "there is a magic barrier at work which will take me time to pierce. I already know where the magic originates."

"And where is that?" whispered Jungir.

"From Asta Khan, sire." Shotza risked a glance to see the effect the name had on the man above him.

Jungir's face betrayed no emotion, but his dark eyes narrowed. "Still alive? How can this be? He was an old man when my father became khan. He left the city of tents to die more than twenty years ago."

"But he did not die, lord. He lives still in the Mountains of the Moon. There are many caves there, and tunnels that go through to the center of the world."

Jungir rose to his feet. He was tall for a Nadir, as his father, Tenaka, had been. He had jet-black hair drawn back in a tight topknot and a short, trimmed trident beard. His eyes were slanted and dark, betraying no evidence of his half-breed ancestry. "Stand up," he ordered the little shaman, and Shotza rose. He was just over five feet tall, wiry and bald. Less than sixty years old, the skin of his face hung in wrinkled folds.

Jungir looked into the shaman's curiously pale eyes and smiled. "Do you fear me?" he asked.

"As I fear the winds of death, lord."

"Do you love me?"

"Love? You are my khan. The future of the Nadir rests with you," answered Shotza. "Why would you need my love also?"

"I do not. But the answer is a good one. Now tell me of Asta."

The khan returned to his throne and sat with his head back, gazing up at the silken roof that gave the throne hall the appearance of a vast tent. The silks were gifts from the eastern kingdom of Kiatze, a dowry for the bride they had sent him.

"After Asta left the Wolves, he passed from the knowledge of men," began Shotza. "We all thought he had died. But at the last full moon, when I tried to trace the silver thread of your destiny, I found that a great mist had settled over the sign of your house. I tried to pierce it and at first had some success. Then it hardened into a wall. I flew high but could not find the top. Using all the arcane powers my masters taught me, I finally breached the wall. But all too briefly. Yet I saw the face of Asta Khan. And I sensed the perils that await you in the coming year."

Shotza licked his lips and once more considered his words. "I saw the gleaming Armor of Bronze floating beneath a star and a swordsman of great skill. But then Asta became aware of me—I was thrown back, and the wall sealed itself once more."

"And that is all you saw?" asked Jungir softly.

"All that I could see clearly," Shotza answered, wary of offering a direct lie to his king.

The khan nodded. "Find Asta Khan—and kill him. Take a hundred of my guards. Scour the mountains. Bring me his head."

"With respect, Great Khan, you could send a thousand

men and not find him. Asta was the greatest of shamans; he cannot be taken by men."

"His magic is stronger than yours?"

Shotza closed his eyes. "Yes, lord. There is not one man alive who could overcome him."

"It is not my way, Shotza, to have inferior men serve me."

"No, lord. But there is a way in which I could defeat him. I have six worthy acolytes. Together, and with certain necessary sacrifices, we could overcome Asta."

"Necessary sacrifices?"

"Blood kin of Asta Khan, sacrificed on the night of midwinter."

"How many such sacrifices?"

"Twenty at least. Maybe thirty. Each one will weaken the old man."

"And you, of course, know the whereabouts of Asta's family?"

"I do, lord."

"Then I leave the preparations to you, Shotza. Now, this peril from the Armor of Bronze—does it herald yet another Drenai uprising?"

"I do not think so, lord. I saw the image of the armor, yet the star was in the north. There can be no Drenai threat from the lands of the Gothir. But once I have breached Asta's wall, I will know more. I will know it all."

Shotza bowed deeply. Jungir waved him away, and the shaman made his way to his chambers and sat down on a silk-covered divan. Free from the piercing eyes of Jungir Khan, he lay back and allowed his fear to show. His heart was palpitating, and he found it difficult to breathe. Slowly he calmed himself, thanking the gods of the steppes that Jungir had not pressed him about the other images.

He had seen a babe, wrapped in a cloak, lying on a cold stone floor.

And hovering over the child was the grim ghost of Tenaka Khan, Lord of the Wolves.

Jungir watched the little man leave, then sat in silence for several minutes. He could smell Shotza's fear and knew full well that there was more the shaman could have said. None of these sorcerers ever gave the whole truth. It was against their nature. Secretive, deceitful, and cunning, they were weaned on subtlety and guile. But they had their uses. Shotza was the best of them, and it must have taken great courage to admit that Asta Khan was more powerful. Jungir rose and stretched. He walked to the hanging tent wall that masked the window and pulled it aside.

The new city of Ulrickham stretched out before his eyes, low single-story dwellings of mud-dried brick and stone. Yet inside all of them were the tent hangings that meant home to the Nadir. Nomads for ten thousand years, they were ill suited to cities of stone. Yet Tenaka had insisted on the building of the cities, with their schools and hospitals.

"It ill behooves the world's greatest nation to live like savages," he had told Jungir. "How can we grow? How can we fasten our grip on the events of the world if we do not learn civilized ways? It is not enough to be feared on the battlefield."

Such talk had made him unpopular with the older Nadir warlords, but how could they turn on the man who had done what the mighty Ulric could not? How could they betray the man who had conquered the round-eyed southerners?

Jungir stepped back from the window and wandered into the Hall of Heroes. There, after the fashion of the conquered Drenai, were the statues of Nadir warriors. Jungir paused before his father's likeness and stared into the cold gray eyes. "Just how I remember you, Father," he whispered. "Cold and aloof." The statue was expertly carved, showing the lean power, the fine jaw, and the noble stance of the khan. In one hand he held a longsword, in the other the helm of Ulric. "I loved you," said Jungir.

A cool breeze caused the torches to flicker, and shadows danced on the stone face, seeming to bring it to life. Jungir could almost see the stone eyes gleaming violet, the mouth curving into that long-remembered cynical smile. He shivered. "I did love you," he repeated, "but I knew of your plan. You trained me well, Father. I had my spies, too. No man should think to live forever . . . not even Tenaka Khan.

And had you succeeded, where would Jungir have found a place? The eternal heir to a living god? No. I, too, am of the blood of Ulric. I had a right to rule, to make my own life."

The statue was silent. "How strange, Father. There is no difference in talking to you now from when you were alive. It was always like speaking to stone. Well, I wept when you died. And I almost stopped you drinking that poison. *Almost*. I reached out my hand to you. You looked into my eyes, and you said nothing. A single word from you and I would have stopped you. But you looked away. Did you know, I wonder, as the poison touched your soul? In those last moments, as you lay on the floor with me kneeling by you, did you know that it was I who put the black powder in your wine? Did you?" He gazed once more into the cold eyes. "Why did you never love me?" he asked.

But the statue was silent.

The twelve days lost beyond the gate cost the questers dearly, for a savage blizzard kept them trapped in the cabin for eighteen days. Food ran short, and Finn almost died after setting off to hunt for meat. After killing a deer, he was caught in a second blizzard and had to take refuge in a cave. An avalanche blocked the entrance, and it was only through the magic of Okas that Chareos and the others found the hunter and dug a tunnel through to him.

The winter storms eased off on the nineteenth day, but even then it took another three weeks before the exhausted group topped the last rise before Tavern Town.

Beltzer led the way down to the inn, pounding on the door and calling for Naza. The little man shouted with delight when he saw the giant and embraced him.

"I feared you dead," he said. "Come in, come in! Mael has just lit the fire. It will soon be warm. Come in!"

"Where is everyone?" asked Kiall.

"They don't fell the timber at this time of year," Naza replied. "There will be no one here for another two months. Most of the passes are blocked. Sit down by the fire. I will fetch you some wine." His smile faded as Okas entered the tavern. "He's . . . he's . . ." stammered the innkeeper.

"Yes, he is," Chareos said swiftly. "He is also a friend who, like us, last ate three days ago."

"Wine first," grunted Beltzer, throwing his arm around Naza's shoulder and leading him back toward the cellar.

The flames took hold of the logs and began to rise, but even so it was cold inside the inn. Chareos pulled up a chair and sat. His eyes were dull, and purple rings showed under them. Even the hardy Finn was exhausted. Only Okas and Kiall seemed none the worse for the ordeal in the mountains. The old man had been untroubled by the cold, and the youngster had grown in strength as the days had passed.

"We're too old for this," said Finn, reading Chareos' thoughts. Chareos nodded, too tired to reply. Returning with wine, Beltzer thrust a poker deep into the fire and waited until the iron glowed red and bright. Then he plunged it into the wine pitcher. He poured five goblets and handed one to each of the questers. He downed his own swiftly and refilled the goblet. Naza brought them bread, smoked cheese, and cold meat.

After the meal Chareos slowly climbed the stairs to the upper guest room, pulled off his boots, and was asleep almost as soon as his head touched the bolster. Maggrig and Finn took a second room, while Okas lay down on the stone hearth and slept before the fire.

Beltzer and Kiall sat together, the giant calling out for a third pitcher of wine.

Mael brought it. "I take it you still have no money?" she asked.

"Oh, yes, he has," said Kiall. "Pay the bill, Beltzer."

Beltzer muttered a curse and dipped into his pocket, producing a thick gold ring. Mael took it, judging the weight. "That should settle about half of what you owe Naza," she said, leaving her hand extended.

"You are a hard woman," grumbled Beltzer. He fished around in his pocket, seeking a small token, but he had only larger items. Finally he produced a wristband. "That's worth ten times what I owe," he told her.

Mael laughed at him as she took the band and examined it. "I have never seen workmanship like it or gold as red as this. Naza will give you a fair price—and you are right. It is worth far more than you owe. I will see to it that you are reimbursed."

"Don't bother," said Beltzer, flushing. "Keep it. I'll probably come back one day with not a copper coin to my name."

"There's truth in that," she told him.

After she had gone, Beltzer turned to Kiall. "What are you staring at, boy? Never seen a man settle a debt before?"

Kiall had drunk too much wine, and his head was light, his thoughts serene. "I never thought to see *you* settle one."

"What does that mean?"

"I took you for a selfish, greedy pig," said Kiall, smilingly oblivious to Beltzer's growing anger.

"I pay my debts," declared Beltzer.

"Truly? You didn't even thank Finn for buying back your ax—and that cost him dear."

"That is between Finn and me. You don't count, boy. Now curb your tongue before I cut it out!"

Kiall blinked and sobered swiftly. "And you are a liar," he said. "You told me Tura was dead, drowned in a dock. All lies. And I don't fear you, you fat-bellied pig. Don't threaten me!"

Beltzer lurched to his feet, and Kiall rose, scrabbling for his saber, but not before Beltzer's fingers grabbed the front of his jerkin and hoisted him into the air. As Beltzer's fist rose, Kiall's foot lashed up into his groin and the giant bellowed with pain, dropping the younger man and staggering back. Now Kiall drew his saber. Beltzer grinned at him and advanced.

"What are you going to do with that, boy? You going to stick old Beltzer? Are you?" Kiall backed away, aware that the situation had careered out of control. Beltzer lunged at him, slapping the saber aside. Kiall hit him with a straight left that slammed into Beltzer's face. The giant ignored the blow and stuck Kiall's jaw open-handed, cartwheeling the younger man across the floor. Half-stunned, Kiall came to his knees and dived headfirst at Beltzer's belly. Beltzer's knee came up with sickening force, snapping Kiall's head back . . .

He awoke to find himself in the chair by the fire with Beltzer sitting opposite him.

"Want some wine?" Beltzer asked. Kiall shook his head. Hammers were beating inside his skull. "You are a game fighter, boy, and one day you may even be a wolf. But wolves know better than to tackle a bear."

"I'll remember that," Kiall promised. "And I'll have that wine now."

Beltzer handed him a goblet. "I love old Finn. And he knows how much it meant to me to have that ax back; he didn't need any words. Back at Bel-azar Finn was dragged from the ramparts by the Nadir. Chareos, Maggrig, and me, we jumped down to haul him clear. It was I who carried Finn on my back and cut a path to the gate tower. He didn't thank me then; he didn't need to. You understand?"

"I believe I do."

"It's the drink. It makes me talk too much. You don't like me, do you?"

Kiall looked at the flat, ugly face under the shining bald head; he stared into the small round eyes. "No, not much," he admitted.

Beltzer nodded solemnly. "Well, don't let it concern you. I don't like myself much, either. But I was on the mountain, boy. No one can take that away from me."

"I was on the mountain, too,' said Kiall.

"Not *my* mountain. But maybe you will one day."

"What is so special about it?"

"Nothing," replied Beltzer.

"Then why should I wish to go there?"

Beltzer looked up from his wine. "Because that's where your lady is, Kiall."

Moonlight bathed the gray stone walls, and a hunting owl swooped low over the deserted ramparts. Chareos could hear the screams of the wounded and the dying, yet there were no bodies sprawled on the stone, no blood pooling by the gate tower steps. As he sat down on the edge of the crenellated battlement, staring out over the valley of Bel-azar, the screams faded into the echoes of memory. The land was now empty of life. Where Nadir campfires had lit the valley like fallen stars, now there was only the shimmering grass, the lonely boulders, and a long-dead lightning-struck tree.

Chareos was alone. He could not remember traveling to Bel-azar, but that did not seem to matter. He felt in some strange way that he was home, safe among the ghosts of the past.

Safe? Dark shapes moved at the edge of his vision, vanishing into the shadows as he swung to confront them. He backed away to the rotted gate tower door and climbed the spiral steps to the circular battlement. There he drew his sword and waited. He could hear the scratching of talons on the stairway, smell the fetid odors of the dwellers in the dark: slime on fur, the sweet, sickly stink from mouths that fed on corpses.

He slammed shut the top door. There was no bolt, and he dropped his sword into the catch, wedging the door shut. Heavy bodies beat on the wood.

"Beltzer!" called Chareos. "Help me!"

But there was no answer. "Maggrig, Finn!"

"It would seem you are alone, kinsman," said a quiet voice, and Chareos turned slowly, knowing whom he would see. The tall man sat on the battlement's edge, his black hair tied at the nape of the neck, his violet eyes seeming gray in the moonlight.

"Will *you* help me?" whispered Chareos.

"Blood always aids blood, my friend. Are you not my kinsman?"

"Yes. Yes, I am. Will you help me? Please?"

The door splintered, and a taloned hand broke through, ripping at the wood.

"Begone!" shouted Tenaka Khan. The hissing cries beyond the doorway faded into silence, and the hand slid back from view.

"Are they your creatures?" Chareos asked.

"No, but they know a voice of power. And they can smell fear like a lion smells blood. Why are you afraid, Chareos?"

"I don't know how I came here. I am alone."

"That is not an answer. Fear brought you, but what caused the fear?"

Chareos laughed, but there was no humor in the sound. "You can ask that? You who slew my father and mother and made me an outcast? I should hate you, Tenaka. Once I thought I did. But then you climbed alone to this tower, and you sat and talked with us." Chareos stared at the man before him. He was dressed exactly as he had been on that night so many years ago, in black riding boots and leather leggings, topped by a shirt of black silk embroidered with silver. "You called me kinsman," whispered Chareos. "You know who I am?"

"I knew you when first I saw you on this tower," answered Tenaka. "Blood recognizes blood."

"I should have killed you!" hissed Chareos, "for all the pain. I was twelve when they sent me from Dros Delnoch. The night when your hordes finally stormed the last wall, I was taken from the fortress and brought to the lands of the Gothir. My father's last words to me were 'Avenge me, my son. And remember the Drenai.' My mother was already dead. And for what? So that a treacherous cur like you could take Nadir savages into the last bastion of civilization. What caused my fear? You dare ask me that?"

"I still ask it," replied the khan smoothly. "And all you tell me is a history I already know."

"You were descended from the Earl of Bronze and raised by the Drenai. How could you destroy them?"

"How, indeed?" replied the khan. "If you truly knew the story of my life, you would not ask such a question. As you know, I was raised by the Nadir until I was fourteen. You think you were the only child who ever suffered pain and rejection? I was hated for being part Drenai. Then I was sent, as part of my mother's marriage agreement, to live among the Drenai. Were they different from the Nadir? No. To them I was a savage from the steppes, something they could bait and torture. Yet I learned to live among them. And I fought for them. I rode with the Dragon. I even made a few friends among them. But when the mad emperor, Ceska, brought terror to the land, I risked my life and my soul to aid the Drenai. I paid my debt to them. I brought the Nadir to crush the emperor's army, and I allowed Rayvan and your father to form a new republic. Why did I take Dros Delnoch years later? Because I was the khan! Because the day of the Nadir had dawned. Yet if I can be accused of treachery, what of you? Why did you not obey your father's command? Why did you not return home?"

"For what purpose?" shouted Chareos. "To die? Achieving what?"

"So that is your fear?" responded Tenaka Khan. "You were afraid to try. Afraid to fail."

"Don't you dare to judge me!" Chareos stormed. "I will not be found wanting by a murderous traitor."

Tenaka Khan spread his hands. "And who did I betray, Chareos? I was the khan of the Nadir. I had saved the Drenai once. I gave them good warning that I would return. But you—you betrayed your father and all your ancestors back to Regnak, second Earl of Bronze. He held Dros Delnoch against seemingly insurmountable odds. Generations of Drenai warriors have died to protect their homeland, but not you. No, you would be content to marry a whore and win a little battle here at Bel-azar."

Chareos dragged his sword from the bolt latch of the door and swung on Tenaka.

"Is this how you repay me for saving your soul?" Tenaka asked mildly. "Only a few moments ago you were asking for my help against the beasts of the night."

Chareos lowered his sword. "Am I a coward, then?" he whispered.

"There are many forms of cowardice, Chareos. One man can face a score of enemies with a sword but not a sickness which paralyzes him. Another can face death with a smile yet fear the years of hardship and toil which are life. Are you a coward?"

Chareos sat down on the battlements, staring at the sword in his hand. "I have never feared an opponent. But yes, I am a coward. I did not have the strength to return to the Drenai . . . I still haven't."

"You found the Tattooed Man?"

"Yes. Yes, we found him. And he will come with us on our . . . journey."

"You feel this quest is below you?" asked the khan.

"We are seeking to rescue a pig breeder's daughter taken by Nadren raiders. Will the sun fall from the sky if we fail?"

Tenaka stood and placed his hands on Chareos' shoulders. "I returned to the lands of the Drenai to kill a madman. Instead I found a friend, and a love, and a home I never knew I had lost. From being the Prince of Shadows I became the great khan, and I took the Nadir to heights undreamed of. Do not judge your quest until you have completed it. You remember that other night on this very tower?"

"How could I forget? You let us live."

"One day soon you will know why."

Chareos awoke. The fire had died, and the room was cold; he shivered and pulled the blankets over his chilled frame. He could still picture the slanted violet eyes and feel the strength of the grip on his shoulders.

The door opened, and Okas stepped in. He moved silently to the bed and sat on it.

"The dawn is up," said Okas. "Your quest awaits."

"I had a dream, Okas."

"I, too. I dreamed of a bed of rushes and a soft woman."

"And I of Tenaka Khan."

"Was he at Bel-azar?" the Tattooed man inquired.

"Yes." Chareos sat up. "How do you know that?"

"I did not," replied Okas, blinking. "It was a question."

"But why did you ask it?"

The old man was silent for a moment. "There is a mystery here. Tenaka Khan was buried with his ancestor Ulric in the great tomb. It was sealed by his son, Jungir, and a thousand spells were cast upon it so that it should never be opened."

"I know all this," snapped Chareos.

"You do not know," said Okas, "or you would solve mystery. I understand magic that is hidden in the world; I can read hearts of men. Yet the Source of All Things has his own secrets, and I cannot read those. Tenaka Khan died and was buried—this we know. His son was anxious that no one should enter the tomb; this also we know. But here is the mystery, Chareos: Why do Tenaka Khan's bones lie hidden at Bel-azar?"

"That is impossible. It would be sacrilege."

"Indeed so."

Chareos shook his head. "Our quest has nothing to do with Tenaka Khan. We will be traveling nowhere near Bel-azar."

"Are you sure?"

"I will stake my life on it."

Okas said nothing.

7

CHIEN-TSU WAS NOT a man who liked to travel. He did not like the dust of the steppes or the arid, inhospitable country; most especially he abhorred the squat dwellings, the stench of the towns, and the barely concealed hostility of the Nadir. It was said back in Hao-tzing that the Nadir were closely related to the people of the Middle Kingdom. Chien-tsu doubted it; despite the similarity of skin color and language, he could not believe that their origins were identical. He put forward the entirely reasonable view that the gods had made the Nadir first and then, realizing the ghastly flaws inherent in the species, had created the perfect people and had given them the Middle Kingdom for their own. This hateful visit only confirmed his theory. The Nadir did not seem disposed toward bathing, and their clothes remained unwashed from season to season—in fact, probably from decade to decade, he thought.

And what a country! Though he traveled light, which did not befit an ambassador from the Supreme City, he still found it difficult to obtain lodgings for his forty-two servants, eleven concubines, and sixty members of the guard royal. He had been reduced to purchasing sixteen wagons to carry necessities such as tents, beds, tables, chairs, soft linen sheets, harps, flutes, two enamel baths, and five full-sized mirrors. And he had brought a mere twenty-five chests of personal luggage containing his own—entirely inadequate—traveling wardrobe.

Chien-tsu found it curious that the emperor should have

allowed one of his daughters to wed a savage, but a wise man did not question the decisions of the divine one. And Chien-tsu, as all civilized men knew, was wise far beyond his thirty-two years.

He reined in his horse before the city and sighed. The buildings were in the main unlovely, and the palace that towered at the center, despite having an arrogant, almost primal simplicity, lacked any sense of aesthetic beauty. There were six square towers and a crenellated battlement. No banners flew. Chien-tsu halted the wagons and ordered his tent pitched. Once this was done, he had his mirrors assembled and a bath prepared. His handmaidens washed the dust from his body and massaged him with aromatic oils; his long dark hair was carefully greased and combed, drawn back from the brow and held in place by ivory combs. Then he dressed in leggings of gold-embroidered blue silk and shoes with golden straps. His shirt was of the whitest silk, and over it he placed a lacquered breastplate of wood and leather decorated with a golden dragon. His long, curving sword hung between his shoulder blades, and two knives in gleaming wooden scabbards were carefully placed within the satin sash tied around his waist. He ordered the presents for Jungir Khan to be carried forward: there were seventeen chests, matching the age of the new queen of the Nadir. It would, Chien-tsu decided, be pleasant to see Mai-syn once more. The youngest of the emperor's legitimate daughters, she was quite breathtakingly beautiful and could play the nine-stringed harp with exquisite style.

He stepped into the saddle and led his entourage of five footmen and thirty-four bearers down toward the palace.

They were greeted by twenty soldiers led by an officer wearing a silver chain who inclined his head in a perfunctory bow. Chien-tsu stiffened, for the bow was some six inches short of politeness. Raising his head, he looked the officer in the eye . . . the silence grew. It would not be good manners to speak first, but Chien-tsu found his irritation growing.

"Well?" snapped the officer at last. "What do you want?"

Chien-tsu was taken aback but controlled his rising temper. It would not be seemly to kill a man on his first day in the city.

"I am Chien-tsu, ambassador of the supreme emperor to the court of Jungir Khan. I have come with suitable gifts on the anniversary of the queen's birthday. Kindly take me to the royal presence."

As Chien-tsu had expected, the man's expression changed; he bowed once more, this time exceeding the distance required. Then he barked out a command, and the twenty soldiers turned. "Follow me," he told Chien.

There was no open courtyard within the great gates, merely a maze of tunnels. They emerged swiftly into a large shrub garden to the east of the gate. A line of stables stretched to the right, and Chien-tsu dismounted, allowing his horse to be led away. The party was passed on to a second officer; taller than the first, he wore a silver breastplate and helm. He bowed correctly to Chien and smiled.

"Welcome, Ambassador. The lord khan was not expecting you so swiftly."

"Is this not the day of the anniversary?"

The man seemed confused. "Please follow me," he said.

Chien and his party moved on into another intricate system of tunnels and corridors that opened on to a wide hallway before huge double doors of oak mounted with silver.

Four guards stood before the doors. They stepped aside as the officer approached and the doors swung open.

Inside, to Chien's surprise, the main hall resembled a giant tent with curtains and hangings of the finest silk. At the far end, on a raised dais, the great khan lounged on a satin-covered divan. Chien entered and bowed low, holding the pose for the obligatory ten heartbeats.

The khan waved him forward. "Welcome, Ambassador; this is an unexpected pleasure." The man's voice was deep and powerful. He rose and stepped from the dais. "We did not expect you until tomorrow."

Chien lifted his hands and clapped them, and the thirty-four bearers moved forward to place the chests in a line before the khan. The men backed away with heads low, eyes averted. Chien bowed once more. "Great Khan, I have come bearing gifts from the Divine Lord of the Golden

Realm to celebrate the first year of your marriage and to inquire on behalf of His Majesty whether Mai-syn has continued to bring exquisite joy to your hearth."

"Indeed she has," Jungir answered. "Now to the chests, if you please."

This was not the response Chien had been expecting, but he hid his consternation and opened the first of the silver-bound chests. Lifting clear a handsome coat of silver silk decorated with pearls, he held it before the khan.

"Pleasant," commented the khan. "Are they all clothes?"

"No, Great Khan," said Chien, forcing a smile. He opened the second chest, which was filled with emeralds, some the size of a man's fist.

"What is this worth in your land in, say, horses and men?" asked the khan.

"A man could equip an army of ten thousand lances for a full summer," Chien answered.

"Good. I like them. And the others?"

Some contained gold, others perfumes and spices or articles of clothing. The last chest produced the strongest response from the Nadir warlord. From it Chien lifted a saber of dazzling brightness. The hilt guard was of gold inset with gems, and the hilt was bound with gold thread. But the pommel stone was milky-white and carved into the head of a wolf.

Jungir took the blade and slashed the air. "It is perfect," he said, his eyes shining. "The balance is beyond belief, and the edge is remarkable. Truly I am pleased. Relay my thanks to your king; tell him I had not realized his lands delivered such wealth. When will you be starting back—tomorrow?"

"As you wish, Great Khan."

"Tomorrow would be good for you, for the winter will be closing in on the ports and I would not like your journey to be uncomfortable."

"It is kind of you to concern yourself over my comforts, but His Majesty has required me to see his daughter and to carry to her a message of his love and devotion."

"I will give her that message," Jungir said loftily.

"And I do not doubt, Great Khan, that you would deliver

it more skillfully than I. But my king ordered me to see her, and as I am sure you will agree, a subject must always obey the order of his liege lord."

"Indeed," said Jungir, "but I fear that will not be possible. The . . . queen is at my palace in the south. It is a two-month journey. I am sure your king will understand that you could not fulfill his wishes."

"But I can, Great Khan. I will travel to the south and then journey home. With your permission, of course."

Jungir's face darkened, but his expression remained friendly. "It would not be advisable, Ambassador. The lands of the steppes are . . . perilous for outsiders. Many tribes continue to harass . . . foreigners."

"I understand, sire. Even within the Middle Kingdom there are bandits and rogues who disobey the emperor's will. But I am sure my soldiers will be a match for them. And I much appreciate your concern over the safety of a humble ambassador."

Jungir gave a tight smile and stepped back to the dais. "Quarters will be allocated to you, Ambassador, and my chamberlain will furnish you with the guides and supplies you will need for your journey. And now I have matters of state to occupy me."

Chien bowed, but not low. He straightened. "I cannot thank you sufficiently, sire, for the time you have allowed me." He backed seven paces instead of ten and turned.

As the great doors swung shut, Jungir turned to a broad-shouldered warrior at his side. "You will guide them south for a week. Then there will be an attack on them. No one survives. You understand, Kubai?"

"I do, sire."

"And see that they do not move around in the palace. I want no one to mention the yellow-faced bitch."

"As you wish, Lord Khan."

The chamberlain led Chien through the maze of tunnels to three large, square adjoining rooms. Windows in the west walls looked out over an exquisitely ugly garden of shrubs. In the first room was a bed, four chairs, a table, and three lanterns. The second contained only a narrow bed and a single lantern, while the third boasted a metal bath, three barrels of water, and several thin towels.

"It is almost too luxurious," said Chien, without a hint of mockery. The chamberlain gave a thin-lipped smile and left. Chien turned to his manservant, Oshi, a wiry ex-slave who had served Chien's family for forty years. "Find the spy holes," ordered Chien, using an obscure Kiatze dialect. Oshi bowed and moved around the room for several minutes.

"There are none, lord," said Oshi finally.

"Is there no end to their insults?" snapped Chien. "Do they feel I am not important enough to spy on?"

"They are savages, lord."

"Go and find where they have put Sukai and the others. Send Sukai to me."

"At once, lord. Or should I prepare your bath first?"

"I will bathe tomorrow. I would not put it past these Nadir to have urinated in the water barrels." Oshi chuckled and left the room. Chien pulled a linen handkerchief from his pocket and dusted one of the chairs. A dark shape scuttled across the room behind him, and Chien swiveled, his hand snapping a small throwing knife from his sleeve. The blade flashed across the room, and the black rat died instantly, almost cut in half.

Minutes later, as Chien stood at the window staring down at the gray-green shrubs in what passed for a royal garden, there came a discreet tap at the door.

"Enter!" he commanded.

Sukai marched into the room and bowed as low as his lacquered leather breastplate would allow. The officer carried his iron helm against his chest. He was neither tall nor especially formidable in appearance, yet his skill with the long, curved *chantanai* blade was known throughout the Middle Kingdom. He had served Chien for eleven years, and not once in that time had Chien seen him without his hair combed, oiled, and lacquered. Now it was hanging lank about his shoulders.

"Why do you come here looking like the basest peasant?" asked Chien, still using the Kiatze dialect.

"A thousand apologies, noble lord," Sukai replied. "I

was preparing for my bath. I did not think you would wish to wait for me to dress properly."

"You are correct in that, Sukai. But it was improper to prepare to bathe without first ascertaining whether I had need of you. However, in a city of barbarians it is difficult to retain hold of civilized behavior. Have you checked your room?"

"I have, lord. There are no passageways hidden and no secret hearing tubes."

"Disgraceful!"

"They are an insulting people."

Oshi entered silently, bowed twice, then saw the dead rat. He retrieved Chien's knife and removed the corpse by the tail. "It has fleas," he said, holding the body at arm's length.

"Throw it from the window," ordered Chien. "If we leave it here, we will probably find it served to us for supper." Oshi hurled the rat to the gardens below and wandered off to the back room to clean the knife, while Chien turned back to the warrior. "Tomorrow we will be leaving for the south."

"Yes, lord."

Chien hesitated and closed his eyes. His concentration hardened, and he felt the floating presence of a spirit within the room. He smiled. So, he thought, they are not quite such savages. His fingers flickered against his belt; Sukai read the message and smoothly moved from Kiatze to Nadir.

"Will the lord khan be supplying us with guides, sir?"

"But of course. He is a noble king, of a noble line. But I do not think we should all presume on his hospitality. You will arrange for a guard of twenty men to take the women and all manservants bar Oshi back to Kiatze. I will send a message to the divine emperor, telling him of the success of our mission and the kind words of Jungir Khan. The journey south would be too hard on my girls."

"Yes, lord."

"We will take only one wagon—with gifts for the queen. All my goods will go back to Kiatze."

"With the exception of your tent, my lord?"

"No, that also. I will take my paints and brushes—that is all. There may be some interesting flowers along the way." His fingers appeared to brush a speck of dust from his sleeve.

Sukai bowed. "I have noticed many red blooms, sir."

"You will see many more."

Sukai's face hardened. "May I be permitted to write to my family, lord?"

"Of course. Now leave me. I will see you at dawn."

As the officer departed, Oshi returned to the room with Chien's freshly cleaned knife in his hands. Chien returned the blade to the oiled sheath in his sleeve.

Oshi moved the cleaned chair to the window, and Chien sat, seemingly lost in thought. He focused his mind on the intrusive spirit in the room and saw a thin, wrinkled old man with pale eyes and a weasel face. He was floating just below the high ceiling. Chien sat silently until the watcher's presence faded.

"Oshi!"

"Yes, lord?"

"Go to the kitchens and find some bread. They will have no fish, but choose me some dried meat that is not full of corruption."

"At once!"

Chien folded his arms and thought of Mai-syn. To her this place must have seemed worse than squalid. He concentrated on the beauty of her face, trying to communicate with her spirit. But there was only a cosmic silence. Perhaps she is too far from here, he thought. Perhaps not, the darker side of his nature told him.

The chamberlain knocked at the door and told Chien that the Lord Jungir Khan had arranged a feast in his honor. It would be that evening at moonrise. It would be acceptable if the lord ambassador wished to bring the chief of his guards. Chien bowed and accepted.

What new humiliation will the savages plan for tonight? he wondered.

The great hall was packed with warriors seated around a score of bench tables pushed together to make an enormous open square. Jungir Khan, in a tight-fitting tunic of black leather embroidered with gold thread, sat at the southern end of the hall, the throne dais behind him. Chien was seated at his right hand, and to his right sat Sukai, ill at ease and eating little. To Jungir's left was a wizened man whom the khan introduced as Shotza, the court shaman. Chien inclined his head to the man. "We have heard much of the skills of the Nadir shamans," he said.

"As we have of the court magicians of the Kiatze," responded Shotza. "Is it true they make tiny golden machines that fly in the air, imitating birds?"

"The divine king has three," answered Chien-tsu.

Shotza nodded but seemed unconvinced.

The feast involved eating an extraordinary amount of meat that back in Kiatze would have been refused by the court dogs. In the main, it was high beyond the point of rotting. To offset this, the guests covered the food with spices. Chien ate sparingly and drank less. The liquor being consumed by the Nadir was distilled, he was told, from rancid goats' milk. "How clever," he remarked. How apt, he thought.

Between the interminable courses there were performances by jugglers or acrobats. They were not especially skilled, though Chien applauded politely.

"We have heard much," said Jungir Khan suddenly, "of the martial skills of the Kiatze. Would your officer honor us with an exhibition?"

"Of what kind?" Chien inquired.

"Swordsmanship."

"With respect, Lord Khan, that is not possible. The soul of a warrior partly resides in his blade. It is not to be drawn unless to take blood—and that, I fear, would not represent an exhibition of skills."

"Then let him fight to the death," said the khan.

"I am afraid I do not understand you, sire. Is this a jest of some kind?"

"I never jest about war, Ambassador. I merely ask that your man show me the skills of the Kiatze. I would take it badly were you to refuse me."

"I hope, my Lord Khan, that you will not interpret my

words as a refusal. I merely ask you to reconsider. Is it not bad fortune for there to be a death at a feast?"

"That depends on who dies," answered the khan coldly.

"Very well, sire," said Chien, turning to Sukai. "The khan wishes to see the battle skills of a Kiatze officer. Oblige him."

"As you order," answered Sukai. He rose and vaulted the table. He was not a tall man, nor did he have great width of shoulder. His face was broad and flat, his eyes dark; he was clean-shaven but for a thin mustache that drooped to his chin. He drew his long, curved double-handed sword and waited; his fingers brushed his chest. Chien read the signaled question and found it difficult to keep the pride from his eyes. "Do you require me to die?" Sukai had asked. Chien lifted his hand to touch his carefully lacquered hair. Sukai understood—and bowed.

Jungir Khan pointed to a warrior at the far end of the hall. "Show our guest how a Nadir fights," he called, and the man leapt into the square.

"Excuse me, sire," said Chien, his face expressionless.

"What is it?"

"It seems hardly fair to have only one man face Sukai. He will be mortally offended."

The khan's face darkened, and he held up one hand. Silence fell. "Our guest, the ambassador for the land of Kiatze, has said that one Nadir warrior is no match for his champion." An angry murmur began. Again the khan's hand cut the air, and silence followed the move. "Can this be true?"

"No!" came a roar from the feasters.

"But he also says that his champion will be insulted if he faces only one opponent. Should we insult so fine-looking a warrior?" There was no response, and the Nadir waited for the lead from their khan. "No, we cannot insult our guests. Therefore, you, Ulai, and you, Yet-zan, will join your comrade." The two Nadir warriors clambered into the square. "Let the battle commence," Jungir ordered.

The Nadir warriors spread out in a circle around the motionless figure of Sukai, his great sword resting lightly on his shoulder. Suddenly the first Nadir ran forward, the others following. Sukai spun on his heel, his sword slicing out and down to cleave the collarbone and chest of the first attacker. He swiveled and blocked a thrust, cut the head from the sword wielder, dropped to one knee, and rammed his blade through the belly of the third man.

Sukai returned the great sword to its scabbard on his back and waited with hands on hips. At his feet lay three corpses, their blood staining the mosaic floor.

"He is a fine warrior," said Jungir Khan, his voice cutting the silence.

"Not especially, my lord," replied Chien, masking his delight. "I thought the last thrust sloppily executed. A fourth man might well have killed him at that moment."

Jungir Khan said nothing but waved his hand. Servants moved into the square, and the tables were pulled back to allow the bodies to be dragged from the hall. Sawdust was spread on the blood.

The feast continued for another hour, but Jungir did not speak again to the ambassador from the land of Kiatze.

Toward midnight the feasters began to drift away. Chien stood and bowed to Jungir. "With your leave, my lord."

The khan nodded. "Good fortune follow you on your journey," he said.

"I am sure that if you will it, then it will be so," answered Chien. "My thanks to you for the feast. May the gods bring you all the blessings you deserve."

With Sukai following, Chien-tsu marched from the hall.

Back in his rooms he turned to Sukai.

"I apologize," he said, "for the affront to your dignity. It was unseemly to have agreed to the khan's request."

Sukai bowed low, dipping his head three times. "No apology is necessary, lord. I live to serve you."

Chien entered his rooms to find that Oshi had stripped the Nadir linen from the bed and covered the mattress with sheets of fine silk and a coverlet filled with goose down. The servant was asleep at the foot of the bed.

Chien removed his clothes and carefully folded them, placing them on the chair by the window. Then he climbed into bed and lay back, wishing that he could enjoy a hot, scented bath.

Oshi rose from the foot of the bed. "Is there anything you require, my lord?"

"Nothing, thank you."

Oshi settled down on the floor once more, and Chien stared out the window at the bright stars. In all probability Mai-syn was dead. He could sense no warmth from her spirit. No more would her laughter be heard under heaven; no more would her sweet singing grace the night. But he could not be sure and therefore would have to begin, at least, his journey to the south. Yet if she was dead, then once away from the city, Chien had no doubt the party would be attacked and slaughtered. Jungir Khan would have no wish for news of his daughter's death to reach the emperor. No, Chien's murder would be put down to robbers or bandits, and thus the flow of costly presents would continue for at least one more year.

There had to be a way to thwart the khan. Honor demanded it.

For several hours he lay awake. At last a smile touched his face.

And he slept.

Despite the closeness of the midwinter solstice, the warmth of an early spring was in the air as the questers rode down the long hills into the valley of Kiall's settlement. The young man found his emotions torn as he gazed down on the wooden buildings and the new stockade. He was home, yet he was not home. All his dreams of childhood were resting there, the ghosts of his youth still playing in the high woods. He knew every bend and turn of the trails, all the secret places, the fallen trees and the hidden caves. Yet the village had changed. The burned-out buildings were no longer in evidence, and twelve new houses stood on the outskirts. Tanai the baker had been killed in the raid, his house and bakery gutted. Now a new bakery stood on the site, and Kiall felt that someone had reached into his memories with a hot knife, cutting and hacking at images dear to him.

Chareos led the small group down into the settlement and on through the unfinished stockade wall to the main square. People stopped their work to watch the riders, and a tall, fat man in a tunic of green wool, a wide leather belt straining to hold his bulging belly, marched out to stand before them with brawny arms folded across his chest.

"What do you want here?" he asked, his voice deep, his tone pompous.

Chareos stepped down from the saddle and approached him. "We are looking for shelter for the night."

"Well, there's no welcome here for strangers."

Kiall could stand no more; he lifted his leg over the pommel of his saddle and jumped to the ground. "I'm no stranger," he stormed. "But who in Bar's name are you? I don't know you."

"Nor I you," said the man. "State your business or suffer the consequences."

"Consequences?" snorted Beltzer. "What is he talking about?"

"He's talking about the bowmen hidden in the alleyways around us," explained Finn.

"Oh," said Beltzer.

Chareos glanced around and saw the archers. They seemed nervous and frightened, their fingers trembling on the drawn bowstrings. At any moment an accidental shot could turn the square into a battlefield, Chareos knew. "We are not Nadren," he said softly. "I came here on the night of the raid and tried to aid the people. The young man here is Kiall, who is of this village."

"Well, I don't know him, and I don't believe I care to," the man retorted sourly.

"My name is Chareos. It would at least be polite if you told me yours."

"I don't need to be polite to the likes of you," said the man. "Be off with you!"

Chareos spread his hands and stepped closer. Suddenly he seized the man's tunic with his left hand, dragging him forward. His right hand flashed up, holding his hunting knife, the blade point resting against the man's throat.

"I have an abhorrence for bad manners," he said quietly. "Now order your men to lower their weapons or I will cut your throat."

The man swallowed hard, the action causing his flabby skin to press on the knife point. A thin trickle of blood traced a line to his tunic.

"Put . . . put down your weapons," the leader whispered.

"Louder, fool!" hissed Chareos, and the man did as he was told.

Reluctantly the archers obeyed, but they crowded in to surround the group. Still holding on to the fat man, Chareos turned to the crowd. "Where is Paccus the seer?" he called. No one answered him.

Kiall stepped forward. "Does no one remember me?" he asked. "What about you, Ricka? Or you, Anas? It's me—Kiall."

"Kiall?" said a tall, thin man with a pockmarked face. He moved closer to peer at the young warrior. "It *is* you," he said, surprised. "But you look so different. Why have you come back?"

"To find Ravenna, of course."

"Why?" asked Anas. "She'll be some Nadir's wife by now—or worse."

Kiall reddened. "I will find her, anyway. What is going on here? Who is this man? And where is Paccus?"

Anas shrugged. "After the raid a lot of families chose to move north, to settle nearer Talgithir. New families moved in. He is Norral; he's a good man and our leader. The stockade was his idea, as were the bows. We are going to defend ourselves in the future, Kiall. The Nadren will not find us an easy target the next time they ride into Gothir lands."

"What about Paccus?"

"He died three days ago."

In the background Chareos sheathed his knife and pushed Norral away from him. Beltzer and the others dismounted.

Kiall looked at the rest of the crowd. "We are not raiders," he said. "I am of this village, and we will be leaving come morning to seek the women stolen in the raid. We will bring them back. These warriors with me may not be known to you by sight, but you do know of them. This one is Chareos the Blademaster, and this is Beltzer of the Ax. The man with the dark beard is the famed archer Finn, and beside him is his friend Maggrig. They are the heroes of Bel-azar, my friends. The other man is a mystic from the lands of the Tattooed People; he will follow the spirit trail that leads us to the saving of our people."

Anas stared hard at Beltzer. "*He* is the famous axman?"

"Yes, I am, goat brain!" thundered Beltzer, drawing his ax and holding the shining blade under Anas' chin. "Perhaps you'd like to see more proof."

"Not at all," Anas said, stepping back.

Norral stepped alongside Chareos. "A thousand apologies," he whispered. "I didn't know, of course. Please make my home your own. I would be honored if you would spend the night at my house."

Chareos nodded. "That is kind," he said at last, forcing a smile. "I also must apologize. You were quite right to be concerned at the appearance of six armed men, and your precautions were commendable."

Norral bowed.

The food he supplied them was excellent, cooked by his two plump, comely daughters, Bea and Kara. But the evening was dominated by Norral, who told them the story of his largely uninteresting life in great detail, punctuating it with anecdotes concerning famous Gothir statesmen, poets, and nobles. Each story had the same ending: how the famous complimented Norral on his sagacity, wit, farsightedness, and intelligence.

Beltzer was the first to grab a jug of wine and wander out into the cool night air. Maggrig and Finn soon followed. Unconcerned by the stream of sound from Norral, Okas curled up on the floor to sleep.

Chareos and Kiall sat with the fat farmer until after midnight, but when he showed no sign of fatigue, Chareos yawned theatrically. "I must thank you," he said, "for a most entertaining evening. But we will be leaving soon after dawn, and if you will excuse me, I will leave you in Kiall's company. He is younger than the rest of us, and I am sure will learn much from you."

Rigid with boredom, Kiall contained his anger and settled himself for more of Norral's history. But with the last of the heroes of Bel-azar gone, Norral had no wish to converse with a former villager. He excused himself and took to his bed.

Kiall stood and walked out into the night. Only Beltzer remained awake, and Kiall sat down beside him.

"Did the old windbag run out of stories?" the giant asked.

"No. He ran out of listeners."

"By the gods, he doesn't need a stockade; he could just visit a Nadren village for an evening. The raiders would avoid this place like a plague pit."

Kiall said nothing but sat with his chin resting on his hands, staring at the homes around him. Golden light showed in thin beams from the closed shutters of the windows.

"What ails you, boy?" asked Beltzer, draining the last of his wine.

"It is all changed," replied Kiall. "It's not my home anymore."

"Everything changes," said Beltzer, "except the mountains and the sky."

"But it was only a few months ago. Now . . . it's as if Ravenna never existed."

"They can't afford to stay in mourning, Kiall. Look around you. This is a working village. There are crops to be planted, cultivated, harvested; animals to be fed, watered, cared for. Ravenna was last year's crop. Gods, man, we're all of us last year's crop."

"It shouldn't be that way," argued Kiall.

"Wrong, boy. It is the only way it *can* be." He picked up the empty jug and passed it to Kiall. "What do you see?"

"What is there to see? You finished it all."

"Exactly. The wine was good, but now it isn't here anymore. Worse, I'll piss it against a tree tomorrow; then no one could tell if it was wine or water."

"We're not talking about wine; we're talking about people. About Ravenna."

"There's no difference. They mourned . . . now they're living again."

Soon after dawn Okas vanished into the hills to seek the spirit trails. Kiall wandered in search of Ravenna's sister and found her at the house of Jarel. She smiled and invited him inside, where Jarel was sitting by the window, staring out over the mountains. Karyn poured Kiall a goblet of watered wine.

"It is good to see you again," she said, smiling. She looked so like Ravenna that his heart lurched: the same wide eyes, the same dark hair gleaming as if oiled.

"And you," he replied. "How are you faring?"

"I'm going to have Jarel's child in the autumn," she told him.

"I congratulate you both," he said.

Jarel swung from the window. He was a strongly built young man with black, tightly curled hair and deep-set blue eyes.

"Why must you pursue this business?" he asked. "Why chase after the dead?"

"Because she is not dead," answered Kiall.

"As good as," snapped Jarel. "She is tainted . . . finished among civilized people."

"Not for me."

"Always the dreamer. She used to talk of you, Kiall; she used to laugh at you for your silly ideas. Well, don't bring her back here; she won't be welcome."

Kiall put the goblet down on the tabletop and rose, his hands shaking. "I will say this once to you, Jarel. When I bring her back, if there is one evil word from you, I will kill you."

"You?" snorted Jarel. "Dream on, Kiall."

Kiall walked forward to where Jarel stood with hands on hips, grinning. He was a head taller than Kiall and far heavier. Kiall's fist slammed into the bigger man's face, rocking him back on his heels. Blood spurted from his smashed lips, and his jaw dropped; then anger blazed in his eyes, and he sprang forward—only to jerk to a stop as he saw the long hunting knife in Kiall's hand. Fear touched him then.

Kiall saw it and smiled. "Remember my warning, Jarel. Remember it well."

"I'll remember," said the farmer, "but you remember this: no one here wants the women back. So what will you do? Build a new place for them? Two of the men whose wives were taken have remarried. Twenty other families have gone, and no one knows where. What do the captives have to come back to? No one cares anymore."

"I care," said Kiall. "I care very much." He turned to Karyn. "Thank you for your hospitality." She said nothing as he sheathed his knife and walked out into the sunlight.

◊ 8 ◊

OKAS SAT CROSS-LEGGED beneath a spreading elm and concentrated on the village below. His vision swam, and the buildings blurred and faded like mist under sunlight. He had no control now, and time ceased to have meaning. He saw mountains of ice swelling on the land, filling the hollows, rearing from the peaks. Slowly, reluctantly through the centuries, the ice gave way and the long grass grew. Huge lumbering creatures moved across the face of the valley, their massive limbs brushing against new trees and snapping the stems. Eons passed, and the grass grew. The sharp hills were smoothed by the winds of time. The first oak tree took root on the southern hill, binding the soil. Birds flocked to its branches. Seeds in their droppings caused other trees to grow, and soon Okas saw a young forest stretching across the hills.

The first group of men appeared from the west, clad in skins and furs and carrying weapons of bone and stone. They camped by the stream, hunted the great elk, and moved on.

Others followed them, and on one bright day a young man walked the hills with a woman by his side. He pointed at the land, his arm sweeping to encompass the mountains. He built a home with a long sloping roof. There was no chimney; two holes were left at the points of the roof's triangle, and Okas saw the smoke drifting from them as the snows fell. Other travelers settled close by over the years, and the young man, now a leader, grew old.

A savage tribe entered the valley, slaying all who lived there. For some time they took over the homes, but then, like all nomads, they moved on. The houses rotted and fell to feed the earth; grass grew over the footings.

Okas watched as the centuries slid by, waiting with limitless patience, judging the passage of time by the movement of the stars. At last he saw the familiar buildings of the near present and moved his spirit close to the village. Focusing on Kiall, he found himself drawn to a small house on the western side. There he watched the birth of a boy, saw the proud smile on the face of the weary mother, saw the happiness in the eyes of Kiall's father as he tenderly lifted his son.

Okas relaxed and let the vision flow. He saw Kiall's mother die of a fever when the boy was first walking, saw the father injured in a fall and losing his life to gangrene from the poisoned wound. He watched the boy, raised by strangers, grow tall. Then he saw the dark-haired girl, Ravenna.

At last he came to the raid, the Nadren thundering into the village with bright swords and gleaming lances.

Okas pulled his gaze from the slaughter and waited until the raiders had taken their captives back into the hills, where wagons stood loaded with chains and manacles.

He followed them for a hundred miles to a stockaded town, but there the vision faded.

He opened his eyes and stretched his back, suppressing a groan as the ligaments above his hip creaked and cracked. The wind was cold on his skin, and he was mortally tired.

Yet still there was another flight to be made. The call was still strong, and he allowed himself to link to it, his spirit lifting from his body to be drawn swiftly across the steppes. The mountains were beautiful from this height, cloaked in snow and crowned with clouds. His spirit fell toward the tallest peak, passing through it deep into the dark. At last he entered a cavern where torches flickered on the walls and an old man sat before a small fire. Okas looked at him closely. He wore a necklace of lion's teeth around his scrawny throat, and his thin white beard had no more substance than wood smoke. When the man's dark eyes opened and fixed on Okas, there was pain in them and a sorrow so deep that Okas was almost moved to tears.

"Welcome, Brother," said Asta Khan. The Nadir shaman winced and cried out.

"How can I help you?" asked Okas. "What are they doing to you?"

"They are killing my children. There is nothing you can do. Soon they will send their forces against me, and that is when I shall require your aid. The demons will fly, and my strength will not be enough to send them fleeing back to the pit. But with you I have a chance."

"Then I shall be here, Brother . . . and I will bring help."

Asta Khan nodded. "The ghosts-yet-to-be."

"Yes."

"Will they come if you ask it?"

"I think that they will."

"They will face nightmares beyond description. The demons will sense their fears and make them real."

"They will come."

"Why do you do this for me?" asked Asta. "You know what I desire. You know everything."

"Not everything," said Okas. "No man knows it all."

Asta screamed and rolled to the floor. Okas sat quietly and waited until the old shaman pushed himself upright, wiping the tears from his eyes. "Now they are killing the little ones; I cannot block out their anguish."

"Nor would you wish to," said Okas. "Come forth and take my hand."

The spirit of Asta Khan rose from the frail body. In that form he seemed younger, stronger. Okas took the outstretched hand and allowed his own strength to flow into the shaman.

"Why?" asked Asta once more. "Why do you do this for me?"

"Perhaps it is not for you."

"Who, then? Tenaka? He was not your lord."

"It is enough that I do it. I must return to my flesh. When you have need, I will be here."

* * *

Kiall's anger was short-lived. As the questers waited on the edge of the woods for Okas, the young man sat beside Chareos and vented his rage.

Chareos cut across his words. "Follow me," he said sharply. The blademaster stood and walked away into the trees, out of earshot of the others. Once there, he turned on Kiall, his dark eyes angry, his face set.

"Do not waste your self-righteous wrath on me, boy. I'll not have it. When the raiders came, you—and all these villagers—did nothing. Of course they *think* they don't want the captives back. And why? Because it would be like looking in a mirror and seeing their own cowardice. They would have to live every day with that mirror. Every time they passed a former prisoner, they would see their own shortcomings. Now, stop whining about it."

"Why are you so angry?" Kiall asked. "You could have just explained it to me."

"Explained . . . ?" Chareos threw back his head and stared at the sky. He said nothing for several seconds, and Kiall realized he was fighting for control of his temper. Finally he sat down and indicated that Kiall should join him. The young man did so. "I don't have time to explain everything, Kiall," the older man said patiently, "and I do not have the inclination. I have always believed that a man should think for himself. If he relies on others for his thoughts and his motives, then his brain becomes an empty, useless thing. Why am I angry? Let us examine that for a moment. How do you think the Nadren know which villages to hit, where attractive young women live?"

"I don't know."

"Then think, damn you!"

"They send out riders to scout?" ventured Kiall.

"Of course. How else?"

"They listen to traders, merchants, tinkers who pass through such villages?"

"Good. And what do you think they are listening for?"

"Information," Kiall answered. "I do not understand where this is taking us."

"Then give me time. How does one village know what is going on at another village?"

"Traders, travelers, poets—all carry news," said Kiall. "My father said it was one way in which they encouraged trade. People would gather around their wagons to hear the latest gossip."

"Exactly. And what *gossip* will the next trader carry?"

Kiall reddened and swallowed hard. "He will tell the tale of the heros of Bel-azar who are hunting Ravenna," he whispered.

"And who will hear of this band of heroes?" asked Chareos, his eyes narrowing, his mouth a thin tight line.

"The Nadren," admitted Kiall. "I'm sorry. I didn't think."

"No, you did not!" stormed Chareos. "I heard of your dispute with the farmer and your threat with the knife. Bear this in mind, Kiall. What we do is easy. Understand that. Easy! What the villagers do is hard. Hoping and praying for just enough rain to make the seeds grow and just enough sun to ripen the harvest, never knowing when drought, famine, or raiders will destroy your life and take away your loved ones. Do not ever ask me for explanations. Use your mind."

Finn pushed through the undergrowth. "Okas is back. He says we have a hundred miles to travel. And it's rough country for the most part. I've sent Maggrig back to purchase supplies. Is that all right, Blademaster?"

"Yes. Thank you, Finn. We'll set off once he's back and camp away from here. I couldn't stand another night with that sanctimonious bore."

"Just think, Blademaster. Tonight he'll be entertaining the villagers with how you complimented him. You'll be remembered in future times as Chareos, the friend of the great Norral."

"There's probably truth in that." Chareos chuckled.

He strode through the undergrowth to where Okas was sitting quietly with Beltzer. The old man looked dreadfully weary.

"Would you like to rest for a while?" Chareos asked him.

"No rest. It is a long journey ahead. I will sleep tonight. There is a good camping place some four hours ride to the south."

"Is the girl alive?" asked Chareos. Kiall moved in behind him.

"She was when they took her to the fort town," Okas said. "I could not see beyond that; the distance is too great for me. And I have no hold on her but for the love of Kiall. It is not enough. Had I known her, I would be able to find her anywhere."

"How long for the journey?"

"Maybe three weeks. Maybe a month. It is rough country. And we must move with care. Nadir tribesmen, outlaws, Wolfsheads, Nadren. And . . . other perils."

"What other perils?" asked Beltzer.

"Demons," answered Okas. Beltzer made the sign of the protective horn on his brow and chest, and Finn did likewise.

"Why demons?" Chareos asked. "What has sorcery to do with this quest?"

Okas shrugged his shoulders and stared down at the ground. He began to trace circular patterns in the dust.

Chareos knelt beside him. "Tell me, my friend. Why demons?"

Okas looked up and met Chareos' dark eyes. "You asked me here to help you," he said. "I help you. What if I ask you to help me?"

"You are a friend," Chareos replied without hesitation. "If you need me—or any of us—you have only to ask. Are the demons hunting you?"

"No. But there is old man—enemy of Jungir Khan. He lives alone in mountains far from here. He is the one I am pledged to help. But if I go alone, I will die. Yet I must go."

"Then I shall go with you," declared Chareos.

"And I," echoed Beltzer, clapping his large hand on Okas' shoulder.

Okas nodded, then returned to tracing his patterns in the dust. He spoke no more, and Chareos left him alone.

Kiall moved alongside Chareos. "I need to speak with you," he said, walking away from the others. Chareos followed him to a shaded spot beneath a spreading elm. "How does this help us find Ravenna?" the young man asked.

"It doesn't, Kiall. We may die here."

"Then why? Did we come so far for nothing?" Kiall stormed.

"Friendship is not *nothing*. That old man will die without us. What would you have me say? There are few virtues in this world, boy, but friendship is one that I prize. But if you want a reason which has naught to do with honor, then consider this: What chance do we have of finding Ravenna *without* Okas?" Chareos gripped Kiall's shoulder. "I have no choice, my friend. None at all."

Kiall nodded. "I shall go, too," he said.

Maggrig returned with supplies of food: dried meats, oats, salt, and a sweet tisane made from dried honey and turmeric root. The questers set off toward the south with Okas and Chareos riding at the front and Kiall, Beltzer, and Maggrig following. Finn galloped off into the distance, scouting for sign of raiders or outlaws.

Kiall rode alongside Maggrig. "The thought of fighting demons terrifies me," he confided.

"And me," owned Maggrig. "I saw the stuffed corpse of a Joining once when we were in New Gulgothir. A wolfman some ten feet high—he was killed by Ananais, the Drenai hero, during the Ceska wars decades ago. But no demons. Finn had a friend killed by them, so he told me. They were hunting him in his sleep, and he would awake screaming. One night he screamed but did not wake. There was not a mark on him."

Kiall shivered.

Beltzer dropped back to ride alongside them. "The Nadir Shamans summon the creatures," he said. "I knew a man once who survived an encounter with them. He'd robbed a Nadir shrine. Then the dreams began. He was being hunted through a dark wood; he had no weapons, and the beasts came closer to him each night."

"What did he do?" Maggrig asked.

"He journeyed to a Temple of the Thirty near Mashrapur. They made him pass over the ornament he'd stolen—a goblet, I think it was. Then two of the warrior-priests sat with him while he slept. He dreamed of the wood again, but this time the priests were with him, all dressed in silver armor and carrying swords which blazed brighter than lanterns. They fought off the demons and took the man's spirit to the Nadir shaman who sent them. They agreed to return the goblet and the dreams stopped."

"He was a lucky man," said Maggrig.

"Not really. He died soon after in a fight over a tavern whore."

Beltzer spurred his mount forward and followed Chareos and Okas over a small rise.

Ahead of them was a long valley, and beyond that the seemingly arid, windswept landscape of the Nadir Steppes.

Tanaki rose from her bed, stretched, and walked to the window, opening the shutters and staring out over the empty square.

Movement from behind made her turn, and she smiled at the newcomer.

"It is considered polite to announce yourself, Harokas," she told the hawk-faced assassin.

He shrugged. "Not in my line of work," he said with a broad grin.

"I had not expected you for some weeks. Tell me you rode day and night to feast your eyes on my beauty."

"Would that I could, Princess. But I did bring news that will interest you. There is a group of men riding here, intent on rescuing one of the slave women. It is likely your life will be in some danger from them."

"How many?"

"Six."

She chuckled. "You think I should fear six men? I could probably tackle that many myself on a good day."

"These men are special, Princess. They are led by Chareos the Blademaster. Among them is Beltzer of the Ax—also the bowmen of legend, Finn and Maggrig."

"The heroes of Bel-azar? What interest can they have in a peasant woman?"

"What, indeed?"

"How did you hear of this?" Tanaki asked.

"They bragged about their mission in a village. The whole of the area is alive with the story."

"But there is something you are not telling me," she said, a trace of a smile on her face.

"You are quite correct, Princess," he replied, opening his arms to her. She stepped in to him, and he kissed her; then she pulled away.

"Later," she told him. "First tell me all."

"Oh, no," he said, sweeping her from her feet and carrying her into the square bedroom at the rear of the hall.

They made love for more than an hour; finally he lay back on the bolster and closed his eyes.

"Now tell me," she said, raising herself on one elbow and looking down at him.

"You know that if I was the sort of man to fall in love it would be with you, Princess. You are strong, intelligent, courageous, and quick-witted. And in bed . . ."

"Yes, yes. I compliment you also. But tell me!"

"And you are so single-minded. I admire that." Her face darkened. "All right, all right," he said, smiling. "The earl has commissioned me to kill Chareos."

"And you would like me to do it for you?"

"Well, I am getting old and tired."

"I noticed that," she said, sitting up. "And now I have work to do."

"Why was Tsudai here?" he asked, and she turned back to him, wondering if the concern in his eyes was genuine. Deciding that it was not, she merely shrugged and stood.

"How is it that you hear everything, Harokas? Are you a seer?"

"No, I am a listener. And when Jungir Khan's general rides across the steppes, I know it is not for exercise."

"He came to buy women; that was all."

"Now it is your turn to hold something back. Would you like him dead, Princess?"

"No!" she said sharply.

"As you wish. But he hates you—you know that?"

"He says he loves me."

Harokas grunted and rolled from the bed. "He wouldn't know the meaning of the word."

"And you do?" she asked, slipping into her tunic.

"Sometimes I think I do. What will you do about Chareos?"

"I will send out riders today."

"Send the best, Princess."

"The heroes of Bel-azar will be dead by the end of the week."

"Perhaps," he said softly.

Despite its bleak appearance, the land leading to the steppes was teeming with life, and Kiall found himself fascinated by the wonder of the wild. He had spent his life in the valley and knew the habits of deer and wild sheep, but out here there were creatures of rare beauty, and their behavior was sometimes both mystical and comical.

High above them on the fourteenth day of their journey he saw great birds with long rectangular wings swooping and spiraling in the sky. Recognizing them as vultures—but of a type he had not seen before—he spurred his horse to ride alongside Finn, who was half a mile ahead of the group.

Finn reined in and waited for the young man. "Is there a problem?" asked the hunter.

"No. I was watching the vultures. Does it mean something is dying?"

"Not death," answered Finn, smiling. "Life. They circle like that to find a mate. Watch them closely and you will see the males gliding around the females. Gradually their actions will become like mirror images."

The vultures soared and wheeled in breathtaking displays.

"Such beauty from creatures of ugliness," whispered Kiall.

"Why ugliness?" countered Finn. "Because they feed on carrion? They clean the land, Kiall. In many ways they keep it beautiful."

"Why do they mate in winter? Does the cold not threaten the eggs?"

"No," Finn replied. "When the female lays, she will sit on the eggs for two months. After they hatch, she will feed the young for a further four months. It is a long period for a bird."

The questers rode on, crossing streams that rippled down from the mountains, which were swollen with melted snow. Finn caught three large trout, which they cooked for supper on the sixteenth day. He caught them with his hands, which impressed Kiall. The hunter shook his head. "No great skill, Kiall. Even for them it is the mating season," he said. "They settle down in grooves on the shallow streambed to lay their eggs. They remain still, and if a man is quick and certain, he can ripple his fingers against their sides and flick them from the water."

As the days passed, more and more wildlife was seen: great crested grebes on shallow lakes; coots; herons in their comical mating dances, leaping on sticklike legs to attract the females; huge black kites swooping, diving, meeting in the air.

Okas withdrew ever more into himself, often riding with his eyes closed, lost in thought. Once he almost fell from the saddle, but Beltzer caught him.

On the afternoon of the seventeenth day Okas moved his pony alongside Chareos. "We must find a hiding place," he said.

"Why? Are there enemies close?"

"Yes, those, too. But this will be the night of the demons."

Chareos nodded and rode to Finn. The hunter galloped off toward the west, where rearing rock faces rose from the snow-speckled ground. By dusk the questers were camped in a deep cave on the side of a hill.

They ate in silence seated around a small, flickering fire. Okas forbade any meat to be eaten and sat with head bowed, eyes closed. At last his head came up, and he looked at Chareos.

"This is a night of great peril," he said softly. "The forces that will come against you are strong in their evil, powerful in their malice. They have been fed with the deaths of many, many people."

"Tell us of the old man we are to protect," invited Chareos. Sweat shone on his face, and he could feel the cool breeze of the night on his skin. Watching the swordsman, Kiall felt his fear. Beltzer, too, remained silent, his small round eyes peering intently at Okas.

"His name is Asta Khan, and for many years he was shaman to Tenaka Khan, Lord of the Wolves. When Tenaka . . . died . . . he left tribe and traveled—eventually—to Mountains of Moon. Tenaka's son, Jungir, and his own shaman, have decided it is time for Asta to die. They have sacrificed forty of Asta's blood kin to feed the spirits and weaken the old man. Tonight the demons will fly."

"Why is he such a threat to Jungir?" Finn inquired.

"He knows a secret Jungir wishes kept silent. Jungir Khan murdered his father."

"And that is all?" asked Beltzer.

"Not all," admitted Okas, "but all I know for certain."

"Can we defeat these demons?" asked Beltzer. "Can my ax cut them?"

"We shall be entering their world. In that place, yes, they can die. But their powers are very great. You are strong, fat Beltzer, but where we travel it is not strength of body but strength of heart which is important. It is a place of faith and miracles, a place of spirit."

"How do we go there?" Finn asked.

"You do not go there," replied Okas. "Two must remain to protect the fleshly forms of those who fly. You, Finn, are best man for this."

Kiall's breathing became shallow, and he could feel his heart fluttering like a caged moth. But he remained silent.

"I will go," declared Chareos, "as will Beltzer." He looked at Maggrig, then at Kiall. The blond hunter smiled at Kiall, reading his terror.

"I will come with you," stated Maggrig.

"No," said Okas. "You will remain. There are enemies who have discovered our trail, and they will come in the night. Your skills with the bow are needed here."

"Then," said Kiall, his voice shaking, "I must come?"

"There is no *must*, my friend," answered Okas with a gentle smile. "This is a task for ghosts-yet-to-be. Perhaps we can win with only Beltzer, Chareos, and myself."

"I . . . I will come," said Kiall. "I began this quest, and I will walk where the dangers lie." He swallowed hard.

Chareos reached over and patted his shoulder. "Well said, Kiall."

"You stick close to me, boy," Beltzer told Kiall, hefting his ax. "I'll see you safely home."

"It is time," said Okas. "Finn, when we have departed, put out fire and watch trails. With good fortune we return by dawn." He rose and led the three companions deeper into the cave, where they sat in a circle. Okas began to chant in a hissing tongue that the others could not understand. Listening to the chant, Kiall found his mind spinning. Stars swam before his eyes, and the roar of rushing rivers filled his ears. Then darkness fell, a darkness so complete that all sense of being departed from him.

He came to awareness with a sudden blaze of light and found himself standing, with the others, before a fire in another cave. The body of an old man lay there, seemingly asleep. The man's spirit rose from the still form and approached them.

Asta Khan said nothing but bowed deeply to Okas. The Tattooed Man knelt and traced a large circle in the dust of the cave floor, then rose and took Asta's hand, leading him to the center of the circle. Asta Khan sat while Chareos, Beltzer, Kiall, and Okas grouped themselves around him. Black smoke billowed from the cave walls, closing in on the questers. Beltzer lifted his ax and Chareos and Kiall drew their sabers. A sibilant hissing began from within the smoke.

Okas began to chant and was joined by the voice of Asta Khan. White light shone in the circle, blazing from the blades of the questers.

The smoke parted, and a tall figure in black armor came into view. He was wearing a dark, winged helm with the visor down, and his arms were folded across his chest.

"It is time to die, Asta Khan," he declared.

Finn knelt beside the still forms of the departed questers, staring silently at the motionless bodies. Then he took up his bow and moved to the cave mouth, where Maggrig joined him.

For some time the two men sat in silence there, watching the moonlight on the swaying branches of the trees.

"Anything?" whispered Maggrig.

Finn shrugged. "You take the trail to the left; I'll watch over the right. But do not move too far from the cave mouth." Maggrig nodded and smiled. Notching an arrow to the string, he moved swiftly out into the open and vanished into the undergrowth. Finn waited for several minutes with his eyes closed, allowing the darkness to concentrate his hearing. The sounds of the night were many, hidden within the whistling of the wind, the sibilant whispering of the leaves. He opened his eyes and slowly scanned the trail. Satisfied at last, he slipped out into the moonlight and moved to the right. Hiding places were many, but Finn needed someplace that would supply a killing ground. The bow was not a good night weapon. Distances were hard to judge under moonlight, and a good defensive position could prove a death trap unless there was also a second, safe way out.

He crouched behind a screen of bushes and tried to locate Maggrig. There was no sign of the blond hunter, and Finn smiled. At last he was learning something! An hour passed . . . then another.

Finn closed his eyes and pushed his concentration through the sounds of the night, flattening them, flowing with the rhythms of the land, seeking the discordant. There was nothing, and that worried him. Okas was rarely wrong, and if he said there were enemies close, then enemies were close. Finn licked his lips and felt his heartbeat quicken. If he could not hear them or see them, there were only two options to consider: either Okas was wrong, or the men hunting them were as skilled as the defenders. Keeping his actions slow and smooth, Finn dropped lower to the ground and glanced back at the cave mouth. There was no movement that he could see. He stared at the rock face, putting his peripheral vision into play. Nothing. Just rocks and grass and dark scattered bushes.

Easing himself back, Finn strung his bow and notched an

arrow. If their enemies were skilled, then perhaps they had seen him and Maggrig move from the cave. The thought of danger to Maggrig almost made him panic, but he quelled the feeling savagely. If they *had* seen them, then they would now be moving into place to make the kill. Yet Finn had chosen his route with care, and his position was a good one. Boulders protected his right flank, and there was killing ground ahead and to the left. Behind him was a narrow trail that cut to the right back to the rock face. Bellying down, he moved on his elbows until he was screened by the undergrowth. He had now lost the advantage of the killing ground on the left but was protected from immediate attack and knew his enemies could no longer see him.

"This is nonsense," he told himself. "There is no one there. You are being frightened by shadows."

Think, man, think! He put himself in the place of the hunters. You have seen the quarry. What must you do now?

You must make him show himself for a killing shot.

How?

Give him a target. Let him see you. Finn risked a glance to the killing ground now ahead to the right. Yes, that is where I would order a man to walk. Which would mean that Finn would have to rise in order to aim. He flicked his gaze back to the undergrowth behind him. There were only two possible places for an assassin to wait: by the gnarled beech with the thick silver trunk or behind the rounded boulder leading to the cave mouth. Or perhaps both? Finn began to sweat.

The only sensible course was to retreat. The enemy had all the advantages. But to give ground would mean fleeing to the cave, and that would bring him into the open. Even if he made it to the rock face, he would then be trapped inside. And Maggrig would be stranded. Gently placing his bow on the ground, he raised his hands to his face with thumbs pressed together and gave out the low hoot of a night owl four times.

The grunting cough of a badger came from ahead.

Maggrig was still safe. Better still, he knew the danger and had spotted one of the enemy.

Finn dropped below the bushes and edged back, making no sound.

A man carrying a bow moved out into the open ahead of him. For Finn to make the shot he would have had to stand. The man angled toward his hiding place, and Finn took a deep breath and rose, drawing back on his bowstring. Suddenly he swiveled. Another attacker appeared from behind the boulder twenty paces to the rear; Finn sent an arrow that hammered into the man's skull, then dived to the earth. Two shafts sliced the air where he had been standing. Pushing his knees under him, Finn sprinted from his hiding place, hurdling bushes and boulders to drop behind a fallen tree. From there he could see the body of the man he had killed.

Now the game was more to his liking. They had hunted him with great skill, arrogantly confident about their talents. Now one was dead, and the others would be nervous. Dropping to his belly once more, he crawled back from the tree and, staying flat, notched a second arrow to his bow.

The hunters had to attack from the front now. Was there an edge? They had seen that Finn was right-handed; therefore, they should come from his right. It would give them an extra fraction of a second in which to make the kill. He angled his body to the right and waited.

A warrior carrying a long spear hurdled the fallen tree, and Finn shot him in the chest. The man staggered. A second attacker came from the left. Discarding his bow Finn rolled, came up with his hunting knife, swerved away from the lunging spear, and rammed his blade home into the man's belly. He held the dying man to him and scanned the undergrowth. He could see no one. With a curse he let the body drop and ran to his bow, scooping it into his hand. Just as he straightened, he saw a bowman rear up. Finn was dead, and he knew it . . .

An arrow from Maggrig took the bowman high in the shoulder. The man screamed and loosed his own shaft, but it flew to the left of Finn, who scrambled back into the bushes.

"The cave, Finn!" shouted Maggrig, breaking all the rules. Finn swung to see three men running across the open ground. He sent an arrow after them, but the distance was too great and his shot was high and wide. Hurling aside his bow, he drew his knife and raced after them.

But they vanished within the cave, and he knew he would be too late.

"Stand firm or we are all lost," said Okas. Kiall took a deep breath and watched the swirling smoke.

It vanished to reveal a glittering landscape of stark mountains and tall, skeletal trees devoid of leaves. There were six scaled creatures, their huge mouths rimmed with sharp-pointed fangs. They shuffled toward him with arms extended, and Kiall recoiled in horror. They had no hands or paws. Instead, bloated faces hung from the ends of their arms, sharp teeth gnashing and clicking inside the hollow flesh. Each of the demons was more than seven feet tall, and their horned skin appeared to be impervious to Kiall's slender saber. He glanced to his right, seeking encouragement from Chareos.

But there was no one there.

Alone, Kiall looked to his left. An open door stood there, and through it he could see a green field carpeted with spring flowers. Children played there, and the sounds of their laughter rippled through the beckoning doorway.

The clicking of teeth made him spin. The demons were closer now. He had only to run through the doorway to be safe.

"Stand firm or we are all lost," came the voice of Okas in the halls of his memory.

He thought of Ravenna. If he died there, there would be no one to rescue her. He heard a voice from the doorway.

"Quick, Kiall, run! It is safe here!" He risked a glance and saw his mother, her sweet face smiling, her hand waving.

"I can't!" he screamed. His sword came up. The doorway vanished . . . the demons closed in.

Beltzer blinked in surprise. He had no idea where the others had gone; he knew only that he stood alone before six armed men. They wore black armor and carried long swords. There was nothing demonic about them as they waited to attack; their faces were grim but human.

The giant found his ax feeling heavy in his hands and allowed the head to rest against the ground. Looking down at his hands, he saw that they were wrinkled and covered with dark brown liver spots. His arms were scrawny and thin, his legs just bone and wasted muscle. A cool breeze touched his back, and he turned slowly and peered at the land behind him. It rose sharply into a towering mountain. Fresh streams flowed there, and the sun shone in glory.

"Go back to the mountain," said one of the warriors. "We have no wish to slay an old man who cannot raise his ax. Go back."

"Chareos?" whispered Beltzer. He licked his gums; there were no teeth there, and he felt a terrible weariness.

"You will be young again on the mountain," said the warrior. "Then you will be able to face us. Take a single step back and feel the strength in your limbs."

Beltzer moved back a pace. It was true. He felt a quickening of his muscles, and his eyes cleared a little. All he needed to do was move back onto the mountain and he would find the strength to face these warriors.

"Stand firm or we are all lost," came the voice of Okas in the halls of his memory.

It required all of Beltzer's strength to lift the ax. He looked at the grim warriors. "Come on, then," he said. "I'll move no further."

"Fool!" hissed the leading warrior. "Do you think to stand against us? We could kill you in an instant. Why not be strong again and at least give us a good fight?"

"Will you talk all day?" roared Beltzer. "A good fight? Come on, my boys, earn your pay."

The warriors bunched together and charged. Beltzer roared his defiance. His ax was suddenly light in his hands, and he countered their charge with his own. His limbs were powerful once more, and his ax smashed and sliced into their ranks. Their swords cut him, but no deep thrust slowed him. Within seconds the warriors were dead, their bodies vanished. Beltzer looked back to the mountain. It was gone, and in its place was a deep, yawning pit that vanished into the depths of the earth. He stood with his back to it.

And waited for more foes.

Chareos stood once more on the shadowed walls of Belazar, moonlight streaming on the mountain slopes and glistening on the grass of the valley. The dwellers in the dark were moving up the stairwell, and there was no Tenaka Khan to help him.

"This way," came a soft, female voice, and he turned to see a second stairway, which led down into the valley. A woman stepped into the moonlight; her beauty made him gasp.

"Tura? Sweet heaven, Tura?"

"It is I, my love. I cannot bear to see you die. Come with me."

"I cannot. I must help my friends."

"What friends, Chareos? You are alone; they have left you. Come with me. I love you; I always loved you. I was such a fool, Chareos, but it can be right again. It can be beautiful again."

He groaned, and his soul yearned for her.

A huge taloned hand smashed the stairwell door to shards.

"Come quickly!" yelled the woman.

"No!" shouted Chareos. He leapt forward and lanced his sword into the beast's gaping mouth, up through the cartilage beyond and into the brain.

"Help me!" Chareos turned and saw that a second creature had come from the staircase behind her and was hauling her back into the darkness.

"Stand firm or we are all lost," came the voice of Okas in the halls of his memory.

He screamed in his anguish but remained where he was. Two more creatures lunged at him; he sidestepped and killed the first with a thrust to the heart and the second with a slashing sweep that cut through its neck.

The sound of laughter came to him, and he saw the woman locked in an embrace with the monster at the stairwell. Her face turned to Chareos; it was white as a shroud, the eyes staring, the pupils slitted like those of a cat. Slowly she lifted her leg, stroking it against the demon's thigh.

"You never were much of a man," she said. "Why do you think I needed so many lovers?"

He swung away from her, but her words continued to taunt him. "I slept with them all, Chareos. With Finn, with Beltzer. With all your friends. I told them all what you were like. I told them how you cried on the first night we made love . . . they laughed at that."

"Leave me alone!"

Another beast came through the doorway, but Chareos ducked under the sweep of its talons and slashed his saber through its belly. It fell back into the darkness.

Her voice came closer, but the words were softer now. "I said that to hurt you," she whispered. "I am sorry . . . I am so sorry." Closer she came, and Chareos moved back a step. "Through all that I did," she continued, "all the terrible wrongs I did you, you never hurt me. You could never hurt me." Her arm flashed up. Chareos' saber slashed through her throat, and the head flopped to the floor, the body toppling beside it. The small curved knife dropped from her fingers.

"No," said Chareos, "I could never hurt Tura. But you were not Tura."

Kiall hacked and slashed at the monsters around him. The fang-lined paws ripped at his skin and pain flooded him, yet still his sword lanced out to force them back. He slipped and fell, and the demons loomed over him. Just then a warrior in black, armed with two short swords, leapt to stand over him, driving the monsters away. Kiall struggled to his feet and watched the warrior. The man's skill was breathtaking; he spun and whirled like a dancer, yet at each move his glittering blades flickered out against the demons. The last beast died, and the man walked to Kiall and smiled.

"You fought well," said the man. Kiall looked into the slanted violet eyes and the hard cruel face.

"Who are you?" he asked.

"I am a friend to Asta Khan."

Darkness loomed before Kiall's eyes, and he blinked . . .

He was back before the fire in the cave. Okas and Asta were sitting together, with Beltzer and Chareos standing guard over them.

"Will they come again?" Beltzer asked.

"I do not know," Okas answered wearily.

"They will not," said Asta Khan, his dark eyes glittering. "Now it is time for my enemies to see *my* power." He closed his eyes . . . and vanished.

Three hundred miles away Shotza screamed. The first of twelve acolytes, deep in a trance, fell back with his chest ripped open, his heart exploding. Shotza tried to run from the room, but all the doors were barred by a mist that formed like steel. One by one his acolytes died silently, until only the shaman was left.

A figure formed in the mist, and Shotza backed away. "Spare me, mighty Asta," he begged. "I was acting under orders from the khan. Spare me and I will help you destroy him."

"I do not need your help for that," Asta said, floating close to the trembling shaman. Asta's spirit hand shot out, the fingers extending into long talons that slid into Shotza's chest. A terrible pain clamped the shaman's heart, and he tried to cry out—but died before the scream could sound.

◊9◊

BELTZER AWOKE FIRST. His body was stiff, and he stretched. At that moment he saw the attackers running into the cave. He rolled to his knees and came up with his ax. The fire was dead, the light poor. Beltzer bellowed a war cry and charged. Two of the men ran at him, the third ducking and sprinting past the axman. Beltzer ignored the runner and hammered his ax into the first of the attackers. A sword plunged through his jerkin, narrowly missing the flesh on his hip. Dragging his ax clear of the falling warrior, he backhanded a cut into the second man's ribs, the blade cleaving through to the lungs. Then he spun, ready for an attack from the rear. But the third man was dead, killed by Chareos.

Finn raced into the cave, his knife raised. He stopped as he saw Beltzer and Chareos standing over the three bodies.

"Some watchman you turned out to be," said Beltzer.

Finn slammed the knife back into the sheath by his side. "We killed three and wounded a fourth," he said, "but they doubled back on us."

"How many more are there?" asked Chareos, wiping the blood from his blade.

"I don't know," answered Finn.

"Find out," Chareos told him. Finn nodded, turned on his heel, and ran from the cave.

Beltzer sat down and chuckled. "A night to remember, eh, Blademaster?"

"Yes," agreed Chareos absently, turning to where Kiall and Okas still slept. Kneeling, he shook Kiall's shoulder.

The young man opened his eyes and flinched. "Oh," he whispered. "Are we safe?"

"We are back at the cave," replied Chareos. "How safe we are remains to be seen. You did well back there."

"How do you know?" Kiall asked.

"You are alive," said Chareos simply.

"Shouldn't we be out there helping Maggrig and Finn?" queried Beltzer.

"No. The game being played is theirs. We would be a hindrance."

Chareos took his tinderbox from his pack, cleared the ash from the fire, and started a new blaze. The three men settled around it, enjoying the warmth. A scream sounded from beyond the cave, and Kiall jumped.

"That could be Finn or Maggrig," he said.

"Could be," agreed Beltzer. "What about some food?"

"A good idea," pronounced Chareos, and he turned to Kiall. "Prepare some oats. My stomach is starting to think my throat has been cut."

"What about Finn?" demanded Kiall.

"He can eat when he gets here," replied Beltzer, grinning.

Kiall moved back to the packs and took a hide sack of oats. He glanced at Okas. "He's still sleeping," he said.

"I doubt that," said Chareos.

The three questers sat in silence as the oats bubbled and thickened in a copper pot hung over the fire. The thin gray light of predawn brightened the sky as Kiall ladled the food into two wooden platters.

"Not eating?" asked Beltzer as Kiall sat back.

"No, I lost my appetite," answered the younger man, flicking his gaze to the bloodied corpses. "How can you think of food with a stench like that in the air?"

Beltzer shrugged. "It's only meat, boy, and bowels and guts."

Finn entered the cave moments later and sat down, his eyes red-rimmed and weary. Maggrig followed a few minutes afterward. Both men ate in silence.

"Well?" asked Chareos, as the meal was finished.

"There were four more of them."

"Did you get them all?" Beltzer asked.

"Yes, but it was close. They were skilled, very skilled. What do we do now?"

"We wait for Okas," answered Chareos. "You should get some sleep." Finn nodded and moved to the far corner of the cave, wrapping his lean frame in a blanket and settling down with his head on his saddle.

"They almost took us," said Maggrig. "At least one of them had a better position. His shot missed Finn's head by a finger's width."

"Did you find their horses?" Chareos asked.

"Yes. We stripped the saddles and turned them loose. Finn thinks they were outriders for a larger force, probably the same group that took Ravenna."

"Then they were hunting us," said Chareos.

"Of course they were hunting us," snapped Beltzer. "That's why there are bodies everywhere."

"I think Chareos means us specifically," put in Maggrig. "They weren't just trying to rob a small traveling party; they were looking for *us*."

"How did you reach that conclusion?" Beltzer asked Chareos.

"Tell him, Maggrig," said Chareos.

"First their skill. They were extra careful, which suggests to Finn and me that they knew our strengths. Second, they were prepared to take losses and still keep coming. If we were just a traveling party, they would have no way of knowing how much we were carrying, and a few supplies and horses are not worth dying for."

"So," said Beltzer, "the word is out already."

"It would appear so," Chareos agreed.

"It is most curious," said Chien-tsu. "The Nadir shaman no longer watches over us." Sukai reined in his gray and gazed down at the campsite below.

"Perhaps it is because they intend to attack tonight, lord," said the soldier, dismounting. Chien-tsu lifted his left leg over the pommel of his saddle and jumped to the ground.

"No. They will attack tomorrow at dusk—at least that is the plan the man Kubai spoke of when he rode out to meet the killers last night." Chien would long remember the ugly sound of Kubai's laughter as he spoke with the two Nadir outriders about the massacre of the "yellow men." His spirit had floated just above the trio, and he had heard himself dismissed as an "effeminate fool," a "painted doll" man.

"It is galling," said Sukai.

"Galling? I am sorry; my mind was wandering."

"To be forced to meet one's death at the hands of such barbarians."

"Ah yes, indeed so," Chien agreed.

"It would have been pleasant to have had a second option." Below them the twenty soldiers had prepared three campfires. From his position on the hilltop Chien could see the scout Kubai sitting apart from the men. Chien unbuttoned the brocaded red silk coat and scratched at his armpit. "I shall not be sorry to say farewell to this garment," he said. "It is beginning to stink."

"It was part of your plan, lord," said Sukai, smiling broadly.

"Indeed it was, but it is dreadfully uncomfortable. Who will wear it tomorrow?"

"Nagasi, lord. He is your height and build."

"I must apologize to him; it is one thing to die in service to your lord but quite another to be forced to die in a dirty coat."

"It is an honor for him, lord."

"Of course it is, but good manners should be paramount. I will see him this evening. Would it be too great a privilege if we asked him to dine with us?"

"I fear that it would, lord."

"I think you are correct, Sukai. You and I will dine together, though 'dine,' I fear, is too fine a description for a meal of broiled hare. However, I have some good wine, which we will finish."

Chien stepped into the saddle and waited for Sukai. The officer mounted his gelding and cursed softly.

"What concerns you, my friend?" asked Chien.

"The man Kubai. I would dearly like to separate his head from his neck."

"A thought I can appreciate—and share. However, it is vital that the soldiers of Kiatze commit no crime while in Nadir lands. All we can do is react."

"As you wish, lord," muttered Sukai, touching spurs to his mount and guiding the beast down the hill to the camp.

At noon the following day the Nadir scout Kubai, announcing that he was riding off to hunt, galloped away to the southwest. Sukai watched him go, then turned his horse and halted the column.

Chien-tsu rode alongside him. "We have four, perhaps five hours," said Chien. "It is time to begin." Sukai signaled the twenty guards to dismount, and they tethered their horses and stood at attention. Chien walked the line in silence, stopping only to admonish a soldier whose bronze and silver hilt guard showed a trace of tarnish. The man reddened.

"You all know," said Chien, standing at the center of the line, "that treachery awaits us. The Nadir will attack at dusk. It is imperative that they believe they have surprised us; therefore, you will be sitting around fires when they come. You may leave your horses saddled. Once the attack begins, you may fight as your hearts desire. The Nadir greed and lust for battle show us that one day they will march on the kingdom of Kiatze itself. With this in mind, it is vital that you account for yourselves well. I would not expect any man to die until he has dispatched at least four of the enemy. There will be no retreat; you will die here." Chien turned away, then swung around again. "It would not normally be necessary to add to what I have said, but we are standing under an alien sky and far from home. So let me say this: You are the best warriors, the finest of men. If it were otherwise, you would not now be with me. I shall watch the battle from the hill yonder; then I will ascertain whether Mai-syn lives. After that, I will find Jungir Khan and cut the head from his shoulders. That is all."

Chien removed his brocaded coat of red silk and called Nagasi to him. The warrior shrugged out of his breastplate and pulled on the garment, then bowed to Chien.

"I will see that Oshi arranges your hair in a more regal fashion," Chien told Nagasi, then walked away to where Sukai stood close to the wagon. The warrior was staring up at the storm-threatened sky.

"How many will they send against us, lord?"

"I do not know. Why does it concern you?"

"If it is less than a hundred, we might win, and that would not be in keeping with the plan you have so carefully considered."

"That is true," said Chien gravely, "but I would imagine—following your exhibition at the banquet—that they will want to be certain of the outcome. One hundred would be the barest minimum Jungir Khan would send."

"And what if we win?" Sukai asked.

"Then you win, and we will think again," said Chien. "Now would you be so kind as to cut my hair."

"The men will see you," protested Sukai. "It is not fitting."

Chien shrugged. "It is important that I pass for a Nadir nomad. A gentleman of the Kiatze has no hope of survival in this barbarous land. Come now, Sukai," and he sat on the ground. Sukai took a long pair of brass scissors and began to cut away at the heavily lacquered hair, leaving only a topknot on the crown. Chien stood and removed his shirt and trousers of blue silk and his high boots. He lifted the canvas from the back of the wagon and pulled out a Nadir jerkin of goatskin, leather breeches, and an ugly pair of high riding moccasins.

"This has been cleaned, I take it?" he asked, holding the goatskin at arm's length.

Sukai smiled. "Three times, lord. Not a louse or a single flea remains alive in it."

"It stinks of wood smoke," muttered Chien, shrugging his arms into the garment. He clambered into the pair of ill-fitting breeches and tied the rawhide belt. Then he tugged on the moccasins.

"How do I look?" he inquired.

"Please do not ask," said Sukai.

The warrior summoned Oshi, who brought two horses that had been unsaddled and reequipped with Nadir saddles of rough-cut leather. There were no stirrups. "Bury the other saddles," instructed Chien.

The warrior nodded. "Also," Chien added, "it would be better if Nagasi died having suffered facial injuries."

"I have already explained that to him," said Sukai.

"Then it is time for farewells, my friend."

"Indeed. May your paths be straight and your days long."

Chien bowed. "Look down on me from heaven, Sukai."

The warlord took hold of his horse's mane and vaulted into the saddle. Oshi scrambled to the back of his own mare, and the two riders galloped from the campsite.

Chien and Oshi rode high into the hills, hiding the horses in a thick stand of poplar. Then they sat in silence for an hour, Chien praying, and Oshi, looking ludicrous in the clothes of a Nadir warrior, wrestling with the problem of how to look after his lord in the middle of this barren, uncivilized land.

His prayers concluded, Chien rose and moved to a rocky outcrop overlooking the valley below. As ordered, Sukai had cook fires burning, the men relaxing around them. Chien allowed anger to wash over his emotions. It was intolerable that a warrior such as Sukai should be sacrificed in such a manner; there was no honor here in this land of treachery and barbarism. With good fortune his secret messages to the emperor, carried by his most trusted concubine, would mean no further gifts to the khan. Perhaps also the news would encourage the emperor to build up his army.

Oshi crept alongside Chien. "Should we not put distance between ourselves and the action, lord?" the old servant asked.

Chien shook his head. "It would be most unbecoming to allow them to die unobserved. If there is a small risk to us, then so be it."

The sun began its slow descent and Chien saw the dustcloud to the southwest. His heartbeat quickened, and he fought for calm. He wanted to see, with a cool eye, the last moments of Sukai's life. It was his hope—albeit a faint one—that one day he could write a poem about it and deliver it in person to Sukai's widow.

As the Nadir force topped the hills around the campsite, Chien's trained eye swept over them. There were almost three hundred men in the attacking group, and his pride swelled. Here at last was a compliment from the barbarians: three hundred against twenty. Chien could almost feel Sukai's joy, watching as the twenty men ran to their horses. Sukai took up his position in the center, drawing both of his swords. Nagasi, in Chien's red coat, was beside him.

Screaming their battle cries, the Nadir charged. Sukai, forming the point of a wedge, kicked his horse into a gallop to meet them. Dust swirled under the horses' hooves. Chien made to stand, but Oshi tugged nervously at his jerkin, and reluctantly Chien sat. He could see Sukai cutting and cleaving a path through the Nadir ranks and could just make out the features of the traitor Kubai at the rear. Sukai almost reached him, but a spear was thrust through his throat; he killed the wielder, plunged his second blade into the body of a Nadir warrior, and fell from the saddle. The battle was brief, but Chien waited until he could count the Nadir fallen. Almost ninety of the enemy had been killed or wounded.

Kubai rode through the Nadir ranks and dismounted alongside Sukai's body, which he kicked three times. Then he hacked the head from the neck and raised it by the hair, swinging it around and finally hurling it away to roll in the dust.

Chien backed away to the horses, Oshi following.

"They fought well, lord," said Oshi.

Chien nodded and vaulted to the saddle. "The khan will pay dearly for Sukai's death. I swear this on the souls of my ancestors."

Turning his horse to the southeast, Chien led the way toward the distant mountains. His sword on his back, his hunting bow in his hand, he flicked the reins and let the stallion run. The wind was cold on his shaved head, but his blood was hot with the memory of the battle.

The distant mountains rose jagged against the sky, awesome in their size, clouds swirling about their peaks.

"Will we cross them, lord?" asked Oshi fearfully.

"There is a narrow pass that does not offer perils to the traveler. We will go there."

"Do they have a name, these mountains? Do spirits wander there?"

"They are the Mountains of the Moon . . . and spirits wander everywhere, Oshi. Do not concern yourself."

"I am concerned only for you, lord. Where will I find food to prepare for you? Where will you bathe? How can I clean your clothes?"

Chien smiled and hauled back on the reins, allowing the stallion to walk. He turned to Oshi. "I did not bring you with me so that you could serve me. I brought you because you are an old man and a friend, Oshi. You served my father with diligence and loyalty, and me with loyalty and affection. I still remember sitting on your knee and listening to fanciful tales of dragons and heroes. I remember you letting me drink *seichi* and eat rice cakes by your fireside. It was you, Oshi, who cured me of my childhood fears: my nightmares. Do not call me 'lord' any longer. Call me Chien, as you used to when I was a child."

"You have decided to die, then, lord?" whispered Oshi, blinking back tears.

"I do not think that even I can hope to take on the Nadir nation and survive, Oshi. I am pledged to kill Jungir Khan. If necessary I will walk into his palace and do it before all of his generals. Do you believe I can walk away from such a deed?"

"You could kill him with an arrow," ventured Oshi.

"Indeed. But then he would not know for what crime he was slain. No, it will be with a sword. But first we must ascertain the fate of Mai-syn. Once that is accomplished, we will find a ship for you to return home."

"I could not leave you, lord . . . Chien. What would I do? What would you do without me? We will kill the khan together."

"Someone must take the news back to the emperor. I will also give you letters to my wives. You will execute my will."

"You have it all planned, then?" asked Oshi softly.

"As much as can be considered at this time. It is all subject to change. Now let us ride and seek a good camping site."

They made camp in an old, dry riverbed, lighting a fire against the vertical bank and eating a light meal of dried fruit. Chien was in no mood for conversation. Unrolling the blanket from behind his saddle, he wrapped it around his shoulders and settled down.

"No, lord, here," said Oshi. "I have pushed aside the pebbles, and there is soft sand beneath. I have bunched some for a pillow. You will be more comfortable."

Chien moved to the place Oshi had prepared; it was indeed softer and away from the cold wind. He settled down to sleep. He dreamed of home in the ivory-white palace with its terraced gardens and landscaped streams and waterfalls. It was a place of tranquillity. But he awoke sharply when he heard the sound of boots on the pebbles of the riverbed. Rolling from his blanket, he rose. The moon was high, full and bright. Kubai stood staring at him with a wide smile on his face; beside him were four Nadir warriors. Oshi awoke and huddled against the rocks.

"Did you think I could not count?" asked Kubai. "I searched for you among the bodies. You know why?"

"Pray tell me," said Chien, folding his hands across his chest.

"Because of him," he replied, pointing at Oshi. "His body was nowhere. So I examined the corpse we took to be yours. There was a gash on the face, but not enough to fool me."

"Your intelligence staggers me," said Chien. "You are quite correct. I took you for an evil-smelling, stupid, treacherous barbarian. I was wrong; you are not stupid."

Kubai laughed. "You cannot make me angry, yellow man. You know why? Because tonight I will hear you scream. I will take your skin an inch at a time." Kubai drew his sword and advanced, but Chien stood waiting, arms still folded. "Are you not even going to fight, yellow man?"

Chien's arm flicked out, and Kubai stopped in his tracks, the ebony handle of the throwing knife jutting out from his throat. Chien leapt, and his foot cracked against Kubai's head, cartwheeling him from his feet. The other Nadir rushed in. Ducking under a sweeping blade, Chien stabbed his hand, fingers extended, to the man's midriff. The warrior doubled over, all breath gone from his lungs. Sidestepping a thrust, Chien hammered the edge of his palm into a second warrior's throat. Hurling himself forward, he rolled to his shoulder on the pebbles and came to his feet in one smooth motion. The remaining two Nadir came at him more carefully. Chien's hand snaked out, and one of them crumpled to the ground with a dagger through his eye. The last warrior backed away, but Oshi reared up behind him, plunging a thin dagger through his heart.

"You must not take risks," Chien told him. "You are too old."

"I am sorry, lord."

Kubai had pulled the blade from his throat and was kneeling on the streambed, blood gushing to his goatskin jerkin. Chien knelt before him and gathered his blade.

"In case it is of any interest," he said, "your lungs are filling with blood. It is said that a man can experience the most delightful visions at such a time. You, on the other hand, deserve no such joy."

Chien slammed the blade into Kubai's heart and pushed the body onto its back.

"I was having the most wonderful dream," said Chien. "I was in the gardens at home, and—you recall the plant we tried to train by the dry stone wall at the south gate?" Oshi nodded. "Well, it was in bloom, and the flowers were quite the most exquisite shades of purple. And there was a fragrance I recall that put my roses to shame. I wonder if that purple plant ever took root."

"I would imagine so, lord. You have a fine touch with flowers."

"It pleases me to think so."

A groan came from the Nadir Chien had winded, and the

Kiatze warrior stood and hammered a kick to the man's temple. His neck cracked, and Oshi winced.

"What was I saying? Oh, yes, flowers. This land could do with more flowers. Perhaps then the Nadir would become interested more in poetry than in war. Saddle the horses, Oshi. This ugly place is making me melancholy."

For three weeks the questers traveled only by night, hiding by day in the woods and jagged hollows that stretched across the land. The journey in darkness was taken with great care as the land descended in giant steps from rocky plateau to rocky plateau. The trails were scree-covered and treacherous, and the questers were often forced to dismount and lead their horses.

Four times Okas warned them of hunters, and twice the hidden questers saw bands of Nadren riders searching for sign. But Finn had obscured their trail, and the hunters passed on.

Water was scarce on the steppes, and they were compelled to take wide detours to seek rock pools in the plateaus. Most of them were guarded, and many times the questers were forced to move on, their throats dry. What little water they carried was used to rinse the dust from the nostrils and mouths of their mounts.

"Our enemies have all the advantages," said Finn, as they made their third dry camp in as many days. "They know we cannot travel without water, and they have stopped trying to track us. Now they guard all the wells and pools."

"Not all," said Okas. "There is rock tank an hour's ride from here. The water is shallow but good to drink."

"Why is it not guarded?" Chareos asked.

"It is, but not by men."

"If there are more demons," croaked Beltzer, "I'd just as soon suck grass for another day."

"Not demons," said Okas. "Lions. But do not fear; I have a way with beasts."

With a half moon to guide them, the questers set off across the plateau, their horses' hooves muffled by cloth shoes. The trail wound down at first, then cut to the right, rising steeply. The horses grew increasingly nervous as the smell of lion droppings filled the air. Okas led the way on foot, and the trail opened to a wide bowl-shaped arena. They saw eight lions by the pool: one male, three females, and four cubs. The females rose first, baring their fangs. Okas began to chant softly; he walked slowly toward the beasts and sat some ten paces from them. The sound of his rhythmic song echoed in the rocks, and a lioness padded toward him, circling him, her tail thrashing. She pushed her face against Okas' shoulder and head, then settled down beside him. The other lions ignored the old man.

Okas' voice sounded inside Chareos' mind: *"Lead the horses to the pool. Let them drink their fill. You do likewise and fill the water sacks. Then withdraw. Let no one speak."* Chareos turned to the others and lifted his fingers to his lips. Finn nodded, and silently they made for the water.

The song of Okas continued as the questers led the frightened horses to the pool. The need for water overcame their fear, and they dipped their heads and drank. Chareos dropped to his belly and filled his mouth with the cool liquid. For some moments he held the water there, then he allowed it to trickle into his dry throat. Finally he drank until he felt he could contain no more. Only then did he fill the water sacks. The others followed suit.

Kiall ducked his head under the surface of the pool. "That was good," he said as he sat up.

The lion roared. The horses reared, and Beltzer almost lost his grip on the reins. The lion rose and padded across toward Kiall.

"Make no move!" came the voice of Okas in Kiall's mind. *"Sit still. Absolutely still."*

The lion prowled around Kiall, baring its yellow fangs. The song of Okas came louder now, hypnotic in its rhythm. The lion's face loomed before Kiall's eyes, the fangs brushed his skin, and he could smell the creature's fetid breath. Then the lion padded back to the pride and settled down. Kiall rose unsteadily. Chareos had gathered the reins of Kiall's mount and passed them to him silently; slowly the group retreated from the pool, down the long slope, and out onto the plateau.

Okas joined them and the party rode on for an hour, camping just before daybreak in a shallow lava ditch.

Finn clapped Kiall's shoulder. "Not many men have been kissed by a lion," he said. "It will be something to tell your children."

"I thought he was going to tear my head off," said Kiall.

"I thought of doing the same," snapped Chareos. "Did you not see the sign for silence? Did you take lessons in stupidity, or does it come naturally?"

"Leave him be, Blademaster," said Finn. "You were young once. Do you know why the lion nuzzled you, Kiall?"

"No."

"He has scent glands in his mouth. Lions often mark their territory with them. You were lucky; mostly they urinate to establish the borders of their domain."

"In that case I feel doubly lucky," said Kiall, smiling. He turned to Okas. "How long before we reach the Nadren settlement?"

"Tomorrow . . . the day after." The old man shrugged. "The hunters are everywhere. We must continue to move with care."

"Will Ravenna still be there, do you think?" Kiall asked Chareos.

"I would doubt it. But we'll find out where she went."

"I'm sorry for that mistake," apologized Kiall, seeing that Chareos was still angry.

The older man smiled. "Finn was right; we were all young once. Do not allow mistakes to become a habit. But there is something we must talk about. There is no way we can rescue all the women who may be held by the Nadren—we are not strong enough—so prepare yourself for disappointment, Kiall. It will be wonderful if we can establish where Ravenna was sent, but there is no more than that to be gained. You understand?"

"But if they are there, we must make the attempt, surely."

"What purpose would it serve? You have seen yourself the difficulty we are experiencing just getting to the settlement. Can you imagine what chance we would have of getting out?"

Kiall wanted to argue, to find some compelling reason why Chareos was wrong. But he had seen the arid lands of the steppes and knew that they would have no chance to escape if they were encumbered by perhaps twenty freed captives. Yet he could not bring himself to answer Chareos. He looked away and stared at the stars.

"I know that you made a promise, Kiall," continued Chareos. "I know what that means to you. But it was a foolhardy promise. All life is compromise, and a man can only do his best."

"As you say, I made a promise," returned Kiall. "And yes, it was foolish. But perhaps I can buy them back. I have gold."

"And they would sell them to you, and a day later, or even before, they would ride after you, kill you, and take back what they sold. We are not dealing with men of honor."

"We shall see," said Kiall. "It may all be as you say. But let us not decide until the day comes."

"When the sun rises, the day has come," said Chareos.

Kiall settled down to sleep, but his thoughts were many. He had dreamed of riding off like a knight in pursuit of his love; he had pictured her returning beside him, her gratitude and love sustaining him. But it was almost four months now since she had been taken, and he was as likely to find her wedded to a savage or dead. As for the other women, many of them he had not known too well. He had always been shy in female company, and they had laughed at his blushes. Lucia, the baker's daughter, had always been kind to him. But what could he offer her now? Her father was dead, her home burned. If he took her back, she would have nowhere to live and would probably be forced to find employment in Talgithir. Then there was Trianis, the niece of Paccus the seer. Again there were no living relatives. He ran the names of the captives through his mind: Cascia, Juna, Colia, Menea . . . so many.

Chareos was right. How could they attempt to rescue

twenty or more young women and then spirit them across the steppes?

Yet if they did not at least try, then Kiall would have branded himself both a liar and a braggart.

Kiall slept fitfully into the day. Soon after dusk the questers set off, avoiding skylines, keeping to the low ground. At last Okas led them up a winding deer trail and halted within a clearing surrounded by poplar trees. There he dismounted and moved off to the brow of a low hill. Chareos and the others joined him there and found themselves overlooking a large settlement. A tall stockade wall was built around the town, with four wooden turrets at each corner. Inside there were some sixty dwellings and a long hall. Guards paced the battlements, and lanterns were hung over the gates.

"It's more like a cursed fortress," said Beltzer.

"We're not here to attack it," Chareos told him.

"Thank the gods for that," said Beltzer.

Chareos studied the layout of the buildings and the movements of the people within the town. It was just after dawn, and few of the town dwellers could be seen. Two women carrying wooden buckets on yokes walked to the rear of the stockade and out through a side exit. Chareos focused his attention on this; it was shaped like a portcullis, with a heavy metal block that was raised by turning two spoked wooden wheels situated on the battlements.

Chareos eased his way back from the skyline and joined the others.

"I can see no way for us to gain entry without being seen," he told them, "unless we have someone on the inside."

"Who?" asked Beltzer.

"I'll go myself," proposed Chareos.

"No," said Kiall. "It makes no sense to send our leader into peril. What would the rest of us do if you were taken? No, I will go."

"What will you tell them, boy?" chortled Beltzer. "That you've come for your lady and they'd better surrender her or else?"

"Something like that," said Kiall. He pushed himself to

his feet and walked to his horse. Swiftly he emptied his saddlebag of gold, keeping only a single red gold ring, then he returned to the group. "I shall tell their leader, whoever he is, that I am willing to buy back the women taken. If he is agreeable, I will signal you from the ramparts; I will raise my right arm and wave. If I think there is treachery in the air, I will raise my left."

"What are we supposed to do then, General?" Beltzer sneered. "Storm the citadel?"

"Be silent, you oaf!" snapped Chareos. "So far the plan is sound. At midnight Finn and I will be at the southern wall. If you have not signaled in that time, we will come in and look for you. Be careful, Kiall. These men are killers. Life means nothing to them."

"I know," Kiall replied. As he walked to his horse and mounted, Okas' voice came into his mind.

"I will be with you, seeing through your eyes."

He smiled at the Tattooed Man and touched heels to his horse.

The sun was bright as he headed down the grass-covered slope toward the settlement. Looking up at a sentry who had notched an arrow to his bow, Kiall waved and smiled. The gates loomed, and he rode through. Sweat trickled to his back, and he could not bring himself to look up at the archer. He guided the mount to a hitching rail and dismounted. There was a well nearby, and he hauled up the bucket and drank from a rusty iron ladle.

He heard the sound of moving men and turned slowly to see four guards approaching him with swords drawn. He spread his hands. "There is no need for violence, my friends. I am here to buy a woman—maybe two."

"Let's feel the weight of your gold," answered a tall man.

Kiall dipped his hand into his pocket and came up with the ring. He tossed it to the man, who examined it closely.

"Very nice," he said. "And the rest?"

"Hidden until we complete our business."

"Hidden, eh? Well, I know a few tricks that always make a man sing out his secrets."

"I am sure that you do," said Kiall. "Now take me to whoever is the leader here."

"How do you know it's not me?" the man asked, sneering.

Kiall's temper flared. "I do not. I merely assumed the leader would have more than half a brain."

"You cowson!" The man's sword came up, and Kiall leapt to the right, drawing his saber.

"Leave him be!" roared a voice, and the men froze. A tall man dressed in black came walking through the crowd that had gathered beyond the group.

"What has this to do with you?" the swordsman asked.

"I know this man," he answered, "and I do not want to see him killed." Kiall looked closely at the speaker. He was hawk-faced and lean, and a jagged scar showed on his cheek; his nose was hooked, his features dark and hard. But Kiall had never seen him before.

"Why push that long nose of yours into another man's business, Harokas?" the swordsman sneered.

The man smiled coldly and drew his own saber. "You brainless dolt, Githa! You never saw the day dawn when you could best me with a blade."

Githa swallowed nervously and backed away, aware that he had gone too far.

"Enough!" bellowed Kiall, doing his best to copy the authoritative tone used by Chareos. Both men froze. "You," said Kiall, moving forward to stand before Githa. "Hand me the ring and go back to the ramparts." The man blinked sweat from his eyes and happily obliged. He did not look at Harokas but sheathed his sword and hurried away. With the excitement over, the crowd dispersed. Harokas grinned and shook his head.

"Not bad for a farm boy," he said. "Not bad at all. I see that Chareos has trained you well. Is he close by?"

"Perhaps. Are you a friend of his?"

"No, but I need to see him. I have been looking for you for almost four months."

"Why?"

"I have a message from the earl," said Harokas. He lifted

a ladle of water from the bucket and sipped it. "But what are you doing here, Kiall, so far from home?"

"If you are from the earl, then you must know already. This is where the women from my village were taken."

"And you have come to win them back? How noble of you. A shame, though, that you have arrived too late. The last of them was sold off months ago. This is only a market town, Kiall. Every three months or so Nadir merchants and princes come here to buy slaves."

Kiall swallowed back his frustration. "How is it, then, that you, an earl's man, are welcome here?"

"I am welcome in many strange places. Come, I will take you to the leader you inquired about. Perhaps then you will find answers."

Kiall followed the tall man through the alleyways and out into the main square. Here was the hall he had seen from the hill. Harokas entered the building and led Kiall to a curtained area at the rear.

A woman rose from a satin-covered divan and strode to meet them. Her hair was short-cropped and dark, her eyes wide and slanted, her lips full. She wore a black tunic belted at the waist, and her long legs were bare. Kiall blinked and tried not to stare at her. She stood before him, too close, and he shifted his feet, trying to put more distance between them. He looked into her eyes, noting that they were blue tinged with purple.

"Well," said Harokas, "you have your wish, Kiall. Here is the leader you asked to meet."

Kiall bowed, aware that he was blushing. "I am pleased to . . . that is . . . I . . ."

"Is he retarded?" she inquired of Harokas.

"I do not believe so, Princess."

"What do you want here?" she asked Kiall.

He took a deep breath. "I am seeking a woman."

"Does this look like a brothel?" she snapped.

"No. Not at all. I meant that I was seeking a special woman. She was taken from my village, and I want to buy her back."

"To buy? Our prices here are high. Can you afford her?"

"I believe that I can. How high?"

"That would depend," said the woman, "on how beautiful she is."

"Her name is Ravenna. She is the most beautiful—" He stumbled to a halt and found himself staring into her eyes. In that moment he realized that Ravenna could never be called beautiful, not compared with the woman before him. He felt like a traitor even to think such thoughts. "She is . . . I think she is . . . beautiful," he stammered, at last.

"You are riding with the heroes of Bel-azar?" she asked. Her words sent a cold chill through him. For a moment only he hesitated, considering a lie.

"Yes," he answered.

She nodded. "It is always better to be truthful with me, Kiall," she told him, taking his arm and leading him back to the divan. With a wave of her hand she dismissed Harokas; leaving Kiall standing, she stretched herself out on the couch, her head resting on a blue silk-covered cushion. "Tell me of the heroes," she said.

"What would you have me say? They are strong men, courageous, skillful in the ways of war."

"And why would they be interested in this . . . this girl?"

"Merely to see her safe and restored to her . . . loved ones."

"And you are a loved one?"

"No. Well . . . yes."

"Is it no or yes? Sit by me and explain it." He perched on the edge of the divan, feeling the warmth of her leg against his. He cleared his throat and told her of his love for Ravenna and her decision to marry the farmer Jarel.

"I don't blame her. She was right, of course. I was . . . am a dreamer."

"And you have no other woman?" she asked.

"No."

"No stolen kisses in high meadows, no soft touches during secret trysts?"

"No."

She moved up to sit alongside him, her arm draped over his shoulder. "One last question, Kiall, and be sure to answer it honestly. Much depends on it. This quest of yours—

have you told me the whole truth? All you seek is the girl, Ravenna?"

"I have told you the whole truth," he said. "I swear it."

For several seconds she looked into his eyes, then she nodded and smiled. Her hand slipped from his shoulder, and she replaced the small dagger in its hiding place behind the cushion.

"Very well. I will consider what you have said. But I make no promises. Go out into the square and find Harokas. He will see that you are fed." He rose and bowed awkwardly. As he turned to leave, she suddenly spoke. "Tell me, Kiall, do you trust me?"

"I would like to, my lady. It ought to be that a man could put his faith in beauty."

She rose smoothly and moved in to him, her body pressing against him, her arms on his shoulders, and her mouth only inches from his. "And can you put your faith in beauty?"

"No," he whispered.

"You are quite correct. Go now."

◊ 10 ◊

"I AM GROWING tired of sitting up here," declared Beltzer. "What is he doing? Why does he not signal?"

"He has met the leader," said Okas, moving in to sit by Beltzer. "It was interesting meeting." The old man chuckled. "It will be more interesting yet."

"Why?" asked Chareos. "Who is he?"

"It is not a *he*, Blademaster. It is a she."

"Then he is in no danger at present?" Chareos asked.

The smile faded from Okas' face. "Of that I am not certain. There was a moment when he spoke with her when his danger was great. I felt she would kill him. But something stayed her hand."

"We shouldn't have sent him," said Maggrig. "He does not have the experience."

"Not so," said Okas. "I believe it is lack of experience which keeps him alive down there. The woman is hard, very hard. But whatever else, she finds Kiall . . . of interest."

"She wants him in her bed. Is that what you're saying?" put in Beltzer.

"Perhaps; she is certainly a predatory woman, and it is often the way that such people find innocence attractive. But there is more; I can feel it. She questioned him about all of you."

"And he told her?" Beltzer hissed.

"He did. That is what, I believe, saved his life."

"But if she is the leader," said Chareos, "then it is she who has been sending out the hunters to kill us."

"Exactly," replied Okas. "Curious, is it not?"

"There is something missing here," said Chareos.

"Yes," Okas agreed. "There is something else also. There is a man in the settlement who saved Kiall. His name is Harokas and he told Kiall he wishes to talk with you, Chareos."

"Harokas? The name is not familiar to me."

"He says he has a message from the earl, whatever that may mean."

"Nothing good, I'll wager," muttered Beltzer. "So, what do we do?"

"We wait," said Chareos.

"She could have armed men moving in on us," Beltzer argued.

"Indeed she could," agreed Chareos. "Even so—we wait."

"I do not know why you are still alive, farm boy," said Harokas as he and Kiall sat at a bench table in the crowded eating house. "Tanaki is not usually so gentle with enemies."

"I am not her enemy," Kiall told him, spooning the last of the hot broth to his mouth.

"Are you not?"

"Why should I be?"

"It was here that your beloved was dragged to the auction block. Does that not make you angry?"

Kiall sat back and stared into the cold eyes of the scarred man. "Yes, it does. Are you saying it was . . . Tanaki . . . who led the raid?"

"No," answered Harokas. "Tanaki merely controls the auctions. Nadren raiders travel here from all over the steppes. You should see this place at market time; it's a revelation."

"I still do not understand how an earl's man is welcome here," said Kiall.

Harokas chuckled. "That is because you do not . . . yet . . . understand the ways of the world. But I see no harm in instructing you. You will learn soon enough. You know, of course, that the lord regent outlawed the slave trade a decade ago."

"Yes. And ended the serf laws. It was good policy."

"That depends on your viewpoint. If you were a slave or a serf, indeed yes. But not if you were a nobleman. The wealth of the nobility used to depend on land. Not anymore, not with the fear of Nadir invasion. Crops bring profits, to be sure, but then, the Gothir lands are rich and food is cheap. No, the real profit was always in slaves. The lord regent did not take this into account with his new laws. Are you beginning to understand me?"

"No," admitted Kiall.

"So slow? I took you for an intelligent man, but then, you are also a romantic and that must cloud your reason." Harokas leaned forward. "The nobility never gave up the trade; they merely found another way of continuing. The raid on your village was sanctioned by the earl. He takes a share of the profits, and I am here to make sure his share is just."

Kiall felt the taste of bile in his mouth. He swallowed hard and took a sip of the ale Harokas had purchased. "We pay him taxes. We look to him for protection. And he sells us out to line his pockets?"

"It is not a nice world, is it, farm boy?"

"Why tell me this? Why?"

Harokas shrugged. "Why not? Your chances of leaving here alive are negligible. And anyway, perhaps I am sick of it, too." He rubbed his eyes. "I am getting old. There was a time when I believed in heroes—when I was young, like you. But there are no heroes, at least not the ones we want to see. Every man has his own reason for every deed. Usually it is selfish. Take your friends. Why are they with you? You think they care about Ravenna? No, they seek to recapture lost glories, lost youth. They want to hear their names in song again."

"I do not believe that," Kiall said. "Chareos and the others have risked their lives for me—and for Ravenna. And you cheapen them merely by speaking their names. Thank you for the meal."

Kiall rose and left the table. The air outside was crisp and fresh, and he strode to the battlements. The two sentries ignored him as he gazed out over the land. He did not look in the direction of the camp but waited until the voice of Okas sounded in his mind.

"What do you have to tell us?" asked Okas.

"Nothing," replied Kiall. "Tell Chareos not to come to the wall. I am waiting to see the woman Tanaki."

"Be careful in her company. She has killed before and will kill again."

"I will be careful. But she . . . disturbs me."

He felt Okas drift from him and returned to the central square. The auction platform was large, supported by six piers of round stone. He pictured Ravenna standing on it, surrounded by Nadir men ogling her, desiring her. He closed his eyes and tried to imagine her. But all he could see were the eyes of Tanaki, wide and slanted.

A man tapped his shoulder, making him jump.

"I thought it was you," said Chellin. For a moment Kiall did not recognize the stocky warrior, but then he smiled.

"You are a long way from the mountains, Chellin. I am pleased to see you made it safely."

The man sat down on a bench seat and scratched at his black and silver beard. "It wasn't easy. You came a long way. How are your friends?"

"Alive," answered Kiall.

"No mean feat, considering the number of men sent out to kill them."

"I'm glad you were not with them," said Kiall.

"I was. We got back this morning. Still, with luck you'll sort out your difference with the princess, and we won't have to meet on a battlefield."

"The princess?"

"Tanaki. Did you not know she was Nadir royalty?"

"No, I did not."

"She's the youngest child of Tenaka Khan."

"What is she doing here?" asked Kiall, amazed.

Chellin laughed. "You don't know much about the Nadir, do you? To them women are nothing, worth less than horses. Tanaki had some sort of falling out with her brother, Jungir; he had her banished here."

"She is very beautiful," said Kiall.

"She is that—and the most desirable piece I ever saw. A man could die happy if he bedded her."

Kiall reddened and cleared his throat. "Where will you go from here?" he asked.

Chellin shrugged. "Who knows? North again. Maybe not. I'm tired of this life, Kiall. I may head south to Drenai lands. Buy a farm, raise a family."

"And have raiders descend on you to steal your daughters?"

Chellin nodded and sighed. "Yes. Like all dreams, it doesn't bear close examination. I hope matters work well with you and the princess. I like you; I hope they don't ask me to kill you." Chellin rose and wandered away, but Kiall sat where he was for another hour. Then a warrior came seeking him.

"You are wanted," said the man. Kiall stood and followed him back to the long hall.

Tanaki waited, as before, on the divan. She was dressed now in a short tunic of white linen, her legs and feet bare. She wore no jewelry or ornaments except for the silver buckle on her wide black belt.

As he approached, she rose. "Welcome to my hearth, Kiall. Sit and talk with me."

"What would you have me say, lady?"

"Very little. Just give me a compelling reason why I should not have you killed."

"Do you kill for no reason?" he asked.

"Sometimes," she told him. "Is that so surprising?"

"I am becoming inured to surprises, Princess. Tell me, will you help me find Ravenna?"

She took his hand and led him to the divan, sitting beside him with her arm resting on his shoulder. "I am not sure that I will. You know I sent men out to kill you?"

"Yes," he whispered, aware of her breath warm on his cheek and neck.

"I did that because I heard that a group of heroes was

riding out to avenge a raid. I thought you were coming to kill me."

"That was never our intention."

"And then I find a tall, handsome young innocent seeking a woman who does not care for him. This man intrigues me." Her lips touched his neck, and her right hand moved across his chest, sliding down over the tense muscles of his stomach. His face felt hot, and his breathing was shallow. "And I wondered," she went on, her voice low and dreamy, "how it was that a man who has never known love could risk so much." Her hand slid lower.

His fingers clamped to her wrist. "Do not toy with me, lady," he whispered, turning in toward her. "You know that I find your beauty . . . irresistible. But I have little . . . self-worth as it is. Just tell me where Ravenna is and let me leave you."

For some time she held his gaze, then she pulled back. "How delightfully you turn me away—not with strength but with admitted weakness. You put the decision in my hands. Very well, Kiall. But you do not wish to know where she is. I mean that almost tenderly. I asked you to trust me this morning, and now I ask it again. Leave this quest and return to your home."

"I cannot, lady."

"You will die. Your friends will die. And it will be for nothing."

He lifted her hand and gently kissed the palm. "Then that is as it must be. But tell me."

She sat up. "The girl Ravenna was bought by a man named Kubai. She was sent to a city not far from here and given as a gift to another man. Then she was taken far across the steppes to Ulrickham."

"I shall go there. And find her."

"She was given to Jungir Khan." The words struck Kiall like knife blades, and he closed his eyes, his head bowing. "So you see," she said tenderly, "there is no point to this quest. Ulrickham is a fortress city. No one could enter the khan's harem and spirit away one of his brides. And even if you did, where could you go to escape his vengeance? He is the great khan; he has half a million men under his command. Where in all the world could you be safe from him or his shamans?"

Kiall looked at her and smiled. "Still I must make the attempt. And somehow it is worse now not because of Jungir but because of you."

"I do not understand you."

He stood and shook his head. "I cannot say it. Forgive me. Do I have your permission to leave?"

For a moment it seemed as if she would speak, but she merely nodded her head. He bowed and walked from the hall.

His thoughts were many as he rode from the town, and a great sadness filled him. He knew now that he did not love Ravenna; she was the dream of an adolescent, the unattainable beauty. But what could he do? He had made his promise. And even if it cost him his life, he would keep it.

He heard the sound of hoofbeats and turned in the saddle.

Harokas cantered alongside him and drew rein. "May I ride with you?" he asked.

Kiall reined in his horse. "I do not desire your company, sir. But if you wish to meet with Chareos, then I will not stop you."

"Then that must suffice," said Harokas. Kiall spurred his horse into a run, and the beast was blowing hard by the time they reached the hilltop. Harokas followed at a more sedate pace. Chareos, Beltzer, and Okas were seated in the clearing, but of Maggrig and Finn there was no sign. Kiall dismounted and started to tell Chareos about Ravenna, but the blademaster waved him to silence. "I know," he said, his gaze fixed on the rider following Kiall.

Harokas slid from the saddle and bowed to Chareos. "I have searched for you for a great length of time," he said. "I have a message from the earl. You have been cleared of all charges and would be welcome at any time in the city of Talgithir. Captain Salida told the earl of your valiant assistance at Tavern Town."

"Is that all?" asked Chareos coldly.

"Indeed it is. Now will the bowmen show themselves?"

"I find it hard to believe in the earl as a forgiving man,"

said Chareos, "and I am wondering why he should send a warrior in search of me. Could it be that you are an assassin?"

"All things are possible, Chareos," replied Harokas, smiling.

"I think we should kill him," said Beltzer. "I don't like the look of him."

"And I do not like the look of you, you fat oaf!" snapped Harokas. "Now keep silent before your betters."

Beltzer pushed himself to his feet and chuckled. "Let me break his back, Chareos. Just say the word."

Finn emerged from the undergrowth. "Chareos!" he called. "You'd better see this: there's an army of Nadir warriors moving toward the town. I don't think they're here to visit."

Tanaki watched the young man leave the hall and then rose, stretching her arms over her head and arching her back. Her feelings were mixed as she wandered back into her living area. Kiall's innocence was both appealing and surprising, like finding a perfect flower growing on the edge of a cesspit. She poured herself a goblet of wine and sipped it. A young man in search of his love, a dreamer. Her eyes narrowed.

"The world has some savage shocks in store for you," she whispered. A cold breeze rustled the heavy hangings, touching the bare flesh of her legs. She shivered.

"I miss you, Father," she said, picturing again the tall lean warrior, seeing his slow smile, watching it soften his cruel face. Tanaki had been his favorite despite her birth having been responsible for the death of her mother, Renya. Tenaka Khan had lavished all his love on his only daughter, while his sons had fought for a kind word or even a nod that might be interpreted as praise. She thought of her eldest brother, Jungir. How he had longed to be accepted by his father.

Now that Jungir was the khan and Tanaki's other brothers had been murdered, she was merely living out her life awaiting the inevitable.

She smiled as she remembered her last meeting with

Jungir. He so wanted her dead. But the khan's generals would never accept the complete obliteration of Tenaka Khan's bloodline, and as everyone knew, Jungir Khan was sterile. Not one of his forty wives had conceived. Tanaki chuckled. Poor Jungir. He could ride the wildest horse and fight with lance or sword. But in the eyes of the Nadir he was suspect because his seed was not strong.

Tanaki pressed her hands to her belly. She had no doubt that she could conceive. And one day, perhaps, when Jungir grew desperate, she could be back in favor and wedded to one of the generals. The face of Tsudai leapt into her mind, and she recoiled. Not him! Never him. His touch was like the feel of lizard skin, and the memory of his tomb-dark eyes made her shiver. No, not Tsudai.

She pushed him from her mind and thought of Jungir as she had last seen him, sitting on the throne and staring down at her. "You are safe, bitch, for the moment. But know this . . . one day I will see you humbled. Live for that day, Tanaki."

So instead of death Tanaki had been banished here, in the desolate wastelands of the south. There were few pleasures to be found in this land, save for the heady joys of alcohol and the succession of young men she took to her bed. Yet even those pleasures soon palled. Bored with her life, she had watched the inefficiency of the slave trade, alternating between glutted markets with the price low and no trade at all. Added to this, there was no central point where slaves could be auctioned and prices could be guaranteed. It had taken Tanaki less than four months to establish the market town, and within a year she had also coordinated all raids into Gothir territory. Prices had stabilized, the new improved market was buoyant, and enormous profits were being made. The gold meant little to Tanaki, who had spent her childhood surrounded by the wealth of conquered nations. But the trade kept her agile mind busy and away from thoughts of Jungir's revenge.

No matter how great the pressure from the generals, she knew there would come a time when Jungir would feel strong enough to have her killed. So strange, she realized, that she did not hate him for it. It was so easy to understand what drove him. He had yearned for his father's affection and, failing to win it, had come to hate that which his father loved.

Tanaki pulled aside a velvet curtain and gazed out of a narrow window.

"He left you nothing, Jungir," she whispered. "He conquered most of the world; he united the tribes; he founded an empire. What is there left for you?"

Poor Jungir. Poor sterile Jungir!

Her thoughts turned to the young man Kiall. His face loomed in her mind, the gray eyes gentle yet with a hint of steel. And there was passion there, too, raw and unmined, volcanic and waiting.

"It would have been pleasant to swallow your innocence." She smiled, and her expression softened. "No, it would not," she realized with sadness.

"Princess! Princess!" yelled Chellin, running the length of the hall. "Nadir warriors!"

She stepped out to meet him. "What of it?" she inquired. "There are always Nadir warriors near here."

"Not the Royal Wolves, Princess," said Chellin. "And Tsudai is leading them."

Tanaki felt her mouth go dry. "Is the gate shut?"

"It is, lady. But there are three hundred of them, and we have less than fifty. And most of those will run, given the chance."

Tanaki moved to a chest of dark oak and lifted the heavy lid. She took out a wide belt from which hung two short swords.

"We cannot fight them, lady. Why are they here?"

She shrugged and did not reply. So, she thought, the day has come. No more to see the blue of the sky, the eagle riding the wind currents over the mountains. No more men to possess her and, in possessing her, give away their souls. Anger flared. Ignoring Chellin, she walked from the hall and onto the wall, climbing to the ramparts to watch the approach of the khan's Wolves. As Chellin had said, there were more than three hundred warriors, their pointed silver helms ringed with wolfskin, their silver breastplates edged with gold. They rode seemingly without formation, and yet at a single order they could wheel and charge in a flying wedge or break into three units. Their discipline was incredible. Tenaka Khan had formed the royal guard a quarter of a century before and had trained them to a degree never before experienced among the Nadir. Among the tribesmen it was still regarded as a badge of honor to be accepted into the Wolves. For every hundred applicants, only one was given the helm and the Wolfshead-embossed breastplate.

And there at the center rode Tsudai, a fighting man without equal, a general without peer.

Men gathered around Tanaki. "What shall we do?" asked one.

"Why are they here?" asked another.

"They are here to kill me," said Tanaki, surprised that her voice remained calm.

"Will they want to kill the rest of us?" asked a burly warrior.

"Shut your damned mouth!" roared Chellin.

Tanaki raised her hands for silence. "Get your horses and leave by the iron gate. Do it swiftly! They will kill all they find here." Some of the men ran from the ramparts, but Chellin stood firm.

"I'll not let them take you while I live."

She smiled and placed her hands on the old warrior's bearded cheeks. "And you cannot stop them. But it would please me to see you survive, Chellin. Now, go!"

For a moment only he stood, then he cursed and ran for his horse.

The Nadir were closer now, and the face of their general could be clearly seen by Tanaki. Tsudai was smiling. He raised his hands, and riders swept out on either side of him in a skirmish line.

"What do you want here?" Tanaki shouted.

"We want you, whore!" called back Tsudai. "You are to be brought to Ulrickham for trial."

Tanaki's anger rose, but she fought for calm. "By what right do you call a daughter of the great khan a whore, you who were suckled by a scabrous goat?"

Tsudai chuckled. "I have here three hundred warriors, *Princess*. Each one of them will use your body between here and Ulrickham. Now, the journey will be sixty days. Even my simple mind tells me that five men a day will get to enjoy the pleasures you bestow so freely on the foreigners and scum you surround yourself with. Think of it, *Princess*: three hundred men!"

"Why warn me, you foul-mouthed whoreson?"

"It could be that you will not wish to suffer such humiliation. Surely someone of the blood of the great khan would sooner take her own life."

Through her fear Tanaki forced a laugh. "My esteemed brother would like that, would he not? No, Tsudai. Come and take me. I'll survive. And when the generals hear of my treatment at your hands, I will live to see the skin flayed from your foul body."

He spread his hands. "As you wish, *Princess,* but do not expect too much support from the other khans. The Lord Jungir will shortly be celebrating the birth of an heir. All the omens say it will be a boy."

"You lie! Jungir is sterile."

"I never lie, Tanaki! You know that. One of the khan's wives is pregnant."

"Then she had a lover," snapped Tanaki, before she could stop herself. But her heart sank. The khan's concubines and wives were kept in a walled palace patrolled by eunuchs. There was no way a man could infiltrate such a fortress. And even if by some miracle he did, the scores of spies among the concubines would carry word to the khan.

"Will you come out—or will we come in after you?" shouted Tsudai.

"Come in!" she yelled. "Why not come yourself?"

Tsudai chuckled and waved his arm, and twenty riders raced for the walls, hurling ropes that looped over the pointed stockade timbers. As the Nadir leapt from their saddles and swiftly clambered up the walls, Tanaki drew her swords. The first man to show himself died, his throat ripped open. The second fell, his lung pierced. As the others came in sight, Tanaki waited, blood dripping from her silver blades as they advanced from left and right. She leapt and spun, killing a man with a reverse sweep across the neck, then jumped from the battlement into a wagon loaded with sacks of wheat. Scrambling clear, she ran for the hall. Four men moved to cut her off, but she swerved into an alley, then doubled back and waited. Six warriors raced into view. She charged into them, cutting and cleaving, breaking through their line.

On the battlements knelt a warrior holding a sling. He whirled it around his head and let fly, the small round stone cracking into Tanaki's temple. She staggered and almost fell. A man ran at her . . . spinning, she hurled her right-hand sword. It punched into his chest, and he fell back, scrabbling at the blade. A second stone screamed past her. Ducking, she stumbled to a barn, pushing her back against the door. Her head was swimming, and a terrible dizziness overcame her. Two more Nadir warriors came into view. She half fell, and they leapt at her. Her sword came up, partly severing a man's arm. A fist cracked against her skull, and her swords were torn from her grasp. Twice more the fist pounded at her face. She fell to her knees. Men were all around her now, tearing at her clothes. They dragged her into the barn, hurling her naked to the straw-covered floor.

"Well, well. We do not look like a princess now," came Tsudai's voice, cold and mocking. She struggled to stand, but a foot was pushed against her face and she fell back. "I said five men a day, but these twelve warriors have at least fought for you, Princess. I will leave you in their tender care."

She gazed up through swollen eyes and watched the men untying their rawhide belts, saw the lust in their faces. Something inside her quivered and snapped. Tears ran to her cheeks.

"Make her scream a little," said Tsudai, "but do not mark her unduly. There are many more men waiting."

The general walked out into the sunlight, where he stood for a while listening to the sounds of grunting men and the low moans that came from the once-proud princess. Then she screamed, a long and piercing sound. Tsudai allowed himself a smile. He had waited a long time for this moment. Four years since the haughty Princess Tanaki had first spurned his offer of marriage. He had given her a second chance mere months before. Now she would begin to understand the depth of his hatred. The scream sounded again. More animal than human, he thought. Curious how so much despair could be carried in a sound with no words . . .

The screams drifted on the breeze, carrying high into the mountains. "Dear gods, what are they doing to her?" said Kiall.

"What the Nadir always do," hissed Beltzer. "They're raping her. My guess is they'll kill her soon after."

"Shame," commented Harokas. "Good-looking woman."

"We must do something," said Kiall, pushing himself to his feet. Chareos grabbed his belt, hauling him back.

"Good idea," agreed Beltzer. "Why don't we saddle up and charge all three hundred of them? Grow up, Kiall. She's finished."

"Kiall is right," said Okas softly.

Beltzer turned to him, his jaw dropping. "You think we *should* charge them?"

"No, my friend. But she is part of this . . . this quest. I know it. I feel it."

"We're here to rescue a farm girl," said Beltzer.

"Not anymore," said Okas.

"What do you mean?" asked Chareos.

Okas rubbed his tired eyes. "It is coming together now, my friends. All the threads. And I can see them. The girl Ravenna was sold to Jungir Khan. He has bedded her, and it is she who now carries his child. He has made her the Kian of Wolves, the queen. You are seeking to steal the Nadir queen."

Beltzer began to laugh. "Better and better. In that case we *should* charge them. It'll be good practice for when we take on the entire Nadir army!"

"The woman down there is Tenaka Khan's daughter, Jungir's sister. She will know the palace. She will be of great help to us," Okas said.

"Help?" said Chareos. "We can't go on with this. It is madness now to even consider it."

"There is more to this quest than you realize, Chareos

Blademaster," Okas continued. "Far more. Can you not see it? The dream of Bel-azar, the ghost of Tenaka Khan? It is all part of a great whole."

"What part?" asked Finn, kneeling by the Tattooed Man.

"The child," answered Okas. "He will be born early . . . twelve weeks from now. The stars show that he will be great king, perhaps greatest who ever lived. He will be bloodline of Ulric and Tenaka Khan and of Regnak, Earl of Bronze. He will be warrior and statesman. As Nadir khan, he will take his armies across the world."

"Are you saying we should kill the babe?" Beltzer asked.

"No. I am saying you should continue with this quest and see where it leads."

"It will lead to death for all of us," declared Chareos. "We are no longer talking of buying or stealing back a farm girl. We are talking about the Nadir queen!"

"Let me speak," Kiall said softly. "You are right, Chareos. It is all too . . . too overpowering. May I then suggest we take one step at a time? Let us first think of a way to rescue Tanaki. After that we can decide what to do."

Chareos sighed and shook his head. "We are six men in an alien land. And you want us to consider a plan to steal a prisoner from three hundred of the fiercest warriors in the Nadir nation? Well, why not? How many ways can a man die?"

"You don't even want to consider that question," said Harokas. "In Nadir hands a prisoner could be killed slowly over a score of days, with each painful day worse than the last."

"What a sack of comforts you are," snapped Beltzer.

"The sun is going down," said Finn. "If we are going to get the girl, then tonight will be our best chance. Especially if the main force camps outside the walls. Then all we have to do is get down there, sneak past them, climb the walls, kill anyone inside, and carry the girl out."

"Oh, that's all?" Beltzer sneered. "And I know who gets to carry the bitch. It's me, isn't it?"

"Correct," admitted Finn.

"I'll come with you," said Harokas. "I rather like the

woman. You don't mind if I stick close to you, do you, Chareos?"

"Not at all. But stay in front of me, Harokas."

Chareos knelt on the hillside as the sun faded into dusk. The Nadir warriors had dragged the girl out into the open and dropped her naked body in the dust of the square. She was limp as a doll. Two of the men then hauled her up, lifting her onto the auction platform and bending her over the block. Chareos averted his eyes and switched his gaze to the riders beyond the town. They had settled down in the open, setting campfires. The general and four of his men had entered the long hall, which left seventeen men inside the town.

Too many . . .

Kiall brought Chareos a meal of dried meat and fruit, then sat in silence beside him.

What am I doing here? thought Chareos. What is this madness? The woman means nothing to me; this quest is of no consequence. What will it matter to the world in a thousand years if another Nadir khan is born? He gazed down at the still, white form draped over the auction block and the men bearing down on her.

"Do you have a plan?" whispered Kiall. Chareos turned to the pale-faced young man.

"Do you think me some god of war, Kiall? We can get in, possibly without being observed. But then there will be seventeen against seven—six if you discount Okas, who is no warrior. Now, let us assume we could defeat all seventeen. Could we do it silently? No. Therefore, the other warriors outside would be alerted. Can we defeat three hundred? Even you will know the answer to that."

"Then what do you suggest?"

"I don't know, boy!" snapped Chareos. "Go away and let me think!"

The sky darkened, and the moon shone bright. Idea after idea drifted into Chareos' mind, there to be examined, dissected, discarded. Finally he called Finn to him and outlined his thoughts. The hunter listened, his face impassive.

"Is this the only way?" he asked at last.

"If you can think of a better plan, I'll go along with it," answered Chareos.

Finn shrugged. "Whatever you say, Blademaster."

"I say we should all go home and forget this nonsense," said Chareos, forcing a smile.

"That would win my vote," admitted Finn. "So why don't we?"

Chareos shrugged and pointed down to the moonlit town, where the naked form of Tanaki was tied to the auction block.

"We don't know her," said Finn softly.

"No, we do not. But we have seen her suffering. Do I sound as naïve and romantic as Kiall?"

"Yes, but that is no bad thing, my friend. I share your view. Evil will never be countered while good men do nothing."

"Then we are a pair of fools," declared Chareos, and this time the smile was genuine. Finn reached out his hand, and Chareos took it.

"Win or lose, we achieve nothing that the world would understand," said Finn.

"But then, the world does not matter," answered Chareos, rising.

"Indeed it does not," Finn replied. "It is good to understand that."

It was close to midnight when Finn and Maggrig rode from the camp. Chareos, Harokas, Kiall, and Beltzer slowly made their way down the slope toward the stockaded town. Okas remained in the woods, squatting cross-legged, his eyes closed. He began to chant softly, and a mist rose from the grass, swirling out to cloak the four warriors as they moved into the open.

11

THE MIST ROLLED on and down like a ghostly blanket, shimmering in the moonlight. Chareos reached the rear wall of the stockade and located the iron portcullis. Beltzer moved alongside him.

"What now?" whispered the giant.

"We raise it?"

The iron grille was four feet wide and seven feet high. Beltzer handed his ax to Kiall and gripped the lowest bar. The muscles on his neck and shoulders swelled as he applied pressure: the gate creaked and rose an inch. Harokas and Chareos joined him: the gate rose another foot. "That is enough," hissed Kiall, dropping to his back and sliding under the gate.

Chareos turned to Beltzer. "Can you hold it there?"

The giant grunted. Chareos ducked down and rolled under to rise beside Kiall. The two men climbed the rampart steps; there were no sentries posted. Together Kiall and Chareos turned the wheel above the gate, tightening the rope and relieving Beltzer of his burden. Swiftly they returned to the gateway, where Beltzer struggled through, followed by Harokas.

"Now we wait," whispered Chareos.

From beyond the town came the sound of galloping hooves.

Finn rode headlong into the Nadir camp, scattering two fires. Warriors surged up from their blankets as his horse thundered by them. Finn swung the horse to a stop. Notching an arrow to his short hunting bow, he sent a shaft slicing into a man's throat.

From the other side of the camp came a wild yell, and Maggrig galloped into sight through the mist. The Nadir swarmed for their horses. Finn shot a second man, then kicked his mount into a gallop and headed off toward the south. The camp was in an uproar as warriors seized their swords and ran to saddle their mounts. Within minutes the campsite was deserted.

Inside the town Tsudai ran from the hall, mounting the ramparts to watch his soldiers splitting into two groups to hunt down the attackers. He swung to an aide who was running toward him.

"Get out there and find out what is happening!"

The man darted to his horse, vaulted into the saddle, and galloped through the gates.

Chareos and Beltzer climbed through the window at the rear of the long hall and crept forward. Four Nadir officers were sitting around a table, playing dice.

Chareos sprang into the hall, slashing his sword through the throat of the nearest man. Beltzer leapt into action beside him, his ax killing two men before they could rise. The fourth man tried to run and made it to the door, wrenching it open. Harokas' knife plunged into his chest.

Harokas stepped into the doorway, grabbing the man's corpse and lowering it to the floor.

Outside Kiall, keeping close to the shadows, crept toward the auction block where Tanaki lay unconscious. Three men ran into the square, and he ducked behind two water barrels and waited.

The men climbed to the ramparts where Tsudai was watching the chase. Kiall could not hear their conversation. He moved carefully out into the open and climbed to the auction platform, where he knelt by Tanaki and cut the ropes binding her wrists. She moaned as she felt his touch.

"No more," she pleaded. Her eyes were dark and swollen, her lips cut, her body bruised and bleeding. Kiall gritted his teeth and waited. The men on the ramparts came down to the square, and he heard one of them laugh. Hidden behind the block, he saw a Nadir warrior point to

Tanaki, then turn toward her. The others hooted and swung to Tsudai.

"It is still your day," he told them.

The first man clambered to the platform, loosening his belt and dropping his trews. Kiall reared up and plunged his sword into the man's groin.

Tsudai's eyes widened. "Wolves to me!" he yelled, and from the barn came a further nine men, swords in their hands. "Take him!" shouted Tsudai.

The warriors surged forward, but just as they reached the platform, Beltzer came hurtling into them, his ax cleaving and cutting. Chareos and Harokas joined him. Kiall leapt from the platform, cannoning into three men and bearing them down. A sword sliced the skin of his upper arm, but then he was up, his blade slashing at the men beneath him. Harokas ducked under a wild cut and skewered the man before him. His blade sprang clear in time to block a second thrust from another warrior. Chareos dispatched two Wolves, then swung to aid Harokas. Beltzer fought like a man berserk. Within seconds the last Nadir fighting man had been cut down.

Tsudai ran along the ramparts and jumped to the ground, rolling to break his fall. He seized the reins of his horse and vaulted to the beast's bare back. Chareos ran to block his escape, but the horse galloped clear.

"Get the girl!" Chareos shouted.

Beltzer tossed his ax to Kiall and climbed to the platform. Lifting Tanaki, he draped her over his shoulder.

Chareos led the group back to the iron gate and out into the mist-filled night. Slowly they made their way clear, judging their path by the rising ground. Within minutes they heard the sound of horses' hooves. "Down!" hissed Chareos. The group dropped to their bellies. Horsemen passed them by within a few paces. Chareos rose.

"Which way?" whispered Beltzer. They could hear the calling of the Nadir, but the mist had thickened into a deep fog and the sounds were distorted, muffled and eerie. As Chareos led them up the slope, Beltzer was breathing heavily, his face red with exertion.

"I'm not as young as I was," he said, stopping for a moment to get his breath.

A glowing sphere formed in the air before Chareos. "Thank the Source!" he whispered. The sphere floated away to the right. Chareos and the others followed it and soon climbed above the mist into the relative safety of the trees. Okas was still squatting on the grass, but he opened his eyes as the questers entered the clearing. "Sit around me in a circle," he said. "Place the girl at the center." Beltzer gently laid the unconscious Tanaki on the grass, and they formed a circle. Okas closed his eyes and began to chant once more, his voice low and rhythmic. Beltzer looked closely at him. The old man was painfully thin, and his face was streaked with gray, his lips as blue as the tattoos on his chin.

Beltzer nudged Chareos and pointed to Okas. Chareos nodded. Whatever magic the old man was working was taking a terrible toll.

Nadir horsemen rode into the clearing, and Beltzer jerked and reached for his ax, but Chareos gripped his arm. The horsemen seemed insubstantial, like ghosts. They rode slowly past the questers.

Kiall shivered and watched the wraith riders as they passed. Okas opened his eyes and sagged sideways to the grass. Chareos and Kiall moved to him, but the old man waved them away and curled up to sleep. Chareos covered him with a blanket as Kiall turned to the girl. Under the bright moonlight he could see that her face was swollen and bruised. Her left eye was closed tight, the right darkened and discolored. Carefully he lifted the blanket from her body. Her legs and buttocks were also badly bruised and scratched, and there was dried blood on her thighs.

Beltzer knelt on the other side of Tanaki. "You want some help?" he asked Kiall.

"No. There is nothing we can do. But a fire would help; we could keep her warm."

"We cannot risk that," said Chareos. "I don't know how powerful the magic is or how long it will last."

"I do not know why she is still unconscious," said Kiall. "The bruising is severe, but no bones seem to be broken."

"I have seen this before," Chareos told him. "It is not an injury to the body but to the spirit. This is an ugly business, Kiall."

Tanaki moaned softly, and Kiall lay alongside her, stroking her face. "You are well now," he whispered into her ear. "You are with friends. Sleep, lady. Rest." Chareos covered her with his own blanket, while Beltzer removed his jerkin and rolled it for a pillow beneath her head. She turned to one side, her hand outside the blanket. The fingers clenched into a fist, then opened and dug into the earth. Kiall took her hand gently and held it. Tanaki's breathing eased, and she slept.

Three times ghostly Nadir riders entered the clearing. Once a man dismounted within three paces of the questers and knelt to examine the tracks. He looked puzzled and spoke to his companions, but the questers could hear no words. Then he mounted and rode away through the trees.

The night passed slowly. Kiall slept fitfully alongside Tanaki, while Chareos and Beltzer sat talking in low whispers. Harokas moved away to the edge of the trees and slept alone.

Dawn found Chareos and Beltzer on the hillside, scanning the horizon for signs of Finn or Maggrig. The Nadir camp was deserted, the town silent.

"They're canny men," remarked Beltzer. "They'll be all right."

"I wish I could be sure," said Chareos. "The risk was too great; I should never have asked them to go."

"They're grown men; they could have refused. And we did get the girl."

Chareos was tired. His back ached, and he stretched out on the grass. "You should sleep for a while," said Beltzer. "I'll stand watch for Finn."

Chareos nodded. "Keep an eye on the earl's man also. Don't let him move behind you."

"You think he's an assassin?"

"I just think he needs watching." Chareos closed his eyes and drifted off to sleep.

The sun climbed higher as Beltzer sat beside Chareos, his ax in his lap, his mind on the mountain. He felt alive now, almost young again. Almost. Carrying the girl had sapped his strength, as had the battle in the town. His huge hand curled around the ax haft. "There's still a skirmish or two left in us, eh?" he said.

Far off to the west he saw a rider keeping to the low hollows. Beltzer shaded his eyes and tried to identify the man; it looked like Finn. Scanning the hills and hollows, he could see no pursuers. He thought of waking Chareos but hesitated. The blademaster was bone-weary; he needed rest. Slowly the rider made his way up the slope. It *was* Finn. He dismounted and led the horse into the clearing, then walked back to Beltzer.

"Where is Maggrig?" Finn asked.

"He's not back yet," Beltzer told him.

Finn sank to the ground. "I didn't think I'd make it; they almost had me. I killed two of them and then rode into a swirling river. I lost my bow. I thought the horse would drown, and I hung on to the pommel. But he's a good beast. He swam well and found solid ground."

"Get some rest," Beltzer advised him.

Finn shook his head. "I've got to find Maggrig."

"Don't be a fool! The Nadir are everywhere. Maggrig is probably holed up in some cave. He'll wait till nightfall, then make it back. If you ride out there, you'll lead them to him."

Finn sighed. "You are right. I'll sleep for a while. Wake me if he comes."

Beltzer nodded. "We got the girl," he said. "It went well."

Finn did not reply but lay on the grass and closed his eyes. Beltzer sat with his back to a tree and dozed in the morning sunshine. He awoke to see Harokas kneeling beside Chareos. The hawk-nosed warrior was staring intently at the face of the sleeping man; his expression was hard to read, but Beltzer could see that he was troubled.

"Don't wake him," said Beltzer softly, and Harokas looked up.

"I was sent here to kill him."

"I know," said Beltzer. "So does he."

"But there is no need, is there? You have all decided to die. And I am glad to be relieved of the task."

Harokas rose and walked away to his horse. Beltzer watched him mount and ride away.

At the center of the clearing Kiall awoke. He sat up and looked down at Tanaki. Her color was better. Opening his pack, he took out some comfrey leaves, which he mixed with cold water. It was good for swellings, and he labored over the poultice for some time. Satisfied at last, he touched Tanaki's hand, and she awoke with a start.

"You are with friends," he told her, his voice soothing. "It is me, Kiall. I have a poultice here for your eyes. Lie still." She said nothing as he placed the cool cloth over her eyelids. He took her hand and patted it gently.

"The Wolves?" she whispered.

"Gone."

"How did . . . ?"

"Do not talk, lady. Rest. We came into the town last night and slew the men who . . . attacked you. Then we carried you here. You are safe."

"Why?"

"Rest now. Let the poultice do its work." He tried to release her hand, but her fingers gripped his.

"Why?" she asked again.

"Because you were in need," he said lamely. He sat with her for several minutes; then her fingers relaxed their grip, and he saw she was asleep once more. He stood and stretched. Beltzer was asleep by a tree on the crown of the hill, Chareos and Finn lying close by. Of Harokas and Maggrig there was no sign.

The voice of Okas sounded in his mind. *"Kiall, can you hear me?"*

"Yes," he answered aloud, looking down at the old man's sleeping form. The voice was like a whisper through time, impossibly distant yet clear. "I can hear you."

"Tell Chareos to travel to the Mountains of the Moon. Tell him to seek out Asta Khan. Tell him I am sorry."

The voice faded. Kiall moved to Okas and knelt by the body. It was stiff and cold.

The Tattooed Man was dead.

* * *

They buried the old man on the crown of the hill and stood silently around the grave. "The first of us to die," whispered Beltzer, his words hanging in the air. He walked back to the campsite and sat staring at the blades of his ax, twirling the haft in his hands.

"I am sorry," Kiall told Chareos. "I wish I had never asked you to help me. It all seems so futile now. I don't know why."

"We are free men, Kiall. We make our own choices."

"I know that," said the young man. "It is just . . . there is so much savagery. Look at Tanaki. How could men do that to her? I don't understand."

"Be glad that you do not."

"Do you?"

Chareos turned away, staring out over the steppes. "Yes, sadly I do. I would never contemplate such a deed, but yes, I understand it. It is connected with war, Kiall, and the nature of the warrior. He is competitive, and his desire is to dominate and destroy his enemies. But the word to remember is *dominate*. There is another word to consider also: *arousal*. A man can be aroused to anger as easily as he is aroused to rut. The two emotions are closely linked. Anger and lust. So the warrior is aroused in battle and fights to dominate. Tanaki and others like her are the victims of that. Dominated, abused, humiliated."

"They are evil," said Kiall. "Simply that."

"Would that it were so simple. Some of those men will have had wives and children. They might have been good family men; they knew love and compassion in their lives."

"I would show them no compassion. I am glad we killed them."

"Glad? Never be glad another man has died. Not *ever*. Just be relieved that you are alive. I had a teacher once, a great man called Attalis. He told me that the path to evil often begins with righteous anger. A Nadir band raids a Gothir village; they rape and kill. A group of Gothir soldiers set out for revenge; they want to hurt the enemy, so *they* rape and kill. It never ends. Never . . . ever . . . be glad to kill."

Chareos walked away and stood at the graveside. Kiall left him there and wandered over to Beltzer, who was sitting alone. The giant's face was set, but a muscle twitched in his cheek. His eyes were red-rimmed, and he was blinking rapidly.

Kiall sat opposite him. "Are you all right?" asked the younger man.

"Me? I'm fine. I was just thinking that we haven't eaten. I'm starved." His mouth trembled, but he clamped his jaws tight. "Stupid old fool," he said. "Stupid! He killed himself to protect us. Stupid." Beltzer sniffed, then hawked and spit. "Damned if I'm not getting a chill. It's this weather, cold winds and dust. Only the Source knows how people live out here. Give me a city any time . . . and taverns. What are you staring at?"

"I'm sorry," said Kiall. "I didn't mean to stare. He had a message for you, you know. He said to say farewell to old Beltzer."

"Did he? Truly?"

"Yes," said Kiall, continuing the lie. "He didn't sound unhappy."

"You know what the worst thing is, boy? Do you?"

"No."

"He liked me. For myself. Not because I could swing an ax, or kill a few tribesmen. But for *me*. There's not much to like, but he found it. And I'll tell you something—laugh if you like—but I loved that old man. 'Old Beltzer.' That's something, isn't it? I loved him."

"Why would I laugh?"

Tears welled in Beltzer's eyes, flowing to his cheeks and into the red and silver beard. He bowed his head and wept. Kiall reached out and laid a hand on his shoulder.

"Get away!" said Beltzer. "Leave me alone. Can't a man even grieve in private?"

Kiall rose and backed away. Tanaki was awake and sitting in the center of the campsite, a blanket around her shoulders. Her eyes were still swollen, but she could see.

Kiall sat beside her. "How are you feeling?"

"You wouldn't want to know," replied Tanaki. "Did you kill them all?"

"Yes. No. There was one man—the leader, I think—he escaped."

"Good."

Kiall was surprised, but he did not press the point. "Do you wish to be alone?" he asked.

She smiled, then winced as her lip split and a tiny drop of blood formed. "No. You sit close by. I like your company. Why did you rescue me?"

"Does it matter?"

"It does to me."

"Is it not enough that you were alone and needed help?"

"This is not a song or a fable, Kiall. I am not one of your yellow-haired ladies trapped in a tower."

"But you are a princess," he said, smiling. "One should always rescue a princess." She ignored the smile, and annoyance showed in her eyes.

"What about the others? Why did they help?"

"The Tattooed Man asked them to; he said you were part of our quest. Does that satisfy you?"

She nodded. "I will repay you all."

"There is no need."

"I will judge that. I want no debts hanging over me. Where will you go now?"

"To find a man named Asta Khan."

She looked at him, but he could not read her expression through the bruises she bore. "He still lives? Surprising. My father set great store by him."

"He does still," said Kiall.

"What madness are you speaking? My father is dead; he has been for years."

"It is hard to explain."

"Try!" she snapped. "I may be bruised, but there is nothing wrong with my brain."

As best he could, Kiall outlined the duel with the demons and the violet-eyed warrior who had come to his assistance. "Okas told me it was the spirit of Tenaka Khan."

"How did he fight?"

"With two short swords. He spun like a dancer; I have never seen anything like it."

She nodded. "That is one of the names he carried: Bladedancer. He was also the Prince of Shadows."

"Chareos and Beltzer both knew him," said Kiall, "as did Maggrig and Finn. They are the heroes of Bel-azar; he sat with them on the last night of the battle."

"I know. My father told me. They are the ghosts-yet-to-be."

"What does that mean?"

She shrugged. "I do not know. My father was a secretive man. He told me of the warriors of the Gothir; he said one of them was blood kin, a Drenai prince. I would guess that to be Chareos. It is inconceivable that it could be the bald, fat one."

"I know what you mean. Beltzer is not exactly cultured."

The sound of a walking horse came to them, and Beltzer leapt up, his ax in his hands. Kiall stood, drawing his saber, as Harokas guided his mount into the camp and stepped down.

"I thought you had gone for good," said Beltzer.

"So did I," answered Harokas, wearily, "but I found your friend."

"Maggrig?" Beltzer whispered.

"Yes."

Finn lurched to his feet and ran forward. "Where is he?" he shouted, grasping Harokas' black jerkin.

Harokas put his hand on Finn's shoulder. "The Nadir took him."

"Oh, no! Oh, please, no!" cried Finn, stumbling back. He ran to his horse, but Chareos cut him off, grabbing his arms and holding him tight.

"Wait!" said Chareos softly. "We will all go. Calm yourself, my friend."

Finn seemed to sag in Chareos' arms, his head falling to rest on the swordman's shoulder. Chareos turned to Kiall. "Wait here with the woman. We'll be back."

"There's no point," said Harokas. "The Nadir are everywhere. It's madness."

"Even so," replied Chareos, "will you take us to the body?"

"It means that much to you? You'll risk your lives for a corpse?"

"Yes."

Harokas shook his head in disbelief. "Follow me, then, but ride warily."

Trees were sparse as the questers rode in single file behind Harokas, and the land spread out before them in a series of folds and gullies like a giant's cloak carelessly tossed from heaven.

They moved with care for more than an hour, coming at last to a rocky rise. Harokas dismounted and led his horse up the hill, the questers following his lead. He tethered his mount to a skeletal poplar and waited. Chareos joined him. No one had spoken since they had ridden from the camp. Finn stood by, white-faced, expressionless, his eyes tormented. Beltzer was beside him.

"Follow me," whispered Harokas, "and please . . . no heroics."

He led them to a rock face and on into a narrow fissure that wound down to a ledge. There he squatted in the fading light and pointed to the Nadir camp below. The greater part of the three hundred Wolves were there, and six campfires had been set. At the center of the camp, staked out naked on the ground, was Maggrig, his body covered in cuts and burns. Finn groaned, and Beltzer's hand gripped the hunter's shoulder.

"Have you seen enough?" whispered Harokas. "It does not take a warrior's eye to know the man is dead." Chareos nodded. Maggrig had been tortured, his skin partially flayed, his eyes put out.

"They are still searching for you," said Harokas, "so he could have told them nothing. He had courage. Great courage."

"Yes, he did," agreed Chareos, glancing at Finn. "He was a fine man."

"I think his horse broke a leg," continued Harokas. "It was just bad luck. He almost made it to the slopes."

"There's nothing more to see," said Chareos softly. He touched Finn's arm. "Let us go, my friend."

"Yes," murmured Finn.

Harokas backed away from the rim of the ledge, and the questers clambered back through the fissure. As they reached the horses, it was Beltzer who first noticed Finn's absence.

"No!" he cried. Turning, he ran back for the fissure, Chareos and Harokas behind him. They came to the ledge in time to see Finn walking slowly down the scree-covered slope toward the Nadir camp. Beltzer made as if to follow him, but Chareos grabbed the neck of his jerkin, hauling him from his feet.

Beltzer hit the ground hard. He stared up into Chareos' face. "Leave it be," said Chareos. "He wouldn't want you there; you know that."

Beltzer tried to speak, but no words came. He rolled to his knees, gathered his ax, and stumbled back through the fissure. Harokas knelt beside Chareos.

The blademaster ignored him, his eyes fixed on the small, dark figure closing on the Nadir camp. It would be so easy, thought Harokas, his hand on the hilt of his dagger . . . just slip the blade through his ribs, sliding it up into the heart. So easy. Then he could return to the earl, claim his gold, and get on with his life. But that would mean leaving Tanaki. He cursed inwardly and took his hand from the hilt.

Below them Finn reached the bottom of the slope and walked forward, back straight, head high. There was a roaring in his ears like the distant sea, and his eyes were misted. So many years together, years of joy and fear. It never paid to love too much; he'd always known that. All life was balance. There was always a reckoning. Better by far not to have loved at all. He walked past two Nadir warriors who were honing their swords; they stared at him for a moment, then rose behind him. Steadily Finn walked on. He could see Maggrig now and the terrible cruelty they had unleashed on him. A man seized Finn's arm. Almost absently, Finn plunged his hunting knife into the warrior's throat.

There had been that time when Maggrig had gone down with the red plague. No one survived that, but Finn had sat with him, begging him to live. The fever had burned all the flesh from Maggrig's body, leaving translucent skin stretched tightly over the bones. But Finn had nursed him to health. He remembered the day he had first realized Maggrig was going to live. The sky had been gray and overcast, the mountains covered with mist. Moisture dripped from the trees, yet the day had been beautiful, so incredibly beautiful that Finn had been unable to look on it without tears.

A second warrior came at him. Finn killed him, but the man's sword plunged into Finn's side. There was little pain. He staggered on. Something struck him in the back, but he ignored it. Close to the body now, he fell to his knees and slashed his knife through the ropes binding Maggrig's arms to the stakes. Dropping his knife, he lifted Maggrig's head. Blood gushed into Finn's throat, but he spit it clear.

"You are nothing but trouble to me, boy," he said, struggling to lift the stiffening corpse.

A spear hammered into his back, smashing through his ribs and exiting from the chest. He felt Maggrig slipping from his hands and tried hard to lower the body gently to the earth.

Slowly he toppled, his head resting on Maggrig's chest.

If he could just get Maggrig to the mountains, all would be well. The sky would be gray and overcast, the mist clinging to the trees.

If he could just . . .

Swords and knives plunged into Finn's body, but he did not feel them.

High on the ledge Chareos watched it all. His hands were trembling, and he tore his eyes from the scene, staring down at the ground. He sucked in a deep breath, then leaned back. For several minutes he sat in silence, remembering Finn and Maggrig as they had been back at Bel-azar. Then he turned to Harokas. "You had your chance," he said softly. "It will not come again. Why did you not kill me?"

Harokas spread his hands and said nothing. Chareos backed away from the ledge and returned to the horses. Beltzer was sitting on a rock, his ax on the ground beside him.

"Did he die well?" asked the giant.

"Yes . . . whatever that means," answered Chareos. He stepped into the saddle. "Let's get back."

"What are we going to do, Blademaster?" Beltzer asked. "Yesterday seems so far away now. Okas is dead. Finn and Maggrig are dead. Do we go on?"

"What do we have to go back to? We go on." Touching heels to the gray, Chareos rode out of the clearing. Beltzer gathered his ax, mounted, and followed him.

For some time Harokas waited. Finally he vaulted into the saddle and rode after them. Chareos heard him coming and reined in as the assassin came alongside.

"Well?" asked Chareos.

"You can't take on the Nadir army with three men," said Harokas.

"What do you suggest?"

"Four would even the odds."

12

CHIEN-TSU OPENED HIS eyes. Around him the mountains reared like the spears of the gods, looming and threatening. An icy wind howled through the crags. His servant, Oshi, was huddled by a small fire, his face blue with cold. Chien shivered.

"She is dead," he said, picturing Mai-syn as he had last seen her, radiant and happy, her dress of yellow silk shining in the sunlight.

"As always, then, lord, you were correct," said Oshi.

"I had hoped to be wrong. Come, let us find a cave." Oshi was reluctant to leave even the illusory warmth of the small fire, but he rose without complaint, and the two men led their horses along the winding mountain path. There were no trees at this height, only an occasional stunted shrub cloaked in snow. The walls of the mountains rose sheer to the left and right of the travelers, and there was no sign of a cave or shelter of any kind beyond shallow depressions in the rock face. Oshi was convinced they would die there. It was three days since they had eaten, and that had been a stringy hare brought down by an arrow from Chien's bow.

They walked on. Chien did not feel the cold; he closed his mind to it and thought instead of the beautiful Mai-syn. He had spirit-searched the land, seeking her soul, listening for the music of her spirit.

His mood was dark now and colder than the mountain winds.

The trail dropped into a narrow valley, then rose again. For a while they rode, but it seemed colder to sit immobile on a saddle, and they dismounted. Oshi stumbled and fell, and Chien turned. "Are you weary, old man?"

"A little, lord," he admitted.

Chien moved on. He could not stop the servant from addressing him with his title and had long since given up the effort.

They rounded a bend in the trail and saw an elderly man sitting cross-legged on a rock. He seemed incredibly ancient, the skin of his face weathered like sandstone. He was wearing only a loincloth of pale skin and a necklace of human teeth; his body was emaciated, the bones sharp and jutting like knife blades under leather. Snow had settled on his skeletal shoulders.

"Good evening, old father," greeted Chien, bowing.

The old man looked up, and as Chien met his gaze, he shuddered inwardly. The eyes were blacker than night and cold with an ancient malice. The man smiled, showing several blackened teeth.

His voice whispered out like a breeze across tombstones. "Mai-syn angered Jungir Khan. He threw her to his Wolves, who used her and threw her back. In her despair she cut her throat with a pair of silver scissors. It happened less than a month after her arrival."

Chien felt his stomach heave, but he fought to keep all expression from his face.

"A simple 'good evening' would have been sufficient to open the conversation, old father. But thank you for the information."

"I do not have the time for pleasantries, Chien-tsu, or the elaborate and inane rituals of the Kiatze." The old man laughed. "Look around you—this is Nadir land. It is cold, inhospitable. Only the strong survive. Here there are no green fields, no verdant pastures. A warrior is old by the time he is thirty. We have no energy to spend on pretty words." He waved one hand. "But that is of no matter. It is important only that you are here and that your desire for vengeance is strong. Follow me." Nimbly he leapt from the rock and walked away into the snow.

"He is a demon," wailed Oshi. "That loincloth is human skin."

"I do not care for his lack of sartorial elegance," said Chien. "If he is a demon, I will deal with him, but let us hope he is a demon with a warm cave."

They followed the old man to what seemed a sheer rock face. He disappeared, and Oshi began to tremble, but Chien walked to the rock wall and found a narrow opening that was almost invisible from the outside. He led his horse within, and Oshi followed him.

Inside it was dark and cold. From somewhere in the shadows Chien heard a soft chanting. Torches sprang to life in rusted brackets on the walls. His horse reared, but he calmed the beast, stroking its neck and whispering soothing words. The travelers moved on into a torch-lit tunnel that branched out into a deep cave where a fire was burning without wood.

"Sit," said Asta Khan. "Warm yourselves." He turned to Oshi. "I am not a demon; I am worse than demons. But you have no need to fear me."

"Thank you, sir. Thank you," said Oshi, bowing deeply.

Asta Khan ignored him, locking his gaze to Chien. "And you do not fear me at all, man of Kiatze. That is good. I am not comfortable around fearful men. Sit! Sit! Make yourselves comfortable. It is long since I had visitors."

"How long have you been here?" Chien asked, settling himself by the magical fire.

"I came when my lord was murdered. He was Tenaka Khan, the Khan of Wolves, the Prince of Shadows," related the old man, his eyes shining with pride. "He was the great one, the heir of Ulric."

"I believe I have heard the name," Chien said. Anger flashed in Asta's eyes, but he masked it and smiled thinly.

"All men have heard it, even the soft-bellied Kiatze. But let it pass. Your people are renowned for cynicism, but I watched you fight, Chien-tsu. I saw you kill Kubai and the others. You are skillful and fast. Very fast."

"And you have need of my skills, old father?"

"I see your mind works as swiftly as your body. Yes, I have need of you. And you have need of me. It makes for an interesting debate, I think. Which of us needs the other more?"

"Not at the moment," replied Chien. "As matters stand, I need you not at all."

"Then you know how to get into the khan's palace?" asked Asta.

"Not yet. But I will find a way."

"No," Asta said, "you will not. But I can take you on a path which leads to the throne room. Alone you would not survive, for there are the dwellers in the dark to stop you. I will give you Jungir Khan. I will give you the means of vengeance."

"And in return, old father?"

"You will aid the ghosts-yet-to-be."

"Explain further."

Asta shook his head. "First we will eat. I can hear your servant's belly rumbling. Take your bow and walk from the cave. A deer is waiting there—kill it."

Chien rose and walked back to the cave entrance. The old man had been right, for a doe stood trembling near the entrance, her eyes open and unblinking. Chien notched an arrow and stood for a moment looking at the beast, then turned and retraced his steps.

"Oshi, take a knife and dispatch the beast. There is no sport there."

Asta Khan cackled loudly, rocking back and forth on his haunches.

Chien ignored him. "Tell me of Tenaka Khan," he said, and the old man took a deep breath.

"He was the sun and moon of the Nadir people, but he was cursed with tainted blood. Half Drenai, half Nadir, he allowed himself to love a woman. I do not mean to take her for his own, although he did this. But he surrendered his soul to her. She died giving birth to his daughter, Tanaki, and in dying she took part of the khan's soul to hell or heaven. He ceased to care about his life, allowing the years to drift by. His son, Jungir, poisoned him. That is Tenaka Khan. What more do you wish to know?"

"You were his shaman?"

"I was, and I am. I am Asta Khan. I placed the helm of

Ulric on his head. I rode beside him when he conquered the Drenai and the Vagrians, when the armies of the Nadir rode into Mashrapur and Lentria. He was the fulfilment of our dreams. He should never have died. He should have lived forever, like a god!"

"And what do you seek, Asta Khan?" asked Chien. "Not merely vengeance?"

Asta's eyes shone for a moment, then he looked away. "What I desire is of no concern to you. It is enough that I can give you that which you desire."

"At this moment I desire nothing more than a hot bath."

"Then you shall have one," said Asta, rising. "Follow me." The old man rose and walked to the back of the cave, where a shallow pool had filled with melted snow from a fissure above. Asta knelt by it, dipping his hand to the water. He closed his eyes and spoke three harsh-sounding words that were lost on Chien. The water began to bubble and hiss, steam rising.

"A hot bath for the Kiatze lord," said Asta, standing. "Is there anything else you require?"

"A young concubine to read me the works of Lu-tzan?"

"Make do with the hot bath," Asta told him, striding away.

Chien stripped out of his clothes and slid into the pool. The water was hot but not uncomfortable despite having reached the boiling point. He recalled the story of Hai-chuan, a young man accused of stealing a royal gem. Hai-chuan had pleaded innocence and had been sentenced to trial by ordeal. He had to place his hands in a pot of boiling water. If he was innocent, the gods would protect his flesh; if he was guilty, his skin would blister and burst. He was from the mountains and begged the magistrate to allow him to suffer his ordeal directly under the gaze of the All-father in heaven. Touched by his piety, the magistrate agreed, and Hai-chuan was taken to the top of a high mountain. There they boiled a pot of water, and he placed his hands within it. There was not a mark on him, and he was freed. Later he sold the gem and lived like a prince. Chien smiled. It was due to the altitude, he knew. Water boiled at a much lower temperature in the mountains.

He lazed for a while in the water, then climbed out and returned to the fire to sit naked by the flames.

Oshi had cut the best pieces from the loins of the doe, and the smell of cooking meat filled with cave.

"Now tell me of the ghosts-yet-to-be," Chien said.

Tanaki watched the men ride away, then eased herself to her feet, stifling a groan as pain roared through her. Unsteadily she rose and straightened her back. Nausea threatened to swamp her, but she forced her stomach to remain calm.

"You should rest," said Kiall, who had moved alongside her, one hand held out.

She made no reply. Bending to one side, she gently stretched the muscles of her waist and hips. Lifting her arms over her head, she eased the tension in her neck and shoulders. Her father had taught her those exercises many years before. "The warrior's body," he had said, "must always be supple." More confident now, she spun on her heel and leapt, twisting in the air. She landed clumsily.

"Can I help?" asked Kiall.

"Yes. Hold out your hands." He did so, and her long leg swung up, her heel resting on his palms. She bent forward, grasping the back of her ankle, holding the position for a while and then switching to the other leg. Finally she lifted the blanket from her shoulders and stood naked before Kiall. He blushed and cleared his throat. "Place your hands on my shoulders," she said, turning her back on him, "and gently press at the muscles with your thumbs. Where they are rounded and supple, move on. Where they are knotted and tense, ease them."

"I do not know how," he told her, but tentatively his hands touched her skin. She sat down on her blanket with Kiall kneeling behind her. Her skin was smooth and white, the muscles beneath it strong and firm, as his fingers moved over her.

"Relax, Kiall. Close your eyes. Think of nothing. Let your hands search."

His fingers slid down over the shoulder blades. The muscles on the right side felt as if pebbles had been inserted into them. With great care he rubbed at them, growing more confident as the tautness faded. "That is good," she told him. "You have fine hands, healing hands."

He could feel himself becoming aroused and hated himself for it. After what she had been through, it was wholly wrong for a man to react to her in that way. His hands losing their sureness, he stood and walked away. Tanaki covered herself with the blanket cloak and lay back on the ground. The pain of her body was less severe now, but she would never forget the abject humiliation she had suffered. The memory of the sweating men, the stink of them, the pawing and the pain would remain with her always. She shivered and rolled to her feet. Kiall's horse stood tethered nearby; she saddled him and stepped into the stirrup, easing herself to his back. Kiall saw her and ran forward. "Where are you going?" he asked, his voice full of concern.

"I cannot start the rest of my life dressed like this," she said. "My clothes are down there in the hall. And I will need weapons."

"I'll come with you," he offered, holding out his hand. She took it, and he vaulted to the saddle behind her. "This is not wise, Tanaki."

"The merits cannot be decided until we are done," she told him.

The bodies had been removed from the settlement, but dried blood still stained the ground and the wood of the auction platform. Tanaki slid from the saddle and entered the hall. Kiall tethered his horse and moved to the ramparts, keeping watch for Nadir warriors. As the minutes passed, he felt the tension rise. Hearing the sound of booted feet on the steps, he whirled, scrabbling for his saber. Tanaki laughed at him. She was clad now in trousers of soft oiled leather and high riding boots. Her upper body was clothed in a matching hooded tunic, and two short swords were belted at her hips. Over her shoulder was slung a fur-lined cloak of black leather, and in her hand she carried a canvas pack.

"You have all you need?" he asked.

"Not quite. I need the head of Tsudai—but that will come to me."

They rode back to the campsite and tethered the horse. Tanaki drew her swords. "Come," she said to Kiall, "show me your skill."

"No, I . . . I'm not very good. I am not a warrior, you see."

"Show me."

Embarrassed, he drew his saber and dropped into the stance Chareos had taught him. As she leapt forward, his saber blocked her thrust, but she spun, her second sword blade falling to touch his neck. "You are too stiff," she told him.

"I loosen up when I am afraid," he said with a smile.

"Then be afraid!" she said, her voice low and chilling. Her sword swept toward his head, and he jumped back, but she followed him in. He blocked one thrust, then a second . . . she spun, but he dropped to his knees, her blade slashing the air where his head had been. As her sword sliced down, he dived to his left and rolled. "That is better," she said, "but unless you are a master—which you are not—you should fight with saber and knife. That would double your killing power."

Sheathing her blades, she walked to the brow of the hill, staring out over the land.

Kiall joined her. "You still intend to rescue your lady?" she asked him.

"Yes, if I can. But she is not my lady; she never was. I know that now."

"You blame me for that, Kiall."

"I blame you for nothing, Princess. I was foolish. I had a dream, and I thought that dream was real."

"We are full of dreams," she said. "We long for the unattainable. We believe in the nonsense of fables. There is no pure love; there is lust and there is need."

"I do not believe that, Princess."

"Another dream you think is real?"

"I hope not. There is so much sadness and hatred in the world. It would be a terrible thing if love was an illusion."

"Why did you walk away from me earlier, when you were touching me?"

"I . . . I don't know."

"You lie, Kiall. I could feel the growing warmth in your hands. You wanted to bed me, did you not?"

"No!" he replied instinctively, then looked away, reddening. "Yes, I did," he said angrily. "And I know it was wrong."

"Wrong? You are a fool, Kiall. It was honest lust. Do not be ashamed of it, but do not write poems about it, either. I have had fifty lovers. Some were gentle, some were cruel, and some I even grew fond of. But love? If it existed, I would have found it by now. Oh, Kiall, do not look so shocked. Life is short. Joy is everything. To deny that is to deny life."

"You have the advantage of me," he said softly. "I do not have your experience of life. I was raised in a village where we farmed and raised cattle and sheep. But there were people there who had been together for half a lifetime. They were happy; I believe they loved one another."

She shook her head. "A man and a woman are drawn together by animal passions; they stay together for security. But if a better, perhaps richer man comes along or a younger, more beautiful woman, then—and only then—can you test their *love*. Look at you, Kiall. Three days ago you loved a woman enough to risk death for her. Now you say you did not love her, after all. And why? Because I appeared. Does that not prove my point?"

He remained silent for several seconds, staring out over the horizon. Finally he spoke. "It proves only that I am a fool. That is not hard to do."

Tanaki moved to him. "I am sorry, I should not say these things. I thank you for rescuing me. I will be grateful to you all the days of my life. It was noble of you—and courageous. And I thank you also for walking away back there; that was considerate. But give me a few days and I will teach you joy."

"No!" he said. "I do not want to learn that kind of joy."

"Then remain a fool," she snapped, turning and stalking away to sit alone.

For almost three weeks the questers journeyed more deeply into the lands of the Nadir, moving across the desolate steppes toward the far gray mountains. Occasionally they stayed in small Nadir tent settlements, but mostly they camped in hidden gullies, caves, or hollows. There was no sign of pursuit, and they saw nothing of the soldiers of Tsudai.

Chareos said little during their journey. His face was set and grim, his eyes haunted. Beltzer, too, had little to say. Harokas proved adept with the bow and twice brought down deer. But mostly their food came from the land in the shape of long, twisted roots, purple in color, which made a thin but nourishing soup.

Tanaki recovered well and often entered into bantering conversations with Harokas, but Kiall saw the fear in her eyes when any of the questers came too close, watched her flinch at a touch. For some days he said nothing of it. He treated her with courtesy, though she ignored him most of the time; he guessed she was still angry at what she saw as his rejection of her.

But one night she awoke screaming, rolling from her blankets and scrabbling for her swords. Beltzer was up instantly, his silver ax in his hands. Chareos and Kiall moved to her.

"It is all right," said Chareos, reaching out. "It was only a dream."

"Get back! Don't touch me!" screamed Tanaki. Her sword snaked out, and Chareos leapt back, the blade missing him by a finger's breadth.

"Tanaki?" said Kiall softly. "All is well. You were dreaming. You are with friends. Friends."

She stepped back, her breath ragged, her violet eyes wide and frightened. Gradually her breathing grew more calm. "I am sorry," she whispered, and turning on her heel, she walked from the campsite. Beltzer returned to his blankets, grumbling. Kiall walked after Tanaki, coming upon her sitting on a flat rock. Her moonlit face was pale as ivory, and he was struck anew by her beauty. For a moment he said nothing, then he sat beside her.

She swung to face him. "They must think me weak," she said.

"No one thinks that," he assured her. "But I do not know

how to help you, Tanaki. I can heal bruises, stitch wounds, prepare herbs that will bring down fevers. But I cannot deal with your pain."

"I have no pain," she said. "I am healed."

"I do not think so. Every night you toss and turn. Often you cry out, and sometimes you even weep. It hurts me to see you in pain."

Suddenly she laughed and stood with hands on hips, facing him. "I know what you want," she said. "You want what those soldiers wanted. Admit it. Be a man! Do not come to me with your 'It hurts me to see you in pain.' You don't care for me. And why should you? As far as you are concerned, I'm just another Nadir bitch, to be used when you desire it."

"That's not how I see you," he said. "Yes, you are beautiful. Yes, any man would desire you. But I was talking of friendship—and I do care."

"Well, I don't want your pity, either," she snapped. "I'm not some colt with a broken leg or a blind puppy."

"Why are you so angry with me? If I have said or done anything to upset you, then I apologize."

She seemed about to speak, but her breath came out in a long sigh and she sagged back to the stone beside him. "I am not angry with you, Kiall." She closed her eyes and leaned forward, her elbows resting on her knees. "It is not you," she repeated. "I cannot put it behind me. Every time I close my eyes, I can see their faces, feel their hands, their . . . Every time. When I sleep, they come for me. And in my dreams I think that the rescue was the dream and *this* is the reality. I keep thinking about it. It isn't the rape itself or the beating; it is . . ."

Her voice faded for a moment, and Kiall said nothing, allowing the silence to grow. "I have always known about such atrocities, but until you suffer, you cannot understand the enormity of it. And worse, you cannot explain it. Two of those men were once palace guards at Ulrickham. One of them used to carry me on his shoulders when I was a child. So I ask myself, How could he do that to me? And why would he want to? I feel as if the world was never how I saw it—as if a gossamer veil hung before my eyes which they ripped away, leaving me to see the vileness that is reality. Only a few weeks ago I would see that look in Harokas' eye, and I would take it as a compliment. It would make me feel good. Now? Now it is like the look a fox gives a chicken, and it terrifies me." She looked up at him. "Do you understand any of this?"

"I understand *all* of it," he told her. He held out his hand, but she backed away from it. "Fear," he said gently, "is usually good. It stops us from being reckless; it gives us caution. But Chareos says that fear is a servant who longs to be the master. And he is a terrible master who must be fought, held in thrall. You are strong, Tanaki. You are iron. You are proud. Take my hand."

"I don't think that I can," she said.

"Think back to the woman I first met. You are still her. You have suffered, but you are still the Princess Tanaki, daughter of Tenaka Khan. In you is the blood of greatness."

He held out his hand, and her fingers lifted toward it, fell away, then rose swiftly to hold tightly to his.

Tears welled in her eyes, and she sank forward against him. He put his arm around her and sat with her for some time, neither of them speaking. At last she pulled away.

"Then we are friends?" she asked.

"Always," he told her, smiling.

Together they walked back to the camp, where Chareos was sitting alone, staring up at the eastern sky. He did not seem to notice them, and Kiall wandered over to him.

"How are you faring?" he asked.

Chareos looked up. "I do not need to be comforted," he said with a wry smile. "You did well by her. You are a good man."

"You followed me?"

"Yes. But I did not stay long. She's a fine woman, Kiall. Strong and beautiful."

"I know that," said the younger man, uncomfortable.

"If you were to ask me for advice—which you won't—I would tell you to take her away from here. Return to the lands of the Gothir, marry, and raise tall sons."

"And what would you do?" asked Kiall.

"I would continue this mad quest," answered Chareos.

"Yes, I know. You cannot stop now," said Kiall sadly. "Now that it has cost the lives of three of your friends."

"You are a gifted young man, Kiall. Intuitive and intelligent."

"I wish I had never asked you for aid. I mean that truly."

"I know. Sleep well, boy."

During the weeks that followed Tanaki found herself constantly watching Kiall, enjoying his hesitant, nervous smile, the tilt of his head as he spoke. She had not completely lost her nervousness with the others, but Kiall's friendship had given her strength to battle her fears. During the long evenings Tanaki would walk away from the others and sit with her back to a rock or a tree and watch the men. They talked little, but in their movements there was much to read. Beltzer was a bear, a great ambling powerhouse filled with a bitterness he could not voice. Yet his actions were sure and confident, and his speed belied his bulk. Chareos was the timber wolf, lean and canny, always checking the back trail, always thinking, always aware. Harokas was the leopard, sleek yet savage.

And Kiall?

He was the strongest of them all, confident enough to be gentle, humble enough to be wise. His was the strength born of caring, whereas the others had built their fortresses on their talent for violence.

But what animal? she wondered. She sat back and closed her eyes, allowing her mind to relax into memories. She was back in the cold palace of Ulrickham. Jungir was playing with a set of carved soldiers, setting them out in battle formation, while she was sitting on a bearskin rug snuggled up against Nameas, the huge war hound. He had been a gift to Tenaka from the Gothir regent, and he had followed the khan on every hunt. Nameas was a killer in war, his terrible jaws rending and tearing, yet in the palace he was soft and gentle, turning his great head every now and then to lick the infant curled up beside him.

Yes, that was Kiall. The war hound.

Often Tanaki would smile and beckon Kiall to her, and they would sit long into the evening talking. She would reach out her hand, and he would take it, and they would sit beneath the stars.

One evening, in the third week of travel, she was sitting alone when a shadow fell across her. She thought it was Kiall and looked up, smiling.

"May I join you, Princess?" asked Harokas, sitting down beside her.

She swallowed hard and held the smile in place. "I did not expect you to join this quest," she said. "I have always thought of you as a man who looks out only for himself."

"As always, you are correct, Tanaki," he said. "The quest means nothing to me."

"Then why are you with us?"

"That should be obvious," he told her, reaching out to touch her arm. She shrank back instinctively, and his face darkened.

"You were not so coy back in the settlement, as I recall. Many was the time you invited me to your bed on cold winter evenings."

"That was then," she said, holding her back stiff against the tree.

"And what has changed? We were good together, Tanaki. You were the best I ever had. And did I not satisfy you?"

"Yes, you did. You are an unselfish lover, Harokas. You know how to wait. But I have changed."

He laughed and shook his head. "Changed? No, not you. You are a lusty wench, and in any civilized land you would be the king's courtesan. No, don't fool yourself. You will never change." He moved back from her, his dark eyes scanning her face. "At first I thought it was the rape, but it's not, is it? It's the farm boy. Tanaki of the Blades has fallen for a virgin!" He chuckled. "There's a story to liven a dull evening."

"Be careful, Harokas," she warned him. "My patience is not much spoken of—and with good reason. Leave me alone."

He shook his head, and his face grew grave. "I could never do that, Princess. You are in my blood. I want you more than I ever wanted anything."

For a moment she said nothing, then she rose. "What we

had was good. It was more than good. But it is in the past; there is no more to be said."

He pushed himself to his feet and bowed elaborately. "I think you are wrong, Tanaki. But I will not push myself at you; I will be here when you come to your senses. The farm boy is not for you; he never could be. What does he know? I have seen you holding hands. Sweet! But take him to your bed and he'll rut like the peasant he is. And without his innocence what will he be save yet another farmer? You know what the attraction is for you, don't you? It has been the same since the beginning of time, my love: the desire of the experienced for the innocent, the magnetic lure of virginity. There is an excitement there; you become the first and therefore unforgettable. But what then? No, Tanaki, it has not all been said yet. Good night to you."

Chien-tsu watched the small group as they angled their horses across the pass. He noted that the lead rider paused often to study the trail: left and right, front and back. A careful man, then. Chien nodded in appreciation. He stood, beckoned Oshi, and walked out to meet the riders as they reined in. A huge man on a swaybacked gelding lifted a double-headed ax in both hands and slid from the saddle, but Chien ignored him. He reached the lead rider and gave a bow that was a fraction lower than what was required.

"You would be Chareos the Blademaster," said Chien, looking up into the man's dark eyes.

"And you are from Kiatze," responded Chareos, stepping down to stand before the small warrior.

Chien was both gratified and annoyed. It was good to be recognized as a superior human being, but the man had not returned his bow, and that spoke of ill breeding. "Yes, my name is Chien-tsu. I am the ambassador from the court of Kiatze. The shaman Asta Khan asked me to guide you to him."

"I don't like the look of him, Blademaster," said Beltzer, moving alongside Chareos.

"And I am not overly impressed with you," remarked Chien. "Save for the smell, which is truly awe-inspiring."

"You have a large mouth for such a little man," Beltzer hissed.

"Better that than to be a giant with a brain the size of a pebble," replied Chien, stepping back and dropping into a hand-fighting stance.

"Be silent, Beltzer," said Chareos. "We have enough enemies without adding more." He turned to Chien and bowed deeply. "It is a pleasure to meet you, Ambassador. You will forgive, I hope, the words of my companion. We have been riding for weeks with little food, and we have lost three of our comrades. We are short on provisions, on stamina, and on courtesy."

Chien nodded. "A graceful apology, sir. Perhaps you would follow me, and then we can see to the introductions. There is venison and a warm fire in the cave."

Chien spun on his heel and marched off, followed by Oshi. Beltzer grinned. "Plucky little gamecock, isn't he? I'm damned if I don't like him."

"That is just as well," said Chareos softly. "Had you attacked him, he would have killed you." Without another word Chareos stepped into the saddle and touched his heels to the gray.

At the cave the questers finished the venison with a speed that, to Chien at least, was more gorging than dining. Still, they were barbarians, after all, and little more could be expected of them.

"Where is Asta Khan?" asked Chareos, wiping the fat from his fingers onto the front of his shirt.

"Sleeping," answered Chien. "He will join us this evening. Perhaps we could complete the introductions."

"Of course. Well, that is Beltzer." The giant grinned and thrust out a hand. Chien looked down at it with some distaste. It had all the aesthetic appeal of a shovel: the fingers were thick and short, ingrained with dirt, and there were grease stains on the skin. Chien sighed and gripped the hand briefly. Harokas merely nodded, as did Tanaki, but Kiall also offered his hand. This one at least was clean.

"So why is an ambassador from the east dressed as a Nadir rider?" asked Chareos.

Chien told him of the bridal gift and the attack on his

party. "Unfortunately, treachery is a way of life among the Nadir," he said.

"Not only the Nadir," put in Tanaki, her face blushing. "The Gothir, too, have a long history of betrayal and broken promises."

"I am sorry, Princess," said Chareos. "You are of course correct; it was a discourteous comment. But tell me, Ambassador, what are your plans? Why have you not tried to reach a port for a ship home?"

"All in its own time, Chareos," answered the warrior. "But for now I have offered my aid to Asta Khan, and he is willing to help you. That, I believe, makes us companions."

"You are more than welcome to travel with us, but I would appreciate knowing your purpose. It does not sit well with me to have a comrade whose plans are a mystery."

"That I can understand. But I will follow your lead and even your instructions as leader of the group. You need know no more. When my own plans are more stone than smoke, I will inform you—and we will part company."

Chien moved to the rear of the cave and settled down alongside a second fire that had been built for him by Oshi. He was more relaxed now. Chareos was almost civilized and a thinking man. Beltzer was obviously no great thinker, but he wielded the huge ax as if it had no weight at all. The woman was unusual—great facial beauty but with a body too stringy and boylike for Chien's taste. Yet her eyes radiated strength and purpose. Chien could identify no weak point within the group, and that pleased him.

He settled down to sleep.

Chareos wandered to the cave mouth, looking up at the stars. There were few clouds, and the vault of heaven was enormous, breathtaking in its scale.

"Welcome to my hearth," said a sibilant voice, and Chareos felt the hairs at the nape of his neck stiffen. He turned slowly. Squatting in the shadows was an old man wearing a thin loincloth of skin and a necklace of human teeth.

"Thank you, Asta Khan," replied Chareos, moving to sit opposite the old man. "I am glad to see you well."

"Your aid was vital. I will not forget it."

"Okas is dead," said Chareos.

"I know. Protecting me was a great trial for him, and he had little strength left. Now I shall aid you. I know a way into the city, into the bowels of the palace. There you can rescue the woman."

"Why would you do this, shaman? And do not tell me about paying a debt: that is not the Nadir way. What do you hope to gain?"

"What does it matter?" asked Asta, his face a mask, his eyes cold and impenetrable.

"I do not enjoy playing another man's game."

"Then let me say this: I have no interest in the woman. You may take her. That is what you want, is it not? There is nothing else you desire?"

"That is true enough," answered Chareos, "but now I have two men with their own secret plans."

Asta cackled, and the sound made Chareos shiver. "The Kiatze? He wishes only to kill Jungir Khan. No more. When the time is right, he will leave you. Now you have only one man to concern yourself with."

Chareos was uneasy, but he said nothing. He did not like Asta Khan and knew there was more to be said. Yet he could find no words. The old man watched him, his eyes unblinking. Chareos had the feeling his mind was being read.

"You must rest tonight," said Asta. "Tomorrow we walk the Path of Souls. It will not be an easy journey, but with luck and courage, we will pass through."

"I have heard of this path," whispered Chareos. "It is between worlds, and it is said to be inhabited by evil creatures. Why must we walk it?"

"Because even as we speak, the general Tsudai is riding toward us. He will be in the mountains by dawn. But of course you may prefer to fight three hundred men . . ."

"Three of our party are dead already. I wish to see no more die."

"Sadly, Chareos, such is the fate of the ghosts-yet-to-be."

13

BELTZER COULD NOT sleep. He lay back in the flickering torchlight and closed his eyes, but all he could see was the faces of Finn, Maggrig, and Okas. Rolling to his side, he opened his eyes. His ax was resting against the cave wall beside him and he looked at his reflection in the broad blades.

You look like your father, he told himself, remembering the grim-faced farmer and his constant, unrelenting battle against poverty. Up an hour before dawn, in bed at midnight, day in day out, engaged in a war he could never hope to win. The farmland was rocky, nearly barren, but somehow his father had fought the sterile environment, producing enough food to feed Beltzer and his five brothers. By the time Beltzer was fourteen three of the brothers had gone, run away in search of an easier life in the city. The other two had died with his mother during the red plague. Beltzer stayed on, working alongside the bitter old man until at last, while guiding the plow horses, his father had clutched his chest and sagged to the ground. Beltzer had been felling trees in the high meadow and had seen him fall. He had dropped his ax and sprinted down to him, but when he had arrived, the old man was dead.

Beltzer could not remember one kind word from his father and had seen him smile only once, when he was drunk one midwinter evening.

He had buried him in the thin soil and had walked from the farmhouse without a backward glance.

Of his brothers he heard nothing. It was as if they had never been.

His mother was a quiet woman, tough and hardy. She, too, had rarely smiled, but when he thought back, he realized she had had little to smile about. He had been beside her when she died. Her face had lost its perennial weariness; she had been almost pretty then.

Beltzer sat up, feeling melancholy. Looking around, he saw Chareos asleep by the dying fire. He rose and took his ax, wanting to see the stars, feel the night wind on his face.

He missed Finn. That night on the gate tower when the Nadir had dragged the bowman from the walls, Beltzer had leapt in among them, cleaving and killing. He had been amazed to find Chareos and Maggrig beside him. Stooping, he had lifted Finn to his back and run for the gate.

Later, when Finn had recovered consciousness, his gashed brow bandaged, Beltzer had gone to him.

"How do you feel?" he had asked.

"I'd be a damn sight better if you hadn't rapped my head against that doorpost," Finn had grumbled.

By all the gods in heaven, that was a time to be alive!

Beltzer felt the breeze on his face and strolled into the last tunnel.

He stopped in his tracks . . .

Before him were scores of Nadir warriors, creeping in through the entrance. They had not seen him, and he quickly stepped back into the shadows.

He thought of his friends sleeping peacefully some thirty paces away. The Nadir would be on them in seconds.

But if he stayed where he was, he could be safe. He could live. He had the gold he had buried near Finn's cabin; that would keep him for years.

Sweet heaven, I don't want to die!

He stepped out to stand before the Nadir, the torchlight glinting on his red and silver beard, his ax shining crimson.

"Nadir!" he bellowed, the sound echoing through the tunnels. They drew their swords and charged. Never one to wait he lifted his ax, shouted a war cry, and ran to meet them. The blades sliced downward and wounded warriors screamed in agony as the giant cut and cleaved them in the narrow tunnel. Swords pierced his flesh, but he felt no pain. A man loomed before him, and Beltzer slammed the ax forward, the tips of the butterfly blades skewering his chest. The Nadir fell back. Beltzer staggered but remained upright.

"Well, my boys," he said. "You want to be on my mountain? You want to see the sky?"

A warrior drew his bow and let loose a shaft. Beltzer's ax came up, and the arrow glanced from the blades, ripping the skin of Beltzer's temple. The Nadir charged once more, but in the narrow tunnel they could only come at him three abreast. He roared his anger and lifted the bloodied ax. Four more died, then another three, before they fell back again.

Back in the chamber Chareos had gathered his sword and was sprinting back toward the tunnels, Harokas and the others behind him.

Asta Khan stepped into his path. "You can do nothing!" hissed the old man.

"He is my friend," protested Chareos, reaching out to brush the shaman aside.

"I know!" whispered Asta. "That is why he is dying for you: to give you a chance. Don't let him down now. It would break his spirit if you were to die also. Can't you understand that?"

Chareos groaned. He knew it was true, and the pain of that knowledge was too much.

"Follow me!" said Asta, moving off into the darkness. He took the questers to a second chamber that was smaller than the first; there he knelt and raised his hands, palms outward. No words were spoken, but the chamber grew cold and colder still. Tanaki shivered and leaned in close to Kiall, who lifted his cloak around her shoulders. A deeper darkness formed before the old man, and he rose. "Follow," he commanded. He stepped into the black doorway.

And disappeared . . .

For a moment the questers stood rooted to the spot; then Harokas walked after Asta, followed by Chien and the trembling Oshi.

"Now you," said Chareos to Kiall.

The younger man looked at Chareos, reading the intent in his eyes.

"No, Chareos. We will go through together or back together."

"I don't want you to die, boy!"

"Nor I you, but the shaman is right. Beltzer would not want you there. This is his victory—that we escape."

Tears stung Chareos' eyes as he leapt through the doorway. Tanaki and Kiall followed.

The darkness closed around them.

In the tunnel Beltzer found his strength slowly fading. A dagger was jutting from his belly, and blood was pouring from a terrible wound in his upper left arm. The limb hung uselessly at his side, and he knew the bone was smashed. Yet still he hefted the ax in his right hand, defying the warriors before him. The tunnel floor was slippery with blood, and the moans of the dying echoed around him.

Again they charged, forcing him back. A sword plunged into his side, breaking his ribs. His ax hammered back to smash a warrior from his feet. Blades licked out at his flesh, piercing him. He roared at the enemy and fell to his knees. They swarmed over him, but he surged up, scattering them. Blood was gushing from his throat and chest, and one eye was closed and bleeding.

The Nadir fell back again, but not in fear.

The giant was dying. No warrior needed to die now to clear the path. They stood, staring at the axman, their dark eyes reflecting both hatred and respect.

"Had enough, have you?" croaked Beltzer, spitting blood from his mouth. "You don't want old Beltzer's mountain? Come on? What are you afraid of? It's only . . . death."

He looked up at the men before him and realized he was on his knees, his ax fallen from his hands. He tried to reach for it, but the floor rose up to meet him and he lay quietly for a second or two, trying to gather his strength. Then his arm stretched toward the ax. It was too far away.

But it meant so much. A Nadir warrior knelt beside him, took the ax, and placed it in Beltzer's hand.

Beltzer looked up at the man.

"Watch for me on the mountain," he said.

The man nodded. The last breath rattled from Beltzer's throat, and the Nadir rose and loped off down the tunnel, leaving Beltzer with the eighteen men he had killed.

The shock of beyond brought a scream from Kiall. It was as if black ink had been poured into his eyes, penetrating his skull, covering his brain and his soul with a dark, dark shroud. On the verge of panic, he felt Tanaki's hand gripping his, warm and alive.

Then a golden light grew, emanating softly from the hands of Asta Khan, and Kiall saw that they stood on a narrow pathway of shining silver. The light did not penetrate far into the blackness around them, and it seemed to Kiall that they stood in a spherical cave whose walls pressed down with the weight of worlds.

"Do not stray from the path," whispered Asta. "This is a place of consummate evil. Those who stray . . . die! No rescue. The only safe way is the Silver Path. Follow me."

Asta moved carefully forward, Chien and Oshi following and behind them Harokas, Chareos, Kiall, and Tanaki.

At first the journey was uneventful, but soon a sibilant whispering grew out of the darkness, closing in on them, and hundreds of shining eyes glinted from all around. The path was too narrow for Kiall to keep holding Tanaki's hand, but he kept glancing back to see her face, drawing strength from her presence.

To the right of the trail white wolves loped into view and sat staring at the travelers. They were monstrous beasts, as large as ponies.

Suddenly the creatures howled and hurled themselves forward. Kiall started to back away, but Tanaki grabbed his jerkin. "Stay on the path," she hissed. The beasts came closer—but stopped, fangs bared, inches from the Silver Path.

The party moved on into the endless dark. From close by came a scream, then the sound of laughter, manic and shrill. But they saw nothing. The rustle of wings came from above, but when Kiall looked up, he saw only darkness.

Then there was silence for a while.

Chareos walked on, oblivious to his surroundings. Beltzer was dead. Maggrig and Finn had been slain. His mind reeled back from the tragedies, seeking solace in memories of better times as he followed Harokas blindly, unthinking.

A voice sounded from the left of the path. "Chareos, help me." The blademaster glanced to his left, where Beltzer was staggering toward them, wounded but alive. As Chareos stepped from the path, the skin peeled back from Beltzer's frame and a scaled creature leapt at the swordsman.

Chareos did not move.

Kiall dived at him, hooking an arm around his waist and hurling him from his feet. But the scaled beast moved with terrifying speed, twisting and looming over them. The small figure of Chien-tsu hurdled the fallen men, his silver sword slicing through the creature's neck. Harokas and Tanaki pulled Chareos back onto the path, Kiall scrambling after them, as Chien backed slowly to join them.

Asta stared down at Chareos and shook his head. These fools would never learn, he thought. Their judgments and their reason were built on emotions: love, honor, duty, friendship. The Nadir also understood the value of all four but viewed them differently. Instead of love of the individual, there was love of the tribe. Honor and duty were not abstractions, but realities, earned by serving the chosen leader. And friendship, forged in war, was the least of all. On the word of a khan one friend would cut the head from another. There would be regret but not a moment's hesitation. No Nadir warrior would have stepped from the Silver Path. Asta walked on.

The darkness closed in around them, then Asta's voice sounded. "Stand very still and wait until you see the light once more. Then move swiftly, for I cannot hold the Gateway for long."

Silence followed, broken only by the rustling of wings above and the stealthy padding of claws on the rocky ground beside the path. A shaft of dim gray light lit the scene, stretching, widening.

"Now!" yelled Asta, and the little shaman ran through the opening. Chien, Oshi, and Harokas ran after him.

Chareos stumbled through, followed by Kiall. Tanaki ran forward, but her foot strayed from the path, and instantly a hairy hand grabbed her ankle, tripping her. She rolled, drawing her sword and hacking at the limb. The hand slid away, but she saw the giant wolves bearing down on her. Bunching her legs beneath her, she hurled herself at the shrinking Gateway.

She hit the ground hard, rolled, and came to her knees. The gate had vanished, and she was kneeling on a ledge high above the city of Ulrickham.

Kiall helped her to her feet. "I would not wish to walk that path again," he said. Unable to speak, she merely nodded. Chareos was sitting by himself, staring down at the ground. He looked older, more weary than Kiall had ever seen him.

Kiall walked to him. "He was a strong man. A good friend," he said.

"He was a fool. We are all fools," whispered Chareos. "But I will see out the game." He turned his gaze on the city. "What do you think, Kiall? Shall we surround it and demand they release Ravenna?"

"Whatever you say, Chareos."

Chareos rose and stretched his back. He smiled and clapped his hand to Kiall's shoulder. "Life goes on, boy. Do not be too concerned for me."

Asta Khan walked over to them, squatting to sit before Chareos. "There is an underground river below Ulrickham. The great Tenaka knew of it and linked the city's sewers to it. He also strengthened the side tunnels so that there would be a means of escape if the city was surrounded."

"Is it guarded?" Kiall asked.

"Not by men. It would not be much of a secret if all the soldiers in Ulrickham knew of its existence. No, the prisoners who labored to strengthen the tunnels were slain."

"But it is guarded by something," said Chareos, and Asta looked up, his dark eyes hooded.

"Yes, Blademaster. By something. The blood of the slain was used by me to weave a dark spell. I merged the tunnel with the Void."

"The Void?" queried Kiall.

"You have just passed through it," Asta told him. "Only below Ulrickham there is no Silver Path."

"We must pass through it again? I couldn't!" Tanaki said.

"You can!" hissed Asta. "It is not long, a mere twenty paces. I will lead you."

"And once we are through?" asked Chareos. "How do we reach Ravenna?"

Tanaki stepped forward. "You cannot, Chareos. Asta knows this. No man could enter the Palace of Women, but I could."

"No," protested Kiall. "No, I won't have that. It is . . ."

Tanaki chuckled. "Do not say 'too dangerous,' Kiall. It is your only hope."

"She is right," said Asta, his eyes shining now. "She is truly of the blood of the great Tenaka." Chien-tsu and Harokas joined the group, listening as Tanaki outlined her plan.

"The question is when," said Chareos.

"The time is now," declared Asta. "The journey through the Void took many weeks, though it felt like hours. Ravenna is only a few days from giving birth."

"Should we not wait until after the birth?" Harokas asked.

"No!" said Asta. "Jungir will take the queen and the heir around the kingdom. They will be surrounded by warriors, and there would be no way to approach them. No, it must be now. Tonight."

Chien said nothing, but his eyes locked to the face of the shaman. There was much here that was not being said. He did not like Asta Khan, but this quest meant nothing to the Kiatze. He would aid the questers and then demand his payment. He stood and moved back to Oshi. The old man's face was gray, his eyes wide and staring. The walk through the Void had terrified him.

"Sleep for a while, Oshi," said Chien, but the old man shook his head.

"I would dream of that place, and I would never wake."

Nodding, Chien took a sharp knife from the sheath in his

sleeve. "Then be so kind as to make yourself useful. Shave me."

The little servant smiled. "Yes, lord."

The sun sank beyond the distant, mist-shrouded horizon, and Chareos stood alone, staring down at the city below, where the first lanterns of evening had been lit. He thought of his boyhood and the dream of Attalis that one day Chareos would return to the lands of the Drenai and find the hidden Armor of Bronze.

"You will be a great leader, my boy. I know. I can see it in you."

How little you knew me, thought Chareos. You saw me through the eyes of hope. A great leader? I have brought my greatest friends on a quest of death, and they lie unburied and far from home.

And what did we achieve? he wondered. How has the world been changed by their deaths?

"It is not over yet," whispered a voice in his mind.

"Okas?" he said aloud. But there was no response, and he wondered if he had imagined the old man's voice in the whispering of the dusk breeze. He shivered.

Beltzer had saved them all, standing alone in the dark of the mountain. Chareos smiled, and a weight lifted from him. He looked up at the sky. "You were a cantankerous, foul-smelling, evil-minded whoreson, Beltzer. But you never let down a friend. May the Source take you. May you drink your fill in the Hall of Heroes."

He turned away and saw Harokas standing close by, half-hidden in the shadows. The assassin stepped forward.

"I am sorry, Chareos. I did not mean to eavesdrop on your farewell."

The swordsman shrugged. "It does not matter. What did you want?"

"You intend to go into the city?"

"Yes."

Harokas nodded. "It strikes me that we shall have a serious problem if you succeed. We have no horses. Even if you bring the woman out, how will we get away?"

"The wizard will think of something," said Chareos uneasily.

"Yes, I'm sure," answered Harokas, dropping his voice, "but he is playing his own game, and I don't like to think what it might be. But every time I have heard of Nadir shamans, it has had to do with death and human sacrifice. Is that why he wants the woman, do you think?"

When Chareos said nothing, Harokas nodded, understanding the silence. "Yes, I thought you were worried about that. Look, I will not come with you. I will walk down into the city and buy ponies. I am not known there, and we are not yet at war with the Nadir. Once I have bought them, I will ride south, then turn and meet you beyond that bluff, near the stand of poplar."

Chareos looked deeply into the man's eyes. "Will you betray us, Harokas? Will you sell us for Nadir gold?"

The assassin's face darkened, but he bit back an angry response. Instead he said, "I say this for your ears only, Blademaster; I love Tanaki. I would die for her. You understand me? I would sell you in an instant, but not her. *Never* her."

"I believe you," said Chareos. "We will meet as you say."

Harokas eased past the blademaster and climbed down the ridge. Chareos watched him, but the dark-garbed figure was soon lost among the shadows.

"Far be it from me to criticize a leader's decision," said Chien-tsu, bowing low, "but I do not believe he is to be trusted."

"You move silently, Ambassador."

"Sometimes it is better to do so. Will we truly meet him at the place you agreed on?"

"No. To get there he must pass the trail to the south. We will wait there."

"Excellent. It may be, Chareos, that I will not be accompanying you. If that proves to be true, would you be so kind as to look after my servant, Oshi? See him safely to a port. I will leave him coin to pay his passage to Kiatze."

"You intend to kill Jungir Khan? Alone?"

"Such is my intention. The barbarian mistreated the

daughter of my emperor. Quite rightly she took her own life. Now I must take his. It is a question of harmony and balance."

Chareos looked down at the small warrior, noting the steadiness of his gaze and the proud, stern set of his features.

"It seems to me, Ambassador, that the life of a man like Jungir Khan would not compensate for the loss of Chien-tsu."

"A graceful compliment," said the Kiatze, surprised. He bowed low. "And yet the deed must be done. I will journey with you into the bowels of the earth, and I will wait until the woman is rescued. After that I shall seek out the khan."

Asta Khan led the questers down to the edge of a fissure, a jagged tear in the land's surface. Kiall leaned over and gazed down into the inky depths.

"This is the entrance," said Asta. "Now we climb." The old man nimbly dropped to his haunches and slithered over the edge. Kiall shook his head and looked to Chareos.

The blademaster unbuckled his sword belt and hung it over his shoulders before bellying down and following the shaman.

"Wait here, Oshi," said Chien-tsu. "And if I do not return, take note of the man Chareos. Serve him as you would me. You understand?"

"Yes, lord," answered the servant miserably.

Tanaki and Kiall were the last to begin the dark climb. The hand- and footholds were good, and the descent was less perilous than it had first appeared. Asta Khan reached the lowest level and raised his arms, and a soft yellow light glowed on the walls of the cavern.

"A heavily pregnant woman will not be able to make that climb," said Chareos.

"Nor will she need to," Asta told him. "I have made preparations." Moving to the wall, he reached down behind a jutting rock and lifted a coil of hemp rope. "When we have her, we will climb back to the surface and then haul her up."

Draping the rope over the rock, he set off across the

dimly glowing cavern. The others followed him through a honeycomb of tunnels until, after about half an hour, they reached a point where the glowing light did not penetrate.

Asta pointed to the forbidding wall of darkness. "You all know what is beyond this point: it is the Void. I shall pass through with the woman Tanaki and the warrior Chien-tsu. You, Chareos, and your friend will remain here."

"What purpose will that serve?" asked Chareos.

"If we are pursued, you will cover our retreat. Many of them will be killed in the Void, but others might get through. Also, much could go wrong for us beyond this barrier. You will be able to hear us—and give us aid if necessary."

"You said there was no Silver Path," said Kiall. "How, then, will you cross safely?"

"I am not without power, child," snapped Asta. "But all life is perilously fragile. A man cannot live without danger, no matter how much he may desire it." He turned to Chien and Tanaki. "Draw your swords and be ready to use them."

Kiall touched Tanaki's arm. "Be careful," he said, knowing that the words were ludicrous but unable to find others. She smiled, leaned forward, and kissed his cheek.

"Now stand close to me," ordered Asta, "placing your hands on my shoulders." Chien stood on the shaman's left, Tanaki on his right. Slowly they moved into the darkness.

Once they were inside, a circle of fire leapt around them like a wall. The heat was incredible, and the light burned their eyes.

"I can hold this for moments only," said Asta. "Be ready!" He began to run, the others loping alongside him. The circle of fire remained constantly with them regardless of their speed.

From beyond the silent flames came the sounds of padding feet and talons on stone and the chilling cries of hunting beasts. Still Asta ran on, seemingly tireless.

The flames grew thinner, and Tanaki began to see shapeless forms beyond the fire keeping pace with them. When she glanced at Chien, his dark eyes met her gaze and he gave a tight smile.

A scaled arm lashed at the flames. The skin shriveled, and a ghastly scream sounded.

"Almost there!" called Asta.

Suddenly the fire flared—and died.

Asta screamed. A huge creature swooped down from above them, its leather wings knocking him from his feet. Tanaki plunged a sword into the beast's belly and pulled Asta to his feet; he tore clear of her grasp and sprinted away.

A scaled monster leapt from the darkness. Chien's sword flashed out and down, and the beast fell writhing to the ground.

"As you value your lives, *run*!" came the voice of Asta. Risking a glance back, Chien saw giant white wolves bearing down on them. The small warrior took to his heels. He saw Asta vanish ahead of him, followed by Tanaki. For a moment Chien experienced panic, feeling the hot breath of a beast on his neck.

A great weight landed on his back, and he fell and rolled. As the wolf beast scrambled up, twisting to attack, Chien's sword slashed through its throat. The pack howled and charged. Chien spun on his heel and flung himself forward through the opening, falling to his knees before Tanaki and the shaman.

Tanaki offered a hand, and Chien accepted it, pulling himself to his feet. He glanced back. "How is it the creatures do not follow us?" he asked.

"They cannot pass through. Think of it as a lake," said Asta. "We can dive through the surface, but the fish cannot leave; that is their world. It is possible to make a Gateway for them, but the power needed is great and would require many hundreds of souls."

"I would not wish to sound defeatist, shaman," said Chien, "but upon our return I cannot see the woman Ravenna sprinting away from those wolves. It would be a great pity to rescue her only to see her die in the Void."

"She will not die there," said Asta. "But my power is finite, and I gave you all I could spare. With her I will hold the circle. Now let us move on."

The tunnel widened, and for the first time it was possible

to see the works of men there, the walls smoothed, reinforced with timbers. There was a stairway carved into the rock, and Asta mounted it, moving up to squat beneath a low ceiling. He signaled for silence and called Chien and Tanaki to him.

"Above us," he whispered, "is the throne room. It is now almost midnight. There should be no one there. Are you ready, Princess?"

"Yes."

"If the throne room is not empty, we are doomed," said Asta, for once seeming nervous and unsure.

Chien chuckled softly. "No life is without peril, shaman," he reminded him. Asta muttered an obscene curse and lifted the flagstone above his head. It creaked and shuddered. Chien helped him with the weight, and they twisted the stone to lay it alongside the opening. Tanaki levered herself up into the darkness of the throne room, and Chien followed her.

"I will wait here," said Asta.

Tanaki ran to the main doors, pressing her ear to the crack. Chien moved alongside.

"There should be no guards in the corridor," Tanaki said. "The khan's sleeping quarters are on the other side of the palace. But the women's quarters will have sentries on the outside and eunuch swordsmen within."

Chien nodded. "I will come with you and wait."

She eased open the door and stepped into the torchlit corridor. All was silent. Keeping to the shadows, they moved on, cutting left through a narrow doorway and out into a side street. Tanaki led the warrior through the deserted streets until at last they came to a broad square beyond which was a high wall; three sentries patrolled the outside of the wall.

"How will you get in?" whispered Chien.

Tanaki smiled. "Distract the guards," she said. Removing her sword belt but keeping a curved dagger, she waited until the sentries had passed and then ran to the wall, crouching in the shadows.

Digging into the pocket of his breeches, Chien came up with four golden coins. Tucking them into his belt, he waited for the sentries, took a deep breath, and then began to sing. He staggered out into the open, belched, half fell, and then ambled on toward the men.

"Good evening, my brothers," he said.

"What are you doing here, fool?" asked one of the sentries, moving forward and touching the point of his spear to Chien's chest.

"Fool?" Chien repeated, giggling and swaying sideways. "You think I am a fool? Not me, brothers. I . . ." He looked left and right, as if fearing to be overheard. "I have discovered the great secret. I learned it from a shaman. And never will I be poor again. Fool? No brothers, I am celebrating riches beyond your dreams."

"Riches?" said another. "What nonsense is this? Be off with you!"

Chien glanced over the man's shoulders. Tanaki had begun to climb the wall behind them.

"Nonsense? You don't believe me." He waved his hand. "Give me a copper coin and I will prove it to you. I will turn it into gold before your eyes. Then we'll see. Oh, yes. We'll see."

The men chuckled. One of them laid his spear on the ground and fished in the pocket of his jerkin. He handed Chien a roughly stamped copper coin bearing the head of Tenaka Khan.

Chien rolled the coin in his fingers and flicked it into the air. He caught it deftly and held up his fist, then he began to chant. The words were in an obscure Kiatze dialect.

"Get on with it," said one of the sentries, losing patience.

"It is done," said Chien. "Here is your coin." He opened his hand, and the gleam of gold was caught by the moonlight. The man took it, his mouth dropping open.

"Do one for me," said the second sentry.

Tanaki was almost at the top of the wall.

"Why is it always you first?" retorted the third. "Do mine!"

"I will do them both together," Chien told them. He accepted their coins and repeated his chant.

Tanaki clambered over the wall. "There!" said Chien, handing them the gold coins.

"More! Do us more," urged the first.

"Tomorrow, when I have rested," promised Chien. "Where shall we meet?"

"You know the Clay Pony, behind the Wolves' barracks?"

"Of course," said Chien. "But it must be only you. I could not do this for everyone; it would exhaust me. Just you three."

"Yes, yes, just us. Be there at noon, yes?"

"Oh yes," agreed Chien. "I will be there. And now I am for bed. And you should be at your duties."

He walked away, back into the shadows.

The princess was inside, and that was a victory.

But getting out would not be so simple, he knew.

14

TANAKI ROLLED TO the ramparts, dagger ready. There were no sentries. Swiftly she moved to the steps and ran down to the courtyard below. To her left was the guardhouse. She could see lantern light through the shuttered windows, and hear the sounds of men talking and laughing; these would be the eunuch guards. Straight ahead was the garden walkway, and to the right were the long, elaborately furnished rooms where the khan's women spent their days. Here would be the baths and the pools. Beyond them were the sleeping quarters. Many of the concubines slept in dormitories, only the privileged few having rooms of their own.

Tanaki crept across the courtyard and into the darkened dayroom. Keeping to the wall, she walked to the far end of the chamber, opening a door that led to a curtain-hung corridor. Several cats were sleeping there. She moved on past the dormitory rooms to a set of stairs, which she ascended swiftly.

Knowing the layout of the women's quarters, she tried to decide in which of the major rooms Ravenna would be housed. Not the nearest to the khan's secret corridor; that would be reserved for his latest concubine. No, Ravenna would have been moved closer to the midwives' quarters in the east. She padded on, coming at last to a narrow door that led, she knew, to a suite of rooms overlooking the eastern steppes. Here sunlight bathed the rooms, bringing heat in the morning but leaving the area cool in the afternoon.

Opening the door, she slipped inside. The bed had been moved to the window, and Tanaki could see a young woman lying on her back. As she crept closer, it was obvious she was pregnant. Tanaki moved to the bedside and sat down, touching the woman's arm.

"Ravenna," she whispered. "Ravenna, wake up!"

The woman's eyes opened. "What is it?" she asked sleepily.

"Kiall sent me."

"Kiall?" Ravenna yawned. "Is this a dream?"

"No. Listen to me. I am here to take you from the city. Your friend Kiall has crossed the steppes to rescue you. For pity's sake, wake up and listen to me!"

The woman eased herself to a sitting position. "Kiall? The dreamer?"

"The very same."

"We could never get away from here," whispered Ravenna. "There are guards everywhere."

"I got to you," argued Tanaki.

Ravenna winced and put a hand to her distended belly. "He kicks hard," she said, smiling. She was an attractive girl, Tanaki realized, but no beauty. Her chin line was too strong, her eyes too small. But her smile was radiant.

"Get dressed, Ravenna. I will take you to Kiall."

"Why has he come for me? I don't understand."

"Neither does he. Do you want to leave?"

"You have no idea how much I want to leave. I hate this place, I hate these people. But most of all I loathe the khan. May a thousand curses fall on his bloodline!"

"Be careful what you wish for," snapped Tanaki. "Your babe is of that line."

Ravenna looked instantly contrite. "I didn't mean . . ."

"Just get dressed," said Tanaki. Ravenna slipped into a long robe of soft blue-dyed wool and some silk shoes. "You have no cloak or walking shoes?" Tanaki asked.

"Why would I need a cloak in here? They never let us out."

"Follow me," said Tanaki, leading the woman out into the corridor. Ravenna moved slowly, and Tanaki glanced back, her irritation growing, but there was nothing to be done. The pregnancy was well advanced, the swelling huge.

When they reached the door to the courtyard, Tanaki opened it a fraction and looked out. Two sentries were now patrolling the ramparts, and she cursed.

"What is it?" asked Ravenna.

"Guards. Two of them."

"Can we get past them?"

"Not at the speed you move." She opened the door once more, watching the men, counting the seconds as the sentries passed by one another. Their only chance lay in moving as the warriors reached the angle of the walls, before they turned back. She watched them repeat the maneuver three times, then seized Ravenna's arm. "Now!" she hissed.

They moved from the doorway onto open ground and crept across the courtyard to the wall. "We'll never get out," Ravenna whispered.

Keeping to the shadows, the two women edged closer to the postern gate. The sentries were directly above them now as Tanaki ran her hands over the gate bolts. They were rust-covered, and she cursed softly and eased back the bolt. It moved no more than an inch, then creaked. Tanaki froze. But the guards had not heard, and she moved it again. This time the bolt slid clear. Tanaki swallowed hard, took a deep breath, and pulled open the gate. Glancing outside, she saw three guards standing no more than twenty feet away. There was no way past them, and she could not kill them all.

Then she saw Chien-tsu. He walked across the open ground toward the guards, and one of them turned and raised his spear. Suddenly the little warrior spun and launched a kick that cannoned against the sentry's temple to send the man catapulting from his feet. A second guard fell with a knife in his throat. The third rushed at the Kiatze warrior, but Chien-tsu stepped aside from the thrust of the spear and rammed the blade of his hand into the man's neck.

"Swiftly now!" said Tanaki, leading Ravenna into the open.

A sentry on the wall shouted an alarm as Chien raced to Ravenna, taking her arm and urging her to run. The trio made it to the first alleyway, ducking into the shadows. Ravenna was breathing heavily, her face deeply flushed. "I am sorry," she said, sagging against a wall. "I cannot run any farther."

They could hear the sounds of pounding feet in a parallel street and the calls of the soldiers.

The trio moved on. Chien drew his curved sword and took the lead. The sound of the pursuing warriors faded away. "They are trying to cut us off from the main gates," said Tanaki. "That's good."

Chien felt there was little good in this entire adventure but held his tongue. They reached the palace corridor and ran into the throne room.

Warriors raced from the shadows, but Chien cut the first from his feet, ducked under a wild slice, and skewered another. Tanaki hurled her dagger into the face of a charging warrior and then saw Tsudai. All thoughts of the quest vanished as she dived to the floor, scooping up the sword of a fallen warrior and rolling to her feet. Tsudai ran to meet her, screaming a battle cry. She blocked his cut, spun, and rammed her sword through his chest.

"Rot in hell!" she hissed as he sagged to the floor.

Chien was surrounded now, and Tanaki wrenched the sword clear of Tsudai's body and ran to his aid. There were six warriors against him, but she could hear more running in the corridor outside. She stabbed one man in the back and slashed her blade across the face of another. They all fell back briefly.

Asta Khan rose from the opening in the floor and uttered a weird howl. An icy wind blew across the throne room, and the Nadir staggered back, screaming. The first three warriors stumbled to their knees with blood streaming from their eyes.

Tanaki grabbed Ravenna's arm and dragged her back to the hole in the floor. "Down!" she ordered.

Ravenna clambered into the hole, and Tanaki followed her, leading her down the steps, Chien bringing up the rear.

"Swiftly," said Asta. "The spell will not hold them long." Ravenna staggered but stayed upright, and Chien took her arm.

Behind them they could hear the Nadir pounding down the steps . . .

They reached the darkness. Asta took Ravenna's hand, and she flinched away from the shaman, but he held her tight. "Now is the time for courage, woman," he said, and pulled her into the Void.

As before, a circle of flames sprang up around them, and they moved across the darkness. Behind them the Nadir ran—unsuspecting—into the Void. Their screams were terrible.

The circle of fire began to fade, and the dwellers in the dark closed in. Sweat shone on Asta's brow as he struggled on. Taloned hands reached out for them, but the flames held them back. At last they reached the outer limit and passed through. Asta collapsed to the stone floor. Seeing Ravenna, Kiall ran forward to take her in his arms. Tanaki watched the scene and turned away, her thoughts confused.

Chareos helped Asta to his feet.

The old man shrugged clear of his aid. "We must get out of here," he said. "Help the woman. Carry her if you must."

Back they went through the honeycomb of tunnels, arriving at last at the fissure. Kiall, Chareos, Tanaki, and Chien climbed to the surface, Kiall carrying the rope. They lowered it, and Asta made a loop in which Ravenna sat. Slowly the three men pulled her to the top.

Then they began to walk toward the hills. Chareos glanced back to see that half a mile away the city gates had opened and a column of riders was galloping out toward them.

The sound of hoofbeats came from the left. Chareos drew his saber and spun. Harokas dragged his horse to a halt, a string of ponies behind him.

"You had better mount," said the assassin. They helped Ravenna into the saddle of the first horse, then the others mounted.

"There is only one place we can reach," said Asta Khan. "Follow me." He kicked his pony into a run and set off toward the west. The questers followed him, cutting to the right through a series of narrow passes. After an hour's hard riding with the Nadir closing on them, they emerged at last into a narrow valley.

The moon was high, and Chareos groaned as he saw the broken tower and the stretch of battlements silhouetted against the sky. "No!" he whispered.

But they rode on into the ghostly fortress of Bel-azar.

The eastern gates lay open, and the questers rode their weary mounts inside. Chareos and Kiall dismounted and ran back to the gates, forcing them shut. Harokas found a thick beam, which he and Tanaki wedged into the great bolt plates. Then they mounted the rampart steps and watched from the battlements as the thirty Nadir riders drew rein outside. Asta Khan joined them. He leapt nimbly to the wall and stood looking down at the riders, letting them see him.

"Will they attack?" asked Kiall. Chareos said nothing.

Asta Khan began to dance on the precarious footing, twisting and leaping. He howled like a wolf, the sound eerie and chilling as it echoed in the mountains. Three Nadir riders turned their mounts and rode back toward the city, but the others dismounted and sat on the rocks. Asta turned and jumped back to the ramparts, his dark eyes gleaming.

"They are frightened," he said. "This is a haunted place. They know dark spirits walk here."

In the open ground below Ravenna cried out and clutched her belly. Kiall and Tanaki ran down to her, helping her into a ruined guardhouse where there was a dust-covered bed. Tanaki pulled aside a rotted blanket and placed her own on the mattress; then they lowered Ravenna to it.

"It's coming," cried Ravenna. "I can feel it."

Kiall heard a movement behind him and saw Asta Khan standing in the doorway. The shaman's face was shining, and the glint of triumph was in his eyes. It chilled Kiall.

"Leave us," Tanaki told Kiall, and gladly he obeyed, easing past the shaman and moving out into the dawn light. Chareos was still on the ramparts below the ruined gate tower. Chien-tsu and Oshi had lit a fire near the main barracks building and were sitting together, talking in low voices. Harokas had led the ponies back to a paddock section, where he had unsaddled them and was brushing their lathered frames. Kiall walked to the steps and climbed to where Chareos sat watching the Nadir.

"We did it," Kiall said. "Whatever happens now, we did what we set out to do."

Chareos looked up and smiled. "Yes, we did it. We found your lady, and we brought her back to Gothir lands. That is a feat in itself. But do not hold out any great hopes, Kiall. I do not wish to sound defeatist, but I do not believe five warriors and a shaman can hold off the Nadir nation."

Kiall chuckled. "I cannot explain it, Chareos, but I don't care anymore. All my life I've been a dreamer. Now I feel that a dream has been achieved. I'm not even frightened of dying."

"I am," admitted Chareos. "Especially here." He pointed to the gate tower. "There it is, boy, the scene of great deeds. From there Beltzer leapt to win back the standard. There we sat talking with Tenaka Khan. And it was here we were dubbed the ghosts-yet-to-be. It is not a good feeling to be sitting here waiting for death."

"And birth," said Kiall. "Okas told us the child would be a great king, perhaps the greatest who ever lived. That's something, isn't it?"

Chareos nodded and turned away. The fortress loomed around him, grim and threatening, and he could feel its memories in the cold stone, hear again the screams of the dying and the clash of iron blades.

Tanaki joined them. "It was a false alarm," she said. "She is resting now. Is there any sign?"

"No," answered Kiall. "They just sit there and wait—I don't know what for."

"They are waiting for Jungir Khan," she said. "They don't know why we took their queen, but they dare not risk anything that might cause her harm. Jungir will decide what to do."

She walked off to the gate tower door and pushed it open. Kiall followed her, mounting the cracked steps to the tower itself, where she sat down and leaned her back against the wall.

"Well," she said, "you have seen your woman once more."

He looked down at her and then knelt, taking her hand. "She is not my woman, Tanaki. It was like seeing an old friend. I am not skilled in these matters, but I . . . I want you to know, before . . ." He stumbled to silence.

"Before we die?" she prompted.

"Yes, before we die. I want you to know that I love you. I know you do not believe in love, but I would sooner hold your hand here for a night than live a hundred years without you. Does that sound foolish?"

"Yes," she said, reaching out and stroking his face, "but it is wonderfully foolish. It is beautifully foolish." She drew him toward her, brushing her lips against his. His arms circled her. "Would you like to make love?" she whispered.

He drew back. "Yes, but we will not—not in this cold stone place which reeks of death and misery. Can we just sit together, close?"

"For a man of little experience, you so often say exactly the right words," she told him.

The sun climbed high behind them, the sky cloudless and streaked with red. "It will be a fine day," he said.

She did not reply.

Harokas saw them from the courtyard and sighed. Then he caught sight of Asta Khan moving furtively from the main barracks building; he was carrying something. As Harokas squinted against the sunlight, he saw that the shaman was holding a bleached skull, which he carried to the room where Ravenna lay. Harokas watched him slip inside.

The assassin strolled up to where Chareos sat. "This would be a good time to ride off deep into Gothir lands," he said.

Chareos shook his head. "The woman would lose the babe. She is close to giving birth."

Harokas sighed. "If we stay, we will all die. And women can conceive a second time, Chareos. It would not cause the world to fall into darkness were she to lose this one child."

"The child is special," insisted Chareos. "But more than

that, I am meant to be here. I cannot explain it, but I have known for many years that my destiny lay here."

"I think Asta Khan feels the same way. I have just seen him carrying an old skull into the woman's room. Truly the ways of shamans are beyond me, I am happy to say."

"A skull?" The words of Okas came flooding back to him: *"Why are Tenaka Khan's bones buried at Bel-azar?"* Chareos pushed himself to his feet and descended the broken steps, crossing the courtyard and opening the door to the old guardhouse. Ravenna was sleeping, but at the foot of the bed was Asta Khan, sitting cross-legged, a skull in his lap.

"What are you doing here?" asked Chareos.

The shaman glanced up. "Nothing that will harm the woman, Chareos. You have my word."

"And the child?"

"The child was not part of the bargain, but she will give birth to a healthy babe."

"What is it that you are not telling me, Asta? What foulness are you planning with those . . . those relics?"

"Relics? If you had any idea of what these bones . . ." He stopped and forced a smile. "I have kept my bargain with you, Blademaster. You cannot fault me. But I, too, have a quest, and it is worth more than my life."

"You promise me you do not mean to harm Ravenna or the child?"

"The child will be born," said Asta with a secretive smile. "He will be born strong and grow fast. He will be the great khan. No harm will come to him or to the mother of his flesh."

"Chareos!" came Kiall's voice. "Come quickly!" The blademaster turned from the shaman and ran back to the wall. Beyond, on the open plain, a horde was galloping toward the fortress. Leading them was a warrior dressed in black, riding a gray stallion.

"The whoreson is riding to kill me on my own horse," exclaimed Chareos.

"See who rides beside him," said Harokas. "Now, there is a surprise!"

On a bay stallion, his blond hair glinting in the sunlight, rode the Earl of Talgithir.

The Nadir halted some two hundred yards from the fortress and dismounted, while the earl kicked his horse into a canter and rode up to the walls.

"Open the gate!" he called.

Chareos leaned over the ramparts. "For what purpose?" he asked.

"Because I demand it!" roared the earl, his face reddening. Then he recognized Chareos. "Oh, it is you, is it, Blademaster? I should have guessed. Now open the gate and you will all live."

"I asked you for your purpose," said Chareos.

"I do not need to answer to you, swordsman. I am the Earl of Talgithir, appointed by the lord regent."

"And you have no jurisdiction at Bel-azar," said Chareos. "Talgithir is far from here."

The earl leaned back in his saddle and laughed. "You have been gone for some time, Chareos. I am now the regent's envoy to the Nadir, and as such, my orders are to be obeyed anywhere in the realm. Now, will you open that gate?"

"I do not think that I will," said Chareos. "I care not what appointment you have received. You are a slave trader and a traitor to your people. When the lord regent hears of your dealings, you will hang."

"You are hardly in a position to threaten me. But I will wait." Swinging his horse's head, he cantered back to the Nadir.

"I don't understand this," said Harokas. "Why is he so calm?"

Chareos shrugged. "I have an uncomfortable feeling we are going to find out."

Throughout the morning the Nadir remained where they were, but as the sun reached noon and the shadows disappeared, there came from the west the sound of walking horses. Chareos and Kiall ran to the western gate, dragging it open. Three hundred lancers were riding to the fortress, led by Salida.

Kiall cursed. "That's why the earl was so calm—his soldiers have come to meet him. Now we are truly trapped."

"Do not be so sure," whispered Chareos. "Salida is no lickspittle."

"He's unlikely to take on a Nadir army and his own earl," said Kiall.

Chareos moved out before the riders. Salida drew rein and stepped from the saddle. "Well met," greeted the officer. "You do turn up in the most unlikely places." He lifted the water canteen from his saddle and drank deeply.

"The earl is outside the fortress," said Chareos softly. "He is with Jungir Khan and a thousand Nadir warriors."

"There is a treaty being negotiated. It does not concern you," Salida said.

"There is a *slight* problem," Chareos told him.

Salida walked to a boulder and sat down. "Somehow I did not doubt it," he said wearily. Chareos joined him and swiftly outlined the journey into Nadir lands and the secrets they had discovered concerning the earl's dealings with the Nadren. Finally he told of the rescue of Ravenna and the imminent birth.

"What is it you have against me, Chareos?" asked Salida. "Why must you turn up like a bad smell just when life is looking good? I have had a raise in pay, and I now command three hundred men. We have a treaty in prospect, and my career is golden. Now you tell me the earl is a traitor—and you have kidnapped the Nadir queen. Excellent!"

"What will you do?"

"What would you have me do?" snapped Salida. "The lord regent is expecting a treaty, a treaty he believes will safeguard the Gothir nation. Do you think he will risk a war because of a stolen peasant girl?"

"It is your decision, my friend," said Chareos softly. "All Jungir Khan wants is my life and the lives of my friends. Such a small price to pay for peace, is it not?"

"For the guarantee of peace I would pay more than that," hissed Salida. The captain stood and looked to his men. "Dismount!" he called. "Take the horses inside. Beris!" A young officer came forward. "Twenty groups to the wall, eight groups in reserve. Let the others look to the horses and prepare some food."

"Yes, sir. Sir?"

"What is it?"

"Are we here to fight? I thought we were to accompany the earl back to New Gulgothir with the treaty."

"So did I, my boy. Isn't life full of nice surprises?" He turned back to Chareos. "I assume you have the proof to back up your accusations?"

"Of course. The finest proof of all: the word of the Nadir queen and the man who collected the earl's profits. And lastly, the Nadir princess who dealt with him."

"This is insane, Chareos. You know that, don't you?"

"I know that you're a better man than the one you serve."

"You can forget the compliments," snapped Salida, marching into the fortress and ascending the battlement steps. Seeing Harokas, he scowled.

"Welcome, Salida, old friend," greeted Harokas. The soldier grunted and watched his men fan out along the wall.

The Nadir rose as the line of armored men took up their positions. Once more the earl mounted his bay and galloped to the wall.

"Good to see you, Salida," he called. "Arrest those people and open the gate." Behind him the Nadir had mounted and were riding slowly forward.

"You have been named as a traitor," answered Salida. "I ask you now to surrender yourself to me. You will be taken to New Gulgothir for trial before the lord regent."

"Are you mad?" stormed the earl. "Who accuses me? Chareos? A man I forgave for murder?"

"I do," said Harokas. "You trafficked in slaves, and I collected your gold. The Princess Tanaki is also here. Answer that—*my lord.*"

"I need not answer to you. Come, Salida, think of your position. You have three hundred men. There are a thousand here and a thousand thousand still to be called upon. You cannot prevail. Open the gates and we will ignore this . . . this insubordination."

"I ask you again, my lord, to surrender yourself."

"I'll see you dead, you miserable cur!" the earl shouted.

Jungir Khan spurred the gray alongside the nobleman. "Why are they not opening the gate to you?" he asked mildly.

"They are traitors," snarled the earl. "Kill them all!"

"You cannot even control your own captain," Jungir said. "How, then, can you serve me?"

The earl started to answer, but Jungir's hand flashed up—and the curved dagger blade plunged into the earl's heart. Slowly he slid from the saddle. Jungir rode the gray stallion forward.

"Who commands this castle?" he called.

"I, Salida."

"I am Jungir Khan. Come down. I wish to speak with you. It is not fitting that two commanders should negotiate in this manner."

On the wall Harokas turned to Salida. "Don't listen to him; it is a trick. Once the gate is open, they will storm through."

"These broken walls would not stop them," answered Salida. He strode down the rampart steps and ordered the gate to be opened. Chareos walked with him and waited in the gateway.

As Salida walked onto the open ground, Jungir touched his heels to the gray, which suddenly reared up, almost toppling him from the saddle. He clung on grimly as the stallion ducked its head and bucked. Jungir wrenched the beast's head, and the horse fell, the khan leaping from the saddle and falling to the dust. The stallion—ears flat to its skull, eyes rolling—lashed out at the Nadir leader, who fell back. The horse reared above him, hooves ready to smash his skull, as Chareos ran forward. "Be calm, gray one," he called. "To me!" The stallion swung to the sound of his voice and trotted away from the fallen khan. Chareos stroked the beast's long neck.

Jungir rose and brushed the dust from his breeches. He was acutely aware that his men would be avidly watching what followed. The khan had lost face. Worse, he had been rescued by the enemy.

"Are you all right, my lord?" Salida asked.

"I am well. You!" called the khan to Chareos. "You may keep the horse. It is a gift." He swung back to Salida. "Now, Captain, you say the dead man was a traitor. I have dealt with him. Now I ask you to return to me my property. To refuse will be taken as an act of war against the Nadir people. Is this what you wish, Captain?"

"No, Highness, it is not," answered Salida. "But you are standing on Gothir lands, and Bel-azar is a Gothir fortress. Will you be so kind as to wait for me to seek orders from my superiors in Gulgothir? I will send a rider, and an answer will be forthcoming within the day."

"I could take this ruin within an hour," said Jungir.

"The Nadir are indeed a ferocious enemy," Salida agreed. "But allow me the day."

For a moment Jungir was silent. He walked away, as if considering the request, and glanced at his warriors. The incident with the stallion had worried them. The tribesmen put great weight on omens; the horse had unseated the khan and now stood in the gateway, allowing itself to be petted by the tall, dark-eyed warrior there. A good shaman would find a positive omen even in this bizarre circumstance, but Shotza was dead and Asta Khan was standing on the ramparts in full view of the Nadir. If Jungir gave the order, his men would attack, but they would do so less willingly, fearing bad omens. And if they should fail to take the walls swiftly, there was a chance that, believing the gods were against them, they would turn on their leader. Jungir thought it through. The risk of failure was remote, but on a day like this? He swung back to Salida. "Men should have time to consider their actions," he said. "I give you your day. But hear this: not one person is to leave the fortress, save for your messenger. And all who are not soldiers will be handed over to me. Otherwise I will destroy you all. Let that message be carried to the lord regent."

The khan strode back through his lines, the Nadir flowing after him. They stopped and made camp a half mile from the wall.

"You are a man with nerve," Harokas told Salida.

"And you will need to be," said Salida, "if the lord regent sends the message I expect him to."

* * *

The day wore on, dusky shadows stretching across the valley. The Nadir lit campfires, and Salida ordered most of the men back from the ramparts. The soldiers started their own cook fires, and Salida brought a bowl of thick soup to where Chareos sat on the wall.

The blademaster accepted it and put it aside to cool. "I am sorry, Salida. Once more I seem to have caused trouble for you."

Salida shrugged. "I am a soldier, Chareos. Trouble is what I am paid for. But—and I hope you will not take this amiss—when this is over, I do not want to see you again."

"In the circumstances that is understandable," Chareos agreed with a wry smile. He looked down on the body of the earl. "Strange. He was a man of many talents, and yet he always told me he envied my role at Bel-azar. He often said he would like to have had the chance to fight here. And he did . . . on the wrong side."

"*That* is a question of perspective, Chareos. The wrong side is the losing side. We have yet to see which side we are on."

"What do you think the lord regent will decide?"

"Let us wait and see," said Salida, looking away.

"My thoughts exactly," agreed Chareos. "He will sell us out. Better that, I suppose, than a costly war he cannot win."

An ululating chant began in the guardhouse, and Salida shivered. "I do not like that man," he said. "Like all Nadir shamans, he reeks of death."

Tanaki joined them on the battlements, Kiall beside her. "That is a birth chant," she said. "I'll go down and help."

Chareos yawned and stretched out on the battlements. He was weary, and his bones ached. Rolling his blanket to make a pillow, he lay down in the shadows and tried to sleep.

"Defend the babe, Blademaster," came the voice of Okas.

Chareos awoke with a start. Salida had returned to his men, and only six sentries walked the walls. Chareos sat up. Asta Khan had promised him that the mother and the babe would be safe. What, then, was the danger? He recalled again the words of Okas back in Tavern Town.

"Why do the bones of Tenaka Khan lie buried at Belazar?"

Tenaka Khan, the King beyond the Gate, the Prince of Shadows. A man Asta believed should never have died. Now the shaman sat in the birth room, holding the skull of the great khan. Chareos' mouth was dry, and the thoughts tumbled together. What had Asta said? *"No harm will come to the mother of his flesh."*

What of his spirit, his soul?

He glanced down at the guardhouse. In there, at this very moment, Asta Khan was waiting to slay the child's soul. Chareos rose and ran down the rampart steps.

He had reached the guardhouse door and was about to enter when he heard a sound from behind and swiveled, but he was too late. Asta's dagger slashed out to nick the skin of his face. As the little shaman jumped back, Chareos tried to draw his saber, but his limbs were sluggish and heavy.

"I knew," whispered Asta Khan, "that you would divine my purpose. But it is too late for you, Chareos. Die in peace."

The poison flooded his veins. His legs gave way, and he did not feel himself hit the ground.

Asta pulled the body to the side of the building, then returned to his place at the bedside. He sat on the cold floor and closed his eyes, his spirit soaring free.

Ravenna was moaning with the pain of the contractions, Tanaki beside her. Kiall was asleep by the far wall, but he awoke and sat up. "What is happening?" he asked.

"Her water's broken. The babe will be born any time now," answered Tanaki.

"What can I do?"

"What all men do at this time—nothing," she answered, a smile robbing the words of venom. Kiall rose and walked from the room. Outside the night was fresh and clear. Most of the soldiers were asleep, except for the guards on the walls. He looked around for Chareos, but there was no sign of the blademaster. Seeing Chien-tsu rise from his blankets, Kiall strolled over to him.

The little warrior stretched and lifted his sword belt into place, the long blade hanging between his shoulder blades. His servant slept on, snoring softly.

"Where is Chareos?" asked Chien.

"On the wall, I think."

"Let us hope so," said Chien, trotting toward the rampart steps. They searched the wall and the gate tower. Chien seemed anxious now. He turned to stare back into the fortress, his eyes alighting on the still figure by the guardhouse wall. Both men ran to the body, and Chien turned it over, feeling for a pulse.

"What happened to him?" asked Kiall.

"I do not know. I heard his soul cry out. It woke me."

"Look, there is a cut to his face."

"It could have happened when he fell," said Chien. "We must get him to a fire. His body is cold, but the heart still beats."

Chareos awoke to a bleak landscape, the sky a pitiless gray, the land devoid of life. A dead tree stood like a skeleton on the brow of a distant hill, and a light shone there. Chareos shook his head. He had no recollection of traveling to this barren land. As he walked toward the light, wolves howled in the distance, the sound eerie and hollow. Chareos climbed the hill and sat by the light, which was emanating from a point just above the ground. He reached out to touch it, but a voice stopped him.

"It is fragile, Chareos, and pure," said Okas, and Chareos turned. The Tattooed Man smiled and held out his hand. Chareos took it.

"What is the light?" asked the blademaster.

"There are two lights," said Okas. "They are the souls of the twins Ravenna carries."

"They are beautiful," Chareos whispered.

"All children have bright souls, but these two are special. They will change the world, Chareos. For good or ill."

"How did you come here? For that matter, how did I come here?"

"Asta Khan poisoned your body. Even now you are

dying in the world beyond. He plans to kill what he sees as the soul of the child."

"I remember," said Chareos. "He wants to bring Tenaka Khan back to life. Can he do it?"

"Yes, if his timing is right. That is why the bones were at Bel-azar. That is also why Jungir placed a thousand spells on the tomb of Ulric—not to stop robbers from getting in but to stop Tenaka Khan from getting out. But Asta fooled him; he stole the khan's bones and carried them to Bel-azar to await the ghosts-yet-to-be."

"So we fulfilled his dreams?"

"We kept him alive when he was weak. But now he is strong again."

"What can we do?"

Okas shrugged. "We can defend the child."

"Can we succeed?"

"No, Chareos. But when has that ever been important?"

A cold wind blew across the hilltop, and a dark mist formed. The mist hardened to become a horde of demons with dull red eyes and long talons. In their midst stood Asta and, beside him, Tenaka Khan, the King beyond the Gate.

Chareos stood and drew his saber. It shone with a silver light.

"Still you oppose me?" sneered Asta Khan. "It will avail you nothing. Look now upon my army!" As far as the eye could see there were creatures of darkness, and Chareos could sense their lust for blood like a physical force pushing him back.

"Step aside, Chareos," said Tenaka Khan. "You have done all that you were intended to do. The ghosts-yet-to-be have fulfilled their quest. They have given me a second chance at life."

"No, Great Khan," replied Chareos. "You had your life, and it ended. This child deserves to see the sky and live his own life. And I do not believe that my friends and I died for your glory. If anything, it was for the babe."

"Enough of this!" shouted Asta. "You think to stop us alone?"

"But he is not alone," said Beltzer, walking to stand beside Chareos. When the blademaster looked at his friend,

Beltzer was no longer old and fat, no longer bald. Red hair framed his face in a lion's mane, and his silver ax blazed with light.

Maggrig and Finn appeared on his left, white bows in their hands.

Chareos felt a swelling in his throat, and tears formed in his eyes. He brushed them away with the sleeve of his shirt.

"Now you know, Tenaka," he said, "the meaning of the ghosts-yet-to-be. Bring on your demons. We defy you all!" Beltzer hefted his ax, and Maggrig and Finn drew back on their bows. Asta raised his arm, but Tenaka held on to it. The khan walked forward, his violet eyes sad and thoughtful.

"I thought you were created for me," he said. "I knew you had some purpose—it is why I let you live, why I scarred my life of victories with that one defeat." He gazed down at the light and sighed. "But you are right, Chareos. My day has passed. Let the child see the sky."

He turned away and walked back to the demon horde. A path opened before him, and he vanished from sight.

Asta walked toward Chareos, but the blademaster blocked his way to the light.

The shaman looked old now, wretched and desolate as he looked up at Chareos, blinking and confused.

"You must let me have the babe," he said.

"No."

"I do not mean to kill it. I cannot now, not without Tenaka's blessing. But the Nadir must have a khan. You see that, do you not? He is of the blood of kings. Let me have him."

"What do you offer, Asta Khan?"

"I have an antidote to the poison. You will live."

"You misunderstand me. What do you offer the child?"

"My life. I will defend him all the days of my life. I will teach him to be the khan."

"Then you may have him."

Asta's surprise was genuine. "Let me see his spirit."

"No. Return to Bel-azar and give me your antidote. You will see the babe when he is born."

"Can I trust you, Chareos?"

"I am afraid that you can," said the blademaster.

Asta turned and vanished, and the mist formed about the demons once more. The wind howled, the mist swirling away into the gray sky.

And the heroes of Bel-azar were alone on the hilltop. The light from the twin spirits grew, touching the dead tree. Leaves sprang from the branches, blossoms of pink and white flowered into life, and fragile petals fell like snowflakes around the souls.

◊ 15 ◊

FOR SIXTEEN HOURS Chareos lay close to death, scarcely breathing. Asta Khan stayed by his side, pouring a foul-smelling potion between his lips and rubbing his limbs, forcing the blood to circulate. Chien-tsu offered his help, but Asta waved him away.

"Is he doing any good?" Kiall asked the Kiatze warrior.

"I have never seen anyone work harder. I could almost believe he actually cares whether Chareos lives or dies. Almost."

Kiall returned to the guardhouse, where Ravenna had given birth to twin boys, healthy and strong. Tanaki was still at the bedside, but both women were asleep. Kiall was about to leave her when Tanaki opened her eyes; she smiled wearily and stood, moving into his embrace.

"What now?" she asked, looking up at him.

"Now we wait for the lord regent's answer."

One of the babes began to cry, and Tanaki went to where he lay with his brother in a makeshift crib, lifting him clear. She carried him to Ravenna, pulled back the blanket, and held him to Ravenna's breast. The mother did not stir from her sleep.

Tanaki rubbed the babe's back and returned him to the crib. The other babe awoke but did not cry. Tanaki lifted him also and carried him to Ravenna. He, too, drank lustily.

"It is a pity Ravenna was not the woman of Chareos," said Tanaki.

"Why?"

"He could have challenged Jungir Khan to single combat for her. It is the Nadir custom, and the khan could not have refused. That way we could have avoided a war."

"I could challenge him," said Kiall.

Fear flashed into Tanaki's eyes. "You will do no such thing! I have seen you in action, and you are not one-half as skillful as Jungir. He would cut you into pieces."

"I could strike a lucky blow," he argued.

"Luck does not enter into a contest of that nature. Put the idea from your mind."

He paused in the doorway. "I do love you," he said. "You know that?"

"Yes. I know."

He left her then and walked to the ramparts, where Salida was standing with Harokas and Chien-tsu. Glancing back at the unconscious Chareos, he saw that the shaman was still beside him.

"I think his heart gave out," said Harokas.

"He is not a young man," Salida said, "but I hope he pulls through."

The Nadir began to stir, rising from their campfires and saddling their horses. Salida glanced at the sky. It was almost time.

A rider came galloping through the western gate, leaping from the saddle of his lathered mount. He ran to Salida, handing him a scroll of parchment sealed with green wax and stamped with the lord regent's seal. Salida walked away from the others, removed his battle gauntlets, and opened the scroll. He sniffed loudly and read the document slowly; then he rolled it once more and tucked it into his belt.

Pulling on his gauntlets, he returned to the others.

The Nadir began to ride forward with Jungir Khan at their head. They halted below the battlements, and Jungir looked up.

"You have your answer, Captain Salida?"

"I do, Highness. I am instructed to hold this fortress in the name of the Gothir people and to deny access to any foreign power."

"Then it is war," said Jungir, drawing his sword.

"Wait!" shouted Kiall. "May I speak, Highness?"

"Who are you, boy?" called Jungir.

"I am Kiall. Ravenna was my woman, stolen from my village. We were betrothed. Now I demand the right of combat to decide what happens to her."

Jungir leaned back in the saddle, his dark eyes fixed on Kiall. "You wish to challenge me directly?"

"It is my right and the Nadir custom to do so."

Jungir glanced to his left, watching the men around him. Each of them knew the custom, and he felt with certainty that the boy's daring appealed to them.

"And when you lose?" called Jungir Khan. "What then? I get my woman back—and what else?"

"I can speak only for Ravenna, sire."

"Very well. Come down and we will fight man to man. And I promise not to kill you slowly, for you have followed your woman as a man should." A grunt of approval came from the Nadir warriors around him.

Inside the fortress Asta Khan heard the exchange. As Kiall descended the rampart steps, Asta ran to him, grabbing his arm.

"What do you want?" asked Kiall, trying to pull away.

"Listen to me, fool. There is no need to die! I will help you in this battle if you trust me."

"I want no trickery or magic," said Kiall.

"No tricks," Asta assured him. "Just say these words after me. Will you do that?"

Kiall shrugged. "What are they?"

"Merely a good luck charm which will open you to a friend. Trust me, Kiall. Can you not see I am with you? I am fighting to save the life of Chareos. Does that mean nothing? I am your friend."

"Speak the words," said the former villager.

Asta Khan closed his eyes, and began to chant:

Nadir we
Youth born,
Bloodletters,
Ax wielders
Victors still.

Kiall spoke the words. "What do they mean?"

"Life," whispered a cool voice inside his mind, and Kiall reeled back. "Do not be afraid," said the voice of Tenaka Khan. "I am the warrior who aided you against the demons, and I will aid you now. I want you to relax, to allow me to live for but a brief moment. It is all I ask in return for the aid I gave you."

Kiall could feel the rising tension in him like a pressure building. "Give way, Kiall. And let me save your friends."

"It is my fight," he argued weakly.

"Jungir Khan poisoned me," said Tenaka. "He poisoned his own father. You must allow me my hour of revenge."

"I . . . I don't know."

"Trust me. Relax," said Tenaka, and Kiall felt himself give, felt the power of Tenaka Khan flow through his veins. Their memories merged, and Kiall felt the thrill of countless battles, saw the fall of the mighty Dros Delnoch, experienced the great love the khan had known for Renya, the Joining child. But more than this he felt the confidence of the warrior born. He tried to will himself forward but found to his terror that he could no longer control his limbs. His arms stretched out, and his lungs filled with air.

"Oh," came his voice, "oh, it is good to breathe again!"

Tenaka Khan moved to the postern gate. At that moment Tanaki ran from the guardhouse. "Kiall!" she screamed. "Oh, please don't do this."

She flung herself into his arms, and Tenaka kissed the top of her head.

"I will come back," he said softly. "He cannot beat me."

"But he *can*. He is the greatest swordsman since my father. There is not a man alive, save perhaps Chareos, who could best him."

"Did you love your father?" he asked.

"You know that I did. More than anything."

"And do you love me?" he asked. Trapped behind his own eyes, Kiall despaired of the answer.

"Yes," she said simply. "I am for you, Kiall. Now and always."

"Your father loved you," he said. "You were the joy

Renya left . . . him. Watch from the battlements and fear nothing. Kiall will come back to you. I promise, Naki."

He turned to the gate, opened the bolts, and walked toward the waiting horde. For a moment Tanaki was stunned. He had seemed so different, and he had used her pet name, the name she had carried as a child. She swung to Asta Khan.

"What have you done?" she shouted. The old man said nothing but returned to the still form of Chareos. The blademaster opened his eyes.

"I kept my bargain," whispered Asta. "Will you keep yours?"

"I will," answered Chareos. "What is happening?"

"Kiall has gone outside to battle Jungir Khan."

"By the Source, no," groaned Chareos. "Help me to the battlements." The wiry shaman pulled Chareos to his feet and half carried him to the steps. Painfully Chareos eased his way up to the ramparts.

Out on the valley floor Tenaka Khan strode out confidently to meet his son. Jungir carried the jeweled blade given to him by Chien-tsu. Tenaka drew the cavalry saber, tested it for weight, and then hurled it aside. He walked past the surprised Jungir, halting before an old man on a gray pony.

"They told me on the battlements that you were Subodai, the oldest friend of Tenaka Khan," he said.

The grim-eyed old man nodded his head.

"Would you lend me one of the short swords Tenaka gave you on your last meeting?"

The old man looked closely at the figure of Kiall, at the stance and the tilt of the head, at the gray eyes that fixed to his own. He shivered and drew his sword, reversing it and handing it to the young man without a word.

Tenaka turned and swung the blade twice. He returned to Jungir Khan.

"When you are ready, Highness," he said.

Jungir launched a lightning thrust. Tenaka parried it and stepped in close. "Did you think the poison would keep me from you, my son?" he whispered.

Jungir blanched. His face darkened, and he attacked

again and again. But each time the dazzling blade of Tenaka Khan blocked his approach. As the battle moved farther from the watching warriors, Jungir aimed a wild cut. Tenaka blocked it and stepped inside once more.

"Asta smuggled my bones here years ago. Yet I can still taste the poison from your cup."

"Stop it!" screamed Jungir. His sword lowered a fraction and Tenaka Khan leapt forward, twisting the blade from his grasp. It fell in the dirt ten paces away.

"Pick it up," ordered Tenaka. Jungir scrambled for the blade and ran at Tenaka, offering no defense. Before he could stop himself, Tenaka instinctively rammed his sword home into his son's chest. Jungir sagged against him.

"I loved you, Father," he said, "and you never cared for me. Not once."

Tenaka seized his son and sank with him to the earth, tears filling his eyes. "Oh, my son! I was so proud of you. But I wanted you to be a strong man, a Nadir man. And I never showed my feelings, save for Tanaki. Yet I loved you—and your brothers. Jungir . . . Jungir!"

But the khan was dead.

Tenaka stood with head bowed by the body. He wrenched the sword clear and flung it from him, then knelt by his dead son.

The old general rode forward and dismounted. He walked now with a limp, but he was the same man Tenaka Khan had rescued all those years before.

"Who are you?" hissed the general. *"Who?"*

"I am merely a man," said Tenaka, turning to stare at the battlements and his only daughter. The foolish boy had given him life, and he had used it to kill the last of his sons. And he knew in that moment that he could not rob his daughter of her love. No, better finally to accept death and fly in search of Jungir. "Kiall, come forth," he said softly.

Kiall found the tension lifting from him. He stretched and turned back to the general. "I thank you for the use of your sword, sir. The spirit of Tenaka Khan bade me ask for it."

"Just for a moment . . ." said the general. He shook his

head. "It doesn't matter. Return to your fortress; you will die soon enough."

Asta Khan leapt to the battlements. "Subodai!" he called.

"What is it, warlock?"

"The son of the khan is born!"

"Is this true?" Subodai hissed at Kiall.

"Yes. In the night."

"I will bring him to you," shouted Asta. "Do not attack."

Kiall walked back to the fortress, where two soldiers opened the postern gate. Asta was moving toward the gatehouse when Chareos stopped him.

"Wait," he said. "I will bring out the child."

Chareos walked into the guardhouse, where Ravenna was awake with one child at her breast; the other was sleeping.

He sat beside her. "I do not know how to say this, my lady. But, to avert the war I promised one of your sons would be khan. And now I am trapped by that promise."

She looked at the anguish in his eyes and reached out a hand to him.

"One of them is born to be khan. The other would be slain; it is the Nadir way," she said. "Let Asta have what he wants. I will raise the other." She lifted the babe from her breast and kissed him tenderly. "Take him before I change my mind."

"I will help you raise him; I swear it." He took the babe. "Now let there be no sound. Asta must not know there are twins."

He walked to the door and out into the sunlight. Asta ran forward, holding out his thin arms for the child.

"A new great khan," he said gleefully. Chareos passed the babe to him, and it began to howl, but Asta leaned down and whispered in his ear. The babe became quiet and fell asleep.

"I did what I had to do," said Asta. "But I am grateful to you, Blademaster." Chareos nodded and watched the shaman walk out to the waiting army.

Within minutes they had departed from the valley. As Chareos sat down in the sunshine and sagged back against the wall, Salida joined him.

"I would not have believed the lord regent could be so heroic," said Chareos.

"No," said Salida, lifting the parchment from his belt and tossing it to Chareos' lap.

The blademaster opened it. The message was simple: "Give Jungir Khan all he asks for."

"I think we did that, don't you?" observed Salida.

Epilogue

KIALL AND TANAKI did not wait to be wed in the Gothir fashion. They cut their palms in the Nadir way and pledged their troth before witnesses at Bel-azar. Then they rode from the fortress back to the steppes and out of the pages of Nadir history.

Chien-tsu and Oshi journeyed back to the empire of the Kiatze, where the ambassador was covered with garlands and given lands of great wealth and greater beauty.

Harokas journeyed with Salida to New Gulgothir, where the lord regent grudgingly gave the captain a fine award and a promotion.

Seven years later three riders halted before the first great gates of Castle Tenaka.

"Once, my son," said Chareos, "this was Dros Delnoch, the mightiest of the Drenai fortresses. In those days it was ruled by the Earl of Bronze. One day that title will be yours."

The boy turned his violet eyes on the six massive walls rearing back along the pass. "I will take it from the other side," he said softly.

Chareos smiled and turned to his wife, Ravenna. "Do you have regrets?" he asked.

"None," she said, taking his hand. The boy twisted in his saddle and stared back over the northern steppes.

A thousand miles away another violet-eyed child stood, staring south.

"What are you looking at?" asked Asta Khan.

"The enemy," whispered the boy.

THE WORLDS OF DAVID GEMMELL

Author David Gemmell is hailed as Britain's king of heroic fantasy, and through twelve of his most famous battle-charged fantasies, Del Rey brings the action to American audiences.

Epic fantasy invades the era of Alexander the Great in tales that unite heroes of history with those of legend.

LION OF MACEDON

In every possible future, a dark god was poised to reenter Greece. Only the half-Spartan Parmenion had any hope of defeating its evil. And an aged seeress made it her life's mission that Parmenion would become the deadliest warrior in the world, no matter what the cost.

And as the seeress had foreseen, Parmenion's destiny was indeed tied to the dark god, and to Philip of Macedon, and to the yet-unborn Alexander. And all too soon the future was upon them . . .

DARK PRINCE

The chaos spirit had been born into Alexander, but the intervention of Parmenion had prevented it from taking over the boy's soul completely.

Now a demon king, in another Greece where the creatures of legend still flourished, sought the power of the Chaos Spirit that lived within Alexander. And he called the boy into his world . . .

Only Parmenion could hope to rescue Alexander from the demon king, but could anyone save the boy from himself?

Praise for LION OF MACEDON *and* DARK PRINCE

"Nobody writes better fantasy than David Gemmell . . . A totally engrossing novel . . . It's an enduring and compulsive epic."

—*Starburst*

"Gemmell works the reader's emotions adroitly . . . The novel has the potential to be quite popular as a dramatic historical, with fantasy elements . . . It's a satisfying, often exciting fantasy that will thrill many readers . . ." —*Locus*

"The enjoyable historical fantasy set in ancient Greece spans three decades in the career of Parmenion, a Spartan of mixed ancestry whose life is being shaped and monitored by an aging seeress . . . Particularly enchanting is the appearance of Aristotle as a wizard and guide through the underworld . . ." —*Publishers Weekly*

KNIGHTS OF DARK RENOWN

The legendary knights of the Gabala had been greater than princes, more than men. But they were gone, disappeared through a demon-haunted gateway between worlds.

But one tormented knight had held back—Manannan, whose every instinct told him to stay. But as murder and black magic beset the land, Manannan realized he would have to face his darkest fears: He had no choice but to ride through that dreaded gate and seek out his vanished companions.

Praise for KNIGHTS OF DARK RENOWN

"A sharp distinctive medieval fantasy. Dramatic, colorful, taut."
—*Locus*

MORNINGSTAR

Jarek Mace was an outlaw, a bandit, a heartless thief. He needed nothing and no one.

But now Angostin hordes raged over the borders. Evil sorcery ruled, and the Vampyre kings lived once more. The Highland people were in great need of a hero. And when Mace's harassment of the Angostins inadvertently aided the common people, he found himself hailed as that hero, a legend, the great Morningstar returned.

But Mace was an outlaw, not a savior of the people. Or was he?

Praise for MORNINGSTAR

"It is with some reason that he [David Gemmell] is called Britain's king of heroic fantasy. Here [MORNINGSTAR] . . . he looks at the nature of legend—how a man who is basically self-centered and unfeeling becomes the inspiration for a nation in the grip of evil . . . The setting is half-familiar: a place much like the Scottish Highlands at a time like the Middle Ages . . . It is a fine piece of writing."
—Tim Lenton, *Eastern Daily Press*, England

"It seems that every time I read a new David Gemmell novel it is better than the last—and MORNINGSTAR is no exception . . . The main difference between the book and the myths it draws upon is that Gemmel includes some of the less savory characters who we suspect may have been at the basis of both Robin and Arthur." —*Starburst*

Now experience the Drenai saga that was launched with the international bestseller LEGEND.

Meet the heroes of the Drenai people . . .

WAYLANDER: He was charged with protecting the innocents and journeying into the shadow-haunted lands of the Nadir to find the legendary Armor of Bronze. But Waylander was an assassin, a slayer, the killer of the king.

LEGEND: Druss was a legend even in old age. And he would be called to fight once more, to defend the mighty fortress Dros Delnoch, the last possible stronghold against the Nadir hordes . . .

THE KING BEYOND THE GATE: Tenaka Khan was an outsider, a half-breed, despised by both the Drenai and the Nadir. But he would be one man against the armies of Chaos . . .

QUEST FOR LOST HEROES: Among the companions—the boy Kiall, the legendary heroes Chareos the Blademaster, Beltzer the Axman, and the bowmen Finn and Maggrig—was a secret that could free the world of Nadir. One was the Nadir Bane, the Earl of Bronze . . .

The Drenai Saga
WAYLANDER
LEGEND
THE KING BEYOND THE GATE
QUEST FOR LOST HEROES

"There isn't a British writer in this area [fantasy] who can hold a candle to his knack for plot-weaving, narrative impetus, and the ability to meld wizardry and high adventure so seamlessly." —*Fantasy Bookshelf*

And, beginning in 1996, the eagerly-awaited Stones of Power cycle makes its American debut . . .

Tales of dark magic, sorcery, and conquest in the books of the Sipstrassi Stones of Power . . . A new dark age, a witch queen, a hell-born army, and a man seeking a child born of a demon. Bold heroes . . . The brigand slayer, Jon Shannow, known as the Jerusalem man . . . Uther Pendragon . . . Culain . . .

The Stones of Power Cycle
WOLF IN SHADOW
GHOST KING
LAST SWORD OF POWER

And a new Jon Shannow Adventure, going beyond the gates of time itself . . .

THE LAST GUARDIAN

Join Del Rey for the action-filled stories of heroes and battles, of demons and evil armies, of the fantasy novels of David Gemmell . . .